JAMES
THE
THIRD

MAGGIE BALLINGER

UNIVERSE

This edition first published by Universe in 2022
an imprint of Unicorn Publishing Group

Unicorn Publishing Group
Charleston Suite, Meadow Business Centre
Lewes, East Sussex
BN8 5RW

www.unicornpublishing.org

A catalogue record for this book is available from the British Library

ISBN 978-1914414-56-5

Typesetting by Matthew Wilson
Cover design by Felicity Price-Smith and Matthew Wilson

Printed and bound in Great Britain

To everyone who doesn't know the difference between an heir apparent and an heir presumptive... yet

1948

1

The Morning Room, Clarence House

'I'm worried, Phillip.'

The Duke of Edinburgh wondered what was coming: he'd been pushing his luck recently on the partying front, which hadn't gone unnoticed. His Majesty was still not best pleased about the latest report, and that was putting it mildly. Word had it that the King had kicked a corgi across the room, so great had been his anger.

'What's bothering you, Lilibet?' the Duke ventured.[1]

'I'm worried about Mummy.'

'That makes a change. It's usually your father.'

'I'm constantly worried about Papa, but Mummy's not been herself recently.'

'Something to do with her age?' queried Princess Elizabeth's husband. 'Not that I'm an expert. Has she been having these – what are they called? – flushes?'

'You're the one who has those, Phillip!'

'That's because it's always too damned hot in most of the palace rooms. Servants are constantly trotting in with more coal. It's a wonder there's any left to fuel industry.'

Elizabeth laughed and looked towards her lap. 'Oh, he's off

again. See! There's a foot or an arm, or a limb at any rate.'

'It might be a she. Not long to go now before we find out,' said the father-to-be. 'At least you won't have to have the Home Secretary present for the birth, not that Ede's a bad chap – for a socialist.'[2]

'He does seem to be quietly getting on with things,' mused Elizabeth, recalling her parents' horror at the post-war election of a Labour government and the ousting of poor old Winnie, whose inspired leadership had seen the country through the Second World War. 'I think Papa's getting used to the new regime. He seems to quite like Attlee. Not so sure about Mummy, though. Once she's made up her mind, she never budges.'

'You don't need to remind me. I'll always be the dangerously subversive Hun, plotting to overthrow the monarchy.'

'I think the term used was "dangerously progressive"!'

'And here am I,' said the Duke, mock-seriously, 'doing my bit to secure continuity of the Mountbatten line!'[3]

Elizabeth, assailed by another kick, winced.

'How are you feeling, Cabbage?'

'Like I've swallowed one whole. A new, specially cultivated variety known as the octopus cabbage. Growing a human being is a rather strange experience.'

'So, what is it about your mother that's worrying you?'

'I gather she had a bit of a rant in the palace kitchen this morning. She can sometimes be rather imperious, but I've never known her to shout at the servants. I've never known her to shout at anyone.'

'A rant about what?'

'Apparently, there's a shortage of brown trout, and she specifically wanted it for dinner.'

'Well, if there's no brown trout, then let her eat red mullet. Or better still, tell her to pack her rods and waders and take herself off to Scotland. She can catch her own.'

'She often does, but she won't go anywhere now, for two good reasons. She wants to be here for the birth of her first grandchild. Secondly, the fishing season's closed until next spring!'

'Is a downstairs rant all? Shouldn't think a bit of an outburst is anything to be concerned about, even if it is out of character. Maybe the cold critical stare of disapproval isn't doing the trick any more?'

'There's more to it than that. She was supposed to be having a dress fitting yesterday and refused point-blank to go through with it. According to Margaret, she sent poor old Norman[4] and his assistants packing – though she was all right with the milliner.'

'Perhaps she thought she had enough frocks, but is possibly in need of another few dozen fluffy hats? I shouldn't worry about it too much, Cabbage. If you think she's behaving oddly, take a look at my own mother. She's got all sorts of – shall we call them unconventional? – ideas. Start fretting when Her Majesty declares her intention to train as a nurse and establish an order of nuns somewhere near Athens.'[5]

'That is, at least, a worthy cause with some purpose,' said the Princess.

Just before midnight, on Sunday 14th November 1948, it was announced by Buckingham Palace that Princess Elizabeth had been safely delivered of a prince.

The child was born by caesarean section in the Buhl Room of the royal residence, which had been kitted out as an operating theatre. When Prince Phillip first saw his son, he described him as a 'plum pudding'.[6]

18TH NOVEMBER 1948

BUCKINGHAM PALACE

Professor Eustace Heggarty from University College London[7], an institution more commonly known as UCL, was a world-renowned historian, who seemingly knew everything about Britain from the Dark Ages onwards. He had a particular expertise in constitutional matters and absolutely no idea why he was at Buckingham Palace. Since yesterday's summons, a few possibilities had gone through his mind, none of which seemed realistic.

Only one other person was in the imposing room. This was no lesser a personage than His Majesty King George VI, who seemed nervous. Eustace took a sip of the rather fine dry sherry, which he'd thought twice about accepting and was now glad he had. He was sure he'd wake up any second to the reassuring discovery that this had all been a dream. Shifting position slightly, he wondered whether it would be impolite to fully stretch out his long legs away from the fire. Would that seem overly casual? The sofa was low slung, and Eustace was a tall, lean man. Were it not for his wife's excellent culinary skills, which ensured there was always a bit of flesh on his bones and some colour in his cheeks, he might have been described as cadaverous.

The man opposite cleared his throat.

'Thank you for coming, Professor. I've asked you here to s- s- sound you out – informally you understand – about a m- matter of some delicacy. This conversation is, n- n- naturally, in confidence.'

'Of course, Sir.'

'It's about a point of law.'

'But surely, Sir, might I respectfully suggest that the business would perhaps be better discussed with Sir Hartley Shawcross?'[8]

The Attorney General was the main legal advisor to both Crown and Government.

'Sir Hartley is at present in the United States of America, and I see no need to recall him. This isn't r- r- really his field either. I'm hoping it's something that can be quickly and easily determined.'

'I'll certainly do whatever I can to assist Your Majesty. What is the nature of your enquiry?'

'I've been considering making my older daughter Princess of Wales. Would that be possible?'

'The title – at least that of Prince of Wales – is indeed in your gift, Sir. But it's reserved exclusively for the heir apparent.'

'B- but what's the p- point in having a gift to g- give if there's no one who's eligible to receive it?'

'No point at all, Sir. May I enquire what the Private Secretary's view is on the subject?'

'Tommy has no opinion because I haven't asked him for one,' said His Majesty, with a touch of belligerence.

This was very odd. Sir Alan Lascelles[9], generally known as 'Tommy', was the obvious source of advice on constitutional questions such as this. Although they didn't move in the same social circles, Eustace was acquainted with the man and didn't like the idea of bypassing him. So why was the King doing so? Fear of getting the wrong answer was the most obvious explanation, which meant that the professor had to tread carefully and tactfully. Asking a blunt 'Why not?' would seem far too confrontational.

'Regrettably, Her Royal Highness is only heir presumptive,' he ventured. 'There have been Princesses of Wales before, but never in their own right. They've only ever held the title by dint of marriage to a Prince of Wales. No queen of England has ever been regarded as an heir apparent prior to taking the throne, so the matter has never arisen.'

'N- n- not even Queen Victoria?'

'Your esteemed great-grandmother was, before her accession, only ever heir presumptive.'

Heggarty, not liking where this was heading, took a larger sip of sherry and glanced towards the decanter, which sat on a side table.

'How so?' George asked. 'I'm afraid this is an area I've never properly looked into before.'

'Queen Victoria's predecessor, her uncle King William IV, died when he was seventy-one and was definitely still considered capable of fathering a child.'

The King looked startled. 'Definitely?'

'Yes. When Victoria became queen, a special clause was inserted into the declaration. This was to the effect that, if the King's widow was discovered to be pregnant, any living child she bore would be monarch instead. William's wife, Queen Adelaide, was only forty-four at the time of his death, and therefore regarded as being of child-bearing age – even though she had not produced issue for fifteen years. None of their children had survived infancy, but the possibility had to be accommodated.'[10]

'I see,' said George, 'or I think I see. Is there any point at which – well, to put it bluntly – there is deemed to be no p- p- possibility of further children?'

Eustace, resisting the temptation to pick at the skin around his left thumb, again looked longingly at the sherry decanter. He hadn't known what to expect, but it certainly wasn't this. He fleetingly wondered whether it was treasonable to suggest that the King's consort was past it in terms of her reproductive capacity. There also remained the possibility that if, heaven forbid, Her Majesty should die, the King could remarry. That almost unthinkable scenario could result in a son.

'Let me replenish your drink, Professor,' the King offered, rising to his feet. 'This isn't going to g- get any easier for either of us.'

A bewildered Eustace accepted a second glassful with humble gratitude, even though his usually clear head was already spinning. It was a more generous measure than the one poured by a footman, before the servant had discretely withdrawn.

His host continued. 'Let's approach this by c- c- continuing with our example from the last century. If Wi- Wi- William had lived on to a ripe old age, when would Victoria have been declared heir apparent?'

'I'm not entirely sure that would ever have happened, Sir. Until his death, the possibility of his fathering another child would have remained.'

'Even if his queen reached her dotage by then?'

Eustace was reluctant to say more, and there was an uncomfortable silence, which His Majesty broke.

'Ah, I think I see what you mean. So let us return to the present circumstances. There's never been any woman in my life, other than my dear wife. And nor, I can assure you, would there ever be[11]. My younger daughter is eighteen. So where does that leave us?'

In just about the most embarrassing situation any person could find themselves, thought the professor. In the absence of any mention of the Queen's undergoing what would have coyly been described as 'an abdominal procedure', he was fairly sure that she had not had a hysterectomy. So how could he possibly enquire into Her Majesty's fertility? Or, indeed, Their Majesties' private relationship? One didn't venture anywhere near such matters with lifelong friends, let alone the sovereign.

18TH NOVEMBER 1948

DEPTFORD HIGH STREET, SOUTH LONDON

Lil tucked a gloved hand under her sister Peggy's arm, as the two set off home.

'Thank Gawd for that,' she said. 'You'd fink people were stockin' up for an invasion, instead of just a couple of days. I've never known it so busy on a Fursday.'

'Bedlam,' Peggy agreed. 'The 'ole world's gonna be gettin' vases[12] for Christmas, the rate I was sellin' 'em. Did you get a box of those glass baubles Mum wanted?'

'No. They'd run outta the assorted small ones by the time I 'ad a moment to meself. She said not to bovva if they only 'ad medium or large.'

'Four years ago, 'oo'd 'ave fought we'd be buyin' ornaments made by the Japs? I got 'er some of that shiny lametta stuff though. Now all we need is a tree. Dad should never of chucked that artificial one out.'

'It was almost bald, but I s'pose it would 'ave done annuva turn. Gawd knows where we're gonna get a proper tree from.'

'The market 'ad plenty, Peg.'

'Yes, but they was all too big to fit on the side table. I bet there's loads of nice littluns at Windsor Castle, what wiv that 'uge estate an' all.'

Lily and Peggy Faulkner both worked at Woolworths on Deptford High Street[13]. Peggy was on glassware and china, and Lil dodged between the broken biscuits and sweets counters. They'd have preferred their jobs the other way round. Peggy had the better head for figures, which you needed for weighing out sweets and dealing with ration books.

'Are you seein' your Terry tonight?' Peggy asked.

'Yeah, but we're not goin' out or anyfin'. I'm too knackered. Run off me feet today. All I want to do is soak 'em in a bowl of 'ot water for a few hours.'

'I was busy too,' said Peggy. Not to be outdone, she added, 'And didn't get a wink of sleep last night, what wiv your snorin' and that blessed baby next door screamin' 'is lungs out. 'ow come you didn't 'ear 'im?'

'Dunno. Clear conscience I s'pose.' Lil could have bitten off her tongue, but the words were out and the damage was done. Peggy went rigid, shook off her sister's hand and stomped ahead.

'Don't be like that.' Lil hurried to catch up. 'I didn't mean it. And it wasn't your fault.'

They walked in silence. Next-door's baby could be heard from the end of their street.

'I bet Princess Elizabeth doesn't 'ave that problem,' said Lil. 'Prob'ly 'as a nursery miles away and a ton of nannies to look after the new prince.' To her relief, Peggy turned and smiled. These huffs weren't frequent and never lasted long. Even so, it was a worry to her family that they happened at all, after such a long time.

'Remember when we sent our clothin' coupons for 'er weddin' dress?'

'Us and the 'ole world. But it was nice, that letter we got. Somefin' to treasure for ever.'

The sisters had always felt a close association with the King and Queen's daughters. They were almost the same age as the princesses and, with a bit of a stretch of the imagination, shared the same names. 'Lil', actually short for Lillian, was similar to Elizabeth's family nickname of Lilibet, and Peggy was a form of Margaret. They even imagined they looked like their idols. They studied the latest royal photographs and slavishly curled and styled their dark hair accordingly.

There were a few lifestyle differences. The 'palace' in which they lived was a two-up, two-down terrace on Standford Street[14], which, unlike others further along, had blessedly escaped the bombings. The house did at least have the luxury of a bathroom. Their parents were called Ron and Joyce. During the war, instead of being inspirational figureheads, Ron worked the river and Joyce had done a three-year stint at the Royal Arsenal in Woolwich. In the First World War, she would probably have worked with TNT and been a 'canary girl'[15], but the explosive filling there had ceased in 1940, and she was employed instead on making shells. Ron had made her give up when a metal filing lodged in her eye, almost blinding her.

In common with almost every young woman in the country, the sisters thought that Princess Elizabeth's husband, Prince Phillip of Greece, was wildly attractive. Peggy, especially, often declared that she 'wouldn't say no to a bit of that'. Lil, who was courting, felt that to echo such remarks would be a bit disloyal, though she did agree that the Duke of Edinburgh was a rather dashing and romantic figure.

2

18TH NOVEMBER 1948

HYDE PARK

He had declined the offer of a chauffeur-driven ride to his Bayswater home, in the hope that the gas-lit tranquillity of Hyde Park would soothe his worries. He could still not quite believe that the recent conversation had actually taken place and felt a deep sense of foreboding. 'I knew you were the right man for the job' had been His Majesty's final shot, as the two men parted company.

No matter how often he mentally went through it, the professor still couldn't work out how the course of the dialogue might have been channelled in a different, and less disturbing, direction.

Back in that sweltering room, and just as the academic was about to drown in the depths of discomfiture, the King had unexpectedly laughed. 'Are you a married man?'

Eustace nodded.

'Well then, let me put you out of your misery. It's been many months since Her Majesty – well, I'm sure I need go no further into the mysteries of women's concerns. So shall we put that to one side? There's no real precedent for simply creating a

Princess of Wales. Is that what you're telling me?'

'Absolutely,' declared Eustace, pleased to be back on safer territory. 'But, given the right circumstances, the idea is not inconceivable.' (Damn! Unfortunate pun!) He added a hasty proviso: 'Should such unlikely circumstances ever arise.'

'So, in that case, what are the legalities about Princes of Wales, now I have a grandson?'

'Yes, Sir. May I offer my hearty congratulations on that happy event?'

The King beamed with pride. 'Indeed you may. It's not yet been announced, but he's to be named Charles. So tell me, has a statute concerning the title ever been passed?'

'No, Sir. The principle has been established over the years by virtue of a tradition dating back to 1301 and the reign of Edward I. The body of constitutional law is a complicated mixture of customary law, conventions, statutory law and so on.'

(Don't talk down to the King, Heggarty reminded himself.)

'I'm sure you are very well aware of this, Sir. Before we go any further, the exact status of some traditions might forever remain uncertain, simply because they're never challenged. Even if they were, I could guarantee that there would be almost as many differing opinions as there are legal experts and academics. Some would argue that, for traditions to acquire the status of law *sui generis*, there must be a test of recognition.' Eustace stopped abruptly. He was in lecture mode.[1]

'My apologies, Sir. It's always a sign that I've rambled on too long when I start introducing the Latin. To briefly summarise, it's all extremely complex, and it has taken me decades of study to reach my present level of incomprehension.'

'"The law is an ass", eh? I believe we have Charles Dickens to thank for that particular wisdom.'[2]

Eustace, pleased to note that the King had lost his stammer, considered it prudent not to correct His Majesty.

'Indeed it is. The Easter Act, passed by Parliament as recently as 1928, has since been totally ignored as a means of calculating when Easter should fall. In favour, I might add, of the method first established by the Christian church some sixteen hundred years earlier.'

'Perhaps I should explain my, or rather our, thinking on the matter in hand.'

Noting the well-disguised rebuke, Eustace gave his brain a mental kick for shooting off at a tangent.

'Her Majesty is very keen to lay to rest the ghost of my predecessor, a former Prince of Wales and, all too briefly, a former king. He didn't exactly live up to his '*Ich dien*' motto[3], in that he singularly failed to serve. My wife's got a bit of a bee in her bonnet about it, but we are both in agreement that a new prince or princess of the principality would help to expunge that whole sorry abdication business. I don't suppose there are any loopholes we might exploit?'

Eustace took no longer than a second to process the basis of a possible challenge, then decided with equal speed against mentioning it.

'There are none that would prove straightforward, Sir. Any debate on the subject is likely to take years and, at the end of it all, the outcome may not be the one you wish for.'

'Well then, what about an Act of Parliament? I presume traditions can be altered by such means? Possibly on an exceptional basis?'

'Undoubtedly, Sir. For example, male-preference primogeniture, only implied in statute, is one such ingrained tradition that could, in theory, be changed in that way.'[4]

'I can't envisage that ever happening.'

'Neither can I,' the professor agreed.

'Though a change to absolute primogeniture would have spared us the present debate. You know, I always found it odd that, had Margaret been a boy, she would have overtaken

Princess Elizabeth in the line of succession. Even as a four-year-old, my older daughter was a monarch in the making. My late father certainly recognised it. She always had that strong sense of commitment and applied it to everything she did. But things are as they are, and I suppose I would have got used to it.'

'May I ask about the timing of any move you might be considering, Sir?'

'I was thinking about my birthday next month, as a sort of very special personal gift to myself – and to the Queen, of course. It would cheer her up immensely. She's a little under the weather at present.'

Heggarty, a kindly man, felt desperately sorry for His Majesty, who had valiantly assumed a role to which he was entirely unsuited. With an unfailing sense of duty, he'd succeeded both in restoring the popularity of a teetering monarchy and in bolstering the nation's morale during six years of war. The challenge had taken its toll.

'I wish there were a clearer way forward, Sir.'

'I should know this, but do Princes of Wales have to have reached a particular age before they can receive the title?'

'No. Your grandfather – ' (Eustace just managed to avoid saying 'Edward VII'; there was no need to remind the King who his grandfather was!) ' – was only a month old when it was bestowed upon him. Indeed, the future George III was just a week old.'

'That's something, I suppose. I know Acts of Parliament take a while to go through the process, but can they be retrospective?'[5]

In favour of brevity, Heggarty dismissed another Latin phrase that came to mind. 'In some exceptional circumstances, yes, it has happened.'

'So what are my options, Professor?'

'As I see it, there are three possibilities. The first two are better avoided, because both would require some form of, er, regularisation. Firstly, you could create, as Princess of Wales, Her Royal Highness The Princess Elizabeth. This would, as things stand, be both unconventional and unconstitutional. Secondly, you could bestow the title upon Prince Charles. At present, that's again unconstitutional. He will, in the fullness of time, become first in line and certain to succeed, thereby becoming eligible.' Eustace added a hasty, 'But not, God willing, for many years to come.'

Relieved to have uttered the afterthought, the academic continued. 'Thirdly, and by far the most prudent course, would be to wait. At the very least, ask Tommy to informally sound out his fellow Privy Counsellors – '[6]

Heggarty was interrupted. 'And what do you suggest?'

It was clear to Eustace that, by ignoring the strong steer given in favour of option three, the King had already reached a decision.

'So what you're saying is that, by acting in favour of Charles, this would only amount to being somewhat premature?'

'That appears to sum it up, Sir,' Eustace warily agreed.

'I'm not, by nature, an impulsive man, Professor. Nor have I ever been known for being the most decisive. But on this matter I am inclined to the belief that it would be far easier to seek forgiveness rather than to ask permission,' declared His Majesty.[7] 'My mind is made up. By way of endorsement, I shall tell the Privy Council what you've advised and what is therefore to happen. I'm sure I'll be able to out-stand any of them!'

The sovereign always stood at Privy Council meetings, which meant that no one else could sit down. This usually ensured that proceedings didn't last long. Eustace felt his heart plummet. Why hadn't he been more assertive?

'The necessary letters patent[8] will be produced by the Crown Office and, if needs be, a retrospective Act must be passed,' continued His Majesty, now in full and completely articulate flow. 'I'm sure, once a *fait accompli* has been presented, the whole thing can be resolved. There will certainly be no problem with royal assent, should that be required!'

A troubled Eustace abandoned the path by the Serpentine and began to head diagonally across Kensington Gardens. To his left, he could see the lit windows of Kensington Palace. Would Tommy be at home? Would he be receptive to an unexpected visitor on a dark late-autumn evening? More to the point, how could the matter possibly be broached, given that the King had deliberately excluded his private secretary?

The professor shoved his hands more deeply into his coat pockets and dismissed the idea. He attempted instead to focus on reaching the sanctuary of his own home, where he most definitely wouldn't be sharing with his wife of twenty years any of the astonishing confidences to which he'd been party. Edith was no gossip, but who knew what she might let slip. When she asked what the King wanted to see him about, he would tell her that it was to do with a minor legal technicality, then start spouting Latin. That would ensure she'd seek no further explanation.

By the time he reached Porchester Gardens, the backfriend on the edge of his left thumb nail was bleeding – something which hadn't happened since second-year geography lessons.

On Tuesday 14th December 1948, King George VI marked his fifty-third birthday by bestowing upon his new grandson the title of Prince of Wales. The following day, the child was baptised Charles Phillip Arthur George by the Archbishop of Canterbury.

Aside from a handful of nationalists and republicans, the news that they had a new prince of their own was well received by the Welsh, and joyously so in some parts. The *Western Mail* pronounced that the country was 'now again a Principality, in the true sense of the word' but did, however, view as disappointing the fact that none of their prince's names was Welsh.[9]

On learning of this, the Duke of Edinburgh asked why Arthur, being of Celtic origin, was not sufficient, adding, 'We should have spelt Charles' second name with a couple of 'y's.'[10]

3

15TH DECEMBER 1948

WINDSOR CASTLE

Once the christening was over, the family moved to Windsor Castle, where they would be spending Christmas.

Four days later, after dinner, the King quietly asked his daughters to go to the drawing room and wait. There was something he and Mummy wanted to discuss with them. The two princesses obliged.

'What do you think is going on?' asked Margaret. 'It isn't as if we haven't just spent more than an hour with them. And why just us? It must be something serious, and I don't like it. Gilliatt was here this morning.'

The Princess was referring to Sir William Gilliatt, gynaecologist to the royal household.

'That's because he came to see me,' Elizabeth said, 'and all's well.'

'Well he saw Mummy, too.'

'But not Papa?' Elizabeth was anxious.

'Not as far as I know. Why would he? Oh oh. Here they come.'

The King and Queen entered the drawing room, and the small family were soon comfortably settled beside a roaring fire, with the girls sharing a sofa, opposite their parents.

'Just like old times,' commented George, lighting a cigarette. Margaret followed suit. 'Only, it would seem, things are about to change.'

For a moment, Elizabeth panicked, fearful that Mummy was seriously ill. But, if that were the case, Papa wouldn't be smiling. Nobody about to impart bad news would be looking so pleased.

The King patted his wife's hand and coughed. 'I have some rather marvellous news. "We four" are about to become "we five".'

There was a pause as his daughters tried to absorb the implications of what he had just said.

Margaret was the first to find her voice. 'No. Surely not! When? How?'

The King laughed. 'There would appear to be something of a gap in your education, Margaret. I admit it was a bit of a shock, but we're not exactly past it. As to the when, well quite soon apparently – in a couple of months' time.'

'How could you not know, Mummy? How could you both do this to us?'

Their mother, rather hesitantly, began the delicate explanation. This was not a subject area commonly or easily discussed.

'I mistook the, er, signs,' she said, reddening. 'I just thought, well, at my time of life, there was a much more obvious reason. But, according to William, this can and does happen more often than people might think. He told me about some island in the Pacific where it's by no means uncommon for women over fifty to have babies.'

Margaret interrupted. 'We don't live on an island in the Pacific, Mummy. We live on a chilly island in the north Atlantic. For heaven's sake, you're a grandmother. Charles will have an aunt or uncle who's younger than he is.'

'Then he will soon have a ready-made playmate of his own

age. Think how lovely that will be,' said the Queen, beaming.

'Did Sir William say anything else, Mummy? I mean about how you are and how he expects the delivery to go? Will it take place at the palace? Or would a hospital perhaps be less risky?' asked Elizabeth.

'I'm sure the palace will be perfectly adequate. The Buhl Room was kitted out for you. It may still be, for all I know. It can be again, if everything has already been removed. He did mention having a backup team of paediatricians present and some extra equipment, just in case they're needed, though I really don't see why they should be.'

'You don't look pregnant,' argued Margaret.

'I shall by tomorrow. I simply thought I was putting on weight. What do they call it? Middle-aged spread? So I took to wearing very strong corsets, but I'm now told that they must go immediately, in case they constrict the baby's growth.'

'Didn't you have any suspicions at all?' Margaret's voice was a mixture of bewilderment and accusation.

'I was beginning to. That's why I requested Sir William to look in on me. But it was still a bit of a shock.'

'That must be the understatement of the decade,' commented the younger princess grimly. Then her mood suddenly switched. 'Ha ha, Elizabeth. Just think, if the baby's a boy, you won't ever be queen! We'll both just end up as pair of spare sisters.'

The King's high spirits seemed to have evaporated somewhat. 'We'll just have to wait and see who arrives. The most important thing is that he or she is strong and healthy, and that your mother gets through it all safely. Nothing else signifies.'

Margaret leant forward to stub out her second cigarette of the session and stood up. 'Good job the Australian tour was cancelled, even though I was looking forward to it,' she said as she left the room.

Elizabeth remained only long enough to tell her parents that she was genuinely delighted 'for all of us' and that she was sure everything would go smoothly, because there was no reason why it shouldn't. Sir William was highly regarded and would ensure the attendance of people with the requisite skills to cover every eventuality.

As she went to seek out Phillip, the weight of destiny, which had been resting on her shoulders for so long, felt a little lighter.[1]

'What was that little confab all about?' asked the Duke of Edinburgh. His wife told him. His response to the news was complete silence. For at least a minute, he didn't utter a single syllable, after which came the admission, 'Words fail me.'

'It will probably take a while to get used to the idea.'

'By the sound of it, we don't have that long. A couple of months, you say?'

'Apparently.'

'Which just about sums things up. A boy would become heir apparent.'

'Everyone's already worked that one out, Phillip. You may not be married to the future Queen of England after all.'

'Would it surprise you to know I'd find that a relief?'

'No, because I'm already starting to feel the same way myself.'

'Isn't there another serious matter to consider? Charles holds the title of Prince of Wales, even though he doesn't qualify. One short week ago that probably wouldn't have mattered, because it had not yet been announced and there might have been a chance of backtracking. But what now?'

'If there's a little sister on the way, it won't be a problem. But if it's a brother, I have no idea, except that it might well give rise to a ghastly constitutional muddle. I'd ask Papa but, firstly, he probably doesn't know either and, secondly, he may well say, "Let's cross that bridge if we come to it."'

JANUARY 1949

BUCKINGHAM PALACE

There were five of them in the sitting room. Six, if you counted the one whose birth was now imminent. This forthcoming obstetric event had not been publicly announced, though a number of engagements had had to be cancelled on minor pretexts.

Saying first that it didn't matter to her on a personal basis, Princess Elizabeth had raised the question of Charles' title with her father. His reply had not been a model of elucidation.

'I'm sure someone will be able to sort it out. A new statute or something, to clarify what already appears to be a legal uncertainty. In retrospect, I'm afraid I did act a little hastily, but Charles will retain his title. It might result in even more of a mess if I have to rescind something so recently bestowed. Besides, any brother of yours would have plenty of titles in his own right from the moment he's born – Cornwall for one. An heir apparent doesn't have to be made Prince of Wales. Of that much I am absolutely sure.'

With that subject clarified as far as it was ever going to be, the King and Queen, the two princesses and the Duke of Edinburgh had now convened to discuss possible names for the coming child.

'We definitely need to recognise the Welsh somewhere,' said the King. 'We should include David.'

'Absolutely not!' declared his wife. 'Never!'

Elizabeth and Margaret looked at each other, knowing full well the strength of their mother's feelings towards Uncle David, now Duke of Windsor, whose decision to abdicate had propelled their shy and unassuming Papa onto the throne. Mummy's feelings of resentment ran high and increased a further notch every time their father's health gave rise to renewed concern. Some ill feeling was directed towards the Duchess of Windsor, the twice-divorced American Mrs Simpson, whom she referred to as 'the lowest of the low' or as 'that woman'. There was always an unspoken venomous adjective sitting between the two spat-out words. But, to an even greater extent, the Queen's bitterness was directed towards her brother-in-law. She hadn't forgiven the former king, and nor was she ever likely to.

The princesses did, in fact, have a second Uncle David – their mother's beloved younger brother. But the Queen's fondness for her sibling was trumped by an anger directed elsewhere, so still failed to carry the day.

'I would, however, like the names of two of my other brothers included. Patrick – '

'That neatly ticks off Ireland,' Phillip observed.

' – and Fergus, naturally.'

'Another nod to the Irish,' Margaret said, siding with the Duke in an attempt to lighten the mood. The conversation was threatening to become too serious. 'And to the Scots as well.'

'Fergus certainly,' the King agreed, remembering his wedding day and the moment when his bride had unexpectedly paused to lay her bouquet on the grave of the Unknown Warrior. It had been a poignant tribute to a brother who'd sacrificed his life in the Great War. He chuckled quietly as he also recalled that, much to his relief, the marriage service was not allowed to be broadcast because, as noted by the Archbishop of Canterbury, 'men in pubs might listen with their hats on.'

Everyone agreed that George would be fitting. But Albert was rejected, even though it was the King's first name and, as such, was used in its alternative form of 'Bertie' within the family. The King's grandfather, Edward VII, had been baptised Albert Edward but, probably predictably, had chosen to reject his father's name. This was contrary to his mother's dearest wishes, and in all likelihood, she would not have been amused. Edward VIII could have elected to adopt it, but hadn't done so. The conclusion was that it didn't seem to have an especially monarchical sound to it.

'Alfred would fit the bill better,' suggested Phillip. 'That's if we're looking for an "Al" of any sort. Or maybe Alan's more modern?' This earned him a glare from the Queen.

Frederick was considered but, as a regnal name, it had already been taken by Denmark.

Having made what seemed like a reasonable start, they turned to girls' names, a subject upon which the King seemed surprisingly well informed. The truth was that, following his meeting with Heggarty some two months earlier, George had realised that his knowledge of British royalty was sadly lacking. In addition, he hadn't liked any of his wife's suggestions for a third daughter. Mainly drawn from amongst the Bowes-Lyon clan, these had included Violet and Cecilia.

Rose, the name of one of the Queen's sisters, had already been given to Margaret. In consequence, he'd decided to do a bit of preparatory research, ahead of this little conference.

He started by offering Matilda, as someone who would have been a queen had she not been usurped by her cousin Stephen. Next, he tried Eleanor, which had cropped up a few times throughout history. Alexandra was rejected: not only was it Princess Elizabeth's second given name but, more significantly, it had also been bestowed upon the late Duke of Kent's daughter. Charlotte, George IV's heir, who had tragically died in childbirth, remained in the frame, as did Mary in honour of the present King George's mother. The Queen Dowager had been invited to join the discussion, but had declined without giving a reason. She didn't have to give a reason.

The other seven of Queen Mary's generous complement of names were considered in turn. Victoria, Augusta, Louise,

Olga, Pauline, Claudine and Agnes. Margaret quite liked Louise and Pauline, but Olga sounded too Russian, and look what was going on there! Elizabeth thought Augusta might have been suitable had the baby been due to arrive in that month. Going back a further generation produced the option of Adelaide. The Queen thought it inappropriate to name a princess after an Australian city. Her husband reminded her that the city had been named after a queen. He went on to say that William IV's wife also gave rise to the possibilities of Amelia, Louise (again), Theresa and Caroline.

His Majesty strongly favoured his first suggestions – Matilda and Eleanor. Charlotte, along with the twice-mentioned Louise, emerged as contenders, but nothing was firmly decided upon.

'I suppose Wallis is out of the question?' said Phillip, earning another fierce look from his mother-in-law.

On Monday 14th February 1949, an announcement from Buckingham Palace told the world that the 48-year-old Queen had been safely delivered of a prince.

As heir to the throne, he automatically assumed the titles of Duke of Cornwall, Duke of Rothesay, Earl of Carrick, Baron of Renfrew, Lord of the Isles, and Prince and Great Steward of Scotland.[2]

The new prince would forever miss out on the Prince of Wales, plus the associated Earl of Chester titles, because these had already been bestowed upon his nephew.

'What do you fink of these, Peggy?'

Lil laid out her purchases on the eiderdown.

'Very nice, but 'ow many more tea towels are you gonna

need? That bottom drawer of yours is stuffed full already, and Terry ain't even popped the question yet.'

'He will, and 'e sent me that lovely Valentine's card,' Lil said confidently. 'We've bin goin' steady for two years now. 'e's done his national service[3], so what's to stop us?'

Doreen Carmichael might, thought Peggy, as she plonked down on her bed. Today hadn't been busy, so there'd been time to stop and chat. Sometimes she thought that people came into Woolies more to gossip than to actually buy anything. That morning, Mrs Bailey had asked, in a confidential whisper and with the occasional covert glance in the direction of broken biscuits, whether Lil and Terry had split up. He'd been seen canoodling with another girl. Peggy sincerely hoped that the tale had been embroidered and that there was an innocent explanation, but Doreen had a reputation for being easy. If the trollop ended up getting pregnant, Terry might well be forced into marrying her – like it or not. Shotgun weddings were far from uncommon in these parts, and the ugly cow was never likely to get a husband any other way.

Peggy didn't know how to broach the subject, but was denied the chance because, at that moment, the girls' mother burst into the room.

'You'll never guess,' Joyce said, 'It's just bin on the news. The Queen's 'ad a baby.'

'Never! You're windin' us up, Mum,' Lil exclaimed.

''onest to God, I'm not. It's a boy. Both doin' well.'

Peggy, all worries about her sister's threatened happiness banished from her mind, flopped backwards.

''oo'd 'ave fought it. At 'er age, too.'

'Does 'appen,' said Mrs Faulkner, patting her ample tummy. 'Only kiddin',' she laughed.

For want of anything else to do, the girls rushed downstairs, grabbed their coats and dashed out into the street. Everyone, it seemed, had had the same idea. Words were tumbling out of mouths, barely heard by ears, let alone processed by brains. It all seemed too much to take in. Snippets registered. What a right turn-up for the books! Nobody had known the Queen was pregnant. Well, they wouldn't, would they? Just in case something went wrong. Mrs Salmon from the fish shop was also expecting, and she must be fifty if she was a day. These change-of-life babies did happen. Prince Charles should never have been made Prince of Wales. A right old hoo-hah that was going to cause. Fancy that pretty Princess Elizabeth not being heir any more. She'd have made a lovely queen one of these days.

Just before she switched off the bedside lamp, Lil was musing about whether the King and Queen shared the same bedroom.

'They must've done at some point,' declared Peggy, 'but I bet they 'ave their own rooms as well, in a palace that size. Perhaps they even 'ave their own bathrooms.'

'Bet they 'ave plenty of 'ot water, too. It was all used up by the time I got a look-in this mornin'.'

'I 'ope Mum was just windin' us up earlier on. D'you fink they still do it?'

"oo?'

'Mum and Dad.'

'If they do, it's to be 'oped they use a Johnny. Last fing we want is another kiddie. There'd be nowhere to put it. We ain't got enuff room as it is.'

'We'd 'ave to get bunk beds. Baggy me the top bunk!'

Lil giggled.

4

BUCKINGHAM PALACE

All manner of thoughts had been flitting through Eustace's head.

He had a fondness for fiction, especially if the subject matter related to action during the Second World War. He had just finished reading *The Naked and the Dead*, a debut novel by a young American writer called Norman Mailer. He'd found parts of it rather disturbing, and some of it was over-wordy, but there was one particular phrase that had firmly stuck. 'The shit hits the fan.'

It perfectly described the fallout from the King's move to declare his grandson Prince of Wales, which had caused consternation enough in government circles, even before the shock arrival of a new prince and incontestable heir apparent.

Over and over again, the professor asked himself one question. Could he – indeed, should he – have done more to prevent it? The endless analytical reruns of that discussion with His Majesty had failed to produce an answer. His name had been kept out of it, though he knew that it would have been mentioned amongst the elevated Counsellors of State, as well as by members of the Privy Council.

The status and numbers of those who might be holding him culpable wasn't a concern. Far more depressing was his inability to rid himself of guilt. For days, he'd been accompanied by his own personal Jiminy Cricket[1], who sat on his shoulder sanctimoniously singing, 'Always let your conscience be your guide.'

He hadn't expected to be invited to the palace a second time. He hadn't expected to be invited ever again, but the summons had come. Eustace was grateful that George VI wasn't Henry VIII, or he would surely have been doomed to a public beheading. Worse still, the dreadful fate of being hanged, drawn and quartered might have awaited him. Nevertheless, he could still be facing the monarch's extreme displeasure.

Instead, and with some relief, he found himself being greeted in a genial manner by his sovereign. He was even more surprised to be invited, in a casual way, to help himself to the sherry. As before, his host was not drinking, so Heggarty poured only a small measure and dispensed the necessary congratulations on the recent birth.

The King flicked his lighter to the end of a cigarette and began.

'You hail from Cheshire, I understand, Professor?'

'Yes, Sir.'

'Then how does the Earl of Willaston sound?'

Eustace was confused. Surely His Majesty wasn't thinking of opening a public house in the county? The academic could bring to mind a hotel called the Earl of Crewe, close to the railway station, but couldn't immediately recall any other establishments that might warrant a place in Debrett's. This was all very strange.

'I was born there,' he ventured uncertainly.

'And would you accept the title?'

It took the bewildered professor a few seconds to absorb the fact that he was being offered a peerage.

'I should be honoured to, Sir. But an earldom? Come my retirement, even a knighthood for services to academia would be almost unimaginable.'

'You have children, I believe?'

'Yes, Sir. One daughter and one son, in that order. Catherine and Howard. But we've always called her Cathy.'

'Is that some sort of historical joke?'

'Indeed it is, Sir, although not many people recognise it as such.'

'Well, it will be a hereditary peerage. You may wish to consider an appropriate subsidiary title and location. The Lord Chancellor or someone from his office will need to discuss it.'

'But may I ask why? Especially after the consequences of my advice?'

'I chose to ignore that advice and, on balance, have no regrets. What's done is done, and Wales is only titular after all.'

'Not just any old title,' screamed a voice inside Eustace's head, but no comment emerged from his mouth.

'As to the why, the simple fact is that I like and trust you. I find you easy to talk to. As easy as dear Lionel[2], but he's only around when there's a tedious speech on the horizon, so I can never be at my most relaxed with him. Besides, he's pushing seventy.'

Eustace, unaware that he was one of several men who'd been considered for a very particular role, wasn't sure what the voice coach's age had to do with anything, but allowed the King to continue uninterrupted.

'Even with Tommy, whom I encounter almost every day, the conversation invariably concerns matters of state, plus the occasional observation on the weather. So you see, I'm in a somewhat isolated position. As one of five brothers, my family should have provided all the male companionship I need. But poor John didn't reach adulthood, I lost another during the war, and I'm not on proper speaking terms with a third. That only leaves Henry, whom I don't see as often as I'd like.'

The professor blinked. 'But in view of what's happened?' he persisted.

'Come, come. It isn't as though Charles was given Cornwall, together with the Duchy's valuable revenue. I have since been led to understand that that particular course of action would certainly need to have been unravelled.'

'That particular course of action could never have been possible in the first place, Sir. It would have been completely out of the question, so unravelling wouldn't have come into it.'

'I'm trying my best to reassure you here, Professor. You weren't the only one I bamboozled into agreement. A number of Privy Counsellors are not best pleased with the way I chose to bulldoze through my decision, and that's putting it mildly. But it doesn't bother me if I go down in history as "Jump the gun George", so we shall say no more about it.'

'Thank you, Sir.'

Heggarty noted that the King appeared remarkably relaxed and had not once stumbled over his words.

'What is more, Professor – or may I call you Eustace? – I would like you to be one of the new Prince's sponsors. No date has been set, as yet, for the christening but you will be advised of the arrangements in good time. You have, I presume, been confirmed?'

'Yes, but I'm not sure I'd be an appropriate person to provide, er, spiritual guidance.'

'He'll have plenty of that. I'm thinking more about a secular influence. My son will be in need of a good man who can provide a decent example to follow. I believe an American has suggested the term "role model".'[3]

Eustace again thought it better to maintain a silence. On the last occasion he'd been sitting in this room, the difficult issue of the Queen's fertility had been raised. Now it sounded like he was being confronted by the equally tricky matter of the King's mortality. In late November, it had been announced that the royal tour of Australia, planned for the coming spring, had had to be cancelled as a result of the King's declining health. The professor's reaction had been the same as almost everyone else's, but the initial alarm had quickly given way to reassurance when the King sent a message to the Australian people, saying he regarded his present illness as causing a postponement only. The royal couple were due to be accompanied Down Under by their daughter, Princess Margaret. Eustace reasoned that, while His Majesty was not an old man, nor was he a young one. Surely such a lengthy and gruelling trip would be a daunting prospect for anyone that age, no matter how fit they were.

The King was continuing. 'He'll require someone who's steady, who's sensible and who is untainted by any suggestion of, well let's say, notoriety.'

The professor added 'homosexuality' to his mental list of tricky subject matters. One couldn't live, and socialise, in the capital without picking up rumours concerning certain people close to the throne, such as the Queen's own brother and the revered Lord Louis Mountbatten. Similar speculation had also surrounded His Royal Highness The late Duke of Kent. But there remained the King himself (please God, long may he reign), his son-in-law the Duke of Edinburgh (surely the finest possible exemplar?) and the Duke of Gloucester.

As though thought-reading, the King was saying, 'As I've already mentioned, there is my remaining brother, of course. But, when he's not away, he's usually at Barnwell. Northamptonshire is not that far, but someone who's invariably London-based would be more readily to hand. I may not – well, who knows what the future holds?'

He stopped short of admitting that he had been attended by two royal physicians a couple of days after the birth of Prince Charles. The verdict on his health, and consequently the prospect of his making old bones, had not been encouraging.

Hoping he was not being too familiar by enquiring, Eustace ventured, 'Has His Royal Highness been named yet, Sir?'

'Almost. We are hoping to make an announcement very soon, which means it won't be confidential for much longer.'

Eustace listened. Seven names were reeled off, and he commented that Their Majesties had provided a decent number of well-established options for a regnal name. However, the matter had not been fully settled.

'Tommy suggested that, by way of making some amends, a distinctively Welsh name should also be added,' explained the King, 'so that remains under discussion.'

'It's a splendid idea, Sir. May I enquire how far you've got?'

'Patron Saint or not, David's been ruled out, even spelt D-a-f-y-d-d. So have Andreas, which sounds too Italian, and Geraint, because nobody was sure they'd ever remember how to pronounce it. Llywelyn and Owen have both cropped up as possibilities.'

'If it's of any assistance, Sir, there were two especially notable Llywelyns. One was "the Great". The other – "the Last" – was defeated when England conquered Wales. So, arguably, that could be viewed as a slightly tactless reminder. Owain Glyndŵr, on the other hand, proclaimed himself Prince of Wales a century or so later. His revolt was ultimately unsuccessful, but he's very much regarded as a national hero. In fact, he's apparently still awaiting the call to return and liberate his people!'

'Thank you, Eustace. That's been useful, though we don't want to do too much to stir up nationalist sentiments. So do I have your undertaking that you'll do your utmost to act in the best interests of James Alfred Fergus Patrick Edward Richard George (probably) Owain? Yes, I do like that.'

'You have my most solemn commitment, Sir. And good luck to your son's future bride, when she's standing in front of the altar!'

'I, in turn, will ensure that everyone who matters understands my decision to involve you in the Prince's future. This principally means family members, but I shall also ensure that Tommy is fully aware of my wishes. Might I suggest, if it isn't too much of an imposition, that you invite him to dinner or lunch at your club, so the two of you could discuss this further?'

'It would be a privilege, Sir.'

'I'm sure, between you, you'll be able to come up with a suitable role. We can't have you floating around the palace like some sort of minister without portfolio, can we? I was thinking along educational lines. It's not traditional, of course, to contemplate sending James to school, but a governess is unlikely to suffice indefinitely. One must keep up with the times, eh?'

'Absolutely, Sir.'

'Even before that stage is reached, you should be well placed, perhaps as an occasional and coordinating tutor, to identify any deficiencies in what he's being taught. You are certainly well equipped to ensure he fully understands his legacy, and I should like you to do that. Elizabeth received private tuition in constitutional history from the Vice-Provost of Eton. Did you know Henry Marten?'[4]

'Sadly, only by reputation, Sir. I was sorry to hear of his passing. I shall do whatever I can to emulate him.'

'But, most importantly of all, it is to be hoped that you will also become someone in whom James can confide. Someone with whom he will always feel able to freely discuss any concern, whatever its nature.'

'I'm deeply honoured, Sir,' said Eustace, who also felt deeply saddened that His Majesty was so clearly planning for a time when he'd no longer be around. 'And, if I may briefly refer back to the constitutional backlash resulting from our decision of two months ago, several of us at UCL are working on a way of justifying it.'

'Which is?'

'That the creation of the first English Prince of Wales was not lawful. If you'll forgive a little more Latin, Edward I arguably violated the legal maxim *nemo dat quod non habet*. This translates as "one cannot give more of a right than they themselves possess". Edward may have conquered the Welsh, but did that give him the right to make his son, in effect, their king? It's sure to be a lengthy and complex debate.'

As he once more trod the route through Hyde Park to Bayswater, the professor summoned a name from his extensive memory bank: Roger Ascham, tutor to the future Tudor Queen Elizabeth and, via that role, informal tutor to her half-brother, Edward VI. These were two extraordinarily bright children of royal blood, who benefitted from unconventional and 'fun' teaching methods. The pair absorbed information without realising they were learning. Ascham, the person, would be a good 'role model' to emulate when it came to the education of a future king of England. Ascham, the name, might also be rather fitting for a viscount.

The new earl now had only to consider territorial designation. His maternal grandparents had lived in a small village, not far over the border from Cheshire. He'd spent many happy holidays there as a child. Its adoption would be his own deeply satisfying gesture towards the people of Wales, as a secret apology for the part he'd played in denying them their rightful prince.

He glanced at his watch, which confirmed that he'd be home just in time for dinner. After they had eaten their main meal, and while they were all still seated round the table, he would inform Edith that she was now Countess of Willaston, Howard that he was now Viscount Ascham of Hanmer in the county of Denbighshire[5], and Cathy that she would henceforth be styled Lady Catherine Heggarty.

Assuming no one had choked to death on their Government

cheese and biscuits, they could all have some fun dreaming up the requisite coat of arms. Perhaps their two pet bulldogs, Clive and Oscar, could feature? He'd already decided upon his Latin motto.

At least the King hadn't said, 'Call me Bertie.'

5

WOOLWORTHS, DEPTFORD HIGH STREET

His Royal Highness Prince James Alfred Fergus Patrick Richard George Owain was christened on Wednesday 30th March. The ceremony took place in the Music Room at Buckingham Palace. The infant wore the same Honiton lace gown that his nephew, Prince Charles of Edinburgh, had been dressed in for a similar ceremony, held a mere fifteen weeks earlier. It was a garment that had been commissioned by Queen Victoria for her eldest child.

The heir apparent had nine godparents, one of whom was the newly created Earl of Willaston.

An official photograph marking the event appeared in the newspapers the following day. It featured two noticeably proud parents sitting together on a sofa, flanked by the couple's two grown-up offspring. Her Majesty was holding the infant.

Accompanying narratives commented that the picture demonstrated a 'touching intimacy'. What nobody realised was that the King was unable to stand because he'd just undergone a procedure on his right leg. This was to correct an arterial blockage which had threatened the loss of that limb.

Despite the cosy image, the expectant public, who'd been

43

eagerly awaiting their first glimpse of the newborn, felt hugely let down.

Peggy and Lil were sitting in the canteen. Although their lunch breaks didn't always coincide, more often than not they managed to have dinner together.

Lil pushed her plate to one side. Most of the meal remained uneaten.

'That meat was disgustin'. It was just gristle. And the potatoes were as 'ard as rocks.'

'Mine was OK,' said Peggy. 'You should've 'ad the fish pie.'

'What was Mrs Bailey talkin' to you about? A right old tittle-tattler is that one. And she seems to 'aunt your china section. 'ave you ever actually sold 'er anyfin'?'

Glad that some of the aforementioned conversation had veered away from the subject of her sister's boyfriend, Peggy shook her head and explained.

'She was only goin' on about Prince James and 'ow you couldn't see 'is face. That fancy frock was so bunched up, 'e might as well 'ave been a doll and 'ooda known any different? You could see all of Prince Charles' 'ead in 'is picture.'

'Quite a few people 'ave said the same. Mrs Russell finks there's somefin' wrong with 'im, like there is with Mrs Salmon's baby.' The aptly named fishmonger's wife had recently given birth. The new arrival had conspicuously not been paraded around.

'I 'adn't 'eard that.'

'Yeah, apparently 'er nipper is Mongolian[1] or somefin', for all that 'is Dad's English. Edith Duffy was tellin' me the same. It's what 'appens when the mother is old, like the Queen.' Lil paused. 'I'm gonna get a puddin'. Let's hope the treacle tart's better than the stew. And cheer up Peg. It might never 'appen.'

Peggy, mulling over what Mrs Bailey had been saying about Terry and Doreen, was worried that it already had.

August 1949

Clarence House

'Lord Mildmay's buying us a horse,' said Princess Elizabeth.

'That sounds jolly kind of him, but why would he want to do that? Have I ever said I wanted another horse?' queried her husband.

'By us, I meant Mummy and me. It'll be a racehorse, not a polo horse.'

'Your father already has plenty of those.'

'Ah, but this will be a steeplechaser. Mummy has it in mind to become the patron saint of National Hunt. She's already chosen her colours[2]. A pale blue jacket and sleeves, with buff stripes. The silks are based on the Strathmore coat of arms.'

'Sounds surprisingly tasteful and understated, I must say. Teamed with a flower-strewn tartan cap?'

'That would be silly. It'll be a black cap with a gold tassel.'

'There had to be a catch somewhere. Now let me guess, Cazalet will be training the beast?'

'Correct. Mildmay rides for him.'

'And I suppose your mother will be nipping down to Fairlawne[3] at every opportunity to see how it's getting on?'

'Has she ever needed an excuse?'

11TH OCTOBER 1949

DEPTFORD

Peggy's huffy moments were getting worse, not better, over time. Not only did she still clam up whenever anyone got anywhere near the subject; she'd also started being ratty for no particular reason. Peggy had lost a couple of boyfriends as a result of being such a moody cow.

Lil didn't like seeing her sister upset and had decided this couldn't go on. She had a plan, which was to get Peggy drunk and force her to talk. A night on the port and lemons, with just the two of them, would make a dint in her savings but, if the scheme worked, it would be money well spent. The problem was that they didn't often socialise with each other. They walked to and from work together, which afforded plenty of opportunity to chat. There was also a nightly chance to talk, in their shared room, as they were getting ready for bed. But a suggestion that they spend an evening in a pub on no pretext whatsoever would arouse suspicion, and the barriers would already be firmly up, alcohol or no alcohol.

Their father came to the rescue. Ron worked as a lighterman[4] and was based at Rotherhithe Docks. He knew every one of the currents and tides on that part of the Thames and spent his days transferring goods from ships to the quaysides and factories. It was skilled work that earned him both good money and respect.

There was a lot of camaraderie amongst those who worked on the river. Most of Ron's friends were drawn from amongst his fellow lightermen. Like many dock workers, he supported West Ham United. The team played their home matches at the

Boleyn Ground across the Thames. It was five miles away, and he cycled there via the Greenwich foot tunnel. Millwall was nearer, but he'd never been interested. There was a good deal of rivalry – not always friendly – between the two teams.

He also enjoyed an occasional flutter on the horses, but placing bets was a tricky operation. It could only be done trackside at race meetings, so there was always great excitement if anyone was planning a day out to visit one[5]. They'd act as courier for their mates and go armed with everyone's selection lists and stake money. The previous day, Ron's luck had been in, as he told them at teatime.

''ad a good run on the chasers at Fontwell yesterday,' he announced.

'Didn't you say the Queen's 'orse was runnin' for the first time?' asked his wife.

'Yeah. Monaveen. Romped 'ome. Not bad for a nag what used to pull a milk float! But it was odds on.'

'You can't 'ave won much on that then.'

'Backed a few outsiders as well.'

'So 'ow much?'

'Enuff to treat all me girls,' he said, fishing in his trouser pocket. He pulled out a handful of change, sorted through it and distributed three coins round the table.

'There you go! Buy yourselves somefin' nice, now clothes is well and truly off ration.'

''alf a crown! Thanks Dad!' exclaimed Peggy. 'There's a scoop on in 'osiery. Nylons at a shillin' a pair! I'll be able to buy two, plus an odd stockin'.'

'We could get five pairs between us,' reasoned Lil. 'I got anuvva ladder today, so I could do wiv some new ones.'

'Didn't you put nail varnish on, to stop it runnin'?' queried Peggy.

'Yes, but it'd gone a long way before I noticed it. And it wasn't the first. My legs look like they've got some 'orrible rash.'

'You should 'ave used some of me Cutex clear lacquer,' said Peggy.

'You wouldn't let me when I asked. So I 'ad to use me red.'

'Well that was because you wouldn't let me 'ave your acetone.'

'That was because I only 'ad a drop left.'

'Stop bickerin' girls. 'ere!'

Their father tossed them an extra shilling each. 'Now let's 'ave a bit of peace and quiet please.'

Lil seized her chance.

'Why don't we go to the Three Tuns, Peg? Just to celebrate. It'd make a change. My treat.'

'Aren't you seein' Terry?'

'No. 'e's got an extra night school class this evenin'.'

Peggy didn't like the sound of that and readily agreed to accompany her sister, who went upstairs to fetch her larger bag.

'What you playin' around at?' Peggy shouted after her. ''urry up, or there'll no point goin'. We've got work tomorrow, and there's a big delivery of new tea sets arrivin', so I don't wanna be dead on me feet before I've even started.'

The pub was crowded, but they managed to find a corner table, next to the dartboard. It wasn't the ideal place, but the girls soon got used to ignoring the game that was in progress and the noisy banter that accompanied it. Lil had ordered a double port for her sister and asked for extra lemonade in her own drink, so that the amounts looked the same. They drank a toast 'to the milk 'orse', after which Peggy tentatively broached the subject of Lil's boyfriend.

'What's Terry up to these days? We don't see much of 'im any more.'

'He's doin' this night school course. Not sure exactly what 'e's learnin', but it's to do wiv electrics and telegraph wires. 'e's keen to get on and make somefin' of 'imself, now 'e's workin' for the GPO[6]. I'm ever so proud of 'im.'

Peggy felt she'd reached a dead end, so they spent a while discussing what to buy for their Mum's forthcoming birthday. Halfway through the third round, Peggy said, 'Don't know about you, Lil, but I'm startin' to feel a bit tiddly.'

At that moment, a misaimed dart landed on the floor at her feet. Instinctively dodging it, Peggy nudged the table, almost causing her glass to tumble. Grabbing at it just in time, she took another mouthful and started to laugh.

'That was a close shave. Managed not to spill any though. It's warmin' me frough good and proper. Hee hee hee!'

'You'll need it for the walk 'ome. It's pretty chilly out.'

'I know. I wish I'd put me scarf on.'

This was the cue Lil needed.

'Lucky I brought a spare then,' she said, rummaging in her bag and producing the knitted blue length that her sister kept hidden in the bottom of a drawer.

Peggy stared at it, all traces of mirth banished at a stroke.

'Where did you get that?'

'You know where I got it.'

'You shouldn't 'ave done. You've no right to go pokin' around in me fings.'

'You've got to talk about it sometime,' said Lil softly.

'I don't want to. And it's not even my scarf. It's Marjorie's. I only borrowed it.'

'Marjorie 'asn't got a lot of use for it now, though, 'as she?'

Peggy started to cry. Apart from when she first heard the news, the girl hadn't shed a single tear. Instinct told Lil that this reaction now had to be a good thing, so she waited until the sobs subsided, waving away any gestures of concern shown by the pub's sympathetic clientele.

''ere. I've got a clean 'anky.'

Peggy took it and blew her nose.

'Better?'

'Not really.'

'I've said it before and I'll say it again: *it wasn't your fault*. This can't go on, Peg. It's bin nearly five years. You gotta talk it out, or you'll never get over it.'

'I *am* over it.'

'Like 'ell you are. And it's not gettin' any better. Why do you feel so guilty?'

'It was my fault. I ill-wished 'er.'

'Tommy rot. I know for sure that you didn't wish a bloody great German rocket would land on 'er and kill 'er stone dead.'[7]

The whole community had been affected by the V-2 attack on Saturday 25th November 1944. It resulted in the death of 168 people. The missile hit the New Cross branch of Woolworths at lunchtime, when many workers from the immediate vicinity were in the cafeteria. The shop was more crowded than usual because there had been a delivery of saucepans, a scarce commodity which customers were clamouring to buy.

Peggy's eyes welled up again. 'But I did wish somefin' would 'appen to 'er though. Somefin' bad.'

'And what sort of fing did you 'ave in mind?'

'I dunno. She'd just bought a new pair of Oxfords[8], and I do remember hopin' the 'eel would drop off one of them, preferably down a drain, so she couldn't 'ave got it stuck back on again. Somefin' like that I s'pose.'

'That doesn't sound dreadful. That just sounds 'uman. I'd 'ave been finkin' exactly the same sort of fing. Marjorie always 'ad all the luck, din't she? Right from when you was just kids. Always won pass the parcel. Remember that ten bob note you bofe spotted at the same time?'

Peggy managed a wan smile. 'Yeah. She was the one who picked it up an' then wouldn't split it. An' she went with John Sykes when she knew I fancied 'im rotten.'

'Well then. If you 'adn't told 'er there was a Saturday job goin' beggin' at New Cross, she'd prob'ly never 'ave applied for it – and never 'ave beaten you to it.'

'That's sort of what makes me feel so guilty. That an' the ill wishin'.'

'Stop talkin' like this, Peggy. You needn't 'ave mentioned it to 'er. You could 'ave just sneaked off and applied for it yerself without sayin' anyfin'. That's what would 'ave been the really mean thing to do.'

'If only – '

'The 'ole world's full of "if onlys", Peg. If only 'itler 'ad never been born, for one. If only Woolies 'adn't bought in a load of pans, maybe less people would 'ave been killed.'

'She'd still 'ave been killed, even if the store hadn't been packed out.'

'I know. And if only I'd set off ten minutes earlier to queue for one of them pans, I'd 'ave been killed an' all. As it was, the explosion knocked me off me feet. Never 'eard a bang, so I fought it was an earthquake. I still 'ave nightmares about it.'

'Do you?' Peggy was surprised to learn that she wasn't the only one experiencing long-term effects from that dreadful day in November 1944.

'Yes, I do.'

'She was me best friend, Lil.'

'I know. Look, 'ow about me and you go and visit her grave next Sunday? We could return this scarf, praps. Make sure she's snug and warm, now winter's comin'?'

'Maybe.'

By allowing her to let go of her innermost feelings, Lil hoped she'd helped Peggy begin to heal. What she didn't know was that the sisterly worrying hadn't been all one-sided, and that Peggy had also been agonising about how to find the best solution to the problem of Doreen Carmichael. Mrs Bailey hadn't reported much recently, but that didn't necessarily mean that nothing was going on.

6

The focus of Eustace's life had shifted. UCL had agreed to make him professor emeritus. This meant he could continue part-time at the university, in a semi-retired role. Relinquishing academic life completely was unthinkable, especially as he was only part way through a book on the life of Henry III, the king who had reigned for a large chunk of the thirteenth century and who was generally regarded as weak and ineffectual. Eustace was keen to set the record straight, mainly because he had developed a strong affection for a man who'd been such a loving husband and doting father – rare enough qualities in quite recent times, let alone the Middle Ages.

He'd been introduced into the House of Lords, but intended only to turn up for debates and votes on legislation that mattered. He was godfather to the infant heir apparent, and even had his own modest 'suite' in the staff quarters of the palace. This comprised a small bedroom, a bijou bathroom and a sitting room-cum-office, which included the wherewithal to make coffee and tea. He rarely used the accommodation, but whenever he went there, he found it well stocked with basic necessities. In the tiny 'kitchen' corner, there was always fresh milk, biscuits and a bottle of sherry. He thought about asking the Lord Chamberlain if this could perhaps be changed to gin and tonic, which he much preferred.

More importantly, having his own quarters afforded him easy *bona fide* access to the premises, and thence to his sovereign. With a twinge of renewed sadness, he also suspected that the King was thinking ahead and making provision for him to be readily to hand, should the need arise. The thought that he'd been chosen, on so short an acquaintance, made him feel truly humble.

At the new prince's christening, he had met all the other key members of the royal family and been warmly welcomed by most of them. Only Her Majesty had been a little cool. He could understand why. She would probably have been suspicious of anyone who'd suddenly become such a firm favourite. The King, he knew, was not even that close to his equerry, Peter Townsend.

When, a few days later, Eustace next went to the palace, it was apparent that the allocation of rooms to the new earl had been queried. This wasn't stated outright, but mention was made of the fact that it would be some time before Prince James was old enough to need any sort of tutor. This had prompted the King to suggest they should find some sort of nominal royal appointment, preferably to a completely meaningless role.

There followed one of the most frivolous and relaxed conversations Eustace had ever experienced with anyone, let alone His Majesty. Eustace smiled every time he thought about it.

'We must think of what post you could hold, Eustace.'

'Post, Sir?'

'Yes. It doesn't have to involve any work. I was thinking of something like "Keeper of the King's Swans".'[1]

'You already have one of those.'

'Oh? Do I?'

'Indeed, Sir. It is he who arranges the annual Swan Upping on the Thames.'

'Ah, yes of course. Well then, what about the dolphins? I gather I own any that are in coastal waters?'

'That's true. And other cetaceans like whales. Plus all the sturgeon.'

'Think anything might be doing in that department? I do like dolphins.'

'No. They all come under the Keeper of the Wreck, Sir.'

'Oh dear. Never mind. I suppose we don't really have to give you any sort of honorary role. I just thought it would be rather fun to dream up something which could have obscure associated rights. Then, in centuries to come, it will be an ancient quirk started in 1950. Embodied, maybe, by force of tradition? I'm sure we must have a corgi keeper.'

'I'm not very good with animals,' declared Eustace, 'though I am fond of my own dogs.' Entering into the spirit, he added, 'Perhaps I could be a housemaid, Sir?'

'I don't think the outfit would suit you. The role is not specific enough either, and does, I believe, entail work. No, we'll have to find you some ruined castle to look after. Do you know of any?'

'Actually, there is one to which I was often taken as a child.'

Thus it happened that Eustace became Custodian of Beeston Castle[2]. An excursion there would fit in very nicely with his planned visit to Willaston for the summer's Worm Charming Championship.

The next time he visited his little apartment, Eustace was amused to find that a small brass plaque, engraved with the title of his new post, had been affixed to the door. In addition to totally unnecessary palace accommodation, his appointment entitled him to an annual stipend of one groat and three pork pies, plus the right to shoot haggis on the Balmoral Estate.

And, this time, the discussion had ended with a 'please call me George.'

7TH JANUARY 1950

Peggy was still fretting about the problem of her sister's boyfriend. The store had been quieter than usual that Saturday, and the garrulous Mrs Bailey had been in full gossipy flow. She'd even examined, and actually purchased, a sugar bowl when another customer had threatened to divert Peggy's attention. The upshot was that Terry had twice been spotted with Doreen in a pub the other side of Greenwich. Peggy knew for a fact that, on one of the occasions mentioned, he was supposedly at night school. She could no longer put off saying something to Lil, and saw no way of doing so, other than by coming right out with it.

Lil, however, beat her to opening up the conversational agenda.

'I've been finkin' today, while I was dolin' out broken biscuits,' she announced, as the two set off for home.

'Oh yeah?'

'I've decided to learn shorthand and typin.'

'Why?'

'Because I'm fed up standin' on me plates³ all day. I want to better meself. I wish now that I'd done it straight from school, when Mum first suggested it. Don't know why I didn't. You could do the same.'

'No fanks. I don't wanna be stuck in some typin' pool all day, needin' to ask permission to blow me nose.'

'It wouldn't be like that if you were a secretary. You might even get to marry the boss!'

'Huh.'

'Well I wanna propa career.'

'If you got married, you wouldn't need a propa career. 'oo'd run the 'ome and look after the kiddies if you was out workin' all day?'

'While I *am* out workin' all day, I wanna be doin' somefin' different. So I'm goin' to sign up at the technical college.'

'And what does your Terry fink of that?'

'I 'aven't told him yet. Like I said, I've only just decided.'

'You seein' 'im this evenin'?' asked Peggy, finally able to get onto what she really wanted to talk about.

'Yes. 'is Mum and Dad are out, so we've got the place to ourselves.'

'Maybe you should make the most of it, then.'

'What d'you mean?'

'You know very well what I mean.'

'No I don't. You're always tellin' me to be careful. And I am. We don't go all the way. 'e says that if I really love him I would. But then everyone says that once a bloke's got what 'e wants, 'e ups and leaves a girl.'

'Which never seemed to make much sense to me. Surely 'e'd stick with 'er if 'e's gettin' what 'e wants so easy? But it's a diff'rent matter if he ain't. 'ave you ever fought that if Terry's not gettin' 'is way with you, 'e's lookin' for it somewhere else?'

'He wouldn't!'

'Accordin' to Mrs Bailey, 'e is.'

''oo with?'

'Doreen Carmichael.'

'That slut! Never!'

'Where did he tell you he was last Fursday?'

'Night school.'

'That's not his usual evenin' though, is it?'

'It was an extra class.'

'Think about it, Lil. 'e's always havin' extra classes, and last week's was held at the Angerstein, which just 'appens to be an 'otel with rooms.'

'I don't believe you.'

'Why would I make it up? Why would Mrs Bailey make it up?'

'Because she likes nuffin' better than to cause trouble. 'ow long is this supposed to 'ave been goin' on for?'

'Monfs.'

'Then why didn't you say somefin' sooner?'

'I didn't know 'til now. Lil, you must take this seriously, or you know what will 'appen. That schemin' bitch will end up pregnant, and he'll 'ave no choice but to make an 'onest woman of 'er.'

'I'll confront 'im tonight and see what 'e's got to say for 'imself.'

All that evening, Peggy waited impatiently for her sister's return. Such was her agitation, she could muster no interest in what was on the radio, even though she usually enjoyed 'In Town Tonight'. When the announcer said, 'Carry on, London,' she could recall almost nothing from the programme and decided to go to bed. There, she tried to immerse herself in Agatha Christie's latest Miss Marple novel, *A Murder is Announced*. After turning several pages without taking in a single word, Peggy finally gave up, put down the book, switched off her bedside lamp and nodded off with remarkable speed. How long she'd been asleep, she didn't know. Still drowsy, she was vaguely aware of movement in the room. The only illumination was the faint glow of a street lamp outside. A loud 'Ouch!' jolted her into full consciousness.

'Bloody 'ell, Lil,' she said, switching on the lamp and sitting up. 'What you playin' at?'

Lil was hopping around. 'All right. Keep yer 'air on. It's not easy fumblin' around in the dark, but I was tryin' to be quiet and not wake you. Then I went and stubbed me toe. It really 'urts.'

'What time is it?'

'One firty.'

'So what 'appened?'

''e denied it.'

'Well 'e would, wouldn't 'e? And what did you say?'

'I said I could always check, because Dad's a big pal of the landlord at the Angerstein.'

'Is 'e?'

Lil shook her head. 'But Terry doesn't know that.' She sat on her bed and started to rub the injured right big toe.

'And?' prompted Peggy.

''e got down on one knee and asked me to marry 'im!'

'And?'

'I got what I wanted.' Lil paused. 'And 'e got what 'e wanted.'

7

Tuesday 15th August 1945 was VJ Day, when the allied nations had rejoiced in their victory over Japan. Announced by Emperor Hirohito in the wake of the atomic bombings of Hiroshima and Nagasaki, the Japanese surrender had been marked by parades and street parties.

Exactly five years later, Britain was again in celebratory mood when HRH Princess Elizabeth gave birth to her second child. On the same day, three weeks prematurely, Lillian Dagley gave birth to her first.

Both the new arrivals were girls. One was born at Clarence House in the City of Westminster, the other at Lewisham Municipal Maternity Home[1]. One was subsequently baptised Anne Elizabeth Alice Louise, the other Janet Patricia.

Lil and Terry had queued outside the local registry office the previous March. Some of the other happy couples who rushed to tie the knot that month did so in order to take advantage of a full-year married man's tax allowance[2]. For the soon-to-be Mr and Mrs Dagley, the tax loophole had been a secondary consideration. After the ceremony, they'd spent one night in Southend-on-Sea by way of a honeymoon, before returning to Oareboro Road, Deptford.

The groom's parents' house was their first marital home. Harold and Daisy Dagley allowed the young couple to occupy the larger bedroom because it would, in due course, also need to accommodate an infant. It was a bit of a tight squeeze, the more so after Janet's arrival, but the arrangement suited Lil because Terry's mum provided a ready-made, and usually more than willing, babysitter. This meant that Lil could continue with her commercial studies, which she took very seriously. Every evening, she practised her Pitman shorthand by 'taking dictation' from the radio news broadcasts.

Peggy, too, was delighted to finally have what she'd always dreamed of – a bedroom to herself. Despite the extra space, it was a lot less tidy than it used to be when she'd shared it with her older sister.

THURSDAY 3RD MAY 1951

LONDON

On 1st May 1851 in Hyde Park, Queen Victoria opened the Great Exhibition. Housed in a specially constructed Crystal Palace, it was a world fair, celebrating industry and culture across the globe.

Almost exactly a century later, another large event began in London and elsewhere throughout the land. This time, the focus was exclusively on British inventiveness and genius. Described as 'a burst of primary colours', it was intended to bolster morale after years of gravy-brown and dull-green austerity.

At noon, after an interdenominational service of dedication at St Paul's Cathedral, Victoria's great-grandson, His Majesty George VI, declared open the Festival of Britain in 'England, Scotland, Wales and Northern Ireland.' From the cathedral steps, in a broadcast to the world, he said, 'This is no time for despondency, for I see this festival as a symbol of Britain's abiding courage and vitality.'

The flower-decked route taken by the royal procession from Buckingham Palace had been lined with thousands of people. Amongst the crowds were Lil and Peggy, who'd managed to wangle the day off work. The sisters found a spot at Temple Bar, the only surviving gateway to the City of London. It was a fortuitous choice of location, for the carriage containing Their Majesties and Princess Margaret halted just before it reached them.

'Why've they stopped?' asked Peggy, standing on tiptoe and craning her neck.

'Looks like there's some sort of ceremonial goin' on,' Lil replied, as the Lord Mayor presented the King with a sword, which was touched and offered back.[3]

'Can you see what Margaret's wearin'?'

'Pale grey. The Queen's in blue, with a matchin' feathery 'at. Oh, they're off again.'

Their Majesties drove past and were followed by the mounted household cavalry. A further open carriage came into sight.

Lil shoved Peggy in front of her and tried to lift her up a few inches. 'Go on then. 'ave a good swoon. Gawd, you're gettin' 'eavy.'

'I am not,' Peggy protested, as the Duke and Duchess of Edinburgh and Queen Mary drew level. The Queen Dowager sported a paler blue and wore flowers in her signature toque. Princess Elizabeth had chosen moss green.

Once all the lesser royals had gone by, the girls decided to walk along the Strand and cross the river to the South Bank, which was the festival's main focus in London. This was easier said than done. While quite a number of people seemed to have the same idea, others stayed put, which made for slow going. At one point, they came across a woman who had fainted in the crush.

'We'll never get in anywhere,' complained Peggy. 'There'll be queues for everyfin' a mile long.'

'That don't matter. It'll be nice just to be part of it. We'll see the Dome and the Skylon and the Festival 'all. Then we can go 'ome. Maybe find a place a bit quieter to 'ave a bite to eat a bit furver out.'

'We don't need to go spendin' our 'ard-earned money on eatin' out when we've brought sandwiches. We can visit the South Bank some other time, when it's less packed. And the Pleasure Gardens at Battersea, come to that. I'd rather go to somewhere on the royals' route back to the palace.'

'We don't know which way they'll go. They always say 'ow they get to any place, but never 'ow they get back. Maybe they'll be comin' along 'ere again? That's prob'ly why so many people are still hangin' about.'

'Well let's 'ead towards St James's Park. We just keep goin' straight instead of cuttin' off to the Embankment. We can 'ave a sort of picnic on the grass and enjoy a bit of greenery. It'll be grand.'

'If you want greenery, we've got Greenwich on our own doorstep, and you 'ardly ever go there.'

'Please, Lil. I want to make the most of me day off.'

Lil shrugged. Getting anywhere at all was going to prove difficult.

They'd just skirted Trafalgar Square when the bells of St Paul's started ringing in the distance, and the sound of cannon fire seemed to come from all directions, including (they guessed) nearby Hyde Park. 'Blimey. I'm glad I'm not any closer. 'alf the population of London must be stone deaf by now. What sandwiches did you bring, Peg?'

'Marmite.'

'You know I don't like Marmite. Pity, or we could've swapped. I've got fish paste.'

'Well I'm not keen on that, so we'll stick to our own. I brought a bottle of pop but I daren't drink any of it or I'll need a wee. Where d'you fink the nearest toilets are?'

'Dunno. 'yde Park maybe? Otherwise, Waterloo station? We need to get a move on, wherever we're 'eaded. So start doin' a bit more bargin' and elbowin.'

And that's how the sisters happened to be part of the crowd outside Clarence House when the two little princes, both in pale blue coats, were standing on the garden wall. Urged to wave by their accompanying nurses, James and Charles were rewarded with a huge response from those who were gathered, as well as smiles and waves from the personages sitting in the carriages that, before long, were passing by at quite a clip. The added bonus was catching another glimpse of Princess Elizabeth and her husband.

'Was that uvva boy James?' Peggy asked, as they reluctantly turned away, now the show was over. 'I mean, I recognised Charles, but we never get to see anyfin' at all of 'is uncle.'

'Must've been. Don't see 'oo else it could've been. But I don't know why they keep 'im 'idden away. 'e looked normal enough to me.'

'Maybe 'e's sickly, and they don't want 'im catchin' anyfin' nasty?'

It had indeed been a rare public appearance for James. His mother was highly protective of his privacy and did her best to ensure that no photographs of him were made public. Whilst James's young nephew and niece were not exactly being thrust into the public eye, they were already familiar to most people. The same could not be said of the invisible heir.

The newspapers the following day were full of the events. In the evening, the royal party had attended the opening of the Royal Festival Hall. Lil and Peggy devoured all the details. The Queen was wearing a crinoline-type gown of pink patterned with silver. Her older daughter wore a cyclamen silk dress ornamented with roses in the same material, and Margaret's all-white net and silk confection was topped with an ermine cape.

Peggy wanted an ermine cape.

25TH DECEMBER 1951

STANDFORD STREET, DEPTFORD

As they'd done the previous year, the Faulkner and Dagley households joined forces to celebrate Christmas. The Dagleys had hosted the gathering in 1950, when Janet was only four months old. This time, it was the Faulkners' turn. Initially, the presence of a one-year-old toddling around kept them all mindful of her safety, but then they relaxed, figuring everyone else was staying alert.

The centrepiece of the festive dinner was roast chicken, a rare treat indeed, even though it was slightly overcooked. 'Better that than underdone,' said Joyce, by way of apology.

Janet, who'd managed earlier to find and consume some chocolate, had been uncontrollably super-charged. No one admitted to the covert administration of the offending chocolate, but Joyce blamed Daisy, Daisy blamed Joyce, and Lil knew it had been her father-in-law Harold. He and Ron were now engaged in a lively debate about the National Health Service. Harold sided with 'Nye' Bevan, who had rejected a proposal to charge for 'spectacles and teeth'. Ron, a lifelong Conservative voter, argued that the population should regard themselves lucky that they now had free access to medical services. Where would it all lead, if people became dependent on the welfare state to provide for their every need? The split between the left- and right-wing factions within the previous Labour government had resulted in a snap general election last autumn and Churchill's return to power. When the men's conversation escalated into the openly argumentative, Joyce intervened by throwing a tea towel at her husband and telling him to 'stop bangin' on about bloody politics'.

By 3 p.m., the dishes had been cleared away, the table flaps folded down and enough chairs mustered to enable everyone to sit around the radio. Janet, her energy finally exhausted, was dozing on her mother's lap.

The King's voice filled the room. 'Though we live in hard, critical times, Christmas, as always, will be a time when we can, and should, count our blessings.' His Majesty went on to say, 'We are a friendly people. If there is anything that we can offer to the world today, perhaps it is an example of tolerance and understanding that runs like a golden thread through the great and diverse family of the British Commonwealth.'

Most of those listening in homes worldwide were unaware that, for the first time ever, the seasonal message had been pre-recorded.

By the end of the broadcast, Peggy was crying silent tears. Lil asked her why she was upset.

''e sounded so frail.'

'No 'e didn't,' reassured their mother Joyce. ''e's always been nervous about makin' speeches, so it's not surprisin' that 'is voice was a bit wobbly.'

'And 'e spoke of his recovery, didn't 'e?' contributed Daisy. ''e fanked all them doctors and nurses 'oo'd made 'im better.'

Peggy caught her father's eye. Ron, his expression sombre, nodded in confirmation that he agreed with his younger daughter.

8

At 10.45 a.m. on Wednesday 6th February 1952, it was announced from Sandringham that His Majesty King George VI, who had appeared to be in his usual health when he retired on Tuesday night, had passed away peacefully in his sleep.

The world heard the news of George's sudden death by radio broadcasts, which began at 11.15 a.m. After several repeats, the BBC was respectfully silent for five hours. Across London, the bells at Westminster Abbey tolled, as did the Great Tom Bell at St Paul's Cathedral. The single dong, sounding every minute for two hours, was the complete antithesis of the previous May's merry pealing. Britain was plunged into mourning.

On 7th February, Prime Minister Winston Churchill addressed the nation in a moving tribute, referring to the King as greatly loved by all his peoples. 'He was respected as a man and as a Prince. We thought of him as a young naval lieutenant in the great Battle of Jutland. We thought of him when calmly he assumed the heavy burden of the Crown. During these last months, the King walked with death. In the end, death came as a friend. The newspapers and photographs of modern times have made vast numbers of his subjects able to watch with emotion the last months of his pilgrimage.'

Along with her parents, Peggy listened. She and Ron were weeping unashamedly. Peggy had never before seen her father cry – not even when Grandma died – though he'd been close to tears of anger during the '49 and '50 dock strikes.

7TH FEBRUARY 1952

ABOARD BOAC FLIGHT FROM ENTEBBE (UGANDA) TO LONDON

Lady-in-waiting Pamela Mountbatten had withdrawn, leaving Princess Elizabeth and Prince Phillip alone in a private area of the plane.

'So, do we know what being Princess Regent[1] actually entails?' Phillip asked his wife.

'Yes. It was all discussed last September, in case Papa didn't come through that awful operation. In effect, I'm king.'

'Well I hope that doesn't involve anything drastic biologically. So what's the phrase? *In loco rex*?'

'*In rege locum*, apparently. There's such a lot to think about, Phillip, and I can't think clearly about anything at the moment, beyond getting home to Mummy and Margaret. They'll be utterly devastated. Poor Papa. I hope he didn't suffer.'

'I'm sure he slipped quietly away.'

'But it's all so sudden.'

'I suppose we're facing no bigger an adjustment than your suddenly becoming queen.'

'It's as big. I'm so sorry. This isn't good news for either of us, is it? A few more years and you'd have been Admiral of the Fleet, entirely on your own merits and fully deserved.'

'It would have taken longer than a few, but there's no point getting upset over what might have been. Has Britain ever had a Princess Regent before?'

'Not to my knowledge. There was the Prince Regent, of course. The one who had the park, and street and even the canal named after him.'

'I never knew that. Or, rather, I never thought about it before. The first decision will, I suppose, be how your brother is to be known. He's got plenty of names to go at. Or could something completely different be chosen?'

'In theory, I think so. Eustace would know. But one that James already has would be more usual. I did always wonder why Victoria opted for her second name. Everyone talks of "the Victorian era", but it could equally have been "the Alexandrinian era".'

'Doesn't have quite the same ring to it, does it? But then nobody would be thinking any differently, had it been the other way round. The most obvious choice here would be James III. I know that the Old Pretender styled himself that way, but that was centuries ago, so it shouldn't be a problem?'

'I don't imagine so. The Young Pretender was known as Charles III, but we didn't think twice about that when we named our own "Bonnie Prince Charlie". It seems strange now, that when he was born, we expected he would succeed to the throne one day.'

'True enough. How quickly everything changed. Our new monarch could alternatively be declared George VII, or Richard IV, or even King Patrick, King Fergus, King Owain or King Alfred. Or would that be Alfred II?'

'I'm not completely sure. Alfred the Great was only king of Wessex. It would upset the Scots if James followed it with a regnal number, and it might upset the people of Wessex if he didn't! I think we can rule it out as a serious contender anyway.'

'So who will decide, given that James isn't old enough to choose for himself?'

'Officially, the Accession Council, I suppose. But then again, not. They're really only part of the complicated ceremonial surrounding the dea – ' The Princess stopped before uttering the word which carried such finality. ' – this particular eventuality. They'll have met yesterday evening, but will need to meet again, so I can take the oath on James's behalf. Only then can an official proclamation be made. We shall need to be quick about deciding on a regnal name. Oh no! What a mess!'

'How so?'

'As Queen Consort, Mummy was automatically a Counsellor of State[2]. But, equally automatically, is not anymore, so she can't represent me at the Privy Council. All of a sudden, she'll have found herself shut out from all the decision-taking bodies. That seems very wrong. It seems wrong, too, that it's technically down to me, and not her, to choose the name under which her own son is to rule. It's a matter of such great magnitude. I'll have to talk to her and then recommend whatever she prefers. That's unless she comes up with something ridiculous. Thank goodness we have Winnie to help steer us.'

'Is that the royal "we" already?'

'No, silly, I meant you and me. I've already made one decision. I'm going to be styled Duchess of Edinburgh[3] first and Princess Regent second. That's only proper.'

'Only, sweet thought though it is, I have a feeling it won't prove to be "proper" and therefore won't be allowed,' said Phillip. 'Duty to king and country first – and all that.'

Elizabeth was almost whispering. 'Yes, of course. Duty first and always. '

Pamela tapped on the door and entered discreetly. 'We're an hour away from landing, ma'am. Time to get changed.'

Phillip squeezed his wife's arm. 'Best foot forward, Cabbage. Paste on the smile.'

'Yes. Best foot forward.'

At Churchill's suggestion, the Counsellors of State met the following day, prior to the full Accession Council gathering at St James's Palace. These were the Princesses Elizabeth and Margaret, their uncle Prince Henry of Gloucester, and their aunt Princess Mary, Countess of Harewood, King George V's only daughter. Styled the Princess Royal since 1932, she was only eleventh in line to the throne, but most of those who ranked higher were still minors: Charles and Anne, the two sons of the Duke of Gloucester, and the late Duke of Kent's three children. Princess Mary would only be relinquishing her Counsellor role – and thus her place on the Privy Council – when her nephew, the young Duke of Kent, turned twenty-one in 1956.

There was no doubt that the Queen Dowager should also attend the meeting, at which a unanimous decision was endorsed.

Once the formalities had been completed, the official announcement could finally be made. 'We, therefore, the Lords Spiritual and Temporal of this Realm, being here assisted by His late Majesty's Privy Council, do now hereby with one voice and Consent of the Tongue and Heart publish and proclaim that the High and Mighty Prince James Alfred Fergus Patrick Richard George Owain is now, by the death of our late sovereign of happy memory, become King James III, by the Grace of God, King of this Realm and of all His other Realms and Territories, Head of the Commonwealth, Defender of the Faith. And we do further declare that, under the terms of the 1937 Regency Act, the Royal Princess Elizabeth, as heir presumptive, does become Princess Regent and has, accordingly, taken the oath to govern on behalf of His Majesty.'

This was first read out on Friday 8th February by the Garter Principal King of Arms, The Honourable Sir George Bellew. He did so from the Proclamation Gallery overlooking Friary Court at St James's Palace. It was then repeated by the heralds of the College of Arms in various traditional London locations. In Edinburgh, the heralds of the Court of the Lord Lyon read the same proclamation from Mercat Cross.

15TH FEBRUARY 1952

WINDSOR CASTLE

'Mummy's distraught.'

'Well that's only to be expected. She's just buried her husband and managed to get through it all without shedding a tear. Hurrah for the British stiff upper lip.'

'She's certainly making up for it now,' replied Elizabeth, fighting back her own tears. 'That stiff "upper" doesn't always stop the lower wobbling. They were so devoted, despite the spats.'

'Is anyone with her?'

'When I left, Grandmamma was still there. We mustn't forget that she's just buried a son. It's all too horribly much to take in.'

'Do you know what she will do now?'

'Return to Marlborough House, I suppose.'

'Your mother?' asked the Duke, clarifying what he'd meant in the first place.

'Back to the palace, but not for very long. Her declared intent is to withdraw from public life completely and forever. Oh Phillip, that would mean I've lost both parents. Mummy's going up to Caithness. Doris has already invited her,' said Elizabeth, referring to Doris Vyner, one of the Queen Dowager's closest friends.

'The north coast of Scotland can be very chilly at this time of year. It's to be hoped that Doris can afford the heating bills. We'll certainly be saving on ours!'

The quip didn't strike quite the right note.

'It won't be so amusing if we find ourselves meeting the restoration costs of Barrogill!'

'Where?'

'It's a barely habitable sixteenth-century castle near John o' Groats. Fine views of the Orkney Islands on a clear day, so I'm told. Mummy wants to have a look at it, with purchasing in mind.'

'What! Wouldn't she prefer another racehorse? Less expensive than buying and doing up a derelict castle, I imagine.'

'One can't hide away in a thoroughbred, or even in its stable. Besides, I've already suggested to her that it would be easier to get down to Fairlawne from here. But, much though she's always loved going, its attractions are proving strangely resistible.'

'Aren't there any suitable caves up there? We could do one up if she really is intent on becoming a hermit? Or maybe my mother could employ her? Then she'd only need a wimple. It would save on hats.' Once again, the attempt at levity failed.

'Seriously, Phillip, I'd far rather she stayed here. First and foremost, there's James to consider. I'm not even sure that Dunnet Head can accommodate a nursery suite, and it would mean uprooting him from everything that's familiar. But, unless she takes him with her, he's bound to wonder where both she and Papa have gone. He won't even have Crackers around to terrorise any more.'

Elizabeth stooped to pat Susan, the pet who'd been an eighteenth birthday gift and who had accompanied the Princess and her new husband on their honeymoon. Crackers, a Pembrokeshire corgi, was an equally cherished companion of the Queen Dowager. Woman and dog were almost inseparable.

'I'm sure the boy will quickly adapt and transfer his less-than-gentle gestures of affection to some other unfortunate creature. Poor little chap. He's aware that something serious has happened, even if he doesn't understand what.'

'I know. He fell about laughing when I curtsied to him.'

'We can probably dispense with that formality for now, except in public.'

'He has no concept whatsoever of what being king is all about, let alone the fact that he is one. He has a much better understanding of reaching the ripe old age of three, and catching up with Charles. It was such a nice little nursery party yesterday. Took everyone's mind off things, for just a short while.'

'Until he and Anne were sick, so I understand?'

'The cake was rather rich. Even Mummy said so.'

'I'm glad she hasn't lost her appetite. It sounds like we need to talk some sense into your mother. But don't look at me – she won't listen to anything I say.'

Elizabeth sighed.

'Perhaps it's a little early. She may need a period of private mourning. And it's not just Papa she's lost. It's her whole status. It really packed her a wallop that she's no longer Queen Consort. She's not even a Counsellor of State any more. It's all terribly upsetting.'[4]

'But she could still have a big say in things, couldn't she? It isn't as though you're going to quibble about her every suggestion. The way I see it, she could end up with the best of both worlds. You get to deal with the tedious stuff, like the daily despatch boxes, and she gets to decide on pretty much everything else.'

'If she doesn't have any official status, it still leaves her in a sort of wilderness.'

'She could carry on being the real power behind the throne though, couldn't she? That wouldn't be so very different.'

'Except for the tiny point that she's no longer queen. She'll keep the title, of course, but it won't be the same. She'll just be another widow of a king, like Grandmamma. Grandmamma never seemed to mind, but Mummy does.'

'Well then, perhaps some sort of diversion would be useful? Maybe we need to find her a cosy domestic hobby? Your grandmother has been perfectly content all these years working, and spending excessively might I add, on the Royal Collection.'[5]

'I'm wondering if there's any way of formalising a role for Mummy. It would help enormously if we could. Reinstating her as a Counsellor would be a step in the right direction, but I doubt it would be enough. And I wish there were a way of distracting Margaret, too. There's no comforting her. Papa was her whole world. She always relished being his joy.'

'And never forget that you were his pride, Lilibet. And quite rightly so. It's not everyone who would add to their own sadness by taking on board the grief of others. Not to mention the weight of all your new responsibilities.'

Phillip took out his handkerchief and gently wiped away a tear from his wife's cheek.

'There, there, Cabbage. Let your mother go up to Scotland for now, but have a word with Winnie at the next audience. He'll know how best to handle things.'

'If he can think of anything, I'll agree to whatever it takes, and I'll do whatever it takes.'

Peggy cried very easily these days. From Lil's point of view, this tendency was preferable to an unnatural stoicism and periods of moodiness, which had been so characteristic of her sister in the years following the V-2 bombing of New Cross Woolworths. Peggy was sobbing now, as she had been in Westminster Hall, when the two of them, along with more than 300,000 others, had filed past the coffin at the late king's lying-in-state. Peggy hadn't been alone in her grief then, and wasn't now. Throughout the auditorium, people were mopping their eyes, and many were blubbing loudly.

The sisters had come to see *The Greatest Show on Earth*, and Lil had to admit that the Technicolour film about a travelling circus was in stark contrast to what they were now watching: the sombre black-and-white Pathé news footage covering George VI's funeral. She herself was almost moved to tears by the narrative and by the power of tradition, especially when it came to the section outside St George's Chapel, where the navy piped His Majesty 'over the side'.

The King's coffin, borne on a gun carriage, was draped in the royal standard, atop of which was a widow's wreath of orchids and lilies of the valley, along with the Imperial State Crown, the cross-mounted orb and the sceptre – symbols of kingly power and justice. Just behind, in the mile-long procession, was a coach, in which the grieving ladies of His late Majesty's household – a wife and two daughters – travelled. This was followed by four men, walking side by side: the Duke of Edinburgh, the sixteen-year-old Duke of Kent and the late king's surviving brothers, the Dukes of Windsor and Gloucester. Monarchs and presidents from other nations were there, all paying their respects to the perfect embodiment of a constitutional ruler, 'George the Good'. The royal guard marched with weapons reversed in mourning. All that could be heard was the rhythmic pounding of footsteps, as London fell silent and still along the three and a half mile route to Paddington station, where a train waited to convey the King to his final destination. '"Grant him thy peace oh lord we pray, who of us all has earned it best, who wore for us his life away, give thou this king a warrior's rest". And so to Royal Windsor, where His Majesty and family found respite from the many cares of state which he had made his own. Let us all strive to make our young king's reign prosperous and great.'

The two women left the cinema in subdued mood, although Peggy did have the distraction of fancying herself in love with Charlton Heston.

9

JUNE 1952

BUCKINGHAM PALACE

Winston Churchill had travelled to Scotland and managed to persuade the Queen Dowager to come out of hibernation. He'd reported the resultant proposals earlier that day.

'How did it go?' Phillip enquired.

'Mummy's about to emerge from her chrysalis.'

'And return as a butterfly – or moth?'

'As soon as the Act's gone through, she'll officially be taking over the regency from me and will become Queen Elizabeth, the Queen Regent. But there are certain conditions.'

'I thought there would be. Those being that you end up as the drudge?'

'I honestly don't mind.'

'Will she have the patience to bone up enough on current affairs in order to have a meaningful discussion every week with the PM?'

'She probably doesn't need to, at least for as long as it's Winnie. He's been enormously helpful to me and spends hours explaining things. I'm sure he'll guide Mummy in the same way.'

'And will she read up on the background stuff before she meets foreign dignitaries? It's easy to put one's foot in it.'

'As you know from personal experience.'

'But I have at least managed to avoid creating diplomatic gaffes. Well, major ones at any rate. And what about speeches? I know she did a tremendous amount to help your father cope, but she never undertook any of them on his behalf, did she? "I name this ship" is about the extent of her public speaking. Beyond that, she always just stood there smiling and looking enigmatic. As regent, she can't stay "utterly oyster"[1] forever. At the very minimum, she'll have to open Parliament and read out what His Majesty's government proposes to fail to do.'

'We'll just have to feel our way as we go along. Tommy, or one of his assistants, always drafts the speeches, and I can help her with the finishing touches. We can keep them brief, at least to start with, and gradually build up her confidence. The rest of us, including Margaret, can take the brunt. Uncle Henry is already doing his bit and may agree to take on more – though, like Papa, he's really rather shy, which can make him come across as rather stuffy, so we'll need to ensure we don't overburden him.'

'You seem to have it all worked out.'

'I wish that were true. Oh, and she's decided to buy that dear little castle[2]. She thinks it would be rather fun to have a "small house" as an escape. The old man who lived there wanted to give it to her, but she's paying a hundred pounds for it.'

'I thought it was crumbling?'

'Not quite. Part of the roof's gone, and electricity needs to be installed, but I'm sure it can be managed.'

'Couldn't she go and stay again with Doris whenever she has a hankering for the far north?'

'She wouldn't be alone in someone else's place, would she?'

'She won't be alone at this Barrogill ruin either, unless she's planning on doing her own cooking and housework. So what onerous task is first on the Queen Regent designate's agenda?'

'Hopefully something she'll find rather fun. Approval of

stamps and coinage. The designs for both have just arrived, and they look very promising. It should be straightforward.'

'Something tells me those might be famous last words.'

Thanks to the initial facilitation of George, and the continuing encouragement of Princess Elizabeth, Eustace was now a familiar figure in the corridors of Buckingham Palace, and he'd started to use his accommodation in the royal residence a little more often. Rather than return home to Bayswater after a stint at UCL, he sometimes went straight to his small sanctuary for a quick bath, a change of clothes and a few minutes' relaxation before calling in to see His young Majesty. The sherry supply remained constant, even though he rarely drank it but, following a tentative request, this had long since been supplemented by bottles of gin, tonic water and (initially unaccountably) Dubonnet. He'd later discovered that the Queen Regent's favourite mixer had automatically been provided. In his room, there was now even a small refrigerator with a freezer compartment that contained ice. He brought his own lemons to slice because, despite leaving the evidence, they never materialised. The fruit was one of the food items he'd most missed during the war.

Recently affixed to the entrance door to his rooms was his own personal coat of arms, which had finally got through the College of Arms' approval process. It featured six earthworms rampant flanked by two bulldogs couchant. Above these, a coronet of a British earl was depicted[3]. Beneath was the motto he'd decided to adopt: *Qui cessat esse melior cessat esse bonus* ('He who ceases to be better, ceases to be good'). The inscription had been found in a bible belonging to Oliver Cromwell but, despite this, Eustace considered it an apt refection of a philosophy which he'd embraced all his life. He'd shown the draft design to the King, the day before His Majesty had set off for Sandringham. It had turned out to be their last ever meeting, and he was glad he and his friend had parted for that final time on a high note of shared laughter.

Try as he might, Eustace couldn't recall very much about the early development of his own children. Edith had been the one to point out when they started grabbing objects, rolling over or sitting unaided, all of which were apparently significant. He most certainly *had* noticed when they began to crawl. It was like having an extra dog, and indeed one of them (possibly Howard) had eaten half a bowl of Chappie before they'd noticed. As for talking, they both seemed to jump from unintelligible sounds to words and sentences without his even registering.

It had therefore taken him a while to fully recognise just how prodigious young James was. Eustace took his duty towards the boy very seriously, and ensured, from the outset, that he missed no opportunity to visit the nursery which, for the purposes of companionship and convenience, was often shared by both young royals, even though Charles' parents now resided at Clarence House.

Officially in charge was Helen Lightbody, and she ruled her domain with an iron rod. Her regimented approach was designed to ensure that children did not become spoilt or fussy. The long arm of her influence even extended to the palace kitchen, where dishes for the youngsters often had to be remade in accordance with her personal whims. She seemed to take pleasure in exercising a reign of terror, and everyone was scared to death of her, including Eustace.

He felt a much greater affinity towards Nanny Mabel. Miss Anderson was a disciple of Dr Spock, and the paediatrician's publication *The Common Sense Book of Baby and Child Care* was her bible. She didn't throw routine out of the window, but recognised that not everything could be achieved by enforcement. Little ones needed affection, comfort and gentle encouragement.

It was Miss Anderson who first pointed out the speed at which James was progressing. During her time spent in other households, she had adopted the practice of jotting down careful reminders of what a child might be doing at any given age. But she was wise enough to recognise that her small charges could differ widely in their attainment of each stage.

Around the time of his first birthday, James was already using several words and responding to simple instructions. 'Compare him to Charles,' Nanny Mabel had suggested. 'Charles is doing exactly what I'd expect for his age.'

Eustace had followed Nanny's advice but, at first, couldn't properly see what she'd been getting at. However, over the months, the differences became more noticeable. By the time the royal family had left to spend Christmas at Windsor in 1951, the tot was having simple conversations with adults. He'd also begun to recognise colours and was counting accurately to seven.

That same month, the Earl's nineteen-year-old daughter Cathy started working part-time at the Lollipops kindergarten in Belgravia. This establishment promised a 'caring and learning environment' for children aged two to five years.

The job was intended as a stop-gap measure – something to do before she decided on the direction any future career might take. From Eustace's point of view, it was a happy coincidence.

It provided him with a further source of comparison. The two of them spent many evenings discussing toddler behaviours and attainments. Cathy, in turn, carefully recorded the progress of her privileged young charges and did this much more systematically than had ever been the case. In due course, father and daughter began to classify the milestones of early development. They started with 'linguistic' and quickly added 'social' and 'physical'. 'Artistic/representational' and 'reasoning/logic' followed a short while later.

In Deptford, no one was monitoring the progress of little Janet Dagley, who spent much of the time in the company of her grandparents. Granddad Harold who, since well before Terry arrived, had always longed for a daughter, was especially devoted. He was always on hand to engage in role-play games with her. He was variously cast as shopkeeper, prince, dragon, cat owner (the small girl especially enjoyed pretending to be a kitten) and a lone crocodile that managed to infest an entire imaginary river. The pair also whiled away many companionable hours looking through books together.

Secure in the knowledge that Janet was being well cared for, Lil – now a qualified shorthand typist – had started working for the London, Midland and Scottish Railway Company, in the offices above St Pancras station. Thanks to the Dagleys' generosity, very little of what she earned was spent on board and lodging, so she and Terry were able to start putting money aside.

Peggy, meanwhile, continued to work in Woolworths and dream of finding love.

10

BUCKINGHAM PALACE

The Duchess of Edinburgh was becoming exasperated.

'Every single man in the Windsor family has hair which parts naturally to the left, Mummy, and James is no exception.'[1]

'And therefore his left profile is his better one.'

'And that's what will appear on the new stamps. It's always the left profile on stamps. But it needs to be his right on coins.'

'Why?'

'It's what tradition dictates. The direction the monarch faces on coins should be a reversal of the way their predecessor faced.'[2]

'I seem to remember that a certain person, whose name shall not be mentioned, broke that rule,' Elizabeth's mother argued stubbornly. 'You see, I've done some homework. But feel free to correct me if I'm wrong.'

'No, you're not wrong, Mummy. And why did Uncle David insist on that? There can only be two reasons. Either he wanted to show he was breaking with convention – '

'Which he went on to demonstrate in a far more spectacular way – '

'Or he did it for reasons of pure vanity, to show off what he considered to be his better side.'

Elizabeth let her observations hang mid-air. Eventually, her mother mumbled a few indecipherable words and nodded.

'Well, James needs his own crown. He's only three, so he can hardly feature wearing the Imperial State Crown or, heaven forbid, one of the lighter-weight ladies' ones. It would look like he was wearing a tiara. I'm sure your grandmamma will be able to find suitable adornments from the Royal Collection, and we could get something specially commissioned.'

'Or,' Elizabeth suggested, 'we could simply go along with these very nice designs that feature an invented one. They don't make him look top-heavy. The alternative would be to dispense with a crown altogether, as Papa and Grandpapa did. It's not mandatory.'

'No. He would just end up looking like a baby if we didn't include some symbol of royalty.' The soon-to-be Queen Regent took a closer look at the prototypes. 'I suppose they are quite attractive, and they do make him look very regal.'

'James liked them, too.'

'You've shown them to him?' The princess' mother seemed genuinely surprised.

'Why not? I wondered whether he'd recognise himself.'

'And did he?'

'Yes, after a bit of prompting. I tried to explain his new status and he seemed to understand. He asked if that meant he had to be "coronated"!'

'Well I never. When do the coins go into circulation?'

'It will take a while, I think. Later this year or early next year is my understanding. I don't know which denomination will be struck first, or perhaps they'll all be issued at once.'

'And what about postboxes and public telephone boxes?'

'The telephone boxes won't change. But a cipher is being devised to go on pillar boxes.'

'Do they all have to be replaced?'

'No, only added to, where a new one is needed. I'm afraid

I've already agreed the specification for the cipher. I went for a simple "JIIIR" with no intertwining of initials.'

'You could have consulted me.'

'I tried, but you weren't taking calls.'

'You might have waited. Is there such an urgent need for postboxes?'

'Apparently, yes. Even during the short reign of "he whose name we do not mention", over a hundred and sixty were installed. And we mustn't forget about service medals either, especially with the Korean War.'

'Now we've dispensed with that, can we please discuss the ideas I have for Barrogill Castle? I've decided to restore its original name of the Castle of Mey. Some of those last-century additions will have to go.'

———

The necessary constitutional changes were agreed by Parliament and officially enacted in early 1953. The late king's widow became Queen Elizabeth The Queen Regent and, at her suggestion, Princess Elizabeth and her young family permanently relocated to nearby Clarence House. Prince Phillip, who'd spent a lot of time directing the updating of the residence's interiors, was delighted to return. It was, however, deemed sensible that, during the daytime, the three children should be brought up together and continue to share the familiarity of the Buckingham Palace nursery and staff.

'So, the deed is done?' asked Phillip.

'Yes, it's all official and I'm no longer king.' Princess Elizabeth was at her desk, marking up a typed page of writing, which Tommy had just delivered.

'Are you relieved?'

'I'm not sure how I'm feeling. Mummy will need a lot of

support. The trickiest thing will be getting her to concentrate. You know how she simply switches off and refuses to listen if she isn't interested in a subject.'

'So what's that you're working on?'

'Her first ever speech. She's managed to dodge doing one whilst not officially regent, but she won't be able to avoid it forever.'

'It doesn't look very long.'

'We decided on the shorter the better. And we've chosen an informal event to start off with.'

'You mean she's not addressing the troops at Tilbury?'

'No, she's going to Larne in Northern Ireland. It will be a combination of mingling with the people who were affected by that tragic ferry sinking and then saying just a few words about those who were lost and the bravery of the Donaghadee crew. She'll also have a tour of the –,' Elizabeth consulted the draft script, '– the *Sir Samuel Kelly* lifeboat itself.'

'That bit won't take long. I thought she was going to cut her teeth on some cosy event. Wasn't there a Women's Institute fundraiser in Surrey that she was supposed to be speaking at?'

'Yes. Next Friday. Margaret's doing that one now, because Mummy wants to get down to Fairlawne early.'

'Can't she detour on the way?'

'Seemingly not, and that's a pity, because there are some nice humorous touches in the speech. They'll go down well, which Mummy might have found encouraging. Larne will be an altogether different prospect. No scope at all for levity. Even so, as patron of the RNLI, she'll be amongst friends.'

'I hope these trips to Kent don't get out of hand. We don't want to reach a situation whereby every day except Wednesday is ruled out for fear of ruining both weekends.'

'That won't happen.'

'Well, if these chummy house parties do start to cause an absentee problem, perhaps they should at least be put to productive use. Why not ask Tommy to summarise the key points – those that absolutely must be included in any speech – then get your mother to ask Noël Coward to write the bulk of the text? And, while we're at it, we could perhaps get Mr Coward to keep reminding her that "work is much more fun than fun"?'

'Talking of work, how are your plans for Dartmouth shaping up?'

The couple had optimistically concluded that, once the role of regent had been relinquished, Princess Elizabeth would not be quite so constrained, even if she couldn't manage to feel less pressurised. It had followed that Phillip might therefore be able to continue his navy career, albeit only partially. Discussions had resulted in a proposed posting to Dartmouth Royal Naval College. It was where he himself trained, and now he would be training new generations of officer recruits. He'd have preferred active service, of course, but that was ruled out – it would have meant overseas duties and unacceptably prolonged absences.

As it was, after resuming his new role, he ended up spending a fair amount of time in Devon. Princess Elizabeth missed him. His absence necessitated performing more of her public duties on a solo basis, but Margaret also managed perfectly well without an escort, so this was no cause for complaint. There was, too, some consolation in that Phillip's absence from London kept him away from all those glamorous showgirls and society ladies, who were falling over themselves to attract his attention – and possibly more than just his passing attention. She never forgot the time when her husband had been seen dancing the night away at the Milroy nightclub with musical star Pat Kirkwood. Heavily pregnant with Prince Charles and feeling decidedly frumpy, Elizabeth had known she couldn't possibly compete with a doe-eyed actress, whose famously long legs were described as 'the eighth wonder of the world'. How furious her usually mild-mannered Papa had been![3]

Pat was a member of the Thursday Club in Soho, where Phillip also liked to party. Film star Merle Oberon, known as Queenie, was another woman cast in the role of siren. The list seemed endless and, on occasions, the Princess was haunted by the famous line from *Lady Windermere's Fan*: 'I can resist everything except temptation.'

NOVEMBER 1953

BUCKINGHAM PALACE

The recent arrival at Buckingham Palace of Catherine Peebles meant that the King and his nephew had started to receive formal tuition. The governess, who soon earned the fond nickname of 'Mipsy', had previously been employed in the Kent household and had come highly recommended.

From the outset, Eustace had done his best to fulfil the sketchy brief he'd been given, but some aspects hadn't always proved easy. When James started crowing that he was worth more than Charles and Anne, Eustace had at first been bewildered, but quickly realised that his protégé was referring to the new National Savings Stamps[4]. Those featuring Anne could be bought for only sixpence and the ones depicting Charles, a shilling. James's cost half a crown. Eustace tried to explain that every human life had equal value.

'Even criminals?' the boy had asked. Fearful of being drawn into a debate about capital punishment[5], Eustace issued the challenge. 'How much do you think I'm worth?' After a moment's thought, James replied in all seriousness, 'You're priceless.' Eustace still didn't know how he managed to avoid laughing.

Whilst the Earl of Willaston and the late king had been on the cosiest of terms, and whilst he was certainly a favourite with all the children, Eustace had never reached the same level of intimacy with any other member of the royal family. Most of them were friendly enough towards him, but the Queen, and to a lesser extent Princess Margaret, remained suspicious. With them, he still felt like an interloper.

As he rarely encountered Margaret, Her Royal Highness wasn't a problem. But he knew he had only been invited to today's meeting because of His late Majesty's express wish that he should be directly involved in all decisions affecting James's education. His exclusion would have been in blatant contravention of that wish, but he was nevertheless well aware that the boy's mother would far rather he hadn't been there.

Matters were complicated still further by the fact that they were discussing not only James's schooling but also Charles'. The Duke of Edinburgh was already known to have strong opinions about which establishments his own son should attend. He wanted Charles to follow him to Cheam and then to Gordonstoun. The belief had already been expressed that both youngsters should ultimately go to Gordonstoun. 'It would make men out of the pair of them.'

Eustace didn't disagree that the Scottish establishment would ideally suit James, who was outgoing, sociable and confident. The only reservation he had was that the boy would constantly find himself looking out for his shyer nephew – fine to a limited extent, but not fine if the protector role became too all-consuming and started impacting on James's own friendships and studies. So, in the Earl's mind, different schools from the outset had to be the way forward. He was fond of Charles, but it was with ensuring the young king's best interests that Eustace had been solemnly charged, and those must therefore be his primary concern.

He could only hope that a diplomatic approach today would do the trick.

It was clear from the outset that the Queen Regent didn't want either her son or her grandson to attend a school of any description. A governess, topped up in Elizabeth's case with one-to-one tuition, had served her daughters perfectly adequately. The Duke of Edinburgh was unhappy about this. Both the Gloucester princes and all three Kent children were happily settled at school, or was this being too dangerously progressive?

Princess Elizabeth mentioned that the boys needed the further society of others their own age. Her mother's solution to this was to form a Buckingham Palace Wolf Cub pack. The palace Brownie pack, established for the benefit of the princesses, had always been very jolly.

When these comments were totally ignored, Her Majesty feigned contriteness, pretended to zip her mouth, and the debate continued without any further input from her.

It was rapidly confirmed that, whilst an initial period of home tuition was in order, James and Charles should eventually be sent as boarders to a suitable preparatory school. Keen to stick to his own agenda of separating the pair, Eustace immediately pluralised the quest for one school by offering to investigate a number of potentially suitable educational establishments. Once a shortlist had been drawn up, interviews with headmasters could be arranged. He added that, whilst the Duke of Edinburgh might still favour Cheam for Charles, Her Majesty could possibly take a contrary view when it came to deciding what was best for her own son. This tactic drew from the regent the warmest smile she'd ever bestowed in his direction, and Eustace was jolted into acknowledging the power of her famous charm.

1954

11

Spring 1954

Deptford

Although they didn't live far from each other, the sisters had enjoyed fewer uninterrupted opportunities to chat since Lil moved in with her husband and in-laws. Whenever Lil visited Standford Street, it was as much to see their parents as to catch up with her sister, especially after Janet's arrival. The best the girls could hope for was a short time spent in the bedroom they'd once shared. Peggy rarely called at the Dagleys', even though – or perhaps because – she was always made welcome. Terry's Mum was a hospitable type, who considered it obligatory to provide tea and biscuits, then sit and 'entertain' anyone who dropped in. It might have been different if Daisy had left the girls to themselves, with instructions to have a good old natter, before swiftly making herself scarce.

Lil and Peggy therefore took to meeting at The Soho, an establishment which had been named for its trendy connotations, rather than its geographical location. The café was owned and run by 'Luigi', whose accent and exaggerated gestures were pure Napoli. Very few knew that he'd been born and brought up in Bethnal Green, that his real name was Dave Jarrold, and that he probably couldn't point out Italy on a map if asked.

For a couple of years, The Soho, with its Formica tabletops and the ambience of a greasy spoon, served the girls' purpose well. Then Luigi decided to install a jukebox, and his establishment started to attract increasing numbers of Teddy Boys[1]. Thereafter, Lil and Peggy had favoured the quieter and slightly more genteel atmosphere of a place simply called Tea Room. It was here that Lil made her announcement.

'We've 'ad a look at an 'ouse in Morden.'

'That's miles away! I'd never get to see you if you moved there.'

'Oh come on, Peggy. It's not as if it's on the uvva side of the world. There's a train from 'ere to London Bridge. Don't get the one what shoots off to the Bricklayer's Arms. Then you're straight froo on the Norvvern Line 'eadin' sowf. Stay on right to the last stop, and then it's a bus ride. You get the 118 that says "Raynes Park". The stop's just across the road from the station, next to the new Wimpy Bar, but I can meet you off the tube first time, so you'll know where to catch it and where to get off.'

'Got it all worked out, 'aven't you? It would take me all mornin' to get there. By the time I got to you, I'd be turnin' round to come straight back 'ome again.'

'No you wouldn't. And we can always meet 'alfway somewhere, just for a natter.'

'Why do you need to move?'

'Because it's nice there. Me and Terry can't go on livin' with Daisy and 'arold forever. Janet needs a room of her own. It's awkward 'avin' a four-year-old sleepin' in the same room, if you know what I mean. She'll be startin' school soon. Best go now, rather than uproot 'er the moment she's settled.'

'I'll miss you. Mum and Dad will miss you. And what about poor 'arold? He'd be lost wivout 'is little playmate.'

'I know, but 'e'd 'ave to find somefin' else to do when she starts school, wouldn't 'e? I'll miss everyone too, but it's not as if we're goin' to Outer Mongolia or the uvva side of the moon.

And we want to get a telephone, but it may 'ave to be a party line.'

'What's one of those for Gawd's sake?'

'It means you share a line with someone else. Maybe another 'ouse'old furver along the road. You can't both use it at the same time. But in an emergency, you can tell them to get off the line.'

'Fat lot of use that is, when we 'aven't got one.'

'Well you could. Or you could ring us. There's always phone boxes.'

'It wouldn't be the same. And I don't want to be spendin' all me time lookin' for one that works, then standin' in a box that smells of wee, feedin' money into a machine. The pips will be soundin' before we've 'ad a chance to say 'ello.'

'Well we're serious about goin'.'

'Can you afford it?'

'We wouldn't be off if we couldn't. Terry's got it worked out and done the sums. Fings may be a bit tight, but 'e's doin' really well at the GPO, and 'is parents are goin' to lend us a bit towards the deposit.'

Peggy sighed. 'So what's this 'ouse like?'

'It's a semi. There's three bedrooms upstairs, though one's a bit small. That could be a guest room, or we could give it to Janet and keep the uvva for guests.'

'And what "guests" do you 'ave in mind?'

'You could always stay. We could leave Terry to babysit and go to the flicks. There's an Odeon in Morden, and the man 'oo showed us round said there's the Rialto at Raynes Park. They always show diff'rent films, so we'd 'ave a choice. Anyway, the 'ouse 'as a separate toilet and bathroom, which is where the airin' cupboard is. And downstairs there's a lounge and dinin' room and kitchen, with an 'atch between, to save walkin' from one to the other. And it 'as a garage.'

'I don't see the point of a garage when you don't 'ave a car to go in it.'

'Nuffin' to stop us gettin' one, when we can afford it. You need to fink ahead, Terry says. Before then, 'e wants to put a bench along one side and use it as a workshop. And 'e wants to grow vegetables in the back garden. 'e's got all sorts of plans for a shed and a compost 'eap, where the peelin's could go.'

'Bully for 'im.'

'It will be nice. We already met one of the neighbours, and she's got a little girl about Janet's age 'oo already goes to Sunday school. 'ey! Isn't that Doreen Carmichael?'

Peggy peered through the steamed-up window.

'Where?'

'She just walked by. I swear it was 'er. Still wearin' that pink and blue 'ead scarf, and she was clutchin' 'er coat. 'as Mrs Bailey said anyfin' recently?'

'No. She 'asn't been in for a while. And, come to think of it, I 'aven't seen Doreen for ages.'

The two of them moved on to one of their favourite topics: whether Princess Margaret should be allowed to marry Group Captain Peter Townsend[2]. They were very much in favour of the match and didn't understand what the objection was, even though the newspapers had tried to explain the situation. It was all to do with the fact that he was divorced, as if that mattered these days. They knew that a king had given up the throne to marry a divorcee, but that had been before the war, and she was American, which must have had a lot to do with it.

In many ways, James was taking after the younger of his two sisters. Margaret's mischievousness as a child was legendary. She'd once filled a visiting dignitary's shoes with acorns, and similar pranks were well within James's remit. He'd begun early, covertly feeding cornflakes to Sugar, the nursery pet, from his high chair. This was only discovered when the corgi, despite a carefully balanced diet, started putting on weight. At the age of eighteen months, one gloomy wet day, he painted several window panes with tomato soup 'to cheer them up'.

He was also showing a talent for mimicry. When King Gustav VI and Queen Louise of Sweden came on a state visit in June 1954, he was soon imitating their accents with some accuracy – though no one was quite sure how he'd managed to overhear them or even any of their attendant staff. The child's performance as an Italian footman amused everyone, including the servant in question, and he also did a convincing impersonation of Churchill.

For Christmas 1955, Eustace bought identical gifts for James, Charles and Anne: first editions of a new publication called *The Guinness Book of Records*. James had been instantly engrossed. He already kept a careful log of the winners of every minor 'tournament' that took place in the environs of the nursery and schoolroom, from which he usually emerged victorious.

Board games were favourites, but the children also played pencil and paper games like hangman, battleships and noughts and crosses. Jacks and square stones had been popular for a while. Charles rarely beat him at any of these but Anne, now she was old enough to compete, was providing tougher opposition.

The previous summer, Eustace had deemed it necessary to have a quiet word when James had shown him the latest snakes and ladders statistics.

'Look! I won seven times in a row.'

'And that tells you what?'

'It means I'm the best.'

'And is snakes and ladders a game of skill, do you think?'

The child had pondered, and the Earl could almost hear the brain cogs churning.

'Skill! It's the way you throw the dice.'

'It's pure luck, James, and "dice" is plural. The singular is "die". So the only thing that a winning run means is that you've either been very lucky, or you cheated.'

'I do not cheat.'

'Well then, let's put it down to a very fortunate streak, shall we?'

The Earl had gone on to suggest that James should start competing against himself.

'What do you mean?'

'You could see how many times you can skip, then try to beat that number next time and the time after that.'

'Skipping is for girls.'

'Not necessarily. A lot of champion boxers do exercises like skipping to get themselves fit. But you could try hopping or catching a ball or – well, anything at all. Then keep trying to beat your best.'

While his protégé took this in, Eustace waited. He was wondering whether it was a little early to be pushing things even further. When, after half a minute, James still hadn't said anything, the Earl decided to risk it. He had to get the incentive right.

'The game could also apply to learning. How many capital cities can you name? How far can you get putting the kings and queens of England and Great Britain in their correct order? How many birds and plants can you identify? You have all those atlases and reference books to look at. And, once you've beaten your best over and over again, you could challenge Charles and Anne, to find out who knows most.'

The boy's face lit up and, thereafter, he started soaking up information like a sponge. Tipped off, Charles was inspired to test himself in a similar way. The Prince of Wales concentrated on the natural world, especially flowers and trees. This would kick-start his lifelong fascination with, and concern for, the environment. The King preferred looking at maps and showed a particular interest in what was left of the Empire and Commonwealth.

Within a few weeks, Eustace was being asked to organise general knowledge quizzes in the schoolroom. He bought copies of the books the boys were using and, at home, enlisted Edith to help with cutting out illustrations for the 'what's this?' and 'where's this?' questions. Half their dining table was usually littered with scraps of paper and cardboard, and was often sticky with glue. They didn't always bother to clear away the debris, as they now used only one end of the mahogany oval for its intended purpose. Both their children had moved away, Cathy's having embarked on a ground-breaking career as a child psychologist. Howard, who'd studied physics at Durham University, was now settled in the north-east.

The Earl always tried to ensure a fair balance of subject matter (not that this made much difference to the outcome) and was surprised to discover how much he himself was learning along the way. Miss Peebles, who regularly acted as scorekeeper, was equally enthusiastic.

Like his father, James never tired of hearing about the annual Worm Charming Championship that took place every summer in Willaston. Open to all comers, participants were allocated a plot of ground and provided with a numbered worm pot, but they had to bring their own equipment. Everyone's methods varied, and included vibrating or prodding the ground, or playing music to lure the creatures out of the soil. Organised by a local primary school, the event was run under the auspices of the International Federation of Charming Worms and Allied Pastimes – the IFCWAP. The same regulatory body also controlled other sports, such as underwater Ludo and ice tiddlywinks.

Eustace promised to take the children to the 1956 contest, if that could be arranged. The Queen Regent was reluctant to give immediate permission, but agreed to consider the proposition nearer the time. Meanwhile, the royal gardeners started to report what appeared to be malicious damage to the palace grounds. Someone had been marking out squares on the lawns, and several tools had gone missing. Investigations revealed that James had been practising a number of possible techniques. The grass recovered, but ruined forever was any prospect His Majesty might have had to compete for the coveted golden worm trophy.

12

Glenholme Road, Morden, Surrey

'It's not doin' anyfin'. It's just all fuzzy and white.'

'It will in a moment. It needs to warm up. The tubes or whatever.'

'Remember seein' 'er in *Rear Window*? That first time I stayed? We were clinging onto each uvva, it was so scary, especially when she got caught in the murderer's flat. 'oo'd 'ave fought then that she'd be marryin' a prince?'

A picture emerged on the TV screen, and Lil twiddled a knob to fine-tune it.

'There we are. I'll go and put the kettle on. Nuffin' much seems to be 'appenin' at the moment.'

The sisters were soon happily sipping their tea and watching events unfold.

'Doesn't she look beautiful?' Peggy exclaimed as Grace Kelly, soon to be Her Serene Highness Princess Grace of Monaco, entered Monte Carlo's Cathedral of Our Lady Immaculate. The American film star and Prince Rainier III of Monaco had married in a civil ceremony the previous day, but the religious service was the spectacle that everyone wanted to see. It had been dubbed 'the wedding of the century', and the sisters were just two of 30 million or so viewers worldwide.

The bride, clad in an ivory silk gown, was followed by a posse of page boys and bridesmaids.

'That's a funny way of doin' things,' said Lil. 'Why's she gone in first? He should already be waitin' for her. And she's not carryin' a bouquet.'

'Maybe they do things different over there?'

The groom joined his bride at the altar. The couple knelt together and choral music was playing.

'This is draggin' on a bit, Lil. She looks like she's about to burst into tears any moment.'

'I don't think so.'

The singing came to an end. 'There,' Peggy cried triumphantly. 'Told you. She just dabbed her eyes with an 'anky that was stuffed up her sleeve.'

'Perhaps she's havin' second thoughts?'

'Bit late now, if she is. But 'oo'd be havin' second thoughts about marryin' a prince in a fairytale weddin'?'

'It's the "ever after" bit that matters. Could be she's realised she won't be able to carry on starrin' in films.'

'Why shouldn't she?'

'Dunno. But I don't fink she'll be allowed.'

The brief service was conducted in French and Latin.

'Can't be doin' with this, Lil. Can't understand a word the minister's sayin'. Turn the sound down and we'll watch the pictures. I've got somefin' to tell you.'

'Oh?'

'I've met someone,' Peggy blurted out. ''is name's Ralph Langridge. 'e's a greengrocer from Bermondsey, and 'e's thirty-two.'

'Is 'e nice?' asked Lil.

'I wouldn't be tellin' you about 'im if 'e wasn't.'

'What's 'e look like?'

'A bit like Gregory Peck, only with fairer 'air.'

'You always did 'ave a thing about fair 'air, Peg. 'ow did you meet 'im? Bermondsey isn't your usual stompin' ground.'

'At the Blue Cross Kennels. And, before you ask, no I 'aven't suddenly gorn and got meself a pet. I found a puppy in the street, and it was limpin' wiv a sore paw. It didn't seem to belong to anyone, so I took it there because I didn't know what else to do, and I couldn't just leave the poor little thing to fend for itself, could I?'

'So 'as this Ralph got a pet?'

'No. 'e was there with 'is granny's budgerigar. Anyway, we got talkin', and he asked me if I'd like to go to the flicks wiv 'im, and that was that. We saw *A Star is Born* at the Rex. It was ever so sad. 'e wanted to see *Seven Samurai*, but I said I didn't fancy that.'

'Sounds like you've already told 'im 'oo's boss! Remember when we went to the Rex to see *Mrs. Miniver* with Mum and Dad? And that air raid message came up on the screen? We were the only ones 'oo got up and left. I never did see the 'ole film. 'ave you met 'is Mum and Dad yet?'

'Dead. They were visiting his auntie in Walthamstow and got killed in the 'oe Street bombin'[1]. Ralph 'ad been left behind to mind the shop.'

Amongst the many bombings suffered in London during the war, both sisters remembered Hoe Street for one particular reason. The missile had caused a crater 600 feet wide, at the very edge of which was an Anderson shelter. From this, an elderly lady emerged unscathed. After surveying the devastation, she said to her friend, who was still inside, 'There, I told you it was a bomb, didn't I, Ethel?'

'And why wasn't Ralph off fightin' somewhere? Don't tell me 'e was a conchie,' Lil asked.

'No. 'e was rejected on medical grounds.'

'I 'ope it was somefin' 'armless like flat feet.'

'It was 'is eyesight. Dip – ? Dip – ? Whatever. I can't

remember the exact name, but it means double vision. Only it cleared up after a few monfs and never came back. I said it was a pity, because 'e'd 'ave been able to see me in twice me glory!'

'Is it serious? You and 'im?'

'I 'ope so. It will be if I've got anyfin' to do with it, but time will tell.'

Lil stood abruptly. ''ang on a mo, Peg. That sounds like the coal lorry. I need to make meself obvious.'

Peggy followed her sister into the kitchen, hanging back as Lil opened the door to the garden, positioned herself on the step and waved a greeting. She could hear coal being tipped into the concrete bunker, which was situated by the wooden alleyway gate. A minute later, Lil turned. There was a satisfied smile on her face. 'Full amount,' she said. 'If you don't count them in, you end up a sack short. The milkman's no better. The bill's 'ardly ever right. I did wonder wevva 'e was just bad at sums, but 'e never undercharges, so 'e's anuvva one on the fiddle. Makes you wonder if anyone these days is 'onest.'

Peggy leant her elbows on the worktop. 'I see all that experience tottin' up at Woolies is comin' in useful.'

'Talkin' of which, before you go I want you to double-check my Co-op chits to see 'ow much divi I'm due. It's divi day next week.'

'Where are they?'

'In that bag by the bread bin. There's paper and a pencil underneaf.'

Peggy reached for the bag, opened it, tipped out hundreds of flimsy till receipts onto the worktop and automatically began grouping them in piles of twenty. 'I can tell where you do most of your shoppin', Lil,' she said.

'There's a Co-op on Grand Drive[2], so it's 'andy. One of our neighbours works on the cheese counter. She says that all the shop assistants know everyone's number, so they can gossip as freely as they please amongst themselves, 'cos none of the customers know 'oo they're talkin' about.'

''ow's your Janet gettin' on?' Peggy asked, as she began listing the amounts on the chits and working through the columns of figures.

'She seems to like 'er school, except for the dinners. We dropped lucky livin' 'ere, because there are three uvva girls close by who are the same age and go to the same one. So there's a Mums' rota for takin' them and bringin' them 'ome. Gwen Mariner from number 57 is doin' the 'onours today. It's my turn tomorrow.'

'Sounds a nice little set up.'

'It is. Janet's starting ballet classes, too. She was walkin' a bit pigeon-toed, and the doctor said they'd 'elp.'

'I never noticed.'

'I might 'ave imagined it, but you can't be too careful. She went to a birfday party a couple of weeks ago, and do you know what they 'ad?'

'Sandwiches?'

'Well yes, but the centrepiece was a choc'late blancmange rabbit, lyin' in chopped up green jelly for grass! I need to come up with somefin' better than that for August. Terry was finkin' of makin' a light-up windmill wiv working sails. 'e's always tinkerin' around in that workshop of 'is. 'e's turned cobbler, too. I don't need to take me shoes in to be mended, 'cause 'e can put new 'eels and soles on them. It saves a bit of money, not to mention all the bovva.'

'And 'ow is your Terry?' Peggy swept aside another pile of paper and moved onto the next.

'Fine. 'e'll be stoppin' doin' Saturday mornin's next monf. It'll be nice when 'e's on a five day week. And one of the neighbours, 'oo's a copper and grows standard rose trees, invited 'im to join the Masons.'

''The what?'

'The Freemasons. They're a secret organisation, what lives

in a lodge, and there's a special ceremony to get in. 'e won't tell me what it involves. All these Masons 'ave a way of recognisin' each uvva. A funny 'andshake or somefin'. Apparently, if anyfin' 'appened to 'im, me and Janet would be looked after. 'e 'as a special apron.'

'You mean like a pinny?'

'No, it's all elaborate and ceremonial. It's not for wearin' in the kitchen. I don't fink Terry even knows 'ow to turn the oven on.'

'Talkin' of ovens, I almost forgot to tell you. Doreen Carmichael's gettin' wed.'

'Never! 'oo to?'

'Richard Travis.'

'Spotty Dick?'

'I expect so, given all them nasty germs she'll 'ave picked up! She's prob'ly got 'er own chair at the clap clinic.'

'No, seriously, Peg. 'e works at the foundry, doesn't 'e?'

'That's 'im.'

'Does 'e know about 'er nipper?'

'I should fink so. Everyone else does. It's 'ardly a secret. Praps 'e got 'er pregnant and is doin' the 'onourable thing? Either that or 'e's desperate.'

''e must be desperate, lookin' like 'e does. Acne and greasy 'air ain't the most attractive combination. She must be desperate an' all. The last time she was up the duff, 'er dad didn't know 'oo to aim the shotgun at, given three of them was lined up, all denyin' it.'

'Two pounds, one shillin' and five pence,' Peggy declared. 'What did you get?'

'The same. Surprisin'. I didn't fink you was concentratin'.'

Lil, like most housewives who juggled a fixed weekly housekeeping sum, was always pleased to collect her dividend. The money was a welcome bonus, and this time some of it would be used to cover the cost of Janet's new pink ballet shoes.

OCTOBER 1956

BUCKINGHAM PALACE

The King had planned it all very carefully. He'd practised keeping very still and quiet, as these abilities didn't come naturally. To avoid boredom while he was waiting, he took with him a book and a torch, the latter in case it clouded over outside, making it too dark to read. To ward off any hunger pangs, he also had a bar of Fry's Five Boys chocolate. Eustace occasionally smuggled in a small treat for each of the children, on the excuse that brain work needed energy. Mipsy knew but never told. The young king's illicit source of sustenance was unwrapped in advance, because the sound of paper being ripped off might create too much sound.

He was regretting the chocolate: it had made his hands a bit sticky, which in turn complicated the process of turning pages of *Our Friend Jennings* without making a noise, though that didn't matter while he was the sole occupant of the Audience Room. Luckily, there was enough natural light, so he hadn't needed the torch. He put the book to one side as soon as he heard the door opening and prayed he wouldn't sneeze.

The small space beneath the heavy pedestal desk was the perfect hiding place but, as he quickly discovered, it also provided an element of sound insulation. While this meant the two other people in the room wouldn't be able to hear him if he needed to shuffle around a bit to get more comfortable, unfortunately it also meant that he wasn't able to hear them as clearly as he'd hoped. But he got the gist of the conversation between his mother and the Prime Minister, Anthony Eden.

Eden was explaining the reasons why he believed that the

British should support the Israelis' armed campaign against Egypt. It was, he argued, the only way to claim back control of the Suez Canal, which had been nationalised by President Nasser the previous July. James listened as the Queen Regent sensibly queried the adequacy of British naval and military might in the area, and he heard the PM's assurances that French support for the venture would be forthcoming. Success was guaranteed.

Come on Mater, the boy silently urged. Keep going and get to the nub of it. Tell him we shouldn't be entering into an armed conflict at all, especially as talks with the United Nations are going well. But the topic was abandoned at that point, and the conversation switched to the subject of progress on an implementation programme for the Clean Air Act.

His original scheme had been to listen in on one of these audiences, simply to find out how they were conducted. He would remain concealed until the coast was clear, then slip out undetected and no one would be any the wiser. But, as matters drew to a close, James felt duty-bound to intervene. There was too much at stake here. The retention of Britain's overseas territories wasn't his primary concern: it was very clear the way the wind was blowing on an outdated colonial past. But he couldn't simply do nothing – not when his country's international reputation was at stake. So he emerged from his hidey hole and, with more confidence than he felt, walked up to the Prime Minister, offered an extended hand and said, 'Delighted to meet you, Sir.'

A flummoxed Eden rose hastily to his feet, bowed, shook hands and, with exaggerated bonhomie, uttered, 'Delighted to meet you too, Your Majesty.'

You won't be, thought James, who'd assumed his most innocent expression.

'James!' exclaimed his mother. 'You shouldn't be in here.'

'Sorry, Mater. Just wondered if I might ask Mister Eden a few questions, if that's all right, Sir?'

'Certainly,' replied a confident Prime Minister. 'What do you want to know?' Just in time, the politician stopped himself from adding, 'Sonny'.

'What does General Eisenhower think about your plan to invade Egypt, Sir?'

'The President doesn't know about it.'

'What if he doesn't agree with it?'

'He's bound to agree. I don't suppose you've heard of the Cold War, but it means that two very big countries – the USA and Russia – are sort of enemies, even though they're not fighting each other with armies and guns. Russia is paying for Egypt's weapons, and the president won't like that one little bit. So if Britain started fighting against Egypt, he'd be jolly pleased about it, wouldn't you think?'

'No. I think he will probably be very cross that you didn't tell him first. We owe him lots of money and he's entitled – '

'James!' interrupted his mother. 'That's quite enough! I'm sure Mr Eden knows what he's doing. Now will you please return to the nursery.'

'But Mater, as king, an important part of my constitutional role is to warn – '

'Enough, I said!'

James knew that pursuing this would be futile, so he reluctantly retrieved his book and torch. As he left the room, his mother was saying, 'He's only a boy and doesn't really understand...'

He encountered a frantic Miss Peebles just outside the schoolroom.

'Wherever have you been, James?'

'I'm very sorry you were worried, Mipsy, but I couldn't tell you where I was going, or it would have put you in a very awkward position, and you'd have had no choice but to stop me!'

'And what is it that you've been up to, James?' the governess asked, noting how upset the boy seemed. 'Nothing mischievous

I trust? You've not been looking for entrances to secret tunnels and passages again, have you?'

'I eavesdropped on today's audience with the PM!'

'Oh dear.'

'It is "oh dear", Mipsy. It's dreadful. Britain is, in effect, going to declare war on Egypt.' The words tumbled out in a rush. 'President Eisenhower doesn't even know yet. Not officially anyway. The CIA has probably worked it out, though. It might have been different if we'd responded immediately, as soon as the canal was nationalised, but not three months afterwards. How can the president complain now about Soviet intervention in Hungary, and at the same time not criticise Britain and France for doing exactly the same thing in Gaza? All the Mater asked about was whether we'd win, as if that's going to make any difference.' James was now crying openly. Miss Peebles produced a handkerchief, stooped to mop away the tears, then thought better of it.

This was no little boy, even though he was wiping his nose on the sleeve of his jersey. This was truly a king, knowledgeable and wise beyond his years, who was fearful for the reputation of his country. She'd sat in on some of his sessions with Eustace, when maps of the Middle East had been studied and patient explanations given. She'd witnessed the speed with which the professor's young student had grasped the concept of Russian expansionism. She'd heard the barrage of questions about nuclear capability, the role of NATO and the political doctrines that divided the world. She could understand her sovereign's frustration.

'I wish there was some way I could help, Sir.'

'That's okay. Thank you, Mipsy. I just hope you don't get into trouble with the Mater for allowing me to give you the slip. If so, I'm terribly sorry. I will tell her it wasn't your fault, and you could always repeat what I told you – that I was going to the library to look up something in *Britannica*. That doesn't sound too bad, does it?'

'No indeed, Sir.'

'And, if it isn't too much trouble, please could you telephone Eustace and tell him I tried my best to stop it? The switchboard aren't allowed to let me put through any calls unless I have permission. I'd feel happier if he knew, though there won't be anything he can do to stop it either.'

'Of course, Sir. Anything else?'

'Yes. Can you start calling me James again, please? I don't like trying to be king, and I'd rather carry on being a child.'

It was at that point James made a firm resolution. The regency was to last at least until he came of age on his eighteenth birthday. He would take up the reins of his destiny, when he was old enough. Until then, he was determined to enjoy a carefree boyhood and youth.

The military operation to retake control of the canal proved highly successful, but was greeted with almost universal international condemnation. Khrushchev threatened both to intervene in the area and to launch direct attacks on the territories of the two western aggressors. The USA didn't know whether Russia had the required nuclear capability to do this and feared that the whole situation would escalate into a third world war. Faced with financial pressure from Eisenhower, the British eventually withdrew, despite the fact that they were very close to achieving their military goal.

The Egyptian president thus kept control of the canal. The episode accelerated the process of decolonisation in Africa, which in turn resulted in the establishment of military dictatorships on that continent. Russia emerged triumphant and recognised that nuclear blackmail was an effective tool, the use of which was to continue until the Cuban Missile Crisis of 1962.

Britain, the nation which so recently had started out alone in facing the might of Nazi Germany, now suffered one of the greatest humiliations in its history.

Even before the last British troops left the canal zone, Eden took himself off to Jamaica to recover. He resigned both as Prime Minister, and as an MP, the following January[3]. His successor was Harold Macmillan. It was on Macmillan's advice that both James and his nephew started as pupils at Hill House, a day school in Knightsbridge.

CHAPTER 12

1958

13

The months spent at Hill House as day pupils proved to be a relatively short taster period. Within a year, both boys were heading to Berkshire and their respective prep schools. Being boarders meant leaving home for the first time. Heatherdown, near Ascot, had been chosen for James. It was only a short drive from Windsor Castle, and boasted its own miniature railway that ran around part of the school's extensive grounds. Charles went to Cheam, near Newbury, almost an hour's drive away from the ancient family home.[1]

Once the boys had gone, Eustace's role diminished, but he ensured that he was around when James returned for the holidays. The young king, who always immediately sought him out, simply called the Earl 'Eustace' and, after the initial respectful formalities, Eustace simply called his protégé 'James'. The Earl was never quite sure of the exact role in which he was cast by the monarch, if indeed he was viewed as any sort of surrogate figure, rather than just a watchful friend.

In effect, James had a father. From the very beginning, he'd viewed his brother-in-law as such, calling him 'Pa' from the moment he could speak recognisable words. The relationship worked both ways, as the boy had all the attributes Prince Phillip looked for in a son. When James discovered that 'Pa' was not strictly accurate, he'd begun referring to Phillip as

'Honorary Pa'. This was quite a mouthful for a small child, so it soon got abbreviated into 'Hon Pa' and, equally quickly, became 'Oompa'.

This tag was one which would persist into adulthood. James's use of it, at informal domestic gatherings, always prompted a family refrain of 'Oompa, oompa, stick it up your jumper', which was unfailingly viewed as hilarious.

In the absence of the late king, Charles relied on Uncle Dickie – Lord Mountbatten – whom he nicknamed 'HGF', which stood for Honorary Grandfather. James's own equivalent of an 'HGF' seemed to be the Duke of Gloucester, whom he saw as often as possible. This was partly because the boy was in complete awe of his cousin Prince William, the Duke's older son and heir. This juvenile hero worship of a young man seven years his senior was not at all surprising given William's prowess at football and cricket, not to mention his adventurous spirit. It was, in many ways, something to be encouraged. In Eustace's opinion, James could not do better than model himself on someone who was known for his kindness, generosity and loyalty towards friends. The reckless streak that the two had in common was, however, of some concern, especially given the prospect that it might be taken to dangerous extremes.

SATURDAY 3RD SEPTEMBER 1960

CHURCH OF ST NICHOLAS, DEPTFORD

Ever since she and Lil watched the wedding of Princess Margaret to Anthony Armstrong-Jones in May[2], Peggy had had her heart set on marrying in church. A month earlier, on the fourth anniversary of the day they'd first met, Ralph had finally popped the question. A surprised Peggy thought it was a very romantic choice of date, then Ralph had spoiled the illusion by admitting that the timing of his proposal was accidental. Nevertheless, he was accepted.

The sisters had considered mingling with the London crowds, but decided instead to take advantage of the fact that the royal nuptials were to be televised. It would be much better to enjoy everything from the comfort of Lil's dining room, which was the focus of the Dagley household: the front lounge, with its plain gold carpet and brown three-piece suite, was only used for best.

As soon as she saw the simple white organza dress, Peggy made up her mind.

'That's what I want. For just one day, I wanna look like a princess!' she'd declared.

'Wouldn't you be better off with a smart new outfit you could wear again?' Lil challenged. 'You've never set foot in a church for years. When was the last time?'

Peggy couldn't remember. 'Prob'ly Janet's christenin'. But you don't 'ave to be a reg'lar church-goer to get wed in one. I'm not goin' to miss out, like – '

Lil directed a warning nod in the direction of her nine-year-old daughter, who was on the floor separating and reassembling the coloured plastic popper beads her Auntie Peg had brought her. 'You'll 'ave to go to church at least three times before'and, to 'ave the bans read,' she cautioned. 'And Dad won't be able to afford silk.'

'I don't mind,' Peggy retorted. 'They've said 'er dress will be copied and 'oo cares if it's nylon, as long as it looks the part?' She studied the engagement ring which now adorned her left hand. 'This is a copy, too. Garnets instead of rubies, but no one could tell the diff'rence. Oh, I can't wait!'

'You may 'ave to. For Saturdays, churches get booked up monfs in advance. 'ow are you goin' to get to Woolies from Bermondsey every day?'

'Don't be silly. I'll give up workin' once I'm married, unless Ralph wants a bit of 'elp in the shop. All I'd 'ave to do is pop downstairs if it gets busy. The flat needs doin' up, but I'm sure I can make it cosy. Maybe your Terry can show me 'ow to do wallpaperin'? It can't be that difficult. I can borrow Mum's machine to make curtains, and there's a stall in the market what sells lovely fabrics. They even 'ad some of that green and gold brocade a bit like yours. And some with fruit on, which would be nice for the kitchen.'

Peggy delved into the bag of Smith's crisps she'd just opened, extracted the small twist of dark-blue wax paper and opened it. 'This salt's clumpy. It won't sprinkle.'

'Use the salt on the table instead.'

'No point. The crisps'll be soggy, too, if the pack's got damp.'

'Please yerself, but don't blame me. I only bought 'em yesterday. Won't it be odd livin' above a shop?'

'No. It's plenty big enough. There's a second bedroom, for when we 'ave a nipper, so we won't start out sharin' like you 'ad to.'

At this point, Janet clinched the matter by asking if she could be bridesmaid. Although not concentrating completely on the TV screen, the girl had noted that her time-twin, Princess Anne, was one of the eight attendants at the Westminster Abbey ceremony.

'Please can I have a dress with a frill at the bottom? And a headband with flowers?'

'Of course you can, darlin',' said her fond aunt. 'And that's a lovely arrangement of those pop-it beads. Now, your Mum told me you'd done a drawin' of Prince Andrew in 'is pram. Can I 'ave a butchers?'[3]

When the big day finally arrived, Lil had to admit that Peggy looked beautiful. The groom, in his hired suit, was almost an incidental appendage. But Lil was even prouder of her daughter, who had performed her duties in an exemplary manner. Janet was a pretty girl, with long dark curls and huge blue eyes. In a departure from the white worn by Princess Margaret's attendants, her bridesmaid's dress was pink, and there was a matching coronet of roses in her hair. The effect was simply breathtaking, and several of the guests commented as such. They expressed their wonder in hushed asides, for nobody wanted to eclipse the bride.

Princess Margaret's wedding had been the first such British royal occasion to be televised. The second, just over a year later, was the marriage of the Duke of Kent to Kathcrine Worsley at York Minster. When Princess Alexandra and the Honourable Angus Ogilvy tied the knot in 1963, this too was broadcast to a worldwide audience of an estimated 200 million people. The British public would have to wait more than ten years before the next extravaganza.

Early in 1961, Janet took the eleven-plus exam. The run up to it caused a couple of major arguments between Lil and her husband. Terry thought that, by buying sets of previous papers and forcing the girl to work through them, Lil was putting too much pressure on their daughter. After their second serious row, Lil phoned Peggy seeking sympathy, but got only short shrift. 'If you don't ease up a bit, the poor kid will be a bag of nerves.'

The stress was also telling on Lil, who persisted in arguing that Janet's whole future rested on the result. Because she was by no means his only patient who needed a 'Mother's Little Helper' from time to time[4], the family doctor was happy to prescribe Ativan for the woman.

Janet was sick the evening before she was due to take the first papers and was still very queasy and jittery by morning. To calm her down, Lil handed over one of her tablets, saying they were a miracle medication that would make anyone feel better. She also wrote a letter to the school explaining that, although Janet was unwell, she would nevertheless be attending. This was in the hope that the information would be passed on and that some allowance would be made when the exam was marked.

Lil had taken three Ativans by the time her daughter arrived home but, although very relaxed, she was still desperate to know how things had gone. Janet was non-committal and didn't dare confess that, with fifteen minutes to go, she'd put her head down on the desk and fallen asleep. All she could do now was pray that a bulky envelope would arrive in due course: those who'd failed received thin ones.

14

James was now a boarder at Charterhouse School in Godalming, and Charles was at Gordonstoun.

From the outset, James had settled in well. He regarded any change of environment as an opportunity begging to be explored and enjoyed to the full.

The same could not be said for his nephew, who'd been miserable from the very first day and remained so ever since. The ethos of the esteemed Scottish establishment was completely at odds with the boy's personality. Treated 'no differently from any other pupil', he found himself constantly bullied and isolated. The Queen Regent had wanted her sensitive grandson to go to Eton but, by forcibly saying so, put Princess Elizabeth in a very difficult position. Elizabeth, too, had favoured Eton but Prince Phillip's heart remained firmly set on the school he'd once attended. With family opinions polarised, it had boiled down to siding with her mother or siding with her husband. His wishes had prevailed.

It was not the first time the Princess had ended up as piggy in the middle, and it wouldn't be the last time she was forced to arbitrate between two opposing views.

While ever Eton had remained under consideration for Charles, alternatives for James were necessarily being looked at. One thing that had long since gained general acceptance was Eustace's principle of separating the boys. James's mother, the Queen Regent, was vehemently against Gordonstoun, if only because Phillip was so strongly in favour of it. When it came to her own son, he had no say in the matter. Charterhouse, one of England's 'Great Nine' public schools[1], was a slightly unconventional choice only in that no member of the British royal family had ever been a 'Carthusian'.

Aside from the pleasurable duty of 'being there' for His Majesty, Eustace continued to liaise with Miss Peebles from time to time. Princess Elizabeth had specifically requested this. Mipsy had been retained to look after Princess Anne and act as the young royal's governess. By the time Anne was preparing for her first term at Benenden School, Andrew was three and a half and (known only to a handful of close confidantes and palace insiders) the Duchess of Edinburgh was pregnant with her fourth child. Two more youngsters in the family assured the Earl of a continuing 'educational overseer' function and thus a real sense of purpose.

On every anniversary of his appointment as Custodian of Beeston Castle, Eustace received his yearly 'payment'. This was left in his room. He always made sure he visited his small apartment on the due date, lest the food component go beyond its best. As it was, the pies took some eating. Sourced from Fortnum & Mason, they were very large Melton Mowbray pork pies. The first year's stipend had, despite Edith's best efforts, started to turn mouldy before being fully consumed. This seemed a shameful waste, especially as meat was still on ration. Thereafter, the couple had hosted an annual party, invitations to which became increasingly sought after. All his wife had to do by way of catering was provide a decent range of pickles as accompaniments. The groats were kept on the mantelpiece in a decorative glass jar. The jar was a fifty-fifth birthday gift from Edith, who thought the coins warranted a better fate than simply being left in a bedside drawer.

Janet, too, was now at secondary school: Merton County Grammar School for Girls. Lil had been desperate for her to attend Sutton High. It had an excellent reputation but, of primary consideration, was its distinctive purple uniform. She'd imagined the envy of the neighbouring mothers (none of whose daughters had managed to pass the eleven-plus) when they saw Janet setting off each morning. Failing Sutton, Wimbledon High would have been acceptable at a push. When the letter arrived saying that Janet had been allocated a place at Merton, which hadn't even featured on their list of preferences, she was mortified and immediately set off for the local council offices to complain. The lady she spoke to obligingly looked up Janet's eleven-plus marks, told Lil that the girl had only just squeaked through the exam, and said she was lucky to have ended up at any grammar, let alone one of the more highly regarded ones.

Fortunately, Miss Frobisher, Merton's relatively new and radical headmistress, had been steadily weeding out the less able teachers and replacing them with ones who had excellent academic credentials. This policy was already being reflected in results, and parents with daughters were soon clamouring for places. Lil could start to feel smug again, especially as Janet seemed to be doing so well. She was bringing home glowing reports, which praised her above-average achievements in every subject except PE. Her gym teacher consistently commented that she didn't try hard enough, but failed to add that the girl was regularly joining those who hid by the tree-screened long jump area, from which cigarette smoke occasionally emanated. The school did have a bike shed, but not one that anyone could sneak behind.

FEBRUARY 1964

GLENHOLME ROAD, MORDEN

'Mrs Bailey finks they must've put somefin' in the water,' said Peggy, who was visiting her sister.

'I don't see how. They all live in different places,' was Lil's logical reply. 'And when did you see that old gossip? Don't tell me she's travelling all the way to Bermondsey to buy her fruit and veg?'

'No, I bumped into 'er when I was visitin' Mum and Dad.' Peggy paused. 'Maybe they went to the same party or some other fancy do, and all drank whatever it was?'

'But the babies aren't due at the same time.'

'All within a couple of months. That's near enough in my book. And I fink them royals must 'ave a special trick. 'ow come they all manage to produce a boy and then a girl? I can confidently predict that Princess Alexandra will 'ave a boy, as it's 'er first. And that Princess Margaret and the Duchess of Kent will have girls next.'

'And what about Princess Elizabeth?'

'Not sure. She already 'ad 'er pigeon pair, first time round, so it don't really matter. I'm guessin' she'll buck the trend and 'ave anuvva boy.'

'Whatever they all get will be down to chance. It's not as though you can choose.'

'Gettin' anyfin' would be all right by me, so long as it's 'ealthy.'

'Still trying?' asked Lil sympathetically.

'Of course we're still tryin'. I'm sick of tryin.''

'Maybe you're trying too hard? Have you thought about

adopting? I've heard that, when a couple do that, they very often end up having one of their own. It's all to do with relaxing.'

'Relaxin'? What with keepin' 'ouse and 'elpin' in the shop, I'm usually so relaxed, I'm 'alf asleep. And 'ow come you're talkin' so posh these days?'

Lil, who'd made a special effort to rid herself of the East End accent, said, 'I dunno. It must be the Surrey air.'

'Surrey airs and graces more like. 'ow's Janet doin' at the grammar? Never thought a kiddie in our family would ever get into a grammar.'

'Why not? Terry's clever and you and me both got our school certificates, didn't we? I'm hoping she'll go to university.'

'What? And get letters after 'er name?'

'Why not? Anything's possible these days, if you put your mind to it. A degree could get her any job she wanted.'

'Does she 'ave – what do they call it? – a vacation?'

'Vocation,' corrected Lil. 'At the moment, she's talking about medicine. She seems to be good at science, but you need really high grades at A level to do that. She seems to be getting top marks in languages as well.'

'So what languages is she studyin'?'

'French and Latin.'

'What's the use of Latin? Or French for that matter?'

'I don't know. She needs an O level pass in one or the other to get into any university. I suppose, if she doesn't get the grades she needs, she could always do teacher training, or get a job in the civil service. She works hard. Does her homework and all that. Not that she has any choice. Terry makes sure she gets it all finished before she's allowed to go out.'

'Nursin'. That's what she should go in for. Must be easier to marry a doctor than to be one. Then she'd be well set up.'

'She'll do what she wants. Girls can have careers. And I'm going to look for a part-time job as a secretary through one of those employment agencies. Earn a bit of pin money. I've signed up for evening classes too. Lampshade making.'

'Good Gawd. I know you like cookin' but you'll be doin' this Gordon Blue stuff next!'

'I have thought about that. We do quite a lot of entertaining. At dinner parties, all everyone seems to serve is prawn cocktail for starters, chicken for a main course and Black Forest cherry cake for dessert. It would be nice to try new recipes.'

'Since when 'as puddin' been "dessert"? And when did dinner move to the evenin'?'

'Oh Peg. Get up to date.'

'Talkin' of dates, what do you want for your anniversary?'

'You don't have to get us anything. It's not like it's a special one.'

'Fourteen years and never a cross word is good goin' in my book,' said Peggy.

'I'm not sure Terry would agree with that but, if you insist, a fondue set would be nice.'

'We'll get you one with bells on – once you've told me what one is. Oh and I nearly forgot. I brought you these.' Peggy handed over a paper bag.

'What on earth are they?' Lil asked, with a suspicious prod. 'They're quite hard.'

'What do they look like?'

'Khaki bananas?'

'They're plantains.'

'What do you do with them?'

'Eat 'em, of course. But you 'ave to peel 'em first, then fry or boil and mash 'em like potatoes. Add salt and pepper and a bit of butter. 'ere, I've jotted down a few recipes that someone gave Ralph.'

'Is this what you cook for him?'

'Not on your nelly! That's why I brought them for you, as you've bin turnin' your 'and to such fancy stuff. I can just imagine you at one of your dinner parties, when someone says the spuds taste funny, tellin' everyone, "Oh, that's just a little

Caribbean dish I prepared for you."' Peggy did an impersonation of what she thought her sister might sound like when in posh hostess mode.

'How come you've got hold of some?'

Peggy laughed. 'Ralph's specialisin'. He 'as so many coloureds as customers 'oo've come over from all sorts of tropical places, and they're wantin' these strange vegetables to make into stews. 'e's got an 'ole section, with all sorts of spices and weird-shaped stuff. And the butcher told me the other day that 'e's bein' asked for goat.'

'Goodness. And I thought chicken à la king was exotic.'

Peggy's forecast proved entirely accurate. The first royal arrival, on 29th February 1964, was James Ogilvy, son of Princess Alexandra. The headlines read 'Christmas Day princess gives birth to Leap Year Day baby boy.'

Next was Princess Elizabeth's third son, Edward. He was born on 24th March, three days before the first test transmission from a ship named MV *Caroline*. The new prince's fifteen-year-old Uncle James became an instant convert to the pirate radio station.

On 25th April, Glasgow Rangers won the Scottish Cup, thereby completing the treble for the second time. Rab Rainsmith, a sixteen-year-old cub reporter on the *Evening News*, was sent to the match on his very first assignment. The game was officially being covered by the paper's sports writer, but the editor had decided it would do no harm to give his newest recruit an opportunity to cut his teeth. The lad's instructions were to produce a piece covering 'crowd reaction' and the general 'atmosphere and excitement' of the event, on the basis of, 'If it's good enough, we'll print it'.

Rab had lived in Glasgow almost all his life but, as a native of Dundee, always remained loyal to one of his hometown's two football teams. He therefore decided to sit with the away side's fans at Hampden Park and, as things turned out, ended up concentrating on the perspective of the losing side's fans. His heartfelt coverage was so well received, he was next asked to write an article on the population explosion within the House of Windsor, for possible publication once there was a full complement of royal babies. Determined to make his mark, he spent every waking hour researching the subject matter. Although during his time with the paper he wasn't destined to become a royal correspondent as such, the challenge demonstrated what could be achieved by zealous fact-finding, and it prompted an interest in the Windsors that was never to desert him. Had he known, at the time, that it would take him more than thirty years to finally get his major scoop, he might have decided to change professions.

Lady Helen, the Duke and Duchess of Kent's second child arrived on 28th April and was followed, three days later, by Lady Sarah Armstrong-Jones, Princess Margaret's daughter.

The day after, much to the delight of Ron Faulkner, West Ham won the FA Cup. Captained by Bobby Moore, it was the first time the Hammers had lifted the trophy.

That same month, Earl and Countess Spencer welcomed a baby boy. After three girls – Sarah, Jane and Diana – they finally had their long-awaited son. Princess Elizabeth was one of his godparents.

Beatlemania was gripping the world. The civil rights movement in America finally resulted in a landmark act that represented a big step towards ending discrimination. South Africa was excluded from the Tokyo Olympics, because its pro-apartheid government refused to send a multi-racial team.

On 15th October, midway through the games, Britain went to the polls. The general election resulted in a four-seat Labour majority, and Harold Wilson became Prime Minister.

King James, with the connivance of his protection officers, attended unrecognised the Rolling Stones' concert at the

Wimbledon Palais. It was the first of his many covert sorties into the real world.

At the very start of 1964, Bob Dylan had first sung, "The times they are a-changin." By the end of the year, nobody could deny the truth of that prophesy.[2]

1965

15

BUCKINGHAM PALACE

Her Majesty The Queen Regent, as mother of the King and grandmother of the Prince of Wales, exerted far more influence over the latter than she did her son. The boys, who'd reached adolescence, had long since twigged that she favoured the more compliant of the two. On the other hand, Prince Phillip (aka 'Oompa') had always had more empathy with his young brother-in-law.

When they conversed with each other, the King and his nephew occasionally referred to the family matriarch as 'she who rules'. To her face, they called her 'Mater' and 'Granny', respectively. A long time ago, she'd asked James why he didn't call her 'Mummy' like his sisters did, to which he'd replied, 'Because you're Mater and I'm king.' The subject had never again been raised.

No resentment arose as a result of the blatant familial preferences. Close in age, but very different in temperament, the young men were good friends and enjoyed each other's company.

James had been expecting his honorary brother to turn up, so wasn't surprised when Charles wandered in.

'You managed to escape "Colditz in kilts" then?' noted the young king. 'Did you tunnel out? Or bribe the guards?'

'Neither this time. They let us out for Easter. And what on earth's that racket? I can't hear myself think.'

James ambled over to the record player and turned down the volume.

'It's a new LP. *The Rolling Stones, Now!* You can't buy it here. A friend sent it over from America. It's got a couple of brilliant new tracks on it.'

James lifted the arm. 'I'll play you them.'

'No thanks.'

'You seem a bit fed up, old boy. What's up?'

'Granny won't let me visit Uncle David[1],' Charles stated glumly. 'It would have been splendid to have had a chat with him and maybe find out a bit more about what really went on – from the horse's mouth, so to speak. Everyone in the family clams up whenever the subject's remotely touched upon. I'm not sure that you and I know any more than Joe Public does. I wonder if he's ever rued his decision to abdicate? I wonder what it's like to be so much in love with a woman that you'd give up everything just so you can be with her? Your throne. Your country. Your whole family. Even just meeting him and getting to know him a bit would have been nice.'

'He's an interesting chap,' James observed, casually. 'Naturally, he does regret what happened. More to the point, he regrets how he played things and how everything panned out. In particular, he realises now that the infamous Mrs S would far rather have been the mistress of a king than the wife of an exiled duke. And I get the impression that he didn't expect to be banished completely. I think he banked on remaining part of the establishment, with a useful role, and thought that he and the Duchess would live happily ever after on some quiet estate in England, once the dust had settled.'

'How do you know all that?'

'I went to see him.'

'How come you were allowed, when I'm not?' Charles

asked, slightly petulantly.

'Because I didn't ask permission. It's one of the most useful things I learnt from dear old Eustace at a very early age. Apparently, it's a philosophy my father had started to espouse, so one could almost argue it's a legacy that I'm morally bound to make the most of.'

'That sounds a bit tenuous.'

'Be that as it may, I must say, it comes in jolly handy. *Carpe diem* and all that. Do it and to hell with the consequences. Of course, it's better still if you can make sure there are no consequences. In this particular instance, the Mater is none the wiser. So far, that is. I only popped in yesterday, so there's time for her to find out. But who cares?'

'But surely someone saw you going in?'

'No. Hospitals have plenty of back and side entrances, most with surprisingly little security. You never see anyone being wheeled out the front way from the morgue, do you? Deliveries don't go in that way either. All it took was getting someone to do a quick recce, add a bit of careful planning and everything was sorted.'

'Was he pleased to see you?'

'Surprised first and foremost but, yes, I think he was. Gave me a "man-to-man" warning about not making the same mistakes, especially now the press don't keep things under wraps like they used to do. Getting things wrong in the romantic stakes seems to be something of a family failing amongst us merry men of Windsor!'

'What did he mean by that? Granny and Grandpapa were solid as a rock.'

'They were the exceptions that proved the rule. Apart from Uncle David, Uncle George Kent reputedly had affairs left, right and centre, including with a stage actress and the Mater's dear friend Noël Coward.'

'No!'

'Strong rumours don't occur without substance, old boy. Even Uncle Henry had a scandalous affair with a Kenyan writer called Beryl Markham before he married Aunt Alice. Beryl's still living off the annuity settled on her after it was all hushed up. Uncle David said he was quite grateful to him at the time for deflecting family attention from his own dalliances, as he put it. Moral of the story seems to be "steer clear of married women, anyone in the entertainment industry and Americans".'

'And any girl with a past. It wouldn't do to have old boyfriends leaping out of the woodwork and telling all. And she must be compliant, but strong enough to stand on her own two feet. I'm not sure you and I will ever find women with the right credentials, when the time comes. Given today's free love culture, we're going to be looking at twelve-year-olds or infiltrating convents.'

'As long as they're not Catholic convents, don't forget! Actually,' mused James, 'I'm quite convinced Mrs S did the country a favour. The Mater and Papa were exactly the right people to help see everyone through the war. I don't know what impression a Nazi sympathiser would have made, and that's assuming we'd ended up at war in the first place. Kings don't have much real influence, but who knows?'

'He doesn't still believe that Hitler should have been given free rein, does he?' queried Charles.

'I'm not sure what he believes now, especially after the extent of the atrocities was discovered. But he and his wife are best buddies with the Mosleys. Eustace told me that Sir Oswald and Diana got married in Goebbels' drawing room and that she was having cosy lunches with the Führer only a month before war was declared. Her opinions don't seem to have shifted an inch. That must tell you something.'[2]

'You seem to have found out a lot for someone who only "popped in" on a sick man.'

'Yes, well, not so sick any more. It was only an eye op and he was very chirpy. I suppose I did stay quite a while.'

SUMMER 1965

The date of the coronation had been subject to informal family debate around the time of the King's fourth birthday, not that the planning of it would need to start for many years to come. Eustace had kindly provided a few notes, summarising the situation regarding monarchs who'd acceded to the throne whilst still minors. Twelve-year-old Edward V, supposedly murdered in the Tower of London, had never been crowned. Henry VI, a baby of just eight months, had been crowned when he reached seven. The coronations of four others, whose ages ranged from nine to fourteen, had taken place almost immediately.[3]

At the time of the first discussion, everyone had agreed that the ceremony could not possibly take place until James was old enough to properly understand the full weight and solemnity of the vows he would be taking. From this happy point of consensus, things began to disintegrate.

The obvious timing would be a few months after the regency ended. Under the latest legislation, this would be in 1967, when James turned eighteen. However, the Queen Regent had been insistent that her son would first need to complete his education. Fitting in the preparations for, and rituals of, being crowned between school and a possible period of at least three years as an undergraduate seemed like an unnecessarily burdensome distraction. In the face of this argument, Prince Phillip was quick to point out that, only very recently, his mother-in-law had objected to any form of proper schooling, yet seemed now to be happily contemplating sending James off to university.

The Queen remained adamant, adding that he could not do justice to his studies whilst at the same time properly fulfilling all the duties associated with being king. And, as he couldn't be expected to do both, either the option of further education would have to be dismissed, or the period of the regency extended. 'After all,' she added, 'the rest of the population do not attain their majority until they're twenty-one.'[4]

The observation seemed to make sense until she went on to say, 'Before that age, no person can be regarded as sensible enough to know their own mind.'

This spoilt things rather and Phillip bridled. 'By eighteen, I was training at Dartmouth. I do hope no one's suggesting that, when I joined the navy – at a time when war on a massive scale was inevitable incidentally – I didn't take what I was doing seriously?'

The comment was swept aside by Princess Elizabeth's intervention. She declared that, regardless of when anyone might be old enough to be considered sufficiently mature, the burdens of state were heavy enough at any age. If Charles were in James's position, she wouldn't like to think of his having to forgo the opportunity of realising his academic potential, nor his chance of leading a relatively carefree student existence.

Her grandmamma, Queen Mary, endorsed the sentiment, adding, 'Not if an alternative exists.' The elderly lady rarely involved herself in family debates, and this would prove her last ever contribution. Five weeks later, she died peacefully in her sleep, never having fully recovered from the loss of a fourth son. Her youngest child, the gentle epileptic Prince John, had passed away at the age of just thirteen. The Duke of Kent was killed in a plane crash during the war. She had set eyes on her eldest, the banished Duke of Windsor, only once since his abdication, when he'd visited her in 1945. And now poor Bertie was gone.

Back in February 1953, and given that no one was in favour of crowning a child, the whole debate had been largely academic. But that was then.

Bernard Marmaduke Fitzalan-Howard had just resurrected the matter. Bernard was Duke of Norfolk and hereditary holder of the title of Earl Marshal. As such, he was responsible for organising all state occasions, something he'd been doing since 1917. The most recent, six months earlier, had been the funeral of Sir Winston Churchill. With only a year and a half to go before the King's eighteenth birthday, Bernard tentatively suggested that some indication of likely timescale would be appreciated, as these things took some time to put together.[5]

The Earl Marshal wasn't the only one who was thinking ahead.

Unaware of the distant discussion that had taken place, James had been worrying a great deal about the prospect of kingship once his schooldays came to an end. He had a clutch of eight very creditable O level GCEs and was about to enter the lower sixth form at Charterhouse. All his friends there were hoping to go to university, preferably Oxbridge, but he no longer allowed himself to share their dreams. A few years earlier, he'd even naively envisaged joining one of the armed forces after a period as a student, but Eustace had moved swiftly to clip the wings of any expectation on that front.

As the King saw things, the Mater was old and well beyond the age at which most women retired. It was no wonder she found the job, so patiently tolerated, tiring.

The Earl of Willaston, concerned about his protégé's increasing depression, viewed the situation very differently. He knew that a simple amendment act prolonging the regency could readily be passed, thus dealing with the legalities. He also strongly suspected that, despite the constant complaints, a certain person would be willing to nobly struggle on. He decided to consult Princess Elizabeth and enlist her help: Her Royal Highness was better placed than he to negotiate the family politics.

The fact remained that James and his mother shared the same agenda. 'She who ruled' thoroughly relished her role as monarch. It wasn't proving at all tedious. Her flair for the theatrical enabled her to deliver the short but witty speeches penned by others. She was popular, had easily managed to ride out the occasional surge in republican sentiment and was, in short, a much-loved institution. Someone else, usually her elder daughter, dealt with all the boring stuff.

The Earl Marshal was accordingly informed that he need not start planning a coronation immediately, as it would not be taking place until the autumn of 1970 at the earliest. Meanwhile, the Queen Regent would continue as monarch, and the King himself could look forward to an extended period of youth, even though an army career and leading British troops into battle was out of the question.[6]

16

The whole nation, including fair-weather fans with no interest in football whatsoever, was gripped by World Cup fever. The streets, almost completely devoid of traffic, were silent. Everyone was glued to television sets.

Ron Faulkner was no exception. He watched the final at the Evelyn Dockers' Institute. Having failed to get one of the 97,000 tickets for Wembley, being in the company of dozens of others was the next best thing. He already felt an almost physical association with the Jules Rimet trophy: he knew Dave Corbett, a fellow lighterman, whose dog Pickles had found the stolen cup the previous March.

Even if it had been specially scripted to engender the whole gamut of emotions, the match couldn't have been more thrilling. There was despair when West Germany took a one-nil lead after twelve minutes, followed by jubilation when England scored to balance things up by half-time.

Nobody watched the band during the interval, because everyone was either buying more beer at the bar, or ridding themselves of it in the gents.

There was further delight when England went two-one up in the second half, and needed only to hang on for thirteen more minutes. All were in a state of nail-biting apprehension as the last seconds ticked away. Like those at Wembley, and in common with everyone else in the social club, Ron began whistling to encourage the referee to signal the end of the game. Then disaster struck as, in the dying seconds, the German team equalised.

During extra time, viewers drew in their breath every time England's net was threatened, and sighed in collective relief when danger was averted. A Geoff Hurst goal seemingly put the home side ahead once more, but hearts plummeted as the ball bounced out again, and there was nervousness while a decision was being made about whether it had actually crossed the line. It had![1]

'Some people are on the pitch. They think it's all over,' declared commentator Kenneth Wolstenholme, just before the ball hit the back of the German net to make it four-two. 'It is now!'

Unmindful of the tables that were in the way, and the glasses that were being knocked over, Ron and his mates were jumping up and down. When the Wembley crowd started the victory chant, those in the Dockers' Institute joined in with a paraphrased version. 'West 'am won the cup, West 'am won the cup, ee aye addio, West 'am won the cup.'

As far as they were concerned, this was true. With a bit of help from eight others, Geoff Hurst's hat-trick, Martin Peters' goal, and the captaincy of Bobby Moore had secured the triumphant outcome. All three played for the Hammers.

A relative lull in the celebrations marked the scenes of the team in red climbing the steps to the royal box, where Her Royal Highness Princess Elizabeth presented the coveted cup.[2] Then she and her brother swapped places, and seventeen-year-old King James handed out the remainder of the winners' medals.

Moore was now being carried shoulder-high around the pitch to the refrain of 'Rule Britannia'. The next thing Ron could recall about that day was finally arriving home, being chastised by Joyce for his sopping wet trousers and protesting that it was beer. A sceptical Joyce stomped into the kitchen, chuntering something along the lines of, 'I bet the royal ladies were delighted when it went to extra time.'

LATE AUGUST 1966

THE GROUNDS OF BALMORAL

Eustace enjoyed collecting his yearly dues as Beeston Castle's custodian. They were an annual reminder of one of the best times he'd ever shared with His Majesty. But he had never exercised his haggis-shooting rights on the Balmoral Estate, even though he'd occasionally been a guest there during the summer break. It was on one such visit, when he was about to turn a corner in the gardens, that he happened upon Charles and his younger brothers. He heard, before he saw, the trio and paused unseen to listen. The Prince of Wales was telling a story.

'... the haggis is a small shy animal, native to the hillier parts of Scotland. Colonies of them live in burrows, and the creatures emerge only once a year to get some exercise. For a single day, they enjoy running in circles up and down steep hills. Because of this, and over many thousands of years, they have evolved in a peculiar way. The legs on the right side of their bodies are shorter than those on the left. This enables them to stay perfectly upright, provided that they always go in a clockwise direction. What do you think would happen if they went the other way?'

'They would fall off!' declared Andrew.

'That's right. And this is where the skill of the haggis-catchers comes in. They work in two-man teams. One stands at the top of the hill and scares the creatures so much, they all turn and scurry away in the opposite direction, which means they instantly tumble down. The second catcher is waiting at the bottom with a net. And what happens then?'

'They get caught and cooked and eaten!'

'You always say that, Andrew. No, the catchers put little rings round their legs to keep track of population numbers. We wouldn't want them to become extinct, would we?'

'What does "extinct" mean?'

'It's when a type of animal dies out completely, and there are none at all any more.'

'But people do eat haggis, don't they? And then they play the bagpipes.'

'What people eat are mock haggis. Oh, hello Eustace.'

'Hello, Your Royal Highness. That was a very entertaining tale.'[3]

'Just something I made up to amuse Andrew and Edward. Go on you two. Scoot!'

Story time over, the younger princes raced off. Eustace sat down on the bench.

'You always were very imaginative,' Eustace ventured.

'James seemed to be better at it than I am.'

'That's not true, Sir. Imagination shows itself in many guises. His abilities and yours are channelled differently, that's all. Have you seen him since you returned from Australia?'

'Yes, though only briefly. I barely had time to turn round before we were heading off for a jolly in the Caribbean. But it was long enough for James to berate me for missing all the excitement of the World Cup final, as if that were my fault. And to be honest, I really didn't mind. Soccer isn't something I'm that interested in.'

'It wouldn't do for us all to enjoy the same things. James doesn't seem overly keen on horses. I heard that you played polo in Jamaica?'

'Yes. I was in the same team as Pa.'

'And how was it Down Under?'

'Very enjoyable indeed, thank you. I was a bit apprehensive, as Timbertop[4] is supposed to be the equivalent of Gordonstoun and, true enough, there were a lot of outdoor activities. But they were fun. It actually felt very different. Not quite as, well, brutal, and much more relaxed somehow. The other boys called me "Pommie" and none of them thought that, by being friendly, they were sucking up. That's always been one of the problems at Gordonstoun.'

'I can well imagine how difficult it must be. In a position such as yours, there'll always be toadying creeps, and there'll always be others who go out of their way to show that they couldn't give a damn. And don't forget, it's the bullies who are the ones with the problems. Not their victims.' As he was speaking these reassuring words, Eustace vowed to try to discover James's secret, so he could tactfully pass it on. The King was never short of friends, but then His Majesty lacked Charles' inherent shyness and sensitivity.

'I'd sometimes settle for one or two toads for company,' Charles chuckled. 'It's probably why I talk to trees and other plants![5] But it was all very informal in Oz. We were told to take any old clothes and just one tidy suit, and I only needed that when I saw Granny in Melbourne. It was nice to escape being royal for a while, and I was genuinely treated as no one special, except for being a bit older than most of the other boys there. I can't begin to tell you what a relief all that was.'

'So it's back to Moray next term, I gather?'

'Yes, but only for another year, thank goodness. I'm to be School Guardian, and I mean to be a good one. I don't suppose I'll be able to put a stop to those dreadful initiation rituals that the new boys must endure, but I shall certainly try my best.'

'Good for you. Well, Sir, I'm only here for a few days' haggis shooting so, if I don't see you before I go back to London, the best of luck. I'm sure you'll be an admirable head boy.'

17

BUCKINGHAM PALACE

'How did the A levels go, Jimmy?'

'Not sure, but they'll take me anyway.'

'Definitely Oxford, then?' asked Charles.

'Yes. I've opted to read PPE. Thought it might be useful to understand a bit about politics and economics.'

'How does the philosophy component fit?'

'It might help when my kingly words of wisdom are ignored, and I start to question my own existence. What about you? Still definitely Cambridge?'

'That's the plan. And then the navy probably.'

'You should be so lucky. It'll be nothing but the build-up to the coronation for me. Still, I have three more years of freedom before I have to worry about that. Interspersed with the occasional obligation of course, to keep the peace. A couple of evenings ago, I was dragged along to a performance of *Tosca* at the Royal Albert Hall, would you believe.'

'Was it Southey's production?'

'No idea, old boy. The programme's kicking around somewhere, if you want to check.'

'But did you enjoy it?' persisted Charles. Despite the fact

142

that he preferred Wagnerian operas, he would have savoured every note and nuance.

'I enjoyed the end. When the fat lady stopped squawking and finally felt as suicidal as the rest of us. They'd put a trampoline behind the battlements. She threw herself backwards and bounced straight back up again. Don't think I've ever laughed so much.'

'Oh yes. I do remember reading about that bit. Apparently, she's rather too much of a prima donna and not very popular back stage. But I didn't know it was a royal performance?'

'Nor did anyone else. I sat in the stalls. Insisted on it. If she who rules suddenly decides my cultural education must be "rounded", it will be on my terms. You know, it's sometimes very useful having one of those faces that easily passes in a crowd. All I have to do is ruffle up my hair with a bit of backcombing and part it on the other side. It makes me look completely different from how I am in official pictures. So nobody ever recognises me. Done it dozens of times.'

'Backcombing?'

'Yeah,' said James lazily. 'I'll show you.'

James strolled casually to the desk, opened the top drawer, extracted a comb and proceeded to demonstrate.

'See. Easy as pie, once you've got the technique. Perfect for those little off-piste jaunts.'

'How do you deal with the men in black? I've never forgotten, or forgiven, what happened to Don. Surely it's more than their jobs are worth to allow you take risks?'

Don Green, Charles' own bodyguard, had been instantly sacked after the underage Prince of Wales had ordered a cherry brandy in a village pub near Gordonstoun.

'Ah now. That was a very valuable lesson for both of us, and I'm a quick learner. Mine are all perfectly tame now. Oh, they do come with me, wherever I go, but they're very discreet. Sometimes I can't even see them, but I know they're always somewhere very close. They blend in, you see. It's part of their police training and, better still, for our less-than-official outings, they've all got nice new clothes. Or in some cases, nice old clothes. We had a lot of fun on a few trips to Petticoat Lane and Carnaby Street to sort that out. Gerald even chose a kaftan.'

'He's the new one, right? Big, ginger, burly – right? "Gerald the Geordie". He needs a good haircut.'

'He most definitely doesn't. They've all grown their hair a bit longer, by royal command. The Mater disapproved, but I argued that it's the fashion and that they'd be less conspicuous.'

'I can't believe you've been wandering around street markets? How do you travel?'

'Let me enlighten you, Charles. There are big red things with wheels. They go along roads all over London. These are known as buses. Then there are things that go on rails through underground tunnels. These are called tube trains.'

'Now you're being silly. How do you get out of here?'

'Ah. That bit we do in something called a car. We make sure it isn't a big, black, shiny car with a royal standard at the front. That, you see, would be inconveniently noticeable. No, we use a small pale-green Austin A40. Only cost me £125. Driver drops us off somewhere quiet (different every time) and parks up. Then it's Swinging London, here we come. Easy. It would be better still if I could get myself a slice of the "Summer of Love", but that's proving rather tricky. I'm almost resigned to an "Autumn of Love". It should be easier when I'm living in college. I've already made friends with some of the scouts[1] and porters. Think about it, Charles. We've got all those girls, who've suddenly found freedom for the first time in their lives, to look forward to.'

The Prince of Wales was unimpressed. 'I'm still surprised your protection people go along with all this subterfuge.'

'What can they do about it? Tell the Mater that I'm being a naughty boy, so she'll send me to bed without any tea? Handcuff me to a radiator? Hey, why don't you come with me next time? Let's think of a name for you. How about Charlie Chester?'

'That's already been done.'

'Chas Chester then? Or Phil maybe? Or you could shorten Arthur to Art, as in Garfunkel? That might work. Stick to plain George even, as in Harrison.'

'Why Chester?'

'Wales is a bit of a giveaway, don't you think? Chester's your other title. Just a thought.'

'So do you have an alias?'

'Of course I do. It's Fergus Carrick.'

'Isn't Carrickfergus a town in Northern Ireland?'

'Neat, eh? But that's not how I came about it. The surname "Carrick" is as in one of the titles I used to have as Duke of Cornwall. I do a great Irish accent to go with it, but usually stick to southern English with a touch of Cockney. That gives a nice slightly roughened edge to the smooth plum-in-the-mouth.'

'Who knows about your alter ego?'

'Well, most of my escorts do, the regular ones that is. And close friends. They're all sworn to absolute secrecy though, otherwise there'd be no point. So what do you think?'

'I'm sure I'd be recognised, even if I grew a moustache.'

James studied his nephew critically. 'Ever known me not rise to a challenge? I've got lots of wigs you could choose from, though you'll have to get your own jeans – mine would be too short. Plain black's safest.'

'Wigs?' Charles almost choked.

'Why not? There's one in the style of Peter Noone. It would cover your ears.'

'Peter who?'

'Herman's Hermits. No? Well, never mind. Come to think of it, I'll rename it "the Brian Jones". You must know who he is. Then there's the one I've called the "Merry Monarch". Long, dark and curly. Bit of a bad perm really. It would make you look like Charles II. Though perhaps not. A flea jumped out the other day, so I stuck it in a bar of soap.'

'The flea or the wig?'

'Do you ever wonder what happens to the soap? No matter. Back to the task in hand. We could see what you look like wearing spectacles. I am trying to build up a collection. Already have some "old geezers" and "mad professors", plus a pair with a tortoiseshell frame. All with clear lenses. I find square frames suit me best. Oh, and a bit of extra advice. Never wear dark glasses, unless the sun's shining. Otherwise people will think you might be someone famous trying not to be recognised. Or they start helping you cross the road.'

'Please don't tell me you wear makeup as well, Jimmy.'

'Certainly not, old boy. What do you think I am? Some sort of poof?'

SEPTEMBER 1967

GLENHOLME ROAD, MORDEN

'Are you sure?'

Janet was now in floods of tears and could barely get the words out.

'Yes.'

'How do you know?'

The girl hiccupped. 'Denise and I went to a clinic in Brook Street, and they did a test,' she managed to choke out.

'What sort of test?'

'I had to wee into a bottle. And then phone back six hours later on, to get the results.'

'Did they say how far gone you are?'

'No. Only that the test was positive.'

Lil was too stunned to react, though it was clear her daughter was braced for an angry explosion. The news was every mother's worst nightmare.[2]

'So how far gone do you think you are?'

'I don't know.' This was a lie.

'So who's the father?'

'I don't know.'

'Don't know? Or won't say? Is he one of the boys from the grammar?'

'No.'

'A brother of one of your friends you stay with, then? Or should I say *supposedly* stay with? Gawd knows what you've been getting up to. From where I'm standing, it seems you've had far too much freedom to abuse.'

'I don't have any freedom at all! I always have to be home at least half an hour before anyone else does. It's depressing.'

'It's because your Dad and I want to protect you.'

'That's a joke. How do you think it feels, leaving early, when all the others are still enjoying themselves? Then I end up waiting at the bus stop all on my own, whereas they set off together. Isn't there supposed to be something about safety in numbers?'

'Well, nine-thirty is quite late enough for a girl your age.'

'I'm seventeen. This time next year I'll be away at university and will be able to do what I like.'

'You're only just seventeen. And while you still live under our roof, we set the rules. If other parents choose to let their daughters come home at all hours of the night, that's up to them. I sincerely hope you're not blaming us for what's happened, despite all the care we've taken?'

'No.'

'Well then. I'm not standing here playing guessing games.

Whoever the boy is, your dad will have his guts for garters.'

'I don't know what to do, Mum. Do you think sitting in a hot bath and drinking a bottle of gin would work?'

'If you want to get very drunk, it would. But you're not trying it. And you're not going to any backstreet abortionist either.' Lil only just managed to stop herself saying, 'You've made your bed, now you must lie in it.'

'Are you cross?'

'Of course I'm bloody cross. But that's not going to help.'

'Will you tell Dad?'

'It's hardly something that can be kept secret, is it? But maybe not this evening. We've got the Hendersons coming for dinner. And I need a chance to think things through. Oh Janet, I thought we'd brought you up to be decent. You had your whole life ahead of you, what with just passing that AS level maths exam and everything. And now you've gone and chucked it all away.'

'Why can't I carry on at school? Pregnancy isn't an illness. I could just have the baby, get it adopted, and then it would be like it never happened.'

'Do you seriously think you could forget all about it? It wouldn't be like handing over a sack of potatoes. And do you seriously think Miss Frobisher is going to let you stay on for A levels? She has the grammar's reputation to think about, so she isn't about to turn it into a home for unmarried mothers. What sort of an example would that set for the other girls? The ones who still have some self-respect?'

'I do have self-respect, Mum. It just kind of happened, and only the once.'

'Once was clearly enough, not that I believe you.'

'You must believe me, because it's true. Anyway, you did it before you were married. Don't forget how good I am at maths. I know I wasn't born four months prematurely.'

'That was different. Your Dad and I were engaged. From

what you're telling me, you just had a one-night stand with a boy whose name you didn't even bother to find out, which makes you no better than a common little tart.'

'He did tell me his name, and it wasn't like that.'

'Well, whatever it was like, I hope it was worth getting into trouble for. The next few months aren't going to be easy for any of us. So what *was* his name?'

'He was special, that's all. His name doesn't matter.'

Lil was tempted to slap the dreamy look off her daughter's face.

'It might matter to the poor fatherless baby you're carrying.'

'Well, I'm not going to tell you. And I'm not going to put it on any birth certificate either, so there.'

'Don't shout. The neighbours might hear you.'

'So what? They'll find out soon enough.' Janet looked at her mother suspiciously. 'Or is that what really matters to you? Why don't you just banish me to a nunnery and have done with it, if I'm bringing shame upon the family? Or you could send me to an ancient auntie in the Outer Hebrides, except unfortunately we don't have one.'

'Well, there is always your Great-Aunt Shirley in Sheffield. She and Uncle John visited Mum and Dad only the other week.'

'Sheffield? Why on earth would I want to go there? Why can't I just stay here?'

'We'll see,' said Lil, who was now thinking rapidly and clearly.

'And *I* see too. You're so transparent. One way or another, you're going to find some way of making sure I never again darken your doors.'

'Stop being so dramatic, Janet. We would never abandon you, but there are Mother and Baby Homes that deal all the time with this sort of situation, and make sure that everything goes smoothly. And, afterwards, you could use those GCEs to get yourself a nice little office job. Or you could train for something.'

'I want to be a doctor. It's all I've ever wanted.'

'You should have thought about that sooner, before you had it off with "father unknown". Right now, what's going to happen about your dreams of a fancy career is the least of your worries. Who knows about your condition?'

'Only Den.'

'Well make sure you keep it that way. And tell Denise to do the same. Make her swear it. I'll be straight onto her parents if she so much as breathes a word.'

The thought went through Lil's mind that her daughter was no better than Doreen Carmichael, but she knew, deep down, that this simply wasn't true. Doreen was a calculating cow, who'd spread her legs for anyone if she thought it might be to her own advantage. A mother's instinct insisted that Janet wasn't like that. Clearly the girl hadn't been forced into anything. Seduction was much more likely. Had it not been for the unfortunate consequences, which all of them must now face, Lil might almost have felt envious.

In the autumn of 1967, James began his studies at Hertford College, Oxford. The centrally-located college, known for the iconic 'Bridge of Sighs', was conveniently situated directly opposite the Bodleian Library.

At the same time, Charles set off for Trinity College, Cambridge, initially to read archaeology and anthropology and later switching to history. There, he became involved in the Footlights, an amateur theatrical club. As a member, he appeared in sketches and revues, which did wonders for his self-confidence. He'd thought about the university's Apathetic Society, but that existed in name only. Anyone who actively sought to apply was not considered apathetic enough to qualify.

James, meanwhile, joined his college's boat club and a drinking society known as the Penguin Club[3]. The latter, with its own student-run bar, sounded like fun but he quickly discovered that the discretion of some of its members could not be relied on. Before divulging his alter ego to anyone, he always first ensured that they were trustworthy. Thankfully, for the purposes of socialising, Fergus Carrick remained known only to a few close friends, who included two bodyguards: 'Gerald the Geordie' and another named Melvin. James's small, exclusive set of young men developed an increasing preference for the city's pubs, which offered an escape from the confines of academia. The ancient university's cloisters sometimes felt almost as insulated as any palace or castle walls, but a student existence did offer more opportunity to escape the claustrophobic atmosphere and enter the world beyond.

It was a world that continued to change apace. The inception of Radio 1 meant that the BBC was finally catching up on the modern music front. The Beatles opened the London Apple shop. Rolling Stones guitarist Brian Jones won a High Court appeal against his prison sentence for the possession and use of cannabis. A triumphant product of Anglo-French collaboration, the supersonic aircraft Concorde was unveiled two weeks after French president Charles de Gaulle had again vetoed Britain's entry into the European Economic Community. The Abortion Act was passed, and a rise in Scottish nationalism was signalled with the SNP's first ever by-election victory. Harold Wilson devalued the pound.

Because of an outbreak of foot-and-mouth disease, horse racing events were called off, much to the Queen Regent's chagrin. She'd been looking forward to the Cheltenham meeting, even though none of her growing string of horses was due to run there. Now a firm devotee of National Hunt racing[4], with all its thrills and excitement, her most famous horse had been Devon Loch. Well in the lead in the 1956 Grand National, and looking like a clear winner only forty yards from the finishing line, he'd mysteriously half-jumped and done a belly flop. No one could explain why he'd apparently attempted to leap over a hurdle that hadn't existed. The horse recovered – probably much more quickly than his distraught jockey, Dick Francis, who was reassured with an 'Oh, that's racing'.

Janet's closest friends knew of her predicament, but they were all under strict instructions to pretend they didn't, if ever questioned.

Lil's interview with Miss Frobisher (the woman secretly referred to by the girls of Merton County as 'the Frobe') had been embarrassingly difficult, and an agreement had been reached only because Janet was such an outstanding pupil.

It was eventually settled that she should continue to attend school until the end of the autumn term, during which she would sit her Oxford University entrance test. Hopefully there would be no visible signs of the pregnancy for a few months yet. Janet would not be excused PE, as this might arouse suspicion and – who knew? – the exercise might just fortuitously prompt nature to take its course. Over Christmas, the girl would develop an illness (hepatitis sounded convincing) and be sent away to recuperate. During her absence, she would be expected to continue her studies in line with the A level curricula. At no little inconvenience to several teachers and the grammar's secretary, material would be prepared and posted every week to Aunt Shirley's address in Sheffield. Homework would need to be submitted promptly. While these arrangements couldn't adequately cover the practical elements of missed lessons, as undertaken in the chemistry, biology and physics laboratories, it was the best the school could offer.

Lil gratefully accepted the terms and fleetingly wondered whether the headmistress of Sutton High would have proved as accommodating.

Terry had, as predicted, been furious when he was told of

Janet's plight, but his anger and disappointment couldn't last forever. Appalled by the notion of giving away their own flesh and blood to strangers, he'd been the one to suggest that he and Lil should adopt the baby and bring it up as Janet's little brother or sister. They could easily afford to raise another child. The telecommunications side of the GPO was developing apace and, by virtue of being in the right place at the right time, he had rapidly moved up the ladder in a series of quick-fire promotions. Like his wife, he was mindful of the reaction of friends and neighbours. Unlike his wife, he figured that any scandal would blow over in time. Besides, his thoughts had recently turned to the idea of moving to a bigger house in somewhere like Epsom or Esher. It made financial sense, as bricks and mortar were a sound investment.

Lil remained unconvinced by his arguments. She'd been 'temping' for several years and was now manageress of the agency through which many of her short-term assignments had come. She didn't want to give up work and become a full-time mother but, more significantly, she didn't want to face the vicarious disgrace which would undoubtedly be wrought by her daughter's moment of foolishness. However, it was Janet who decisively balked at the idea. Although no longer blasé about the prospect of handing over the product of such a magical encounter, she couldn't come to terms with the thought of living in the same household as a child who would never call her 'Mummy'.

There was a much more glaringly obvious solution and it was one which might enable the Dagleys to save face, provided they could keep Janet's pregnancy secret. Hence the necessity of the subterfuge negotiated with Miss Frobisher.

On 23rd April 1968, the Race Relations Bill had its second reading in the House of Commons. A thousand London dockers, who'd gone on strike in protest of the sacking of Enoch Powell, marched to the Palace of Westminster carrying placards bearing slogans such as 'Back Britain, not Black Britain'. Three days earlier, Powell's 'Rivers of Blood' speech, criticising mass immigration, had polarised the nation.

'Mrs' Janet Dagley, oblivious to all of this, gave birth to a 7lb 2oz boy in Nether Edge Hospital, Sheffield. She'd spent the previous three months closeted in a house on Ecclesall Road, with only Great-Aunt Shirley and Great-Uncle John for company. Her Mum and Dad visited once during the period of incarceration, and her grandmother Joyce, Shirley's sister, twice. Aunt Peg turned up within twenty-four hours of the infant's arrival, and Uncle Ralph joined her eight days later in order to complete the formalities of adoption at a place called Miss Dickenson's Nursery. The staff there were geared up to ensure that such legalities went smoothly.

By early May, all of them were back home. Janet, now fully recovered from her supposed bout of hepatitis, returned to Merton County and, above the greengrocery in Bermondsey, the Langridges were adjusting to their new life as parents.

The adults involved in this charade had agreed that Janet should be allowed to choose the baby's name. This was a tactical decision, designed (hopefully) to provide a clue as to the identity of the child's father. However, none of the boys she was known to associate with, and none of her school friends' brothers included a Frederick, so this took them no further forward.

Peggy was slightly disappointed that her niece hadn't opted for George, given that her son had been born on England's patron saint's day. He was a beautiful baby. He had a mass of very dark curls and bright blue eyes, just like his birth mother. Everyone knew that this could change after a few months, but it was obvious from the outset that it wasn't going to happen. Granny Faulkner, a renowned beauty who'd had the same distinctive combination of colouring, had obviously passed on very strong genes. None of them knew what genes were, but they sounded impressive.

Although she worked hard, Janet was unable to make up for the missed schooling and failed to attain the three A grades demanded by Oxford. With one A and two Bs, she instead had to fall back on the provisional offer from Reading University to read biochemistry. But it was a bitter disappointment not to be studying medicine.

1970

18

In 1970, the Five Nations Rugby Union Championship did nothing to boost national pride. It was won by France. The one positive was that, despite the political troubles, the Irish team for the then amateur sport was drawn from the whole of Ireland.

The British Home Championship (often referred to as the 'Home Internationals') was played on a round-robin basis between England, Scotland, Wales and Northern Ireland in April 1970. Regarded as a warm-up for the forthcoming FIFA World Cup, when England would be defending the title won in 1966, the whole event was a rather lacklustre and disappointingly inconclusive affair. All finishing on four points, three teams shared the trophy.[1]

Two months later, England, as the UK's sole representative, was knocked out of the World Cup, losing to West Germany after extra time. Due to food poisoning, Gordon Banks had been unable to play. Ron Dagley, who had by now grudgingly accepted the goalie's key role in West Ham's 1966 victory, turned conspiracy theorist and claimed that the Stoke City player had been nobbled by the opposing side, in an act of revenge.

What with the football in Mexico in June, the ninth Commonwealth Games (held in Edinburgh in July) and an unofficial Test series of six cricket matches against a 'Rest of the World' XI, it was a busy summer for sport. All this happened against the backdrop of the usual great events. In horse racing,

157

there was Royal Ascot, Glorious Goodwood and the five classics at Newmarket, Epsom and Doncaster. Australians John Newcombe and Margaret Court won the men's and ladies' tennis singles at Wimbledon, and American Jack Nicklaus emerged triumphant in the Open Golf Championship at St Andrew's.

And then there was the British Grand Prix.

James was a keen follower of Formula One. During the regency, he rarely undertook official duties but, in 1969, he'd agreed to present the Grovewood Awards. These were made by Grovewood Securities, the owners of Brands Hatch, to three British or Commonwealth drivers who showed outstanding promise in the early development of their racing careers. On that occasion, he'd made friends with the second-prize winner, Formula Three driver James Hunt. The King, who was going to the 1970 Grand Prix with his cousin, Prince William of Gloucester, invited James to accompany them. The thriller they witnessed was won by the German, Jochen Rindt. Hunt was the first person His Majesty telephoned, a mere seven weeks later, upon hearing the news of Rindt's tragic accidental death during a practice session at Monza in Italy.

Whilst attendance at both Brands Hatch and the Henley Regatta were personal 'must dos', James was otherwise forced to ration his appearances at events. For the first half of the year, his studies, culminating in a gruelling programme of exams, took priority. He was thus neatly excused from the almost mandatory appearance at Royal Ascot. Under pressure to be seen to be supporting the full spectrum of sporting events, he would make up for this in early September by turning up for the St Leger Stakes at Doncaster, being there to see the legendary Nijinsky, with the equally legendary Lester Piggott as rider, complete the Triple Crown.

There was some talk of his presenting at least one of the trophies at Wimbledon, which had always been associated with the Kents. For Princess Marina, Dowager Duchess of

Kent, tennis was a passion that lasted until her death in 1968, by which time she'd done a great deal to promote the reputation of the All England Club. Her three children inherited this interest, which was also shared by the Duke's wife, Katherine. This year, being eight months pregnant with her third child, Katherine was an absentee. James, who'd finally completed the last of his exam papers, was not especially keen to go, especially given the lack of a serious British contender. Fortunately, Princess Margaret stepped up to help do the honours instead.

On 25th July, the King presided over the closing ceremony of the British Commonwealth Games in Edinburgh, which had been opened by his brother-in-law Prince Phillip nine days earlier. Like most other people, he struggled to cope with the fact that distance events were no longer measured in imperial units. It still felt strange to be thinking in metres, though this innovation did not extend to the marathon, which was still run over 26 miles and 385 yards. In a short speech, he explained how that particular length had come about. In 1908, during the London Olympics, his great-grandmother Queen Alexandra had requested that the race start on the lawn of Windsor castle, to enable the youngest family members to watch from their nursery window. It finished in front of the royal box at the White City stadium.

By the end of July, and despite all that had been going on during the warmer months, planning was well advanced for the Late Summer Festival of Sports[2]. The radical idea behind this was to play games of both football and rugby union on the same day, using eight different major venues across the UK and Ireland. Kick-off times were to be staggered, enabling television coverage of all the scheduled matches. The winners of these tournaments would receive Coronation Cups and be declared 'Champions of the Kingdom'. This caused some controversy because, if an all-Ireland team won the rugby, 'the Kingdom' might be implied to include a country that was most definitely, and defiantly, a totally independent republic and one which was not even a member of the Commonwealth to boot. Most pundits considered an Irish victory unlikely but, as the festival was intended to promote a sense of unity rather than exacerbate division, the title to be awarded to the rugby victors was changed to 'Champions of the North Atlantic Archipelago'.

Hockey, a very popular sport, was also to have its own 'home nations' events for Coronation Cups, with both men's and women's teams competing. The matches, some scheduled for early afternoon, would fit between the male-dominated sports and culminate on Finals Day, Friday 25th September 1970.

To accommodate all the one-off competitions, First Division football fixtures on 26th September were cancelled and rescheduled for later in the season.

Broadcasting rights were allocated between ITV (on condition that the action was not interrupted by advert breaks) and BBC1. Both channels were known to be planning female-orientated programmes as alternatives to match coverage and, in line with this thinking, BBC2 were re-running the entire series of *The Forsyte Saga*.

In many households throughout the land, women began to conspire. It was one thing putting up with *Grandstand*, football and wrestling on a Saturday afternoon; it was quite another to be faced with the prospect of almost a week spent staring at people moving a ball from one end of a pitch to the other. Some wives, and less often husbands, started negotiating for shared rights to choose which channel they watched.

Others, like Lillian Dagley, took a different approach. The three mums from the old school-run rota, plus two other female neighbours, decided to congregate in one or other of their homes on each of the sport-dominated evenings, and claim exclusive rights to the TV. The disenfranchised husband affected by this would need to find refuge elsewhere.

When Janet had disappeared in early 1968, Lil's explanation was viewed with suspicion, or at least she imagined that was the case. Someone had even been bold enough to comment that the industrial city of Sheffield was hardly famed for its fresh air and recuperative environment. Lil had countered by explaining that her aunt lived on the outskirts, close to the Peak District, and that many tourists went to the area for its natural beauty, climbing and other outdoor activities. Once Janet returned, things had remained slightly uneasy for a while, but the girl's story was well rehearsed, and it wasn't long before relationships were back to what felt like completely normal. After all, even if there had been speculation, it couldn't feed on itself forever, could it? Peggy, though, didn't visit as often and, when she did, she left Freddie with Joyce – just in case anyone put two and two together.

When Lil told her sister about the Festival of Sport scheme, Peggy related it to Ralph, who didn't like the idea of babysitting for several nights on the trot. He was very good with their son, but never confident about the possibility of needing to handle an emergency – such as a dirty nappy – on his own. Instead, he agreed to rent a further TV set on a short-term basis and put it in the bedroom, so they could both watch what they liked.

———————

The sports festival meant that, on top of the preparations for his now imminent coronation, James found himself facing a busy agenda. On Tuesday 22nd September, he attended the evening match between Ireland and Scotland at Lansdowne Road, Dublin. The predictions proved correct, and the Scots won by 22 points to 7.

The following day, he was at Hampden Park, Glasgow, for the late afternoon kick-off between Scotland and Northern

Ireland, which resulted in a two-all draw and was finally settled on penalties, again in the Scots' favour.

Thursday saw him sitting in a makeshift stand at Lilleshall National Sports Centre, Shropshire, a facility which his older sister Elizabeth had opened in 1951[3]. For this reason, she agreed to go with him, and they both watched the English ladies being thrashed by a hockey team representing Northern Ireland, who lifted the cup. On Friday, a solo James saw England's men do the same at Twickenham.

Windsor Park, Belfast, was Saturday's venue for the game to determine third and fourth places in the football. This time, the luck of the Irish ran out and the Welsh prevailed, as was also the case at the following day's rugby final, when the principality took on Scotland. At Cardiff Arms Park, James was accompanied by a reluctant Charles, and insisted that his nephew present the trophy, as was entirely fitting. The two royal personages were whisked by helicopter back to London, where Charles retreated to Clarence House.

James made it to Wembley in time to present the last of the cups to Scotland's football team. The whole festival thus resulted in an even split of honours.

On the seemingly rare occasions when he was home, the King trod the carpets of his private rooms with the coronation crown on his head. Its weight made him feel top-heavy and slightly disorientated. Along carpeted corridors elsewhere, the shoes he'd be wearing on the great day were being worn in by a footman nicknamed 'Buttons'.[4]

Meanwhile, in the apartment suite that should now by rights be his, his mother was happily ensconced. She'd be sitting, with a corgi at her side, doubtless sipping a gin and Dubonnet. Now no longer regent, she was supposed to have moved into Marlborough House, the residence occupied without complaint by her two predecessor queen dowagers. But the Mater refused to budge. James wasn't bothered about reclaiming the accommodation. His surroundings mattered little to him. It was more the fact that she kept dropping in, unannounced, wanting to know what he'd been up to, what his plans were and 'how he was managing'. Sharing the same palace, albeit a bloody big one, was proving rather too convenient for these maternal visits, but he was beginning to suspect he'd never get rid of her.[5]

In between all the pre-coronation sporting engagements, James had visited several junior schools which were participating in 'The Great Acorn Quest'.

As had happened on the occasion of his father's coronation in 1937, acorns from Windsor Great Park were to be shipped around the Commonwealth and planted in public parks, private gardens, school grounds and cemeteries to grow into Royal Oaks or Coronation Oaks.

James had added the idea of a national competition, confined to the UK, to find the biggest acorn. The only specifications were that it had to have its cup intact and that it must have been collected from the ground. This second requirement was strictly enforced. It hadn't needed the input of safety experts to recognise the dangers of climbing trees and the unthinkable consequences of a fall from lofty branches. Any child who was discovered breaking the rule risked the disqualification of their whole school.

In acknowledgment of the fact that inner cities might not afford easy access to oak trees, a national programme of exchange was funded. This scheme enabled pupils from urban and more rural areas to swap classrooms for a day and thereby experience a different learning environment.

Although the contest had been his own brainchild, the thought had been prompted by a discussion with Charles. This had taken place shortly before Christmas 1969, when both were part way through the final year of their degree courses. The opulent surroundings of Sandringham House had prompted Charles to comment on how very privileged they both were, especially compared with how very underprivileged many of their own age must be.

'I want to do something to help,' he'd stated bluntly. 'We're not so insulated that we don't know what's going on in the big wide world.'

James, whose covert forays had given him slightly more exposure to real life, was all for it.

'Had any further thoughts on the matter?' he asked.

'As a matter of fact, yes. Something – not sure what yet – for young people who've lost their way. Those in care, or whose parents are struggling when it comes to pointing them in the right direction. The ones who've somehow got mixed up with gangs and end up involved with drugs or petty crime. Or those who didn't bother much about education and were spat out of the system without a skill or qualification to their name – only to wonder whether they had any aptitude for anything at all and with absolutely no idea about how to find out. There must be dozens of ways in which kids can take one wrong turn and ruin the rest of their lives because of it. And there must be dozens of ways to rescue them.'

'I can't disagree with that. It seems like a noble ambition. Do you have an age range in mind?'

'Secondary onwards, probably. That's when the wrong sort of peer influence starts to kick in.'

'You've really got me thinking, old boy. If you're set to focus on older children – and young adults? – then maybe I should target the younger ones. Infants and juniors. That's where it all begins. We could work in tandem. And I've just had an idea about where to start. It will be ecological in a way, so it should be just up your street.'

It was only natural, given his own competitiveness, that James hit on the hook of challenges. Acorns were to be just the start and, because the event was to celebrate his coronation, he commissioned a small gold-plated trophy from Garrard & Co.

Thereafter, it all started to go horribly wrong. The concept behind the biggest acorn quest seemed pretty straightforward but proved far from it. The first problem was how size should be measured. By length, or by width? This was resolved by opting for weight in grams. An oak wasn't just an oak. There were five main species in Britain, and some produced bigger acorns than others. Those from English oaks (*quercus robur*) were generally smaller than those from *quercus cerris*, for example. The Irish complained because 'their' sessile oak was a national symbol, and couldn't the UK have come up with the produce from a different tree? Conkers from horse chestnuts, for example. Then news arrived that the pupils of a school near Bolton were claiming to have found acorns that were far bigger than those being reported from anywhere else in Britain. Investigations into this revealed that a local landowner had successfully grown several burr oaks (*quercus macrocarpa*) imported from their native North America, thus giving the youngsters he allowed into his garden an unfair advantage. As they came from a non-indigenous species, all the oak apples thus collected were disqualified, giving rise to cries of 'foul', because the original rules had failed to state this.

Princess Elizabeth stepped in at this point and suggested a competition to find the most imaginative use of the humble acorn. Classrooms suddenly transformed into craft workshops, the output of which were countless autumnal wreaths, other supposedly decorative pieces, photo frames, items of jewellery, collages, caterpillars, spacemen and sundry representations of humanoids wearing painted beanie hats. A few very minor injuries occurred. These included pin pricks and slight scaldings. The latter were incurred when some Year Two pupils at St Egbert's in Stroud were attempting to make miniature wax candles in acorn cups.

An imaginative teacher in Perthshire, having heard that acorns were full of beneficial nutrients, was chastised for suggesting an acorn picnic. She hadn't realised that the harmful tannins must first be removed by boiling or soaking. Luckily, due to the bitter taste, no child had swallowed more than tiniest quantity, but warnings nevertheless had to be issued.

James ordered a further dozen trophies, which were silver-plated. Given that judging the winners was such a subjective process, geography could (unofficially) enter the equation and these awards ended up fairly evenly distributed throughout the kingdom. The golden acorn trophy was won by a school in Carmarthen. The winning seed weighed in at a verified 9.6 grams. There was some suspicion that the child who brought it in had 'found' it in an envelope sent from a cousin in Michigan. It was mysteriously misplaced shortly thereafter, and the only surviving record was a poor-quality monochrome photograph. This unfortunately meant that the species could not be properly identified.

Despite the problems, the school exchanges were highly successful and fostered proposals for a more systematic, better frame-worked and wider-spread network. The scheme was to become a core element of the new King's Trust, which was officially launched in 1974. Charles' Prince's Trust, supporting vulnerable young people, was established two years later.

19

LONDON

The day of the coronation[1] dawned dull and grey, with a hint of drizzle in the air. However, this did not deter the crowds or dampen their enthusiasm. A bank holiday had been declared, and royalists and republicans alike were keen to make the most of a long weekend.

James wasn't looking forward to the event, but nor was he dreading it. He simply wanted to get it over and done with and then move on, though to where, he wasn't quite certain. The future that stretched ahead seemed to be a relentless round of red boxes, audiences and sundry engagements, interspersed with foreign tours, mainly to Commonwealth countries.

In his mind, he'd broken up the big day into sections. The ceremonial part in the morning, the balcony appearance and fly-past, the enormous palace luncheon, the chatting to dignitaries... But he'd insisted on having the evening to himself and intended to enjoy it.

He'd commissioned three upper-face masks in three different likenesses. One was in his own image, one represented Charles and the third was the Duke of Edinburgh. This last would be worn by Prince William of Gloucester, who was not at the time an instantly recognisable figure, especially as he'd spent the last two years working in the British Embassy in Tokyo. His father's fragile health had necessitated a return to Britain, and James had correctly figured that his cousin could do with cheering up: William hadn't needed nearly as much persuading to participate as the Prince of Wales. James's plan was that the trio would hit the town, with two of them pretending to be who they really were. It was the perfect double bluff, all topped off by three plastic, and deliberately cheap-looking, coronets.

Whereas many folk had decided to celebrate the crowning of their king by heading 'up West', the young men travelled across the Thames and east for a few drinks, followed by a curry at a place on Tooley Street. The restaurant had been recommended by Jenks, one of James's closest university friends who, despite being a supposed connoisseur of Indian cuisine, nevertheless remained addicted to Vesta ready meals.

James had never before succeeded in getting his nephew to join him on any of his incognito excursions, but the concept for this night's outing almost guaranteed anonymity. Even so, the disguised-as-himself Charles was far from relaxed in the Frog and Nightgown, on the Old Kent Road, where the pub crawl began. He was less uptight in the Dun Cow and, by the time they approached the Gin Palace, he was positively enthused, declaring, 'This is more like it!'[2]

The small dining area of the Razala Ritz restaurant was very busy, but advance bookings ensured that the Carrick party had no difficulty securing tables – one for the now tipsy coronet-wearing trio and another for Gerald and Melvin, who ended up squeezed alongside Ralph Langridge and his friend Ken. Ralph later reported events to a highly amused Peggy.

'There were three jokers in the Ritz. Pissed as newts and pretendin' to be royals. I must say, they were very good. Kept up the posh accents, though the "king" lapsed into Irish now and then. 'ad all the patter off to a tee. "Prince Charles" was bangin' on about some bird called Camellia. It was a right laugh. The blokes at the next table to us even claimed to be their security guards, would you believe?'[3]

1ST NOVEMBER 1970

STANDFORD STREET, DEPTFORD

Metrification hadn't so far affected most of the population.

By 1963, some old imperial measures were no longer legally authorised, but few mourned the loss of drachms, scruples, quarters and rods, poles or perches. In 1966, only those in industry were aware that traditional screw thread systems had become obsolete and that all products exported to Common Market countries now had to comply with Handbook 18's 'metric standards for engineering'.

Come 1967, school children were no longer reciting '12 inches equal 1 foot, 3 feet equal one yard, 22 yards equal 1 chain, 10 chains equal 1 furlong, 8 furlongs equal 1 mile'. Parents, when helping with homework, suddenly needed to get their heads around all those noughts relating to the number of millimetres in a kilometre.

In 1969, pharmacists were obliged to dispense in metric units, but a tablet was still a tablet, and a spoonful of medicine was still a spoonful, albeit a 5ml one. A year later, seafarers were dealing with the new international nautical mile but, as this was only 3.18 metres shorter than the old UK nautical mile, it wasn't so very different.

As they'd done on Christmas Day 1951, the Dagleys and Faulkners had convened at Standford Street. This time, the occasion was Peggy's fortieth birthday, which they were celebrating with sandwiches and cake. The only absentee was Janet, who was in her final year at Reading. Her replacement was the newcomer, Freddie, now a bright and inquisitive two-year-old. He'd enjoyed helping his mummy to blow out the candles and, seemingly exhausted by the effort, was now slumped half-dozing on 'Auntie Lil's' lap.

'We've got new neighbours,' said Joyce. 'They're from Vietnam.'

'Are they nice?' asked the birthday girl.

'We don't know, do we Ron? They don't speak a word of English, but she does a lot of washin', and 'angs out the beddin' every week, reg'lar as clockwork.'

'Why would anyone move 'ere?' Peggy wanted to know. 'I fought you were due to be demolished?'

'Not anymore,' said her father. 'They're doin' a rethink. As it is, there's lots of streets, where 'ouses once stood, that are just piles of rubble. They can't redevelop them all at once. But it's prob'ly only a matter of time. All the old employers are closin' too. Stones's Foundry shut up shop last year. Everyfin's changin' so fast since the docks closed. I never fought I'd end up workin' the Bovril boats.'

Joyce patted his hand sympathetically. She knew how hard that had been for him, after decades employed as a lighterman. The final two years before retirement had seen her husband travelling by bus to Beckton every morning, from where he'd operated the sludge boats. These vessels transported London's human sewage away from the capital and emptied it into the North Sea. It had been an ignominious end to a dignified career.

'I expect a lot of Vietnamese 'ave come to Britain because of the war,' Harold mused.

'I don't know what sort of climate they 'ave over there, but it must be warmer than 'ere,' said his wife Daisy. 'And I reckon the weather's got chillier 'ere, ever since they started measurin' temperatures in centigrade. I don't know where I am these days, now they've stopped showin' the Fahrenheit number[4]. 'oo knows now 'ow cold or 'ot it's going to be?'

Lil laughed. 'It all depends on the accuracy of the weather forecasts anyway, so nobody can ever really be sure what's coming! But it's quite easy to work out. Just double the centigrade temperature shown and add thirty. That gives a good approximation of what you're familiar with. And, if they're predicting 16 degrees, simply reverse the digits, because 16 centigrade is 61 Fahrenheit. The same rule applies to 28°C, which reverses to 82°F.'

'That won't 'appen very often, will it? And 'ow do you expect me to remember all that?'

'If you're strugglin' with that, 'ow are you going to cope with decimal money?' asked Peggy.

'I'm dreadin' it. 'ave you seen that programme *Granny Gets the Point*? Well I feel just like poor old Doris Hare.'

'Wasn't she in *On the Buses*?'

'That's the one, dear. Anyway, 'er grandson 'as got it all worked out, smart as you please. It's all right for you young 'uns. So-called public information films won't 'elp the likes of me. I'm wiv Doris. In the last programme she said that, if she woz given 'er pension in the new money, she'd 'and it back "where it 'urt". I'm wiv 'er on that. And she said she would rarva starve to deaf than buy anyfin' using the new money – and, if she did die, she'd write to the King and complain.'

'We could take a stand togevva, Daisy,' declared Joyce. 'Chain ourselves to the railin's at Buckin'am Palace, or somefin' like that to protest. The ten bob note's goin' in a few weeks' time, and we've got those 'orrible coins instead, which aren't even round. We've already lost the 'alf-crown. It's not good enough.'

'You'll soon get used to it, Mum,' soothed Lil, reaching for the purse in her bag. She emptied its contents onto the table, separated out two coins and placed them side by side. 'Look. This five pence piece is the same size as the shilling next to it. And it's worth exactly the same.' After a further similar manoeuvre, she made the same observation about a ten pence piece and a florin. 'Not that difficult after all, is it?'

Joyce sighed. 'And what's a tanner gonna be worth?'

'Two and a half new pence.'

'That don't make any sense at all.'

During the run-up to 'D-Day', James's survival became a real concern in some official circles: if he died before some four hundred million plus newly-minted coins, all bearing his effigy, were released, then the whole switchover could prove a total disaster. Prince Phillip had put forward the idea of changing the images on the new decimal coins. As chairman of the Royal Mint Advisory Committee, he'd questioned the use of Britannia and expressed his feeling that 'quite a lot of crowns and things' already featured. The Queen Dowager was appalled when he suggested the alternative of 'flowers, weeds and vegetables'.[5]

Flowers were acceptable to her. After all, the plant thrift characterised the dear old thrupenny bit, didn't it? But weeds? And who would want to be looking at carrots and Brussels sprouts when they were counting out their money?

The King celebrated his twenty-second birthday on 14th February 1971 and, the following day, everything changed. The pound remained the pound, but how the pound was divided up was radically different. Henceforth, it would contain a hundred new pence. The farthing – there'd been 960 of those in a pound – had been removed from circulation ten years earlier. Old halfpennies, pennies and threepenny pieces disappeared, as they had no direct equivalents in the new system. Harold Wilson's 'save the sixpence' idea, and the decisions of subsequent governments, meant that the beloved 'tanner' would ultimately survive until 1980. Vending machines, phone boxes, ticket dispensers and parking meters all took these small coins. If this were no longer possible, the argument went, it would contribute to price increases. These happened anyway, amidst a soaring inflation rate of almost ten per cent, with much worse yet to come.

After a while, as things settled down, translating from new to old became automatic. Shopkeepers, predictably, tended to round up what they were charging, rather than round down. Ralph Langridge, aware that many of his customers were in poorly paid jobs, was one of the exceptions and, perversely, his profits increased in line with his reputation as a fair trader.

15TH JUNE 1971

OXFORD STREET, LONDON

'Janet's spending next weekend at some stately home,' Lil told Peggy. The sisters had met in the café of the Oxford Street John Lewis.

'Ooh, that sounds very posh. Fancy 'er rubbin' shoulders with the aristocracy.'

'Not sure about that. Her friend, Helen, is an "Honourable", but she isn't a Lady Something.'

'Well, an 'eiress then.'

'I don't even think she's that. Comes from a big family from what I could gather.'

'P'raps Janet'll 'it it off with a son of the 'ouse?'

'Not sure about that either, but it will make a nice change for her.'

'Shouldn't she be studyin'? I fought her final exams were comin' up?'

'She's just finished them, but hasn't had the results yet. She seemed to be glued to her books for weeks, so a bit of a break is probably exactly what she needs.'

'So where is this grand place?'

'Not far from Reading. Somewhere near Henley.' Lil took a bite of her egg mayonnaise sandwich, chewed it and extracted a bit of cress from between her front teeth.

'Will she be goin' to the regatta?'

'I expect so.'

'Really?

'No, don't be daft. I think you have to wear a dress and a hat for that. I haven't seen Janet in a dress for years.'

'So she'll be back 'ome soon, will she? What's she plannin' on doin'?'

'She's not sure. There's a careers centre at the university, and she's signed up. Apparently employers looking for graduates send their vacancies to these centres, and a list gets sent out every week. But, next minute, she's talking about a gap year.'

'Any boyfriend on the scene?'

'She hasn't mentioned anyone special. You'd have thought university was the best place to meet single chaps with decent prospects, but she doesn't seem interested. Hasn't done ever since... How is Freddie?'

'Settled in nicely at nursery. They say 'e's bright.'

'Takes after his Mum.'

'*I'm* 'is Mum.'

'That's what I meant, Peg, so don't get all defensive. And he couldn't wish for a better one. Talking of which, how are Mum and Dad?'

'They're fine. I saw them a couple of days ago. I try to get over on 'alf day closin'. I said I was meetin' up wiv you. They send their love. Are you lookin' for anyfin' in particular?'

'Just something for Terry's birthday. I'll have a quick look in menswear and see if I can find a tie or a belt. What about you?'

'No. I never see anyfin' if I'm lookin', so I'll just browse. Somefin' may take my fancy. All the clothes I like best are ones I've dropped on. So are all the ones that stay stuck in the wardrobe and nevva see the light of day.'

The following week, Lil phoned her sister to say that Janet had been awarded a first class degree. The girl was currently discussing with her tutors the possibility of further postgraduate studies leading, ultimately, to a PhD.

'What does that mean?' Peggy asked.

'A PhD is a doctor of philosophy.'

'Eh? I fought she was doin' somefin' biological?'

'She is. And, if she stays on and qualifies, she'll get called "doctor", but won't be a medical one. Beyond that, I'm none the wiser. Disappointing though.'

'What d'you mean? If it's what she wants – '

'No,' Lil explained, 'what's disappointing is that, because she had to hang around at Reading having all these talks, she couldn't go back to the Honourable Helen's country pile. She was invited for another week. And guess who'll be staying there for a couple of days while the regatta's on?'

'Search me. The Pope?'

'Close. The King! ... Are you still there, Peg? I think we've been cut off.'

1974

20

25TH JANUARY 1974

BUCKINGHAM PALACE

James had always kept in touch with his friends from Charterhouse and Oxford. He made a point of corresponding with them using anonymous stationery. Sometimes, he contacted them by phone. Because many were now getting jobs and moving away from their parental homes, the young king made a point of updating their details.

Keith Bradshaw's number hadn't been changed, which meant that his Oxford chum was still living in the village of Killamarsh. At least this is what James hoped as he was being put through.

Keith's mother answered with a cheery, 'Hello Fergus... yes, hang on, I'll just get him for you.' The woman didn't know she was speaking to the King. That was how things had long since been determined, and subsequently stuck to, amongst His Majesty's friends.

James explained the reason for the call. He wanted to visit a coal mining area and meet some of the pit workers[1]. He needed Keith's help.

'Happy to assist if I can, Carrick, but haven't you got people who arrange this sort of thing for you?'

'Point is, I want to do it off the record and find out what's really going on with this three-day week. I can't do that if I'm confronted with a parade line of men, all scrubbed up and dressed in their Sunday best. There would be no chance to chat properly, even with those who don't clam up completely. Besides, this has to be unofficial: I can't be seen to be dabbling in politics. I take it that there are a couple of collieries near you?'

'Absolutely. We're bang in the middle of the North Derbyshire coalfield. There's High Moor and Westthorpe.'

'Splendid. And is there anywhere nearby where we can lodge? It would only be for one night. I'll have to scoot off first thing next day for a meeting with the Ghanaian ambassador.'

'As you do,' Keith laughed. 'The best place is probably the Park Hall Country Club. The Beatles stayed there in 1964, when they performed at Sheffield City Hall[2]. I actually went to the concert.'

James heard Mrs Bradshaw's voice in the background. 'Tell Fergus he's welcome to stay here!'

'It's OK, Mum. He's bringing a few mates with him,' Keith shouted back, before resuming the telephone conversation. 'How many of you will there be?'

'Four. A driver, two bodyguards and me. It would normally have been only the one bodyguard for an "unofficial" but, after what's just happened to Anne[3], they've upped the ante in the protection stakes.'

'That was terrible. From the reports, it sounds like she was awfully brave. Is she all right?'

'Fine. Water off a duck's back, old boy. There's certainly no messing with my niece! I've asked myself how I'd have reacted if some gun-toting madman had told me to get out of the car. I like to think that I, too, would have said, "Not bloody likely," but I can't be totally sure. Like her, I wouldn't have known that some ex-boxer was handily in the vicinity to whack the would-be kidnapper on the head.'

'Are all those who got shot OK?'

'Yes, thankfully they're recovering in hospital. But SO14 have gone into overdrive, as you might expect. Anyway, unless anything else changes, and they start insisting on bulletproof vehicles and an armed guard from now on, we'll be turning up in a nondescript Ford Escort, and none of us will look like who we really are.'

'Let me know when you're coming and I'll give Park Hall a bell. They shouldn't be full at this time of year.'

'It's OK, thanks. I've jotted down the details, and someone can book from my end. All I need you to do is make sure you're free next Wednesday, so you can take me to a pub where everyone knows you. One that's frequented by miners.'

'That's just about every pub in the village. Plenty to choose from, though they're all shutting at 10.30 and you may find yourself drinking by candlelight. We'll start at The Crown.'

'Sounds appropriate.'

'Will I recognise you?'

'We'll call for you, and you can direct us from there. Do I need any special props?'

'Like what?'

'I was thinking of, well, a whippet maybe?'

Keith gulped. 'Best not. Skip the ferret, too. A donkey jacket would look the part, as long as it doesn't have NCB emblazoned on the back. How do you want to be introduced?'

'Usual name. A mate from Norfolk. It's my best regional accent, and I know the area around Sandringham well, just in case anyone happens to be familiar with it.'

'Occupation?'

'Unemployed.'

'Occupation when not unemployed?'

'Hmm. I usually say ledger clerk. No one knows what one of those does, and it sounds incredibly boring, which means I'm never asked what it involves. By the way, what are you doing these days?'

'Temping until I find my true vocation. Current job, comp op.'

'A what?'

'Comptometer operator. It's a machine that you punch numbers into. Bit antiquated nowadays, but the bakery I work for still uses one. Useful for us purchase ledger clerks. Like to hear all about what trial balancing involves?'

'I rest my case. Didn't you have an ambition to be a writer?'

'Yes. I'm still on with that, but it doesn't pay the rent, not that Mum charges me anything, apart from a bit to cover my keep. I've written a few bestsellers, but they won't earn me anything until someone publishes them.'

'They will, one of these days. Anything else I should know for when we're on this brief outing?'

'Don't be surprised if anyone calls me Robin.'

'Why?'

'As in sidekick of the Caped Crusader. Robin the Boy Wonder. It's a nickname because I went to Oxford. Hardly anyone from round here has been to university, let alone Oxbridge. Most of them go straight down t'pit.'

'Have you seen anyone from our set recently? Stuart phoned me a month or so ago. He's got a job in Montreal, working on components for the American space programme. He sounded fine. He's taking his wife with him.'

'Wife? Blimey. Obviously had better luck than I'm having, but I suppose a high-flying astrophysicist has better prospects than a temporary comp op! I did see Jenks just the other week. He stopped over on his way down from seeing his parents in Edinburgh.'

'Is he still addicted to Vesta beef curry?'

'He said he prefers my Mum's steak and kidney pudding.'

'Well, hopefully we'll get the chance to catch up a bit more when I see you.'

'Fergus' and 'Robin' made their arrangements and, the

following week, HM The King found himself sitting on a stool at one of several small tables clustered around an alcove in the so-called 'best room' at The Crown. The clientele in the crowded smoked-filled area was almost exclusively male. The exceptions were two women who were with two men – their husbands, James assumed – making up an animated foursome a short distance away. Gerald the Geordie and Melvin, who'd gone in ahead of them, had found a small corner table and were settled with a pint of bitter shandy apiece. Melvin's copy of the *Daily Mirror*[4], an appropriate 'prop', was folded up on a shelf beneath the table. Every table was equipped with such a shelf. It was where people put their drinks, thereby freeing up the surface above for cards or dominoes. Several games were in progress.

Thanks to his imposing bulk, ginger hair and purple kaftan – his favourite from a now-extensive collection of similar garments – Gerald was far more conspicuous than local boy Keith's supposed Norfolk pal. Goodness knows what the regular patrons thought the big ginger-haired man and his companion were doing there. This was no central London bar, frequented by tourists who came and went unquestioned. This was a club, almost as exclusive as any private members' establishment in the capital, where the presence of strangers might occasion misgivings. James wasn't concerned. Gerald would have done the ordering at the bar. Melvin spoke only BBC English, which might have raised suspicion, but someone so obviously from the north-east would have prompted only a degree of curiosity. Whatever anyone might be thinking, nobody was going to guess that the pair were royal personal protection officers, who were being far more vigilant than their behaviour might suggest. Nor would anyone know that, carefully concealed, both men carried Glock 17 pistols, radios and first aid kits.

The Ford was parked nearby. Its armed driver would also remain alert.

'Yer Uncle Willis not out tonight, Keith?' asked one of the men.

'He's gone to the Midland, but we'll be heading there in a bit.'

'Of course. I forgot it's Tuesday. I'm losing track of the days already. So Irene will be at the beetle, will she?'

'She never misses.'

'He'll be collecting his mini gold Davy lamp next year, won't he? Not much to show for fifty years' service to t' NCB, is it? Straight from school at fifteen, then half a century of solid graft. He's better off out it.'

'He does get his pit pension and three bags of coal a week, though. Not that the coal's much use: he's just had a gas fire fitted. My Auntie Irene said she'd had enough of getting up at five o'clock every morning to clear out the grate and start twisting paper. And the chimney wasn't drawing like it used to.' Keith added an aside warning to Fergus, 'If we do run into my uncle later, don't start him on the bad old days, or he'll be banging on about how mining used to involve hacking at the seams with picks and putting in some proper graft, unlike our present company.'

'Don't be so cheeky, Robin,' said another of the men, rising to the bait despite Keith's good-humoured tone and concluding wink. 'I grant it's all mechanised now, but that doesn't mean we have it soft. You should try spending hours underground breathing in black dust instead of doing whatever you do in some cosy office, keeping your hands nice and clean. Bloody waste of an expensive education, that's what I say.'

The first speaker turned to 'Fergus'. 'I suppose you're the same, if you're a pal of his?'

'Chance would be a fine thing. I'm unemployed.'

'We'll all be in the dole queue at this rate,' interjected a rotund balding man, who reminded James of the Pillsbury Doughboy. 'Might be better off, too, the rate prices are rocketing. Our table hasn't had a sniff of beef for months, it's that expensive now.'

An elderly chap sitting in the corner said, 'Twenty year ago, meat were still on ration.' It would prove to be his sole contribution.

'Aye, and now there's no limit, we can't afford it. Same difference.'

The price of beef had almost doubled between 1970 and 1973. There was no doubt that sharply rising world prices for food and other commodities had had a big impact on inflation but, as Fergus got in another round for Keith and himself, other contributory reasons were ricocheting around the group of men.

'My missus says the reason they don't print prices on packages any more is because they go up every day.'

'I blame the Common Market. You can't trust Europeans not to rig things in their own favour.'

'That and allowing the pound to float. Far as I can see, it sunk.'

'What we need are food subsidies. And a decent wage rise, like we've been demanding. What's the point having an enquiry into something and then ignoring what it recommends?'

'What we need most is a change of government. Heath's hanging on by a thread. It won't take much,' piped up a chap of about thirty. He wore a grubby red-and-white-striped Sheffield United shirt.

Doughboy, who'd been studying Fergus with a questioning expression, suddenly changed the subject. Staring straight at the King, he said, 'You know lad, there's something familiar about you. Can't quite put my finger on it, but you put me in mind of someone famous. Let me think... I've got it! It's that James somebody... You know, that racing driver bloke. Has anyone told you that before?'

'You mean James Hunt? Yes, once or twice,' admitted a relieved James.

'Well, my wife always says that James Hunt looks a bit like the King,' contributed the man who'd blamed the Common Market for Britain's woes, 'so you must, too. He does, doesn't he, Mick?'

Mick, who turned out to be the one who'd challenged Keith, shook his head. 'Doesn't follow. Can't see it myself,' he said.

'It's a pity I can't do the posh accent, or I'd be able to earn a living as a lookalike!' responded His Majesty, assuming his broadest 'Naa-fuck'.

'Oh, I don't think you're similar enough for that, but maybe you could work on it, as you've nothing better to do.'

'Steady on, Mick. The lad didn't come in here to be got at. And he polishes his shoes. I like to see youngsters taking care of their shoes. Not many bother these days. It even looks like you've ironed your laces, lad!'[5]

'No, it's my Mum who does that. She irons everything in sight. I keep telling her not to bother with my socks and kecks, but she insists.' James smiled at the mental image of Her Majesty standing in front of an ironing board, tackling a pair of boxer shorts. He took a swig of Wards bitter and turned to the football fan.

'We're playing your lot at home next Saturday. Do you travel to away games?' James scratched his head behind his right ear. He'd briefed Keith, who knew what this meant.

'Not usually,' said the Blades supporter. 'You're not doing very well this season, are you?'

'Rock bottom, mate.'

At that moment, the lights flickered, and the pub plunged into darkness.

'Here we go again,' said Doughboy. 'This country can't run without coal. We've got them over a barrel.'

The others had started counting out loud. On five, the lighting was restored. Mick stood up and declared, 'My round. Can I get you two youngsters another? Robin? Fergus?'

'No thanks, Mick. We'll finish these and then get going.'

Gerald and Melvin's glasses, which had been a third full half a minute earlier, were now empty. James wondered if the bodyguards had hastily gulped down what was left or whether, taking advantage of the temporary blackout, they'd poured the remainder into the large pot plant behind them.

'Odd couple o' characters,' observed one man, as the strangers departed, one through the front door and the other via the corridor that led to the toilets and rear exit.

James and Keith left a few minutes later. It was bright outside. The sky was virtually cloudless, and the moon was almost full. James, knowing his team would follow, suggested walking for a while.

'I feel like stretching my legs,' he said, 'it was a bit claustrophobic in there.'

'I thought you'd been rumbled at one point.'

'So did I. It felt a little too close for comfort. Before my coronation, it was easy to play Mister Anonymous. Average height. No distinguishing features. I always felt sorry for Charles. Ears are difficult to disguise. But now I'm doing the Christmas broadcasts, and my face has been plastered all over mugs and tea towels, I'm never quite as confident as I once was. Not sure a false moustache and beard would cut it, though specs still make a big difference.'

'Do you need specs?'

'Only for reading. I'm never photographed wearing them.' The King lapsed into a momentary silence before adding, 'I suppose the main thing is that, when I turn up totally out of context, the last thing anyone would imagine is that I'm me. Did you know that, on VE Day, my sisters left the palace and secretly mingled with the crowds outside?'

'I hadn't heard that.'

'Yes. They'd appeared on the balcony several times and thought it would be jolly good fun to join in the celebrations.

No one recognised them, despite the accompanying guard. And, only very recently, my older sister went into a village shop somewhere and was asked, "Has anyone told you that you look like Princess Elizabeth?"'

'And what did she say?'

'"How very reassuring".'

'You know, it's all very well adopting a regional accent, looking different and being somewhere nobody expects you to be, but you almost blew it back there with the glasses.'

'How?'

'Remember when you sauntered to the bar to get in the second round, and I had to call you back saying, "You've forgotten these."'

'What did I do wrong?'

'Nobody ever gets a clean glass. They stick to the same all night. Some of them even have their own personal ones behind the bar.'

'I fetched them, didn't I?'

'Yes, but you looked completely bewildered. Almost, might I say, as if you were used to being waited on and cleared up after?'

'Well, I am.'

'That's my point.'

'Point taken.'

The pair strolled on up a slight incline.

'We've just passed the splendid parish church of St Giles.' Keith switched to tour guide mode. 'The main feature is the 12th century Norman south doorway: it's really quite rare with an order of colonnettes, capitals with leaves, and an arch with zigzag on intrados and extrados! That's inside the porch, leading to the Gothic nave and tower.'

'Good God. You sound like you've swallowed a volume of *Pevsner*.'[6]

'We had a school trip here many moons ago, and it's where my parents got married.'

'Pity I won't get a chance to see it in daylight. My nephew Charles would be very interested. The older the building, the better, in his view. Anything more modern than Edwardian is highly suspect, if not outright brutalist.'[7]

'I'm sure my mum would make him welcome any time he fancies visiting! So did you get what you wanted back there?' asked Keith.

'Yes. I got a decent feel of the way the wind's blowing, thanks. It does me good to venture forth from my ivory tower into the real world now and again. Would you say your friends were especially militant?'

'This time, the picketing is carefully controlled and is deliberately being kept peaceful, but every single one of them could turn violent if needs be. This area returned one of the highest percentage votes for strike action in the whole country, but that's not surprising: Tom Swain, our local MP, is vice-president of the Derbyshire NUM. He also used to be a prize-fighting boxer.'

'Glad we didn't run into him then, but a handy type for rescuing princesses in distress. There's been some talk of bringing in the army, hasn't there?'

'Yes, and that really would cause trouble. The attitude to that is you can't dig coal with bayonets.'

'It didn't sound like they actually dig coal at all these days. By the way, what's a "beetle"?'

'Beetle drive. It's a competitive game that takes place every week at the Juniors.'

'Is that a school?'

'No, it's a social club. Full title is Killamarsh Juniors Athletic Club and Institute. I've been a member since I was eighteen. Half the village are members. These "beetles" are a strictly female activity, apart from Edna's grandson, but he's what they coyly refer to as a "nudge nudge... well, you know". Anyway, everyone sits round frantically throwing dice and drawing beetles in square boxes. I suggest we steer well clear, unless you fancy a game of snooker in the other room?'

'Not really.'

'So where to now? The Midland's only just across the road from the Juniors. Uncle Willis will be holed up until it's time to escort auntie home.'

'Would you mind awfully if we went back to our hotel? We could have a nightcap there, and Raymond will run you home.'

'Fine by me.'

'Ever thought of moving to London?'

'Not really. Don't think I could afford even the grottiest of bedsits there.' They reached a bend in the road. James halted and stooped to brush a non-existent speck from his immaculate shoes.

'Did your parents ever write to you, when you were at Oxford?'

'No. I phoned them now and then, but that was about it.'

Ten seconds later, as the Ford Escort smoothly drew alongside, James said, 'Then I have a proposition I'd like to discuss with you.'

PARK HALL COUNTRY CLUB, SPINKHILL

'I've never been frisked before,' stated Keith, as they entered James's room at Park Hall.

'Gently patted down, old boy. It won't happen again, but Melvin was only doing his job. He can't afford to take any risks, even though you're a longstanding friend. They don't usually let me out of their sight, and there's a million to one chance you might have become a radicalised republican assassin.'

'Fair enough.'

'Drink? Room service should still be available. Or there are some sachets and a kettle on the desk. I could make us a couple of coffees, if you show me how to switch it on!'

'I do hope you're joking. I'll have something stronger, please, if it's all the same to you.'

James rang through an order for two whiskies and ice.

'Fancy a billet at Buck House?'

'Oh yeah? With a few servants to wait on me?'

'No, seriously. We're an assistant secretary down. I wouldn't want anyone from round here to know where you work, or it might blow my cover, and I'm really very fond of the Fergus persona. But you could tell everyone that you're doing some vague sort of civil service job in Whitchall, and that you keep moving from flat-share to flat-share in Clapham. You could fix yourself up with an anonymous PO box, in case your parents want to send you a birthday card or whatever. Shouldn't be too difficult. Then you could act as my sort of social secretary for those extracurricular outings that don't appear in the Court Circular. It would be enormous fun – a bit like the old days.

'I don't know what to say.'

'"Yes" might be a good word. I also have it in mind, one of these days, to produce a memoir of my early years. I've kept a diary since I was seven. It's not a priority, but perhaps you could make a start on ghost-writing it for me? Guaranteed bestseller, I imagine. What sort of stuff do you write, by the way?'

'Crime.'

'Ever had anything at all published?'

Keith reddened. 'As a matter of fact, yes. Only a couple of short stories though.'

'Where? I could read one. See if you're any good.'

'I promise you wouldn't want to. I contribute to *The People's Friend*. Funny that I used to deliver the magazine to all the old biddies on my paper round.'

'Actually, I think the Mater reads it. I'll have a look. Do you write under a pen name?'

'I'd rather you didn't. But yes, I'm Caitlin Gilchrist. Thought a Scottish *nom de plume* would go down well. It's all pretty formulaic. No swearing. No violence. No explicit sex, though the odd hug or kiss are OK. Certainly no mention of death, because that's a bit too close to home for most of the readership. It has to be cosy "feel good" stuff, which usually means factoring in a few home-made soups or freshly-baked cakes. And I try to include a cat somewhere. That's always a definite bonus. I say, are you all right?'

James, by now, was doubled up and heaving with silent laughter. When he finally caught his breath, he said, 'Seems we both have alternative identities. Worry not. Your secret's safe with me. So, how about it Ms Gilchrist?'

21

'Who will Princess Anne marry? When the world's most eligible bachelor girl goes out, she makes headlines – and so do the men who go with her. Will she marry a prince or a commoner?'

This *Woman's Own* feature, complete with pictures, had also been reported in the *Daily Mirror* in February 1970. Similar articles regularly popped up to assuage the population's appetite for stories about the House of Windsor.

The conjecture about Anne ended in May 1973, when her engagement to Captain Mark Phillips was announced. The two first met in 1968 at a party for horse lovers, and it was their mutual affection for all things equine that cemented the relationship. As her father Prince Phillip had once said, 'If it doesn't fart and eat hay, she isn't interested.'

On Charles' 25th birthday, 14th November 1973, the couple married at Westminster Abbey.

All the speculation about future spouses was now focused solely on James and Charles. Newspapers and women's magazines were constantly reprising possible candidates for 'King Valentino' and the Prince of Wales, both of whom were referred to as the most eligible bachelors in the world. In August 1972, William, heir to the Dukedom of Gloucester, had been killed when the wing of the Piper Cherokee he was piloting hit some trees, causing the plane to crash and burst into flames. The tragic event was a reminder, to the public and royal family alike, that Princess Elizabeth (and thus ultimately her son) was only a heartbeat from the throne. This would remain so until James, who was fast gaining a reputation as a daredevil like his cousin, married and started producing heirs.

Rab Rainsmith, who was still working at the *Evening News,* had produced occasional articles on the subject of potential royal brides. He'd even developed his own shorthand for certain stock phrases – his favourite was 'DOD/ROR/AW', used whenever the same lady had been seen more than twice in the company of one or other of the gentlemen. It stood for 'Despite Official Denials, Rumours Of Romance Are Widespread'.

More interesting from Rab's point of view was the series he had written on 'royal matters from a Scottish perspective'. His first had been printed shortly after the lavish 1970 ceremony, when the newly-crowned king decided to replace the Tudor Crown on telephone boxes with the St Edward's Crown used for coronations[1]. This had prompted protests in Scotland about the use of English insignia with the result that, two years later, the Post Office and all other government agencies began using a representation of the Crown of Scotland north of the border.

Rab was also regularly covering sporting events and crime. His career as a reporter had progressed fairly steadily, though he was the first to admit that it could hardly be described as stellar. He was now married and had started to discuss the possibility of a change of direction with his wife, Jeannie. She was a nurse at the Glasgow Royal Infirmary and had recently been promoted to sister on the Ear, Nose and Throat ward. The couple were not spendthrifts, and both agreed that they could afford to take a risk, provided they were careful. But what options was Rab considering? One was setting up as a private detective. He was a devotee of crime novels and quick to spot their flaws. He also had a few useful contacts. How difficult, and lucrative, would life as a gumshoe be? Or, given that he was good at stringing words together, perhaps writing fiction would prove to be his forte? Maybe he could combine the two, and spend any downtime between assignments working on a book? Alternatively, a book was something he could try his hand at whilst still employed. There was no need to rush any decision.

July 1974

Glenholme Road, Morden

'What on earf do you want five bedrooms for?' asked Peggy, placing the brochure on the dining room table after only a cursory glance. 'It's not as though you 'ave 'oards of kids.'

'Funny, that,' said Lil. 'We got caught first time, and that was that. It wasn't for the want of trying, but it just never happened again.'

'Maybe there's somefin' wrong with the pair of us, when it comes to makin' babies?'

'I don't know. Anyway, we've put in an offer and it's been accepted. Terry's been on about moving for ages.'

'Won't it be further for 'im to commute?'

'Not much. We'll only be a five-minute walk from Ewell West station, then he's straight through to Waterloo, like he is now from Raynes Park. I can drive to Sutton if I want to carry on at the agency, or find something else nearer.'

'I don't see why you need to keep workin' at all, now that 'e's earnin' so much.'

'That's one of the reasons for upping sticks. We're just frittering money away. Houses are good investments, and I've always wanted to live in a village.'

'I s'pose you could always join the WI. Jam and Jerusalem and all that. And I can start visitin' wiv Freddie, once you've got a new set of neighbours 'oo don't know you.'

'There, you see. You could both bring your swimming togs and have a dip.'

Peggy picked up the brochure and studied it more closely. 'Bloody 'ell, Lil. I didn't notice it 'ad a pool. Since when 'ave you been a keen swimmer?'

'I'm not, but I could become one.'

'More likely the water will go all green, and you'll end up wiv ducks.'

'Whatever. Think how nice it would be to sit in the garden and just be able to cool off when it gets too hot.'

'On about free days a year.' Peggy looked at the rain beating against the French windows. 'It's supposed to be 'igh summer.'

'How's Freddie getting on?'

'Doin' really well. 'e reads a lot. 'is nose is always in a book, and not kids' books neivva. 'e's gone beyond Enid Blyton.'

'What sort of books?'

'Science fiction mainly. Janet said she was very impressed that 'e was into Asimov.'

'When did she say that?'

'A couple of monfs ago, when she came to visit Mum and Dad, and for Freddie's birfday. You and Terry 'ad gone gallivantin' off to Spain. Remember?'

'Oh yes. I do now. We may have to draw in our horns for a while with the new mortgage.'

'Not quite Mr and Mrs Rockefella yet then, if you're 'avin' to cut down on holidays? It'll be 'airdos and magazines next.' Peggy nodded towards the rack next to the hearth, which doubled as a side table. 'Oh, is that the latest *Woman's Realm*? Let's 'ave a quick butchers.'

'Be my guest. I haven't had time to read it yet. I'll pop and put the kettle on. The teapot needs topping up.'

Peggy flicked through, found the page she wanted and shouted through the hatch to the kitchen. 'Seems like a Lady Jane Wellesley is in the runnin' now.'[2]

'Which one for?'

'Either, it says, but probably Charles. They're fancyin' some Luxembourg princess for the King, though 'e's also been seen at Annabel's with Lady Jane Curties. Oh, and with a Julietta Alcaraz, 'oo's the daughter of the Guatemalan ambassador. Same club.'

'Can't blame them for being choosey and sowing a few wild oats while they're still young.'

Peggy put down the magazine.

''ave you sold this place then? I didn't see a sign.'

'No, it's not on the market yet, but the estate agent's been and taken photos. He said it would be snapped up, what with all Terry's home improvements. That Barry Bucknell's his god, right from the time he put hardboard over those panelled doors. And we'll be leaving the orange shag pile in the lounge.'

'But you've only just 'ad it fitted.'

'I know, but the new place is carpeted, so there's no point. Besides, it'll be a selling point.'

Peggy reached once again for the brochure. 'Oh yes. And look! It's got a lovely avocado suite in the main bathroom. I fancy that Sun King colour meself. Ours is just plain borin' white, and Ralph refuses to change it.'[3]

24TH OCTOBER 1976

BUCKINGHAM PALACE

James resisted the temptation to hug Eustace, in favour of the warmest of handshakes.

'What can I get you? G and T?'

'That would hit the spot nicely, thank you, Sir.'

The Earl was touched to note that there were plentiful lemons, as well as ice. His welcome here felt reminiscent of his very first meeting with His late Majesty.

'How's it going, James? We certainly live in difficult times.'

'I'm at as much of a loss as the politicians are right now,' James admitted. 'There doesn't seem a clear way forward. According to Keynes, recession and inflation should be mutually exclusive, but both seem to be happening at once. We seem to be suffering from stagflation. Any wisdoms?'

'I'm afraid not.'

'I always thought that my "warn and advise" role would be simpler. Warning, I figured, would be easy. The only pitfall with advising seemed to be avoiding sounding like the opposition, but the opposition doesn't seem to be putting forward any viable solutions at the moment either. Callaghan's trying to peg wage increases, but he won't be able to hold back the tide of union pressure indefinitely. Once he's forced to give way, there'll be mass unemployment and that's definitely not going to help. No matter. I didn't ask you here today to talk economics.'

'If you had, I'd be the wrong person. So how may I help?'

'It's about next year's silver jubilee. It's supposedly to mark my twenty-five years on the throne, except that, for most of them, I haven't been.'

'That ought not, of itself, be a difficulty. If the people want to celebrate, I see no reason why they shouldn't. Goodness knows everyone could do with an excuse to let their hair down.'

'I agree. A lot of plans are already in place. I'll be zooming around the kingdom and the Commonwealth thereafter. Then there'll be the usual beacons. They've become trickier you know?'

'I most certainly do. I've just been drafted onto a small committee coordinating them and, now health and safety has been invented, everyone seems to be more concerned about issuing guidelines to local authority licensing officers than about anything else.'

'How incredibly tedious. No, it's on a more personal basis that I'm in a quandary. You see, although the Mater was officially regent – and please don't get me wrong, she did the job to the best of her ability, I suppose – it was really my sister who carried the main burden.'

Eustace signified his agreement with a slow nod. 'I'm with you entirely. The public don't see the unrelenting day-in, day-out graft that goes on behind the scenes. The red boxes, the Privy Council meetings and all that. And you want to make some gesture of recognition for Princess Elizabeth's sterling contribution. Is that it?'

'Exactly. Her contribution continues unabated.'

'So we firstly need to identify what matters most to her and, secondly, how that can be translated into a meaningful tribute.'

'You always did have that knack of simplifying everything, Eustace.'

'I'm not so sure about simple. Whatever you decide will need to benefit the population as a whole, rather than a specific sector.'

James chuckled. 'I've already dismissed the idea of corgi breeders and the horsey fraternity!'

'But you already know where Elizabeth's abiding priority lies, don't you, James? Beyond the monarchy, I mean.'

'Can I get you a refill, Eustace?'

The Earl's sense of déjà vu upped a notch.

'You really are so very like your father. Think about it a moment or two.'

The King busied himself with pouring exactly the right amount of tonic, turned and said, 'All of us. Her family. If we're not happy, Lilibet's not happy.'

'Quite so.'

The King took his time with the precision slicing of a lemon.

'She's still very distressed about Margot's split from Tony. It will have to be formalised eventually, which seems ironic from what I know about the Townsend affair. Divorce has always been anathema in the House of Windsor. But my guess is that, while Margot's might well be the first, it won't prove to be the last. It's bad enough for ordinary people, let alone for those living in a bloody goldfish bowl.'

'I suppose ordinary people face different kinds of pressures, like making ends meet – especially these days. Even the strongest of couples, who set off very much in love with one another, must sometimes find it a struggle.'

'"Very much in love" has to be the best way to start, though, doesn't it? I don't give much for my own chances on that score. Nor Charles', unless we get very lucky indeed. He's just had another relationship go pear-shaped, poor boy.'

'Yes, I heard about that – or, rather, Edith mentioned it. Davina Sheffield, wasn't it?'

'It was. They were getting on well, and I had high hopes. But it turned out that she had a boyfriend lurking in the background, who was tricked by a reporter into spilling the beans. So it didn't take long for photos of their "love nest" to be front-page news. Nice chap, the boyfriend. He's into powerboat racing, though he's moved from mono-hull to catamarans now, with the stuff he designs.' James paused. 'I can't see myself ever having the right sort of feelings for any woman, pure as the driven snow or not.'

Eustace sensed that there was more behind the impassioned outburst than met the eye and was saddened that the King was obviously not about to confide. He felt he'd in some way let down his friend George. Switching to an upbeat tone, he ploughed on.

'Well James, as it seems to both of us that there should be some sort of family theme, let's think about what form it could take. Your King's Trust is picking up on young children, and Charles' Prince's Trust is concentrating on eleven to thirty-year-olds. The Duke of Edinburgh's Award scheme is benefitting teenagers, by getting them to push their personal boundaries[4]. So should we take a look at older groups?'

'Hmm. I'm not sure about targeting a specific age group. Families span the generations. If we're looking at the fallout from marriage break-ups, what happens when people start taking sides? I've certainly come across kids who feel they've become pawns in power struggles – not only between parents, but involving grandparents as well. One small girl I met last week said she didn't see her granny any more because Mummy wouldn't let her, which Daddy said made her grandmother cry and feel sad. The real tragedy was that the poor child felt she was somehow to blame. Whatever the rights and wrongs of the split, Daddy should have known better than to lay a guilt trip on his daughter.'

'"Mummy" doesn't exactly emerge as squeaky clean, either. But, as you say, no one knows why things fell apart and what the family dynamics might be.'

'The real point, though, is that there's no organisation to turn to – one which might have been able to advise any of the parties on the dos and don'ts[5]. Grandparents may be berating themselves, too, and wondering where the hell they went wrong. Was it the way they brought up their own children? Should they have spotted sooner that trouble was brewing? And, if they had, was there anything they might have done before things reached crisis point?'

'You've clearly given this a lot of thought. All you really needed was a context to set it in. I'm proud of you, dear chap, and your father would have been proud of you, too, if you don't mind my saying so.'

James beamed with pleasure. 'Not at all. I'm jolly glad you think so.'

'Have you thought of a name for this project?'

'I wondered about The Princess's Trust? Or The Princess's Jubilee Trust?'

'Might it not be more diplomatic to call it The Elizabethan Trust? That way, the contributions of both your sister and your mother could be recognised. It's only an idea, and I know it misses the point slightly, but a two-pronged acknowledgement – ?'

'You never were short of ideas, Eustace. The Mater really has been a good foreign ambassador, what with all those solo trips. And she's kept up with all her organisations[6]. Oompa says it's just an excuse to buy more clothes, but he doesn't really mean it, because she doesn't seem to need an excuse. I've threatened to stop bankrolling her, but she just laughs and says I wouldn't.'

Knowing his protégé wouldn't take long to come up with a *modus operandi*, the Earl ventured, 'How do you see this working?'

'Counselling services to start with, perhaps even just a simple opportunity to talk to someone who understands. Easy access. Anonymous access, too, if that's preferred. And information. Not necessarily information on the legalities and financial side of things, but on the emotional fallout. It often helps just to be given permission to feel the way you do.'

'Did you reach that wisdom through personal experience?'

'No,' said James, 'I think I read it somewhere.'

Eustace wondered whether to utter a reminder of his ready availability and willingness to listen, before deciding it wouldn't be very subtle. Instead, he changed the subject.

'I see your pal James Hunt has just won the world championship.'

'Yes, it's tremendous, isn't it? Pity I couldn't wangle a trip to Japan to see him do it. I'm only sorry that he won't get Sports Personality of the Year[7]. I'd like to have presented that to him.'

'Who do you think will win, then?'

'It's got to be John Curry.'

'Edith's very keen on the ice skating.'

'I still don't have a clue about the difference between a triple salchow and a double toe loop. But it all looks pretty impressive, and James did only become champion because Lauda damned near killed himself. They're best friends, you know. Still, a title's a title, even if there's a slight feel of second best about it. Nikki will do it next year. There'll be no stopping him.'

'You've had a go yourself, haven't you?'

'Yes. A few souls have been brave enough to let me loose at the wheel, so I've done a good few circuits. There's something exhilarating about going very fast.'

'You take care.'

'I will. Do you know what I'm looking forward to most about Australia next year?'

'I can't begin to imagine.'

'There's a chap called Ken Warby[8]. He's building a wooden boat in his backyard in Sydney. It's going to be powered by a jet engine – the type they use for aircraft. And in a year's time, he's going for the water speed record. He might be able to give me a few design tips.'

'Oh please, James, don't even think about it. I know you're fascinated, but it's far too dangerous.'

'Not necessarily. If you can get the cockpit spot-on, so that it always floats, even if the rest of the craft is smashed to smithereens, it should be safe as houses.'

1979

22

BALMORAL CASTLE

'I'm so very sorry, old boy. I know how much he meant to you.'

'It's such a shock,' said Charles. 'The last thing I expected to happen. It isn't as though he was in poor health. In that case, I might have been better prepared.'

Lord Louis Mountbatten[1], two family members and a young local boat boy had been killed the previous day, victims of an IRA assassination plot in which their boat was blown up, just offshore, by a fifty-pound bomb. Everyone else on board was seriously injured.

'He'll leave a big gap.'

'Tell me about it, Jimmy. Where have you been, by the way?'

'Quite nearby, as it happens. Just doing a bit of casual work in and around Edinburgh. Cash in hand. It might pay for an ostrich feather.'

'Well, it's good of you to come.'

'Nonsense. You were there for me when William was killed[2]. I know we were both fond of him but – '

Charles interrupted. 'Are you suggesting that we weren't both fond of Uncle Dickie?'

'Well, you were closer to him than I was. Let's put it that way.'

'No, I don't want you to put it any other way than as it is, please.'

'OK. I didn't like the way he breathed when I sat on his knee. It wasn't the same as sitting on Papa's lap.'

'You remember that?'

'Yes. It's about the only memory of him I do have. It felt safe and secure.'

'Anything else wrong with HGF while we're at it, apart from the fact that he breathed?'

James shrugged. 'You're not exactly in the right frame of mind. And, by the time you are, it won't matter anyway. Can we drop it?'

'No. Now you've started, you may as well finish. Go on.'

'India, I suppose,' said James reluctantly. 'It's not so much that partitioning was a disaster, it's more about the fact that it wasn't his fault and that he supposedly had no alternative. Nothing bad was ever his fault. It would have been more honourable to admit to a well-intentioned error of judgment, rather than apply a gallon of whitewash.'

'There was some talk of his joining me on the upcoming tour there, you know. Him and Amanda. That won't be happening now. I'll be going on my own. Uncle Dickie deserves some credit for his war record, surely?'

'Certainly. Bruneval was very successful, and the raid on Saint-Nazaire bordered on the genius. He was impressive throughout, if you edit out the disasters.'

Charles jumped in. 'Before you say anything else, Dieppe was a very important lesson without which D-Day wouldn't have been the success it was.'

'Try telling that to the relatives of the three thousand or so who were killed or maimed. Dieppe was a bloody fiasco. The Canadians have never forgiven him, and who can blame them? And it was, unfortunately, a learning experience for the Germans, too. '

'Does he have any redeeming features from your all-knowing viewpoint?'

'Maybe the fact that he liberated Burma single-handedly, with only a bit of help from the Americans.'

'D'you know, Uncle Jimmy, sarcasm really doesn't suit you.'

'Sorry, old boy. I genuinely came to offer my condolences. Truce?'

'I guess so. Do you know what the real bloody irony of yesterday's ghastly events is? HGF was a keen supporter of a united Ireland.'

15TH SEPTEMBER 1979

RIVER THAMES

Joyce Faulkner hadn't been convinced, and was even less so when her husband hesitated as they boarded the *Countess of Sark* at Greenwich Pier. Once they were underway, for the first ten minutes his eyes seemed to be fixed on the water, as though he were concentrating on the currents. The light drizzle wasn't helping.

'Never fought I'd end up bein' ferried along this stretch,' Ron commented, as the Tower of London came into sight.

Treating their parents to this river cruise, for their sapphire wedding anniversary, had been a joint decision. Peggy had suggested a boat trip. Lil came up with the idea of afternoon tea somewhere posh, and they decided to combine the two.

Once they'd persuaded their father to leave the deck and adjourn to the enclosed dining area, he seemed more relaxed and was positively enjoying himself by the time the sandwiches arrived.

'You certainly get a diff'rent outlook from 'ere,' he said, as Joyce poured tea into Pyrex cups.

'Wouldn't you 'ave fought they'd 'ave provided decent china?' his wife of forty-five years commented.

'Praps they don't trust the punters not to break them? They must 'ave to fink about safety,' offered Peggy, whose mind veered off at a tangent. 'I 'ope Janet's takin' care, what wiv this Jack the Ripper character on the loose.'

'That's Yorkshire, Peg,' soothed Lil. 'Liverpool's miles away.'

'Shirley's in Sheffield,' said Joyce. 'That's in Yorkshire.'

'Aunt Shirley doesn't go out alone on the streets at night though, does she, Mum? He's targeting prostitutes and, as far as I'm aware, she hasn't resorted to selling herself!'

Joyce seemed slightly shocked. 'Well let's 'ope they catch 'im soon, Lil. That Mrs Thatcher said she was goin' to be tough on crime.'

'Nevva fought I'd live to see a woman Prime Minister,' Ron said. 'She needs to tackle the unions first. Seems the 'ole country's on strike.'

The Conservatives had swept to power the previous May, after a general election had been called. This had followed a vote of no confidence in the previous government, which the Labour Party had lost by a single vote. If Tom Swain, the left-wing MP for Keith Bradshaw's North East Derbyshire constituency had not been killed in a recent accident, the vote would have been a tie, and the Speaker of the House of Commons would, by tradition, have declared in favour of the ruling party.

''ave one of these scones, Dad.' Peggy gestured towards the plate that had just been deposited on their table. 'And please don't go bangin' on about politics, or we'll all be jumpin' overboard.'

'Fair point,' said Ron meekly, 'I can see I'm outnumbered, like always. Let's talk about Princess Margaret's toy boy again, shall we? I'm afraid I can't afford to buy you a tropical love nest, Joyce dear, but if you fancy tradin' me in for a newer model, I'll see what I can do about a part-exchange deal.'

By way of a reply, his wife peered suspiciously at the small bowl containing a gooey red substance. 'Is that supposed to be strawberry jam? Go easy, Ron. It's got to do four of us.'

25TH NOVEMBER 1979

BUCKINGHAM PALACE

When Charles called in on James, the King was not sure he'd been forgiven for his apparent lack of sympathy three months earlier.

'At least someone is showing me a bit of understanding,' Charles began.

'Who might that be?'

'Diana Spencer. She was the soul of compassion and didn't have a bad word to say about our Uncle Dickie.'

James refrained from saying that, in all probability, the lady in question had no idea about the war, or indeed where India was situated on a world map, let alone the politics surrounding its independence.

'Got on well with her, did you? That's a pity.'

'What do you mean, "a pity"?'

'She was on my shortlist.'

'Which shortlist?'

'Potential brides.'

'How many are on your list?'

'None, now, if she's interested in you. I could suggest that she's too young for you, though.'

'If she's too young for me, then the same applies to you.'

'You're forgetting our age difference. You're an old man of thirty-one, and I'm still only thirty.'

'Very funny. I didn't realise you knew her that well?'

'I don't, but she and her granny Ruth "happened" to be at Marlborough House a couple of weeks ago when I was summoned to visit the Mater. The oldies were sitting side by side on the sofa, thick as thieves, and there was obviously some sort of plot afoot. The Mater said something like, "You wouldn't expect her to go galloping around the countryside, would you James?"'

'And what did you say?'

'Nothing. I was laughing too much, because Diana was floating around behind them pretending to be on horseback, both hands clutching invisible reins and doing all the actions. She was hilarious.'

'I can well imagine,' Charles said smiling. 'Anyway, she seems to like me. Do you think it's possible to love two women at the same time?'

'No. The reality seems pretty grim. It boils down to a stark choice, I'm afraid. Either stay single, or marry someone who'll always be second best. And given that staying single isn't an option for either of us, we'll each just have to find a girl we can like very much and hope our feelings grow into something approximating love.'

It never occurred to Charles that his uncle might be speaking from personal experience. 'So where do we go from here?'

'Perhaps we should both see the lovely Lady Spencer now and then, and let her decide which one of us she prefers?'

Charles was used to recognising a challenge. Perhaps he had a real chance this time of finally winning a contest against his uncle?

28TH JULY 1981

PRINCE CHARLES' DRESSING ROOM, BUCKINGHAM PALACE

'At least that bruise has faded in time for my big day,' said Charles. 'Who was it who hit you?'

James's hand went instinctively to his right cheek. 'I told you. It wasn't a "someone", it was a something. Everyone was chucking whatever they could lay their hands on. Luckily, it was only a glancing blow. Now I understand why the PPOs are trained in first aid.'

'Good job it wasn't a firebomb, Jimmy. That would have blown your cover.'

'So would getting myself arrested, or ending up in hospital. Gerald only just managed to get me out in time.'

'Well I hope you've learned your lesson. Chatting to the residents of anywhere, disguised as a road sweeper, is one thing. Risking your life in a riot is another.'

'I didn't plan on being involved in a riot. I just wanted to get a feel for what's going on, not that it would make one jot of difference.' The King undid his white tie and threw it onto the floor. 'All those guests that this place was stuffed with an hour ago probably spend more money on a single fancy suit or dress than the people of Toxteth have to live on for a whole year.'[3]

The King and his nephew had spent the evening at a gala ball to celebrate Prince Charles' forthcoming nuptials.

James sighed. 'I've been telling her – '

'As you're about to jump on some bandwagon or another, I assume you're referring to our Prime Minister here?' Charles queried.

'Yes. Who else? As I was saying, I've been telling the lady week in, week out, that you can't solve deep-rooted social problems by simply condemning the violence they spawn. Mrs T could stand on top of Big Ben with a loudhailer and shout for all she's worth, but that wouldn't solve what's really wrong. But, for all she listens to me, I might as well be just another Tory "wet". At least Toxteth can be left in Tarzan's hands now. He's standing up for regeneration in Liverpool 8, rather than letting an entire city rot from the core outwards.'

'Careful you don't become too political, Jimmy. You're starting to sound decidedly left of centre. "Advise and warn" should be as far as it goes with the PM.'

'I am sadly all too well aware of that. I suppose it's too late to restore an absolute monarchy?'

'Only by about three or four centuries. It was your namesake who screwed things up by banging on about the divine right of kings.'

'And it was yours who got the chop because he took that ethos to ridiculous extremes. Even so, there was something to be said for it, especially when the head of an elected government seems intent on ploughing on regardless. I can see myself threatening to exercise the royal prerogative at some point further down the line. I sometimes dream about a Privy Council meeting where I utter the words "not approved", instead of standing there like a nodding dog.'

'Some of her ideas are sound, surely? It's about time the nation stopped borrowing and started earning its way into prosperity. What was it she said? "The problem with socialism is that you eventually run out of other people's money to spend." And, though I'm all for workers' rights, some of the big trade unions could do with having their wings clipped. We've seen how easily the country can be held to ransom, and that doesn't exactly feel democratic,' said Charles.

'And when I think she's right, I tell her so. Take this new

Housing Act. Apparently she'd needed some persuading, as she jolly well should have done. I said I liked the theory of increasing home ownership, but what about the longer-term effects? "Has the likely impact been modelled?" I asked. Not an unreasonable question. "With all due respect, Sir, this isn't a fashion show," says the Prime Minister...'

Charles always found his uncle's impersonation of Margaret Thatcher highly amusing.

'I can't begin to tell you how much that phrase irritates me,' James continued, 'so I retaliated like for like and pointed out, "with all due respect", that there will always be people who need to rent, so wasn't there a risk that the proposals would reduce the amount of money councils have to build replacements? If that happened, housing stocks would become scarcer, so please think carefully about over-incentivising, or we'll end up with a situation whereby too many properties end up in the hands of private landlords.'

'And?'

'And Mrs T got that glazed look that the Mater gets when she doesn't like the way the conversation is going. I ought to be used to the imperial ostrich tactic by now but, even after years of practice, it's not easy to deal with. Anyway, I shouldn't be banging on about politics on the eve of your big day.'

'Feel free. Anything to distract me.'

'I hope you're not getting cold feet?'

'My metaphorical feet are as chilly as metaphorical icebergs of Titanic proportions.'

'That bad? You should have thought about that before you proposed. Or perhaps I conceded defeat too readily? I might have been the one having their jitters soothed.'

Charles nodded. 'Strikes me you didn't put up much of a fight at all. You know, what I'm really struggling with is the "forsaking all others" bit.' He stood up, strolled to the dressing table and extracted a small box from its top drawer. Offering it to James, he said, 'Take a look.'

Inside was a pair of cufflinks, engraved with entwined back-to-back 'C's.

'You don't need to tell me whom they're from. Back on again, is it? I did wonder at the pre-nuptial ball. In fact, it was pretty damned obvious. To me and to everyone else there, I shouldn't wonder – not least of all your child bride. Surely you could have danced more than once with her? And that was only because I eventually succeeded in wresting a certain other lady from your clutches. A final discreet tryst is one thing, Charles. Couldn't you have managed that instead?'

'I'd managed that as well. A couple of days ago, when I took her my parting gift.'

'Which was?'

'A gold "Gladys and Fred" bracelet. Unfortunately, Diana had seen it beforehand, in the office. She was pretty upset, but then her moods have been oscillating all week. One minute, she's jolly and fun. The next, she's in floods of tears for no reason at all. I did tell her it was just a present for an old friend, but she didn't seem to understand. Pre-wedding nerves, I suppose.'

'That's what you really think?'

Charles shrugged. 'Anyway, from tomorrow, I'll have no option but to try and make a go of it. Odd that, in the non-liberated days of yore, royal mistresses were almost the norm. I offer no apology for my behaviour as an engaged man. It's how things are, or (sadly) were. Camilla and Peter P-B have been living separate lives for a while. Their marriage is a definite no-hoper.'

'It sounds as though yours is too, and you've not even got to the starting line yet. If you're contemplating taking these very tasteful accessories with you on honeymoon, may I suggest you don't?'

'You've not been having much luck with your persuasive

technique recently, have you, Uncle Jimmy? That's exactly what my intention is.'

'Why not go the whole hog and pack a few framed photos of Camilla to put at the bedside? Those would go down well with your new bride.'

'The photos are tucked away in my wallet.'[4]

'Oh Charles. I am so very sorry about the way things are, old boy,' said James. Before snapping shut the box lid, he took a last lingering look at the gift, thought longingly of a different pair of interlinked letters and understood perfectly how his nephew was feeling.

WEDNESDAY 29TH JULY 1981

COBOURG ROAD, BERMONDSEY

At Peggy's suggestion, they were watching the second 'wedding of the century' at her house, which Ralph had inherited from his granny – she of the ailing budgerigar which had brought them together. Situated on Cobourg Road, it was a lovely place, opposite the walled boundary of Burgess Park. Granny and Granddad Mills had met at the Peek Freans biscuit factory. He'd been 'in management' there and had spotted his future bride whilst walking the shop floor. Ralph and his grandmother had been close, especially after she became his only surviving relative, and Peggy had got on famously with her. It seemed appropriate that the groom's parents' wedding cake had been made at the old lady's former place of employment.

The flat above the greengrocery on Southwark Park Road, one and a half miles further north, had now been let to a second-generation Caribbean couple. Peggy had learned to refer to them as 'black', which she'd previously thought an offensive description, not that the colour of their skin was mentioned often, because it was irrelevant.[5]

The Langridges' old, rented TV had been replaced by a brand-new one, which had a bigger screen than Lil's, and a street party had been organised, which Peggy thought might add to the atmosphere of the occasion. Bunting was festooned between upper-storey house windows, which had taken some doing, and almost everyone's fridges were stuffed full of food to be brought out later. Only one lot of neighbours, Mr and Mrs Stanton at the far end, hadn't cooperated. They were self-professed republicans, who considered the monarchy to be a waste of public money and, as such, something which should be abolished.

The wedding of Prince Charles to Lady Diana Spencer had provided the sisters with plenty of conversation fodder in recent weeks and, like most people, the pair were keen not to miss a single detail. In case they wanted to see any of it again, Ralph had set up the newly-purchased Sony Betamax video recorder, which promised to 'turn the act of watching television into the art of watching television.' Peggy hadn't fully got the hang of how to work it yet, but she knew how to play, rewind and pause it.

Their mother Joyce had joined them for the event. Ron professed not to be bothered and instead had offered to take Freddie out for the day. The two of them were the best of mates, and Ron doted on his grandson, who was actually his great-grandson, but this was never mentioned.

Daisy Dagley, Lil's mother-in-law, had also turned down the invitation, even though Lil had offered to chauffeur her both ways. Daisy wasn't too steady on her feet these days, and her health in general had declined sharply following Harold's death the previous year.

Janet had also taken the loss of her beloved granddad very badly. Whenever she ventured south, she divided her time between her grieving granny in Deptford and her parents in Ewell. Dr Janet Dagley was now working at the Liverpool School of Tropical Medicine, as a specialist in disease biology. Her parents were very proud of her but, in the absence of any signs of romance in their daughter's life, had started telling people that she seemed to be married to her career.

The three women settled themselves in front of the TV, waiting for the action to start. Before things got going properly, people who'd arrived days before to claim and guard their pitches were being interviewed.

'It's all very well turnin' up equipped with sleepin' bags and flasks and food,' commented Peggy, 'but what on earf do they do when they need a loo?'

'That nevva occurred to me,' said Joyce. 'Pity women don't 'ave 'andy little gadgets like men do. I always fought a willy would be useful at times.'

Her daughters both laughed. Their mother would never have said such a thing, had she not already been hitting the Babycham.

At last, the event proper began to unfold, as an open carriage swept through the gates of Buckingham Palace. In it were their Royal Highnesses The Duke and Duchess of Edinburgh who, as the groom's parents, were taking precedence for the occasion. Behind them came another carriage, in which four people sat: His Majesty The King, Queen Elizabeth The King's Mother, Princess Margaret and Prince Edward.

'D'you think peach would suit me?' Peggy asked, as soon as she noticed what colour her supposed namesake was wearing.

Joyce was more interested in the Queen. 'There she goes again. Three-quarter length sleeves. Never see her in anyfin' else, come rain or shine. I expect it's because her arms 'ave gone all flabby and crinkly, like what mine 'ave. And it's anuvva fluffy 'at. 'ow many birds d'you suppose 'ave been plucked to produce all those fevvas over the years?'

'Aren't they sweet!' exclaimed Lil, when two very young bridesmaids, under the gentle supervision of Princess Margaret's daughter, Lady Sarah Armstrong-Jones, emerged from a shiny black car onto the steps of St Paul's. 'They're a good clue as to what the bride will be wearing.'

'Bit flouncy,' muttered Peggy.

Finally, the Prince of Wales and his best man, Prince Andrew, came into view. Peggy, despite her preference for fair-haired men, proclaimed the younger prince the best looking of all Princess Elizabeth's children. The cameras followed the groom's progress towards the cathedral. Meanwhile, emerging from Clarence House, was a closed carriage, the glass windows of which afforded a first glimpse of Lady Di. She was accompanied by her father, Earl Spencer, but nobody was looking at him or at the police outriders trotting alongside.

'We can't see what the dress is like,' complained Joyce, 'but there seems to be an awful lot of it.'

'Looks like Andrew needs to keep remindin' Charles to smile,' commented Joyce a little later. 'Edward's chivvyin' 'im up too,' she added as the three young men were shown walking along the cathedral's aisle. 'I've always wondered 'ow 'e was really feelin' about it all, ever since 'e wouldn't say outright that 'e loved 'er.'

'Tell us that again, Mum,' said Lil. 'We could do with hearing it for the millionth time.'

'I don't care what anyone else finks. No one will make me change my opinion that 'e's been forced into this.'

'Why should he have been? He could have had any woman he wanted, but he chose her.'

'Or 'ad 'er chosen for 'im, Lil,' protested Joyce, draining what was left of her drink. 'You mark my words. Go on, Charlie boy. It's still not too late to do a runner!'

'I wonder what Dad and Freddie are up to,' chipped in Peggy, who was eager to get her mother off a familiar soapbox.

In mute appeal, Joyce held up her empty glass. 'And, if you want annuva, Mum, get it yourself from the fridge. I'm not budgin' in case I miss anyfin'.'

The bridal conveyance drew up at the cathedral steps, and its door was opened. The moment everyone had been waiting for had at last arrived.

'Oh my Gawd! Just look at that dress. It looks like a meringue and it's crushed to death. Wouldn't you 'ave fought they'd 'ave run an iron over it?'

'I don't expect it was like that when she set off, Mum. That's an awful lot of fabric to cram into a tiny coach. No wonder it's got so crumpled,' reasoned Lil.

'Why don't the bridesmaids straighten out that worst bunched-up bit? 'er petticoat's showin'. A quick tug, and the creases might drop out a bit.'

'Because they're tryin' to straighten out 'er train. There's yards of it,' said Peggy.

The bride walked up the aisle on the arm of her father. The pair were preceded by a group of churchmen.

'I 'ad an 'at like that once,' muttered Joyce.

'Like which?' Dozens of hats could be seen in the congregation.

'Like the gold one what the bishop's wearin'. Got it in a Christmas cracker. Ha, ha, ha.'

Peggy gave in. 'I'm nippin' to put the kettle on. You need soberin' up, Mum. Try to stay awake while I make you a strong cup of coffee.'

'I don't like coffee.'

'You bloody well do. An' you like it black.'

The start of the marriage ceremony itself passed without further comment, except for Joyce's impassioned 'Say no!' when Charles was asked, 'Wilt though?' Then Diana muddled up the order of Charles' names, and the three women collectively winced.

''oo can blame 'er for bein' nervous?' asked Peggy. 'A girl barely out of her teens? She must be terrified, knowin' the 'ole world's watchin''

It also didn't go unnoticed that the word 'obey' was omitted from the wedding vows.

'You mark me words. It won't last,' said Joyce, just before she fell asleep.

23

CLARENCE HOUSE

'Slow down, James,' instructed Princess Elizabeth, putting down her pen and switching the telephone receiver to her right ear.

'Have you heard from Phillip?'

'He phoned last night and sounded perfectly normal. Is he all right?'

'Oops, didn't mean to panic you, Sis. As far as I know he's absolutely fine. But there's trouble brewing in the Falkland Islands,' said the King. 'A bunch of bogus scrap metal workers have taken over South Georgia and claimed it on behalf of Argentina.'[1]

'That doesn't sound at all good. What are we doing about it?'

'Dispatching HMS *Endurance* from Stanley to Leith, to tell the scrap men to take down the Argentinean flag and bugger off.'

'Is that the ice patrol vessel which is due to be decommissioned next month?'

'The very same. My guess is that decommissioning will be postponed, but that depends on what the Argies do next.'

'I do hope it comes to nothing, otherwise Andrew might get involved.'

'He may well not be the only one. If I know Oompa, he'll want a bit of the action, too.'

'Good grief. Surely not? He's sixty and must be too old for active duty.'

'He's fitter than most men half his age. His presence in the thick of it might prove inspirational.'

'I do wish I'd managed to persuade him to retire. Whatever else happens, please don't let him go.'

'If necessary, I'll go instead. I'm still young enough to enlist.'

'You stick to zooming around in your little boats on lakes, James. They're far safer.'

'If there is an upside, Mrs T is all for taking whatever action may prove necessary to protect the islands and our people. On this one, she has my full backing, which makes a change.'

James had continued to find it difficult to handle Mrs Thatcher. He quickly got used to her extreme deference: her legs always crumpled automatically into the deepest of curtsies, though on a few occasions he feared he'd need to help her to get back up again. The thought of literally manhandling a Prime Minister into a perpendicular position was terrifying. He'd also got used to the voice, which had once been likened to a cat scratching a blackboard with its claws – and which now resembled a strangulated parody of received pronunciation.

He agreed with many of her policy ideas, too. He even understood her desire for rapid change, because change was much needed. The main problem was how she planned to go about things. Quangos[2] were a case in point. She'd been right in that many of these quasi-governmental jobs-for-the-boys agencies served no useful purpose and were simply draining public funds. What he did caution against was dispensing with them all in one fell swoop, without first properly assessing what they did and whether alternative mechanisms were needed for some of their functions. The Metrication Board, an early victim, was a good example. It simply didn't make sense for manufacturers to switch from imperial measurements on a purely voluntary basis. British industry needed to keep in step with the rest of the world, and would suffer if it didn't. Joined-up thinking and a plan were required to ensure that the country kept pace.

Worse was to come, heralded by the appointment of tough guy Ian MacGregor as head of the National Coal Board. The NUM's militant president, Arthur Scargill, seemed intent on industrial action, regardless of whether or not any ballot supported strike action. A clash looked inevitable.

In early March 1984, the NCB announced the closure of twenty pits. Others would follow over the longer term. Scargill claimed that more than seventy faced imminent doom, which the government denied. MacGregor even wrote to every NUM member saying that their leader was deceiving them. But the deceptive one wasn't Scargill. When James asked the Prime Minister how many collieries were scheduled to stop production, she admitted to seventy-five over the next three years.

'We're going to be flying pickets. We'll do it when I'm supposed to be in Scotland,' he announced to Keith a few weeks later, after a miners' strike had been called.

'Bloody hell. What if we get arrested by riot police? Didn't you say Mrs T had geared up to resist that sort of action with force? And we could end up being bussed anywhere.'

Grudgingly, the King agreed. 'In that case, we need to infiltrate a mining village again. But we can't do a repeat of Killamarsh. This time, it might be more useful to concentrate on chatting to a few women and children. How about the north-east?'

'And take Gerald?'

'No. He's becoming a bit too familiar as a PPO, so it would have to be Melvin.'

'But he doesn't speak the part.'

'Gerald will just have to give him a crash course. He'll have him saying "Wey aye, man!" and referring to good things as "canny" before you can blink.'

'Maybe it would be better if Melvin developed a sore throat or lost his voice completely. And maybe Yorkshire would be preferable. It's not so far from my neck of the woods, for one thing. I wouldn't be out of place in Barnsley or Rotherham, and neither would you, wherever you chose to say you come from.'

'We can decide later. Meanwhile, I've got some new Adidas sneakers which need to be scuffed up. I'll make doubly sure that nobody irons the laces.'

'I can always go to a charity shop again and get you some old ones.'

'Great, thanks. I'll keep them hidden this time, or they'll mysteriously end up being chucked out. Take Melvin with you. We'll need some scruffy tee shirts and ripped jeans. Whatever you think will make us all look the part. Cheap wallets. That sort of thing. We'll plan to do the trip in one day, but a few beat-up overnight bags wouldn't be the worst idea either, in case we decide to stop over. The official suitcases might give the game away. Oh, and give your Uncle Willis a bell, will you, please? Maybe he'll know why they've chosen the height of summer to kick things off, just when domestic fuel consumption's at its lowest. Not exactly the cleverest piece of timing.'

They'd ended up in the Dearne Valley. No one took very much notice of strangers. There were plenty of those from neighbouring collieries and remoter coalfields, all of whom turned up in the spirit of brotherhood.

In September, at the next prime ministerial audience, James felt better informed. He began by agreeing with the economics of pit closures, but asked whether more preparations were needed. Mrs Thatcher spoke of the six months' supply of stockpiled coal at power stations, the mobile police units and the protection being offered in some locations to those miners who were still working because there'd been no national ballot for action. She added, 'With all this in place, we shall weather the storm and secure our ultimate victory. Have I missed anything, Sir?'

'I was thinking more about the communities which are being torn apart. Families too. Fathers and sons. Brothers set against brothers. Strikers set against "scabs", if you care to put it that way. Feelings are running so deep, some rifts will never heal.'

'We're a free country, Sir. What people choose to do is up to them, and who am I to stop that?'

'There are wives stuck in the middle, trying to make ends meet and wondering what's going to happen about paying the mortgage when their husbands no longer have a job. There are kids being shunned by former friends because some dads have opted to cross picket lines, and there are other kids on the breadline, pathetically grateful for gifts of strange-tasting chocolate sent over from the USSR.'

'My goodness. How on earth do you know all this?'

'Because I've been there and talked to people. Have you?'

'It's inevitable that there'll be a bit of fallout. But there isn't much we can do about that.'

'There's plenty "we" can do if "we" put our minds to it. The "bit of fallout" from "our" ultimate victory will be huge-scale deprivation. We can at least offer hope. If you're aiming for a new prosperous Britain, that Britain should be able to afford to invest in a targeted programme of regeneration. The worst-hit areas would benefit from the promise of new jobs – productive jobs – to replace the ones which will be lost. Or have I got this completely wrong?'

1985

24

BUCKINGHAM PALACE

James, now thirty-six, was coming under increasing pressure to find a wife and settle down, but there seemed to be a shortage of eligible girls. His mother, in particular, was concerned about history's repeating itself. At the same age, her brother-in-law, the late Duke of Windsor, had been given the lease of Fort Belvedere in Windsor Great Park, there to continue his affairs with married women, such as Freda Dudley Ward and Thelma Furness. This had been worrying enough, but worse followed when Edward began a relationship with Wallis Simpson and appeared to be completely infatuated with the still-married American, who already had one divorce behind her.

Thankfully, James did not seem to be following the same pattern of taking lovers, married or otherwise. Indeed, there were some speculative murmurings in the press suggesting that the King was gay. This was never stated overtly but, increasingly, unnamed 'palace insiders' and 'close aides' were being quoted, all of them hinting at a special friendship between the monarch and one of his senior personal secretaries – an (again unnamed) former Oxford University pal.

Queen Elizabeth had no objection to gay men. To the contrary, she very much enjoyed their company. But it was a different matter when it came to her son. Nothing short of heterosexuality, or at least the convincing appearance of it, would do.

The daughters of foreign royalty had been examined as potential brides. Princess Alexia of Greece and Denmark was mentioned. Suitable despite the abolition of the Greek monarchy, at twenty years old she was rejected as too young. The same objection would have applied to the Spanish Infantas Elena and Cristina had they not been automatically excluded as Roman Catholics. Religion also ruled out Princesses Marie-Astrid of Liechtenstein and Marie-Esméralda of Belgium, although they were the right age. In any case, Marie-Astrid was now no longer available. And goodness knows what had happened to Marie-Christine, the older Belgian princess.

A blank was drawn with the Scandinavian royal houses. The King of Norway's daughter was still a teenager, and Sweden's Crown Princess Victoria was but a child of eight. The conclusion reached was that the days of arranged dynastic marriages were over, though there might not have been any harm in engineering a meeting, had it been possible to identify an appropriate candidate.

Since the marriage of her grandson Prince Charles, the King's mother had taken to scrutinising the guest lists for the most prestigious of the surviving debutante balls, in the hope of identifying a young woman of noble British birth. But there was the crux. Her son was getting older, and the girls seemed to be getting increasingly younger and sillier. As Queen Regent, she'd stopped the presentations at court back in 1958, but now fleetingly wondered whether to revive Queen Charlotte's Ball with new and very specific eligibility criteria. The ideal would be a single, well-educated woman in her twenties from the upper echelons of society. Even the gentry might be all right at a push. Most importantly, she must have no former boyfriends who might, for the right price, be persuaded to tell all.

Unwittingly echoing the conclusion that her son and grandson had reached many years earlier, Her Majesty sadly acknowledged that, these days, such a specification seemed well-nigh impossible – even before she added a whole list of adjectives relating to personality and appearance.

Consequently, when one of her ladies-in-waiting drew her attention to a small concern near Sloane Square, she became very interested. The enterprise in question produced capacious bags. These weren't just any old bags: they were designed and hand-stitched by two resourceful young women, one of whom happened to be Lady Dorothea FitzGilbert, daughter and only child of the Duke of Albemarle[1]. Business, it seemed, was booming, and demand almost outstripped supply when it came to owning one of Chakdor's totally impractical silk and fine lace patchwork totes.

According to a recent interview in *The Lady* magazine, the proprietors had met when the gallery, for which Dorothea worked, was exhibiting some of Chakrika Chabra's award-winning textile designs.

'*... The two were soon collaborating on a few experimental pieces and, before long, hit on their winning "must have" formula. The name of their company is a combination of their forenames, and the iconic "Chakdor jackdaw" logo was based on a sketch by a fellow student of Chakrika's, from her days at the Slade. Chakrika, the daughter of a wealthy Indian businessman, was British-born and educated at Heathfield School before going on to study art. Dorothea, who has always had an interest in needlework, started working at the gallery after being "finished" at Château Mont-Choisi in Switzerland. The duo's workshop, fronted by a tiny boutique, is situated just off the King's Road. So, if you have a thousand or so pounds to spare, why not pop along to Aubrey Street?*'

Instructions were issued by the royal matriarch to check out Lady Dorothea's background, which proved entirely satisfactory. Better still, the young woman was from the Scottish aristocracy, which had to be the best of credentials. Why had this potential gem not been discovered sooner, especially as her parents lived so close to Balmoral?

In consequence, the Queen Dowager summoned her son to Marlborough House. She'd been living there for three years. It had taken him twelve years to persuade her to leave the palace, and she'd only gone then when he threatened to block her overdraft facility at Coutts.

She would, she told James, like him to personally choose a Chakdor tote bag as a gift for her forthcoming eighty-fifth birthday, two months hence. He seemed surprised. She went on to explain that she wanted something special in which to keep a copy of the commemorative book of stamps, which was being produced to mark the event. A puzzled James was not convinced, but nevertheless agreed to go along with the request.

Sensing his mother was up to something, he considered sending Keith to the bag shop on a reconnaissance mission. This, on reflection, seemed slightly paranoid – besides which, Keith was about to depart for Derbyshire on a short visit to see his parents. But James did feel he needed someone who could be classed as a friend to go with him.

Since the arrival on the scene of the Princess of Wales, the paparazzi appeared to have undergone a population explosion, and were getting more and more cunning as well. This meant that Gerald the Geordie could no longer join him on his unofficial excursions because, quite simply, the man was far too recognisable a member of the royal protection squad. His hair, which remained as bright ginger as ever, might have acted like a beacon to any photographers who happened to be in the vicinity of a king in non-kingly mode. Both James and Gerald, who'd shared many an interesting outing, were disappointed about this but accepted the reality. Increasing media interest in the sovereign's private life – 'When will the King meet Lady Right?' – had further compounded the difficulties. Most of James's less conventional forays were now confined to the latter part of August, when he was believed to be staying at Balmoral for a summer break.

There was, he figured, no reason why he should have to be in disguise, simply to go inside a shop. He could turn up unannounced, looking like himself, swiftly choose his mother's gift, jump back in the car and be driven away. Doing this as himself meant that his confidante Gerald could accompany him and, if necessary, help to figure out later what, if anything, was going on. It really didn't matter whether or not James was recognised. In the circumstances, he probably would be but, by the time some sales assistant could do anything about it, he'd be long gone. The worst that could happen was that his visit might prompt speculation about the lucky recipient's identity, and he could easily cut that off at the pass by readily admitting who she was. And – who knew? – his patronage might make a small contribution towards promoting British enterprise.

'Park up anywhere round here, will you, please?' instructed James as he spotted what he assumed to be the boutique fifty yards ahead. 'There's a bloody big Bentley outside, and I don't know whom we might walk in on.'

'Sorry, Sir,' said the driver, easing to a halt, 'but there doesn't seem to be a space. I can hover, but will have to move on if another car comes up behind us, or we'll be blocking its way.'

'Fine. Oh, who's that?' James was sitting in the back of the car, craning his neck to get a better view of the lady who'd just emerged onto the pavement. She was carrying a white paper carrier bag. 'If I didn't know better, I'd say that was Alexandra.'

'I believe you're right, Sir,' Gerald confirmed. 'If her car's going, we can take the slot.'

A couple of minutes later, the King and his bodyguard entered the small premises. The sales area was so cramped, there seemed barely enough space to accommodate the two of them. At a tiny square glass counter, a beautiful Indian girl was tidying something away into a box, carefully folding yards of tissue paper over whatever it was. She was talking to someone lurking in the shop's nether regions, through a partition screen of dangling ribbons.

As Gerald was carefully closing the door, the men just caught a snippet of conversation. 'I don't know, first the Duchess of Kent, and then – oh, sorry, can I help you?' The girl at the counter looked up at the new customer and gasped before curtsying. 'Your Majesty. I- I do apologise. How may I be of assistance?'

Her voice was barely a whisper. The whirr of a sewing machine started up behind the scenes.

James smiled. 'I'd like to buy a bag. I see you have a few.'

'A few' was an accurate description. On display, there were no more than two or three basic shapes, replicated in several different pastel colour-ways. Each meticulously-stitched patchwork component was made of either hand-embroidered or hand-beaded silk, with the occasional lace square interspersed.

'I'll take that one please,' he declared, after a quick glance round. The tote bag in question was mainly pale green, which his mother favoured, but also included peach. He wasn't sure about the peach bits, but the whole effect was stunning.

The girl hesitated. 'May I respectfully suggest that we could have a problem here, Sir? Would it be impudent of me to enquire about the bag's intended recipient? It's only that we've sold three very recently to customers who – well, there might be an issue of duplication.'

James was puzzled and turned to Gerald, who shrugged his shoulders. 'Could you explain further, please?' asked the King.

Chakrika took a deep breath. 'Her Royal Highness Princess Margaret bought a very similar item only this morning. Princess Alexandra chose one in pinks and peaches just a few minutes ago. And, yesterday, the Duchess of Kent was also here. I gather that all their purchases are to be gifts for Her Majesty The Queen, on the occasion of her forthcoming birthday. Without meaning to pry – ?' The unspoken question was recognition that the beneficiary could be someone else – a girlfriend perhaps.

The penny was beginning to drop. James sighed and signalled Gerald, who miraculously produced an oblong book from an inside pocket. On the front cover was an enlarged 15c Swaziland stamp depicting the Queen and James's two sisters. James took the souvenir album, showed it to the girl and, with a degree of desperation, again scanned the displays.

'Is there anything different I might look at, please? Something this would fit in?'

'We're working on a new range of envelope clutch bags, which are not yet generally available for retail. But I could show you one or two prototypes if you like?'

When James nodded, the girl called loudly through to the back. 'Thea! Could you bring me through the finished clutches, please?'

The whirring sound stopped.

'What?'

'The new clutches!'

'Yup,' the voice responded. 'Just finishing off a lining. Be with you in a mo.'

'Now, please. And hurry.'

Thirty seconds later, Lady Dorothea FitzGilbert, carrying three samples, was nudging her way through the ribbon screen. 'These what you want, Chak? Oops. Your Majesty.' The curtsy was an inbred reaction, her comment less so. 'I say, we seem to have become very popular with your family of late, Sir.'

James was very relieved to be outside on the street, only a couple of strides away from the security of the car. Looking quickly to his left, in the direction they'd come, he could see a large delivery van blocking the narrow road, possibly creating a fortuitous obstacle. An unspoken enquiry of the driver produced confirmation that, contrary to expectations, there'd been no prying lenses in the vicinity.

'What did you make of all that?' he asked Gerald, as soon as they were settled inside their anonymous vehicle and being driven away.

'There appears to be conspiracy of some sort going on, Sir. But as to its exact nature, I don't quite know.'

'My feelings exactly. The Mater seems to have roped in everyone, but whether they were on some sort of vetting mission, or whether the plan was more complicated than that, is debatable. Possibly, my mother has simply developed a fad for a particular type of shopping bag and has been dropping hints here, there and everywhere?'

'You think so?' The bodyguard was not convinced.

'It's a shame the "clutches" or whatever they're called weren't quite big enough. It's almost as though they were deliberately made not to fit, by a fraction of an inch.'

'That's a bit of a stretch, Sir. It was probably just chance. I don't see how those girls could have been involved. They both seemed as genuinely surprised as you were by the sudden run of royal patronage.'

'Did I do the right thing?'

'The mix of greys and silver you selected was very tasteful. Not to mention more versatile.'

'I wasn't referring to colour choice.'

'It was sensible of you to get one custom-made to exactly the right size.'

'I'm still worried that I made a stupid decision.'

'I shouldn't worry, Sir. They said they could easily produce one to order, with plenty of time to spare.' James's companion was struggling to keep a straight face.

'Are you being deliberately obtuse, Gerald?'

'Me? Ah, I see. By "the right thing", you're referring to the invitation for her to deliver the goods to you at the palace in person.'

'That, as you very well know, is exactly what I meant.'

Rab and Jeannie were spending a week at a caravan park near Wells-next-the-Sea, on the north Norfolk coast, and disappointingly, Sunday 4th August 1985 was dawning overcast.

'Not the best day for it,' Rab commented, looking out of the window.

Jeannie merely turned onto her left side and pulled the duvet over her head. She'd never understood her husband's fascination with the royal family but, as he frequently pointed out, 'They're news. They're what everyone wants to hear about. And news is our bread and butter. One of these days, it may even be our route to fame and fortune.'

'I'll make us a quick cuppa while you're getting ready,' he offered. 'And a couple of rounds of toast. We're almost out of milk.'

'What time is it?' she managed to mumble.

'5.30. You don't have to come with me. Go back to sleep if you want.'

'No,' she said, sitting up. 'Nothing better to do, and I don't want to be stuck here all day, on my own. This is supposed to be a holiday, not that you'd notice.'

Half an hour later, the couple were in the car, heading towards Sandringham. 'Why do we need to get there so early?' Jeannie asked.

'It'll be easier to park and we need to nab a good spot. We won't be the only ones with the same idea.'

A republican at heart, Jeannie began talking on an old familiar theme.

'What I don't understand is why Willie Hamilton[2] thinks the Queen Dowager is so remarkable. The "pride of the family" he called her, when she spends more money than the rest of them put together. And he's someone who is fervently anti-royalist.'

'People have long memories. She'll never be forgotten for all that morale-boosting during the war. It's earned eternal gratitude. Or perhaps it's just that she fills a gap for those who miss their grannies.'

'Not exactly your typical Granny, though, is she? Most grannies don't own a string of expensive racehorses or need hundreds of servants to provide for their every need and whim. They don't have several homes at their disposal either.'

'She looks the part though.'

'No she doesn't. Worn woolies are more typical than chiffon dresses with matching hats. All the ostriches in Australia must be bald by now.'

'My, my! You do seem to have a bit of a downer on her. We'll have to see if you change your mind when she flashes her famous smile in your direction.'

'So are we going just because you want to be smiled at by an eighty-five-year-old with pink teeth?'

'No, we're going because I want to see who else is there.'

'If we wait for tomorrow's papers, we'll find out exactly who else is there.'

'I can tell you right now who'll be reported as there. It's the ones who come out of church behind them that I'm interested in. And those wandering towards the house after the service, who may not even look like they're officially there.'

'You do talk in riddles sometimes, Rab. Did you get your draft resignation finished before we left?'

'Yes, but I'm still dithering about whether to hand it in.'

'You've been dithering for the last ten years. I thought we'd agreed?'

'Let's see how today goes, shall we?'

Rab's twofold plan was both to mingle with the gathering crowds and to infiltrate the group of those covering the event for the media. Locals always had a pretty good idea of what was going on. The younger royals didn't invariably stay confined behind residence walls, and people living in the vicinity were adept at appearing not to notice, should elevated personages decide to pop out for a drink at some pub or other.

Individual members of the press pack rarely knew more than seemingly unimportant facts or observations. But occasionally, when glued together, these fragments could amount to something of greater significance. Today's gathering of cameramen, all focusing on the House of Windsor, represented a good opportunity.

From snippets gained from his contacts, the *Evening Standard*'s reporter already had a few ideas floating around his head. His Majesty had been spotted in London on a few recent occasions in the company of a stunning, and as yet unnamed, Indian girl. These hadn't been outings *à deux*. There'd been no sightings, in high-class restaurants, of two people getting cosy over candlelit dinners, but then there wouldn't be. However, the inclusion of several female newcomers in the King's usual set hadn't gone unnoticed. James and his nephew Charles were known to frequent exclusive clubs like Annabel's in Mayfair. Comings and goings at such places were under close scrutiny, but it was difficult to know exactly who was with whom and what the precise status of anyone was. Compounding matters were the faint rumblings emanating from 'insiders' about a rift in the Waleses' relationship, which were giving rise to unpublished suggestions that the Prince might be in the market for an extra-marital dalliance. Nevertheless, and despite the complications, Rab sensed the imminence of a 'Despite Official Denials' situation.

He was old enough to vaguely remember the run-up to Princess Margaret's marriage to Lord Snowden, who'd been present at any number of events attended by Her Royal Highness. 'Tony' had been seen entering sundry premises for various private parties but, because he was a photographer, and because there were plenty of eligible young aristocrats around, no one suspected he was the real love interest. Prior to the shock announcement of the couple's engagement, there had not been so much as a whisper of romance between the two.

Hiding him in a crowd hadn't been such a bad tactic. Whether it would work again these days was another matter.

25

GLASGOW

'Fuck! Fuck! Fuck!'

'As you've said, many times, in between periods of angry silence,' observed Jeannie. 'Why not condense it to "triple fuck"?'

'Same number of syllables,' grumbled her husband, 'so no point.'

'It would reduce the number of expletives,' she countered.

He pushed away his plate. Even though breakfast was usually what he referred to as birdseed, they always had a traditional fry-up on a Sunday morning. He looked forward to it, but he could only manage a single bite of bacon today.

Rab hadn't gleaned anything of use at Sandringham, though he'd hung around for a while after the main crowds had dispersed. It had been nice to note that the Queen Dowager had declined a ride back to the house, in favour of walking. Although a lovely touch, especially as it was raining, the gesture was hardly something which no one else would pick up on. If Jeannie hadn't told him she was going to need the loo in the not-too-distant future, he might have stayed even longer. As it was, he suggested driving into King's Lynn and finding

237

somewhere cosy for a spot of lunch. They'd gone to the restaurant at the Duke's Head hotel.

The couple had been back in Glasgow for three weeks. Ever since their return, Rab had been brooding. He was convinced he'd missed something, but hadn't been able to put his finger on what it might have been. The exposé in that morning's *Sunday Mirror* had hit him like a physical blow.

'They were sitting right in front of us. On a couple of occasions they were literally staring us in the face, Jeannie. I knew deep down it couldn't have been a coincidence,' he moaned.

'It could easily have been a coincidence,' she soothed. 'Beautiful Indian girls aren't that much of a rarity. Beautiful Indian girls who frequent restaurants in the company of a friend can't be that unusual either. They could have been a couple of random walk-ins off the street, like we were.'

'They weren't. They weren't presented with a bill for their meal, so they must've been guests with an account. It's blindingly obvious that they'd have been booked in for a night or two, keeping a low profile until well after all the birthday fuss had died down.'

'Obvious now, maybe. But there was still no way you could have worked it all out at the time.'

'I might have been able to, if we'd gone for the table next to them, instead of the one across the other side of the room. We were given the choice.'

'I hope you're not blaming me for that?'

'I don't blame you for anything. I was the one who said we'd take the window table. I was the one who'd dragged you out of bed at the crack of dawn. All you did was suffer in soggy silence while I went about my damn fool, and ultimately futile, mission.'

'There's nothing to say that you'd have overheard anything useful, even if we had been able to eavesdrop.'

'I know, but I should have followed them when they left. Any money, they'll have headed to Sandringham.'

'I might have complained if you'd yanked me away when we'd already ordered. Or if you'd gone shooting off and abandoned me completely. Or if we hadn't been able to pay the waiter for our drinks quickly enough, done a runner and become wanted fugitives.'

'That's right. Make a joke of it.'

Rab sighed. 'Sorry. But I *knew*, Jeannie. I could feel it. The word "decoy" had been racing round my head for days. If only I'd taken a quick snapshot of them. It would have made thousands as an exclusive.'

'Rab, you're clueless when it comes to photography. You don't even own a camera.'

'I feel clueless, full stop.'

'Well you aren't. Take it from one who knows.' Jeannie paused. 'Has it occurred to you that they might have set off from the hotel at any time, not necessarily straight after their Sunday roast and not necessarily through the front entrance either?'

Rab didn't respond.

'And, even if you had managed to confirm where they were going, how would that have taken us any further forward? You still wouldn't have known who they were, would you?'

'Carry on, love. You're doing better than I was.'

'OK. It makes sense, too, that there'd still have been a few hopeful paparazzi lurking around the gates of Sandringham House, who'd also have seen them arrive – unless they were travelling in the back of a delivery van. So you would all have ended up on equal terms.'

At last, Rab rallied. 'Ah, but that's where you're wrong. We had the one huge advantage over everyone else, in that we knew where they were staying. And, before you say anything, yes, I would have found a way of sussing out the names they'd been booked in under. Hotels aren't going to hand out registration details to every Tom, Dick and Harry, but everyone has their price.'

'Then, given you were so sure, wouldn't it have been simpler just to have done that anyway, rather than go chasing round the Norfolk countryside?'

'That, my love, hits the nail on the head. It's what really galls. Why didn't I? It was all there for the taking.'

'Oh, Rab. One of these days, your big break will happen. You're not the only one who feels things in their bones. Finish that novel. Finish your letter of resignation, swallow hard and bloody well hand it in. We'll manage.'

Rab couldn't swallow. Sticking in his craw was the front-page headline: 'Could the King have finally found THE ONE?'

With Rab's mantra in mind, Jeannie had a sudden idea. She pulled the newspaper across the table and read, for a second time, the tantalising front page. Next, she turned to the full story on pages six, seven, eight and nine. Unsurprisingly, it contained quite a lot of information about Chakrika, including the highly successful Chakdor enterprise. Although staked out for a while, the premises appeared to be well and truly closed for the summer, so it had not been possible to obtain a statement from the business partner, about whom there was a short piece. Lady Dorothea FitzGilbert was understood to be holidaying with friends in Bermuda. Details of her flight to the island had been checked out, and it was confirmed that she'd left in late July.

In lieu of the lowdown from the girl who was arguably closest to Chakrika, a few of the boutique's aristocratic clientele, all now claiming to be firm friends, had made gushing contributions to the article. There were also comments from former Slade students about what a lovely person and talented designer Chakrika was, and how they'd always known she was destined for great things. The people who knew her were probably the main source of the images that accompanied the feature. There was one other photo, showing a glimpse of her shrouded face as she was getting into a taxi outside a nightclub. The fact that she was wearing a hooded velvet cloak on a warm dry evening (and was therefore apparently trying not to be recognised) added fuel to the fire of frenzy.

Further speculative waffle dwelt on the prospect of an Indian's becoming a member of the royal family. The general view was that the King's mother was unlikely to have any objection on the grounds of ethnic background, and nor should she. Modern society was multicultural and, besides, it was only relatively recently that Her Majesty had been Empress of India. A more likely concern, should there be any concern at all, would be that the girl's background was trade.

By this point, the palace had not issued any statement. This was despite the fact that Chakrika and her companion, named as an old school chum Joanna Boothby, had joined the royal party both at Sandringham and, subsequently, at Balmoral, where the King was still in residence.

Rab had been right. The manager at the Duke's Head confirmed that the girls had stayed there in early August. The pair had been exemplary guests. The chambermaid, who'd cleaned their rooms, said that they always left things very tidy and that the Indian lady hadn't touched the soap and other toiletries provided. Sadly, she couldn't recall which products had been used instead – information which might have upped the cash value of her small contribution.

Jeannie folded up the paper and handed it back to her husband. Then she started to clear the table. Instead of scraping off the untouched breakfast into the flip-top bin, she covered his plate with a casserole lid and put it in the oven, which she set to a low heat. In so doing, she began what would later feel like the habit of a lifetime. Her next tasks were discarding the old filter paper in the coffee machine and setting up a fresh pot. Rab, meanwhile, was reading.

'Well?' she asked, after plonking down two steaming mugs.

'Well what?'

'Doesn't it strike you that the whole seemingly well-camouflaged affair has been leaking like a sieve?'

'Possibly, now you mention it.'

'Question one: where's all the media attention being focused? The answer to that is pretty easy. Question two: where's all the attention being diverted from? Perhaps "where" isn't the right word. Question three: who would make a (let's say) "more traditional" queen? The daughter of an Indian multi-millionaire, or the daughter of a Scottish duke? Question four – '

'Whoa! I'm with you now.'

'"Decoy". You said it yourself, Rab. So, thinking through the hypothesis, where is the alternative candidate?'

'Bermuda.'

'And if she isn't? You'd know better than me, but how easy would it be to lay a false trail with the flight and the ticket?'

'No more difficult than extracting any bogus info from the airline, I guess.'

'So, if she didn't go…?'

'She may have stayed in London and put up the shutters. Her parents don't live a million miles from Balmoral, but that's an unlikely bolthole. If the press can't get a statement from the horse's mouth, they'll probably be pestering the horse's parents. And if anyone's thinking along the same lines as we are, which is very possible, you can guarantee they too will be monitoring the ancient pile.'

'And where is the King?'

'Balmoral, of course. This doesn't work, Jeannie.'

'It might… if he wasn't there.'

'If that's the case, he could be anywhere. So could she. And they might not be together. This could all be one giant smokescreen.'

'Then write an article on that very possibility. Pick over every hole in the sieve until you can demonstrate how everything's been cleverly designed as one big diversion. You were on the verge of falling for it. Possibly, you could even suggest that the travelling companion's name isn't really Joanna Boothby and that His Majesty's real love interest is right here in Scotland, hiding in plain sight. Pity I can't visualise what she looked like. Darkish hair, I think, but that's about it.'

'I can't do any better, but maybe it won't matter. You could perhaps check out the class of whenever it was at Heathfield School. See if there have been any articles on this Sloane Ranger Chakdor shop. Maybe there was a launch? If so, there might be photos of both its owners. Even if that gets you nowhere, you can't be libelled for speculating, can you?'

Rab shook his head.

'I don't need to tell you that you'll need to be quick about it. But first, would you like to finish your breakfast? I've kept it warm.'

8TH SEPTEMBER 1985

BUCKINGHAM PALACE

'His Royal Highness The Prince of Wales, Sir,' the footman announced.

'Hello, old boy. Weren't you supposed to be staying on for a few more days?' queried James.

'No. Decided I'd better get stuck back in. Diana and the boys are still in France, and I thought it might be nice to have KP[1] to myself for a while.'

'Were Chak and Joanna still up there?'

'No, they left a couple of days ago. So, how goes the courtship?'

'Let's say that Mr and Mrs Carrick from Llanfairpwllgwy-ngyllgogerychwyrndrobwllllantysiliogogogoch had a pleasant time.'

'Surely you didn't put all that in the hotel register?'

'No, the landlady said to just put "Anglesey".'

'Landlady?'

'Yes, Keith found us a nice little bed and breakfast. It was one of my best ever decisions, employing Keith. He understands me completely.'

'Pity he isn't a girl then. So where's "Mrs Carrick" now. Safely back in SW3?'

'Not on your life. That would be totally stupid. The shop in Aubrey Street is permanently closed. Sold in fact. The property belonged to Chak's father, though there's no "sold" sign outside of course. The paps are still staking it out and, while ever they're there, they aren't anywhere else.'

'But what about the bag business?'

'The workshop's being relocated to somewhere as yet unspecified. There'll be no retail area any more. That just wouldn't do. The bags will henceforth be sold exclusively through Harvey Nicks.'

'Not Harrods?'

'They weren't the highest bidder. Mr Chabra negotiated that, too.'

'I did think it was a daft idea, having a decoy who lived and worked in the same place as the target.'

'It was a genius idea. They'll be living separately from now on. I'll be able to visit Dorothea secretly if I want. And I can visit Chak, too, a bit more conspicuously. She's more than tough enough to cope with the media attention. You know how difficult all that was for Diana.'

'Tell me about it.'

'So what about the announcement?'

'No hurry. Andy and Sarah seem to be getting serious, and it wouldn't surprise me if there weren't a royal wedding next year to celebrate, which means mine can wait. Even the Mater would have to understand that we can't have two conspicuously extravagant bashes so close together. So you see, I have all the time in the world.'

'To do what?'

'Decide which one I want to marry. That's assuming either of them would be happy to accept me.'

'And if neither does?'

'Joanna Boothby seems like a nice enough girl. I've always thought that a double "J" monogram would work well.'

'PRESS-TIDIGITATION?

A clever magician pulls off his tricks by sleight of hand, or by diverting attention elsewhere. Which leads us to the question: have royal watchers been victims of misdirection? Have the media cleverly "unearthed" what they were meant to see, rather than what's really going on?

If the answer is "yes", then what lies behind the elaborate masquerade? The answer, surely, is a queen in waiting, but she might not be the one upon whom all lenses are currently being focused. Then again, she might.

Let's have a look at how the press were led through the nose, from the flat landscape of Norfolk to the Scottish baronial architecture of Balmoral Castle, with its hilly backdrop...'

It wasn't the cleverest headline Rab had ever come up with, and the piece itself was padded out with lightweight content. Nevertheless, it had taken off. This was mainly down to the fact that he'd managed to source, in a back copy of *Sloane Set*, a photograph of Chakdor's rather low-key opening event.

It seemed that another journalist had just beaten him to it, because he was informed that he was the second person in as many days to be refused permission to use the image. The copyright owners had doubtless belatedly recognised its value and would, in all probability, now be considering how best to capitalise on their asset.

Initially annoyed, Rab soon realised that this worked to his advantage: given they wouldn't be allowed to reproduce the picture, any rivals for a story based on it would be neatly stymied. Rab alone knew that the woman shown standing beside her Indian business partner wasn't the one who'd been staying at the hotel in King's Lynn. Although both girls were brunettes and of below-average stature, there were marked differences in facial appearance. This suggested the participation of a third female – and thus an extra layer of complexity – in the diversionary charade.

His article first appeared in Glasgow's *Evening News* and had then been syndicated to the nationals. Like many stories, it was quickly usurped by the next one to come along, and Mr Rainsmith would never know how grateful his sovereign had been about that.

Nevertheless, James felt it wise to put his dual courtship activities on hold for a while. He concentrated instead on how his new fibreglass power boat in Coniston was coming along. That Australian he'd met in jubilee year had gone on to beat the water speed record twelve months or so later. Ever since then, His Majesty had been intent on reclaiming it for Britain and for himself.

CHAPTER 25

1987

26

For the second time in the space of a few months, the country was once again caught up in wedding fever, and this was the big one. Everyone, or almost every woman at least, was keen to discover what THE dress would be like. On this occasion, speculation was heightened by the fact that nobody knew who'd be designing it. This was usually common knowledge in advance, regardless of whether or not there'd been a formal announcement.

When Lady Dorothea FitzGilbert stepped out of the golden carriage, all was immediately clear. Who'd produced the dress? She had! This put all those who were intent on making instant replicas into a quandary, for it would be impossible to duplicate. The bodice was simple enough – a close-fitting 'V' with short-capped lace sleeves that barely covered the bride's shoulders. But the skirt was a swirling patchwork of many different fabrics, textures and individually-embroidered kite-shaped pieces, which draped in points to form a zig-zagged hem. Harsher commentators said that the queen-to-be looked like she was wearing a Chakdor tote bag, but most could only concur that the ethereal garment was a triumph. There was no doubt about what the theme of the following day's headlines would be: the woman who'd just become Queen of England had done so wearing a 'home-made' frock.

Getting together to watch royal weddings had, by now, become a tradition for the three women. Lil had hosted the gathering on the occasion of Prince Andrew's marriage to Sarah Ferguson the previous year. They'd all concurred that the whole event was nicely done, especially in that the bride entered Westminster Abbey wearing a coronet of flowers and emerged wearing a glittering tiara, thus symbolically marking her transition to royal status. Joyce had been surprised that, for such a seemingly modern girl, she'd promised to obey[1]. Beyond that, the family matriarch had mildly gone along with the usual comments throughout the service, possibly because her daughters had ensured that, this time, she remained sober. It was only much later, after they'd all hit the prosecco, that the elderly woman had become more voluble and shouted at the screen, 'Come on love. Give 'im a good old snog!'

For the King's wedding, the trio had again convened at Peggy's house in Cobourg Road and were once more scrutinising every detail. Dorothea remembered all eight of His Majesty's names and got them in the correct order.

'She's prob'ly bin practisin' for days,' said Peggy.

'Let's 'ope, now she's safely over that 'urdle, she'll start to look a bit more relaxed and 'appy,' remarked Joyce, speaking for almost the first time.

'I don't suppose you'd be looking relaxed, Mum, knowing the eyes of the world are watching your every blink. In her shoes, I'd be terrified about getting a tickle in my throat and needing to cough. Or I'd be worrying about my voice drying up and not being able to get a word out,' Lil suggested.

'She's worryin' about somefin', that's for sure.'

'The thought of suddenly becoming queen must be pretty daunting. In a few minutes, even her sisters-in-law and mother-in-law will have to curtsy to her, not the other way round. That's how it works.'

Even though it later emerged that Dorothea had been

assisted with the dress by workers from the Royal School of Needlework, and by her partner Chakrika Chabra, Her Majesty's industriousness, skill and thrift endeared her to the public. She would never eclipse the Princess of Wales, of course: Diana had carved out her own special place in everyone's hearts. And, compared to the flamboyant exuberance of Fergie, the new queen paled almost into insignificance. Pretty enough in an unexceptional way, she was of shorter stature than her two nieces-in-law, and yet not tiny enough to be remarkable. But she was quickly observed to be a hard-working royal, who'd adopted a number of unexpected causes. The most notable of these concerned drug dependency, and her interests covered every aspect of the problem. The plight of children living with addicted parents, and the overriding message of prevention, dovetailed nicely with certain of the charities embraced by her husband's King's Trust. The need to rescue youngsters, who had sadly become hooked, similarly complemented the aims of Charles' Prince's Trust.

The funds of all the organisations under the Queen's patronage benefitted greatly from the Chakdor enterprise. Dorothea had learned the art of intricate sewing at her grandmother's knee. Having a needle and thread between her fingers always felt soothing and, in her spare time, she continued to stitch squares of silk cloth, each of which, these days, included a distinctive tiny crown motif. The company now had many skilled employees, but Chakrika always took personal responsibility for assembling what became known as the 'Queen's totes'. These incorporated a single patch personally embroidered or beaded by Her Majesty, and they commanded three times the price of the already expensive, but less exclusive, bags. All the proceeds from the special editions went to charity.

This wasn't Dorothea's only contribution to her country's industry. She bought British and she bought off the peg for all but the most formal glitzy occasions. Even if she lacked a fashion model's height, she wore her purchases to pleasing effect, and others rushed out to copy the look. It took her a while to get used to having ladies-in-waiting to help her dress and accessorise. Although not one of the regulars, Chakrika was amongst the small number who had access to the Queen's bedchamber.

The erstwhile business partners remained close, but this might not have been the case if Dorothea had known about James's rejected proposal to her friend.

JUNE 1987

BUCKINGHAM PALACE

'Well, I'm not having anything to do with it,' declared Charles, 'and neither is Diana. I have no intention whatsoever of going anywhere near Alton Towers.'

'Nice to see the Waleses singing off the same hymn sheet for once,' James observed. 'I haven't agreed to participate of course, but I do think I should show some sort of solidarity. Edward's so enthused.'[2]

'The whole idea is totally ridiculous.'

'Raising money for charity isn't ridiculous. They're representing some jolly good causes.'

'I can't argue with that, though there must be more dignified ways of going about it. By association, they're going to make the entire family a laughing stock.'

'It's supposed to be a laugh. It's supposed to be fun. It might demonstrate that we're not all stuffed shirts who never let our hair down.'

'Talking of "Hair", it was bad enough when Anne got up on stage at the Shaftsbury Theatre and started gyrating.'[3]

'At least she kept her clothes on! I think I might toddle along and provide a bit of moral support behind the scenes. Dorothea will be in Scotland.'

'If that's a tactical retreat, well done her. Wouldn't it be easier simply to send a good luck card. Or should that be a "break a leg" card?'

'Yes, but that's not quite the same. Besides, Nigel Mansell's on Andrew's team. I could congratulate him in person on how well he's doing in the F1 World Championship. I'm not sure I'll be able to get to Silverstone next month for the British Grand Prix, more's the pity.'

'So you do have a secondary agenda then?'

'I wouldn't go as far as that exactly, but there are a few other people I wouldn't mind catching up with. Jackie Stewart for one. I'm not exactly sure how it all works, but the participants in "Knockout" must be allocated dressing rooms. Whether or not they'll be sharing them is another matter, but my people can seek them out and lead me in the right direction.'

'There must be a veritable village backstage at this jamboree. I'd say you were taking a big chance of being spotted, or worse still, of being photographed. There are bound to be people with cameras swarming round everywhere.'

'Ah, that's where you're wrong. One thing I do know is that the press are being very strictly controlled, and they'll all be corralled into one place. Can't take the risk of anyone's being caught in an unguarded moment. We're not just talking four senior royals here. There will also be hordes of celebrities. I'll be long gone before the actual filming starts, so it should all be plain sailing, barring the odd character who might happen to have a Brownie camera about their person.'

Charles shuddered. 'It's bound to come out one way or another that you were there, Jimmy. Someone will spill the beans. Edward might even blab.'

'Not if I tell him not to.'

'Well, in my humble opinion, you're simply asking to be tainted by association. I assume you're planning on going as yourself?'

'I thought so. But you do have a point. Hmm. Yes. That's a very good point. It's got me thinking. Fergus can't go, because he couldn't speak to anyone who knows me. But tattier than usual casuals and a Tilley hat or visor might not be the worst ideas. If it's remotely sunny, a pair of shades would just about clinch it.'

SATURDAY 19TH JUNE 1987

DEPTFORD

Lil and Peggy were visiting their parents. The Faulkners had moved to a new ground-floor flat four years earlier. It was in a low-rise block off Evelyn Street, just behind The Black Horse pub, which had always been one of Ron's favourite haunts. The prospect the couple had dreaded most of all was ending up on the fifteenth floor of a monstrous tower block. What if the lifts broke and they had to climb up hundreds of stairs? In truth, they didn't like the idea of a flat at all, but this place was a good compromise. It had a narrow, railed-off outside space – laughingly described as a 'terrace' – and two bedrooms. The second of these, which they didn't need anyway, was very small. Ron joked that there was room to swing a cat, but the poor creature would be knocked unconscious in the process. The neighbours were friendly, which was what mattered most.

'So tell me again. 'ow come Freddie was involved in this Royal Knockout programme?' asked Joyce.

''e wasn't involved in the programme itself, Mum. 'e was

earnin' a bit of cash by 'elpin' out 'is mate's dad, 'oo does all that caterin' for events. "Jacket Joe's" it's called. Our Freddie was mannin' a food bar be'ind the scenes,' explained Peggy. ''e said that if 'e nevva secs a baked spud again, it'll be too soon.'

'Did he see any of the royals?'

''e said 'e saw Nicholas Lyndhurst, 'im what plays Rodney in *Only Fools an' 'orses*. And Anneka Rice. 'e actually served 'er. And a few uvvas, ooze names I don't remember. And 'e met the King.'

''e must 'ave been kiddin'. The King wasn't there,' declared Joyce.

'Well that's what 'e said when 'e rang.'

'And where is Master Freddie now?' asked Ron.

'Still at Alton Towers, I fink. They 'ad a couple of days finishin' up to do, 'cause everything needed to be taken down. Then 'e and 'is pal were 'eadin' to Cornwall, or somewhere that way.'

'And when will 'e be comin' 'ome?'

'When 'is money runs out, I 'xpect, Dad. 'e'll 'ave to be back by September, though, before 'e goes to university, if only to get 'is washin' done.'

'Is Bristol somewhere up north?'

'It's in the west country, Mum,' said Lil, looking at the clock on the mantlepiece. 'Shouldn't we switch on the TV? We don't want to miss the start.'

27

CHURCH OF ST NICHOLAS, DEPTFORD

Lil and Peggy were once again in mourning. The death of Daisy Dagley in October hadn't been unexpected. She'd been unwell for a long time, though the exact nature of her illness was never properly identified. Resisting every attempt to persuade her that she'd be better off in a care home, she'd struggled on alone.

Lil and Terry had suggested on a few occasions that she move in with them, but the prospect of stockbroker belt Surrey had not appealed to the old lady. They'd made the offer in the certainty that it wouldn't be accepted.

They'd made a similar offer last night to Ron Faulkner, also in the knowledge that he'd refuse to uproot from surroundings that were familiar and from the friends he'd known virtually all his life.

Joyce's death had come as a huge shock. She'd been fit as a flea, apart from the arthritic knee joints, which seemed especially troublesome when the weather was damp. When she'd set off on the Saturday to spend a few days with her sister Shirley in Sheffield, no one expected that they'd never see her again.

At first, they hadn't known whether she'd been caught up in the tragic fire at King's Cross station[1]. Ron, expecting his wife home at any time, heard about it on the *Nine O'Clock News*. He was concerned but not excessively so. She sometimes caught a later train, or even stayed on an extra day or two. Real panic kicked in about a quarter of an hour later when Shirley, who'd taken her to Sheffield station in good time, telephoned to find out whether Joyce was safely back. By 10 o'clock, Terry and Ralph had spoken to each other and swiftly made a plan of action. Between them, they were now frantically ringing all the hospitals to which the injured had been taken by ambulance. Peggy, meanwhile, had caught a taxi to her father's flat, so she could be with him as they both waited for further news. Lil, who'd gone into Epsom with a friend to see *Moonstruck* at the cinema, did not discover what was going on until about 11 p.m.

Joyce's body was one of the first to be identified.

The loss of a second grandmother in the space of six weeks was a devastating blow to Janet, and it hit Freddie equally hard. It was not therefore unnatural that the 'cousins' should cling together for mutual comfort at the funeral, and nor was it surprising that so many mourners commented on how alike they were. Except for the age disparity, the pair might well have been taken for twins – and identical ones at that, were it not for the gender difference.

AUGUST 1988

THE GROUNDS OF BALMORAL CASTLE

'How are you feeling, Jimmy? I heard you'd not been too well.'

'Actually, I'm still feeling pretty ghastly. The doctors don't know why. Tests, tests and more tests all seem to indicate that I'm fit as a fiddle. The pathetic conclusion is that they think I have this yuppie flu, but no one's ever got to the bottom of the whys and wherefores of that. It's now labelled ME/CFS, as if giving it a quasi-scientific name helps. I can never remember what the "ME" bit stands for, but the "CFS" is chronic fatigue syndrome, which aptly describes me. I have less energy than a comatose slug.'

'Oh dear.'

'So how goes it with you?'

'Not good.'

'Diana?'

'Mostly. But she is trying to get to the root of her problems. Latest is a visit to a "dowser healer". Here's the thing. This chap, Jack Temple, dangles a crystal above his patients in search of bodily poisons. So the cause of my wife's problems seems to be that some lead escaped into her system when she broke a pencil against her cheek, aged twelve. That and the fact that her aristocratic ancestors drank out of lead crystal glasses.'

'So did ours. I wonder if that's what's wrong with me?'

'Unfortunately, what this practitioner didn't say was how to get rid of the excess, or the bit of lead shrapnel that's floating around.'

'I thought you were into all that alternative medicine stuff?'

'Complementary, yes, where there's some joined-up thinking behind it. Have you tried homeopathy?'

James expended some valuable energy on laughing. 'Isn't that as cranky as crystal dangling? You've certainly come in for a fair amount of stick for supporting it. I'd rather go with something proven.'

'Perhaps you could try sitting in a circle of people, harnessing the energy of the sun, Jimmy. Also one of Temple's ideas, by the way.'

James sighed. 'I wish I could harness some energy from somewhere. It's depressing that, if the medics don't know the cause, they can't produce a cure. I suppose I'll just have to rest and drink lots of fluids, which is the best they can come up with. Apparently, if the cause is viral, that helps to flush it out.'

'Not like you to do as you're told.'

'No choice in the matter, I'm afraid, old boy. It's even a struggle to get out of bed some days. So I sit here and dream.'

'What of?'

'Happier times. One in particular.'

'You'll be writing poetry next. The moon in June… the stars above… falling in love…'

'That pretty much hits the nail on the head. Do you believe in love at first sight?'

'Sort of. The connection with Camilla was almost immediate. I wish I'd proposed when I had the chance, instead of gallivanting off with the navy. Or done both. Mama was the wife of a serving officer, and it worked for them until Grandpapa died. They spent quite a time in Malta, living as close to an ordinary life as it gets for the likes of us. But I stupidly bowed to family opposition and returned to find I'd left it too late. Don't you think it's funny, in a non-hilarious way, that you and I were considered too young to marry when we were twenty-two and yet, just a few short years later, we had all that pressure to find someone and settle down? So tell me. Who was the fair maiden?'

'Which fair maiden?'

'The one you instantly fell for. The one you're still dreaming about. I don't recall your having a crush on anyone, but you must've had a specific woman in mind when you asked the question.'

'Yes, I did. But I lost her.'

'How do you mean, "lost"? Did she refuse you? As you know, I've been turned down a couple or three times. You get over it.'

'I mean lost as in unable to find her again. It was a long time ago, and she wouldn't have been suitable anyway.'

'Camilla wasn't considered suitable either, and I still can't fathom out why.'

'You know why. Uncle Dickie wanted his granddaughter Amanda for one of us, and he always had more influence over you.'

'She was one of my refusals. I did quite like her and, if it hadn't been for that bloody IRA bomb, she might have felt less reluctant about joining the family. But when your little brother and your granny get blown up, it's bound to make a difference.'

'And don't forget that the Mater was in cahoots with her best buddy Ruth, on behalf of the Spencer girls.'

'Whereby I dutifully obliged by marrying one.'

'She genuinely preferred you, Charles. I never really got a look in.'

'I wish you'd tried harder. Not like you to give up on a challenge, especially when you were the one who laid down the gauntlet. With hindsight, you could say I drew the short straw.'

'Not so short. She's taller than I am, so I'd have had to get built-up shoes made, or spend all my time looking for a higher step or kerb to stand on.'

'Like that 50s film star. Who was it?'

'Alan Ladd? Didn't the crews have to dig trenches for his leading ladies to stand in?'

'That's the one. He was in *The Carpetbaggers*. I was too young to see it.'

'So was I but that didn't stop me,' said James. 'And I got a copy of the book. And then there's Tom Cruise. Another short-arse with heel lifts or clever insoles. *Top Gun*'s still one of my favourite films though. Are things really so bad with Diana? There must be happy times, surely?'

'Maybe there were. Things weren't bad just before Harry was born, but not any more. Perhaps it's partly my fault.'

'Why it went all wrong you mean? Must take some doing with someone who's beautiful, popular, a brilliant mother and all round good egg. She genuinely cares for people, you know.'

'Only when the cameras and press are there to record her goody two-shoes act.'

'That simply isn't true, Charles. I ran into her one night a year or so ago, in Cardboard City. She had only one PPO with her and was sitting chatting, carefree as you please. End of. It was quite funny in a way. At first she didn't recognise me at all, which was encouraging. But she did recognise Melvin, even in his scruffs, and then twigged whom he was with and damn near gave the game away. I shook my head in a warning kind of way, and thankfully she didn't say anything. Otherwise, everyone in the Bullring underpass would have found out my true identity and it would have been "goodbye Fergus". As it was, I think they were already getting a bit suspicious, because Fergus always left behind a couple of brand-new sleeping bags and a few bottles of cheap brandy.'

'Good grief. Are you still up to your old tricks?'

'Absolutely. Though tell me one thing: were you surprised to find me here at Balmoral?'

'Yes, of course. You never usually come for the summer.'

'That's because, these days, August is the only chance I get to live in the real world. Officially, I'm holidaying here, hence the instruction to fly the royal standard of England[2]. The paparazzi know I'm here, so I'm not expected to be anywhere else, if you understand. Dorothea doesn't mind, and she's sensible enough not to ask questions. Maybe you don't show Diana enough appreciation?'

'Appreciation for the fact that she draws all the crowds, and no one ever wants to see me? America's obsessed with her. So much for "Chuck and Di". "Chuck" might as well have stayed at home. And she single-handedly transformed Australia from a would-be republic back into a pro-monarchy nation.'

'That sounds rather self-pitying. Personally, I couldn't care less about being the main attraction. It's the women who get to dress up and look glamorous. The tabloids don't give a damn about who makes our suits, or who designs our shoes and ties. Apart from minor details like lapel widths, one lounge suit is pretty much the same as any other. I wonder whether, next time you and I appear together at some premiere or whatever, we shouldn't both break with tradition and turn up in white, or even purple, DJs?'

'Not sure purple's my colour.'

'Lime green then. Do you have plans to rekindle the flame with Camilla?'

'The flame was never extinguished. But I don't have plans, because it's already back on again, though you're the only family member who knows. It was only ever a matter of time, and I did wait until Diana had been unfaithful first.'[3]

'So it's true then? It's been in the papers. Isn't she supposed to be having riding lessons? I don't think I've ever seen her on a real horse.'

'And who better than a household cavalry officer to teach her? There have even been suggestions that it's all been going on longer than anyone thinks and that James Hewitt is Harry's biological father. We always thought that the hair colouring was down to the Spencer influence.'

'That seems the much more likely explanation.'

'And Hewitt probably wasn't the first. One of the Royal Protection Squad officers has been mentioned.'

'Not Gerald?'

'No, not him,' Charles confirmed. 'At least I've stuck to just the one "extra-marital". But then, for years, there's only ever really been the one.'

'In that case, you're lucky. I'd take a mistress like a shot if I could find one I really fancied – and assuming I regain the energy. At one time not so very long ago, it would almost have been obligatory.'

'Things not going well with Dorothea?'

'So-so. Not brilliantly and not badly either. She's harmless enough. She works hard and does what's expected of her when it's expected of her. Says all the right things. Never puts her foot in it. Sits there most evenings, stitching away like some character out of Jane Austen. It's as though she's a pre-programmed replica of a real person, like one of those too-good-to-be-true Stepford wives. I'm fond of her but I'm not in love with her. I'm not even in lust with her. That would at least be something. I guess I'll just have to stick with it. Uncle David was right about the curse of the Windsor males.'

'Not just the males. Don't forget that Aunt Margot[4] divorced. And Anne's marriage to Fog[5] has been on the rocks for a good while. They've both been playing away[6]. Andrew and Fergie seem happy enough but, given current form, it can only be a matter of time before it's a full house.'

'They've only just had a baby[7]. You can't be writing them off already, surely?'

'Don't call me Shirley![8] No, I'm not, but he's away most of the time, and Fergie spent most of her pregnancy alone. She's already complaining about being deserted. All in all, we're a pretty hopeless bunch. Mama's already asking where she went wrong.'

James picked a blade of grass, chewed it, then made to stand up. The effort was too much. Instead, he flopped onto his back and stared at the sky.

'We really should see about getting you better,' said his nephew. 'You need to be up to full speed by November. Fortieth birthday bash and all that. I've asked Phil Collins to arrange it.'[9]

'With or without Genesis?'

'Without.'

'Pity. I could have caught up with some fellow Old Carthusians. Tony Banks and Peter Gabriel were in the year below me at school. Mike Rutherford was there, too. When did you arrange this?'

'Last month, at Wembley. That Prince's Trust Michael Jackson concert you missed.'

'I'm pleased you're finally getting up-to-date on the music front.'

'What do you mean "finally"? We did Live Aid. In fact, I was tempted to jet over to Philadelphia for the second event. I note you weren't at that one either.'

'You only stayed for a couple of hours before you took off to play polo! As for me, there was the slight impediment that I was in Kathmandu at the time. But I admit that the set list might have been a bit cheesy for my tastes.'

'And I did always like Motown,' Charles protested.

'Huh. Rock and roll with Wagnerian undertones.'

'On the subject of Wagner, I could ask whether your tastes have become any more cultured?'

'Problem with opera is that you have to sit through a whole load of singing before you get to the one decent song. When is someone going to do a live production of Puccini's greatest hits?'

'Philistine. Maybe you could commission it for your own fortieth? I'm sure it would go down far better with the wrinklies than a moonwalking Jacko-themed party.'

'And what's Phil going to play at your bash? "If Leaving Me Is Easy"? "It Don't Matter to Me"? How about "Doesn't Anybody Stay Together Anymore"?' James sighed wearily. 'I've been thinking.'

'What now? Are we going to start a new fashion trend by reintroducing the cravat?'

'No. Answer me one question. What illnesses cause the loss of more working days than any other?'

'Not a clue. Stress?'

'I haven't a clue either, and I hadn't thought of stress. I'm thinking more along the lines of those odd days off. People surely can't ring in sick with stress or depression one day, then return the next miraculously relaxed and happy again. So we're left with headaches, tummy bugs, and colds and flu. With me so far?'

'I guess so.'

'And which medical charities have royal patronage, not counting your Faculty of Homeopathy?'

'Quite a few, and most of them are mine incidentally. And then there are the various Royal Colleges like – '

'I'm asking rhetorically,' James interrupted. 'So how many of our charities are dedicated to clinical research *per se*? Answer: only a small handful. Now do you see where I'm going?'

'If you fancy supporting another research charity, I'm sure they'd be more than delighted to have you old chap. You don't need my endorsement.'

'I think I shall. It's weird that scientists can do so much these days but still haven't been able to find a cure for the common cold. Viruses have a lot to answer for, and not just measles and chickenpox. They cover a wide spectrum. They're probably the reason why my "get up and go" got up and went. They cause AIDS – and, incidentally, look what your wife did to transform public thinking on that. Some of them cause cancer. Some cause liver disease – '

'If I remember correctly, that one's Andrew's.'

'Whatever. I'll look into it and see where best to devote my energies, if and when I ever get any.'

'Well hurry up on both fronts. Oompa has been spouting on again about "too many people". He's said that, if he were reincarnated, he'd like to come back as a deadly virus, to help lower human population levels. His mutation might prove a very tough one to cope with.'

28

GLASGOW

Investigative journalist Rab Rainsmith wasn't paying much attention to the TV. He'd switched it on for company. Having spent the earlier part of the evening downing a pint or four with Jock, Rab was more interested in his supper. This consisted of dried-up toad-in-the-hole and mash. He was used to eating food that had spent a while in a warm oven, slowly dehydrating under a plate.

On the box was a Scottish television *Crimewatch*-type special about the reopening by Glasgow police of a number of historic missing persons cases. Glancing up, Rab just glimpsed an on-screen mug shot of a boy of about fourteen. It was one of those school pictures, in black and white. The kid, who was wearing a V-necked pullover, shirt and tie, had obviously been dragged off to the barber's beforehand.

The face was attractive and slightly sad-looking – possibly, Rab pondered, due to the recent enforced scalping. Several more name-captioned photos of different people flashed up, followed by the closing credits. Rab didn't mind that the programme had finished. He had, as always, set it to record and would watch it in full at some point.

That point came a few days later. Jeannie was visiting her mother, which she often did on a Sunday afternoon. He'd made a cup of tea, equipped himself with a pen and notebook (in which nothing had so far been jotted down), and had almost got through the entire thing when he heard the sound of his wife's key in the lock. Pausing the tape, he prepared to greet her. And there it was again – that same boy's face, frozen on the screen and seemingly staring at him in mute appeal.

The following day, he phoned Jock on a further quest for information and suggested they meet up again. This time Rab's enquiry wasn't about the imminent busting of a notorious Glasgow drugs' ring.

'Pushing your luck a bit, aren't you, mate?' Jock said, but agreed to do what he could, provided that Rab bought all the drinks. Rab almost always bought all the drinks, unless the tip-offs were working the other way round. The newshound did, occasionally, have some 'word on the street' titbit to offer his best police contact.

The men sat at their usual table in their usual pub. In front of them were tankards of what they usually drank, reposing in puddles of spillage and overflow.

'Not much to report mate,' Jock began. 'Case is still open but it was never high profile. Seems our Peter Lowry was a bit of a dropout. Last confirmed sighting of him was at a music festival near Pitlochry on 22nd June 1976. He wasn't reported as missing for another eight weeks.'

'Who reported him missing?'

'His mother. He didn't come home for her birthday. No matter how long he'd been away, and no matter what he'd been up to, apparently he never failed to return for that.'

'How recent was the photo?'

'Two or three years out of date.'

'Did she think it was still a good likeness?'

'File doesn't confirm that, except for a jotting saying "longer hair".'

'Was there a father?'

'None mentioned, so presumably a single mother for whatever reason.'

'Friends? Girlfriends?'

'Only the first names of a few local mates, I think.'

'Anything else?'

'No, apart from the fact that his mum thought he'd made a brief visit home in July. Not certain about the exact date. She was at work and didn't actually see him, but she was sure he'd been in his room and taken a few things. She also thought he'd helped himself to food. What sort of food wasn't noted in the file.'

'How far did the police enquiry get?'

'Hardly anywhere. I suspect it was just classed as another runaway. Why the sudden interest? Those antennae of yours twitching?'

'Not exactly. Just something a bit – well, "haunting" shall we say? – about his face. When does the update programme go out? You must've had some interest in the girls?'

The bulk of the TV special had been devoted to three young women, whose disappearances during the 1980s had made headline news at the time. Peter Lowry was just one of about twenty in a footnote group, compiled simply to provide a representative cross-section of people who'd vanished, never to be seen again.

'Off the record, I gather there may be a strong lead on one of them,' stated Jock. 'Looks like a murder case, unconnected to the other lassies. Beyond that, I can't say. I'm drugs squad now, remember?'

'I don't suppose there's any chance of featuring this Peter again in the follow-up? Asking for anyone who'd been at the Pitlochry bash to come forward?'

'You suppose right, mate. There is a limit.' Jock swigged the remainder of his pint, plonked down his glass and looked expectantly at his friend. Rab held his nerve.

'Home address of the mother then?'

With a show of reluctance, Jock nodded and said a grudging, 'Not that it'll do you much good.'

'Same again?' asked Rab.

The purchase of a third round won him the promise of a photo of the missing teen.

Two hours later, he was back at home, eating congealed stew. Jeannie was again on duty at the Royal Infirmary. If she wasn't doing a night shift, she was often out with her friends instead. He couldn't complain. She provided the main household income, and certainly the only steady income, and would continue to do so until he finally got the big scoop he'd been promising them both for so many years. He considered himself lucky to have such a tolerant partner. She kept faith in his dreams and always understood when he was 'on the trail of the big one'. In recent years, especially since he'd begun to accumulate weight around his middle, she fondly referred to him 'my little truffle pig'. It was to be hoped that, in the fullness of time, he'd bring home the bacon.

These days, he had almost given up on another royal exclusive. He'd only just heard, from his contact at *The Sun*, that another big story was about to break – one which even the editors considered 'too hot to handle'. A bunch of steamy love letters, stolen from Princess Anne's personal briefcase, had been sent anonymously to the newspaper. Written by Timothy Lawrence, the King's equerry, they'd been passed to Scotland Yard. Enquiries were ongoing in an attempt to identify the perpetrator of the theft.

'They'll be lucky,' thought Rab, as he chiselled away at the last remnants of dried-up gravy.

March 1990

Laburnum Close, Ewell

'Does Janet want anyfin' special for 'er birthday?' Peggy asked Lil. 'I know it's a bit early to be finkin' about it, but still.'

'She hasn't mentioned anything. She seems to have everything she needs for her house. We got her a new duvet set for Christmas, and I'm not even sure she wanted one of those. She doesn't like clutter, so ornaments are out of the question. Looks like we're going to be struggling with what to buy her, too.'

'Somefin' red might be appropriate, as it'll be 'er fortief.'

'Where did that time go, Peg? It doesn't seem five minutes.'

'It seems a bit longer than that to me, but I know what you mean. If I'd looked ahead forty years ago to now, I'd 'ave imagined us both still in Deptford, sittin' around bein' terrorised by loads of grandkids and comparin' notes. Ah well. What about a lava lamp? They're supposed to be very soothin' to watch.'

'I've only just turfed out that orange one I brought from Glenholme Road!'

Peggy was thoughtful. 'She's 'ad her ears pierced, 'asn't she?'

'Yes.'

'Well, what about ruby studs?'

'I'm not sure,' said Lil. 'She doesn't go in for jewellery much. But you've given me an idea. All she wears is that little silver cloverleaf pendant – the one you gave her.'

'I nevva got 'er no pendant.'

'Oh. I always thought you bought it for her. Perhaps it was from Harold and Daisy then? I don't remember thanking them for it, and it's a bit late now. Anyhow, I'm wondering whether I could get a pair of earrings made to match. Little ones. She doesn't do dangly. I suppose that's because they'd get in the way when she's looking down microscopes. '

''ow are you gonna manage that wivvout 'er knowin'?'

'She's visiting for Easter. That's if she can tear herself away from Liverpool. I'm sure Terry will be able to think of something.'

'Is 'e enjoyin' retirement?'

'Seems to be. He's got his workshop with all the equipment and has started making model traction engines. There's a club nearby, so he has a lot of friends who all like playing with toys. They must be in their second childhood. Some days, I hardly see him from morning to evening, except for lunch. Funny how a man who could rewire Jodrell Bank can't manage to butter a slice of bread.'

'Ralph's the exact opposite. Since 'e sold up, 'e's bin learnin' to cook. 'e's always experimentin' in the kitchen. But ask 'im to change a light bulb, and 'e wouldn't know where to start.'

'We've been lucky, haven't we? I know Terry and I have had our ups and downs, but we've stuck together.'

'Me and Ralph 'ave, too. We 'ad that rough patch, when runnin' the shop was gettin' too much for 'im and 'e wouldn't sell. But 'e saw sense in the end and never looked back. Princess Elizabeth and Phillip must've 'ad a few bumps along the way, but they're still togevva an' all.'

'Which is more than can be said for their kids. It looks like Mum was right after all, when she predicted that Charles and Diana wouldn't last.'

'I never saw it comin'. The romance was straight out of Barbara Cartland, 'cept they didn't live 'appily ever after.'

'Is Freddie still with that girl he met at university?'

'Which one? I've lost count.'

'The one with the red hair, who was on his course.'

'Search me. I fink she was the *only* girl on 'is course. You don't get many doin' civil engineerin'. Why d'you ask?'

'I just wondered whether he'd settle down. He's our only hope for a grandchild. I've given up on Janet, and her biological clock is ticking away.'

Knowing how touchy she could be, Lil always watched her words and was very careful never to remind Peggy of Freddie's origins. The boy had been brought up as Ralph and Peggy's son. Though he knew he was adopted, that was the extent of it. Whether he ever wondered about how closely he resembled his supposed cousin Janet was another matter.

'Don't forget what 'appened to Queen Elizabeth. There's 'ope yet,' said her sister.

17TH OCTOBER 1991

THE EARL OF WILLASTON'S APARTMENT, BUCKINGHAM PALACE

'When's the announcement to be?' Charles asked his uncle.

'Not until they've done another scan. In the circumstances, they want to make as certain as possible that things will turn out well.'

'Are there any twins in the FitzGilbert family?'

'Yes. Her grandmother on the Duke's side is one of twins. Non-identical. Are there any in our family, Eustace?'

Upon his return from a short official trip to Britain's oldest ally Portugal, James had arranged to have a chat with his mentor. They'd later been joined by Charles, who'd called in at the palace on spec. The three men were sitting as comfortably as possible, given the battered state of the sofas. Eustace had poured them a gin and tonic apiece, complete with slices of the lemon he'd brought with him. Neither he nor James could understand why he was never provided with any from the royal kitchens, despite repeated requests from His Majesty. Charles had come up with an idea, and they'd agreed on the theory of the 'Phantom Lemon Snatcher of Buck House'. This mysterious being, who suffered from scurvy, stalked the back stairs in search of life-saving vitamin C.

'They're rare,' answered the Earl. 'William IV's wife gave birth to stillborn twin sons. Before that, you'd have to go back to the fifteenth century, when Queen Joan of Scotland produced twins, also both boys.'

'I don't know how you remember all this stuff,' commented the King. 'Presumably, the first to be born becomes heir, even if it's only by a few minutes.'

'That's the way it works. Although, if the first's a girl and the second's a boy, he will of course take precedence.'

'It doesn't seem very fair in this day and age of equality, does it?' observed Charles.

Eustace laughed. 'Your grandfather and I once had a similar discussion. Neither of us could envisage a time when absolute primogeniture would apply. I have to say that it's now beginning to seem like a more realistic prospect, though I probably won't live to see it happen.'

'What if they're the same sex and delivered at exactly the same time by caesarean section? They did mention that possibility for Dorothea.'

'I'm guessing that the Royal Gynaecologist would then have to decide.'

'What a huge responsibility. I wonder what the criteria would be?'

'Now you really do have me stumped, Charles. Not my territory at all and never was. Perhaps it would be the one which was in pole position to be born naturally?'

'Nice analogy, Eustace,' said James.

'I do think it's terribly clever of you, Jimmy, to be getting two in a single go,' chipped in Charles.

'It's called effort-effectiveness, old boy. Easier on Dorothea and on me. I only had to perform the once and bingo.'

21ST OCTOBER 1991

EWELL WEST STATION

'Exciting, isn't it?' said Lil, giving her sister a hug.

'What?'

'Of course, you won't have heard. It's just been on the news. The Queen's expecting twins.'

'At last. The royals are usually quicker off the mark than that. When are they due?'

'Spring's all they've said. That could mean any time from March to May. Funny to think that Princess Elizabeth won't be heir any more.'

'She must break all the records for someone 'overin' in the wings.'

'No, she doesn't. There was an interview with some old bloke called the Earl of Whatever, and he said that Edward VII was heir for nearly sixty years, because Queen Victoria reigned for so long. But Elizabeth's a close second. Come on, the car's parked just round the corner. Won't take us long to drive there.'

'Where are we goin'?'

'There's a new restaurant in Esher. Connie from the WI recommended it, so I thought we'd give it a try for lunch.'

'Are we celebratin' somefin'?'

'No, I just thought it'd make a change.'

'Well, there may be somefin' to celebrate soon, but I don't

wanna to tempt fate. Freddie's bringing 'is girlfriend to stay next weekend, and 'e says they 'ave an announcement to make.'

'Do you think they might be getting engaged?'

'Could be that, or else she's pregnant. These days, it don't seem to matter no more if the parents aren't married. 'ow fings 'ave changed, eh? If she is up the duff, it might be born the same day as the King's babies. That would be a coincidence.'

'It certainly would, especially as I had Janet the same time as Princess Anne was born. Anyhow, sounds like it might be good news either way. Here we are. Hop in. Drat. Some bloody idiot's parked too close.'

Lil had to perform a series of manoeuvres to liberate the car.

'Is Freddie's girl still the redhead?' she asked, once they were finally underway.

'Yes. 'er name's Laura. She seems very nice.'

'Does she work in Manchester, too?'

'Stockport, I fink 'e said, but they share the same flat, so it can't be that far away. They're not far from Janet, eivva. Funny 'im and 'er both ending up livin' up norf. By the way, I never did ask if she liked 'er earrings.'

'That was more than a year ago. But yes she did, or so she said.'

''ow did you wangle gettin' them copied in secret?'

'It was a right palaver. As soon as she arrived, Terry noticed that the clasp on the chain had worked round to the front, then told her it looked like it was coming apart and offered to solder it. He said that, if it broke, the pendant could drop off and she might lose it. So, very reluctantly, she handed it over, he whisked it away, and I nipped to the little jeweller's shop in the village first thing next morning. I told the man that I wanted the same design, only smaller. He took photos and made an impression, quick as you please, and I was back before Janet was halfway through her breakfast.'

'So did Terry mend the clasp?'

'There was nothing wrong with it, silly. But he put a blob of solder on it, just for the sake of appearances. The earrings were a shocking price.'

'I s'pose they would 'ave been, if they were specially made to match.'

'It wasn't that so much. The jeweller took one look and told me the pendant was platinum, not silver like we always thought. Can you believe that?'

CHAPTER 28

1992

29

Peggy didn't often suffer from migraines. They'd only started after she turned fifty, and were usually heralded by hazy vision. Sometimes, taking a couple of paracetamols could ward them off, but tablets didn't always work. This time, the attack was so severe that she had no option but to close the curtains and retire to bed. To start with, she thought she was imagining things, but the bangs resonated like knives through her brain. She mustered the energy to crawl out from under the duvet, stagger downstairs and ask Ralph what the blazes was going on.

He told her that a royal salute[1] was being fired from the Tower of London, to mark the arrival of two princesses. Briefly wondering where all the cannonballs were landing, she returned to bed and was fast asleep when Freddie rang to say that Laura had just gone into labour.

'*Her Majesty The Queen was this morning safely delivered of a daughter at 04:08 and a second daughter at 04:15. Her Majesty and the two princesses are all doing well.*'

This announcement prompted three immediate questions. How much did the babies weigh? Were they identical? What would they be called? The information that they were both just under six pounds and were maternal twins emerged quite quickly. Following confirmation that 'maternal' meant non-identical, the only speculation that now remained concerned the choice of names.

'And therein lies the problem,' James told Eustace. They were sitting in the palace garden, making the most of the unseasonably warm sunshine. 'Dorothea says she's not going through all that again. It seemed to be a tricky business, so I can't say I blame her, which means that the very angry orangutan with the "Windsor 1" wrist band will end up as queen some day.'

'Before you were born, I once compiled a historical list of girls' names for your parents to consider. The choice was not quite so important, of course, because had you been another daughter, it was unlikely you'd ever have succeeded to the throne.'

'I do know I'd have been way down the pecking order by now. Where would I have ranked?'

Eustace did a swift totting up of Elizabeth and Margaret's descendants.

'By my reckoning, you'd currently have been fourteenth in line.'

'So I might have ended up spending all my days on a tropical island, living next door to Margot.'

'I don't think that sort of lifestyle would have suited you, James.'

'No. Not in the slightest. I might have had a bit more time to mess around with boats though. A Lake District retreat wouldn't have been the worst idea, apart from the fact that it always seems to be raining up there.'

'When is your family returning from hospital?'

'Later on today. I'll be running the gauntlet of the world's press. They've been camped outside the Lindo Wing for days. I only hope I don't trip and drop a baby on the steps. Dorothea wants me to emerge carrying both of them. She thinks it would look modern.'

'Have you and Dorothea got anywhere on the subject of what to call them?'

'We've hardly talked about anything else, apart from referring to them as "Noisy" and "Even Noisier".'

'Does Her Majesty have any preferences?'

'Not really. She's good at ruling things out, but not very good at putting suggestions forward. Worse still, she's leaving the final decision to me, as she usually does.'

'I know your wife's mother, the Duchess of Albemarle, is Agnes – '

'Neither of us is keen on that. Or on her mother, come to think of it. One of her grandmothers is Anne and the other was Beatrice – both already nabbed by close family members.'

'We perhaps wouldn't contemplate a Queen Bee anyway?'

'You see, that's the tricky bit. A Queen Esmeralda would sound like a character from a Disney film, and a Queen Loretta would sound like a drag artist, not that either of those was ever a contender.'

'I'm relieved to hear it.'

'Margaret's also out of the running, in case a certain ex-prime minister should feel unduly honoured. But I did wonder about Mercedes, Ferrari or Porsche,' said a straight-faced James.

'Now we're getting somewhere,' countered the Earl with an equally deadpan expression.

'What would I have been called?'

'That was, I believe, never fully resolved. But should it be of any assistance, I do know what your father favoured.'

'Which was?'

'He liked both Matilda and Eleanor.'

'Perfect. That's settled, then. It would be almost a special private tribute to him, wouldn't it? Do you think our giving those names to his granddaughters would have made him happy?'

Eustace looked at his sovereign's face. The eager trusting puppy-dog expression was one he'd seen many times before. It reminded him of the boy he'd known, the boy who'd never quite been fully absorbed into adulthood.

'I'm sure it would. And that knowledge makes me very happy, too.'

18TH JUNE 1992

GLASGOW

'*2.637 kilograms. That's what the newest members of the royal family weighed in at. Does anyone have any concept of how heavy that is? How does a bouncing 3.63kg baby sound? Doesn't have quite the same ring to it as an eight pounder, does it?*

A friend of mine has recently renamed his property. It is no longer "Five Acre Farm". His address is now "20,234 Square Metre Farm", and he makes a point of ensuring everyone uses it.

Under the 1985 Weights and Measures Act, it became illegal for traders to sell most commodities in imperial units. You can't buy half a pound of mince anymore. Well you can, if you ask for 227 grams. We no longer buy petrol by the gallon, though we still buy beer by the pint. Car dashboards must, by law, feature kilometres but who, on our illogical island where everyone still travels in miles, notices?'

Queen Elizabeth's steeplechasers are still priced in guineas...'

Rab's cynical feature sold reasonably well, which was handy, because the overworked oven had finally given up the ghost.

The journalist had almost forgotten about the missing

youth, despite having begun with such enthusiasm. From a neighbour, he discovered that Peter's mother had died several years earlier, which was disappointing news. Although that same neighbour had been able to suggest the name of the secondary school which young Peter had probably attended, this information didn't promise to be productive, as later confirmed by a visit to the school, and an encounter with a scary secretary. How was she supposed to know which kid had hung out with which other kids more than a decade earlier?

Another neighbour thought Peter might have been mates with the boy from the newsagents, the one who used to deliver her morning papers. She told him where the shop was, and he discovered that it was still owned by the same couple. Their son, though, had emigrated to New Zealand. They supplied an address, but there was never any response from the letter the investigator subsequently wrote.

He tried trawling the internet, but there was nothing about Bannervale School. It crossed his mind that someone should invent a website, allowing pupils and students who'd lost touch to reunite. Keying in other search words proved equally futile. Without much hope, and with a twinge of guilt about almost certainly wasting money they could ill afford, he placed advertisements in *The Scotsman* and in what he considered to be a good spread of regional newspapers, but these were unproductive. Over the next few months, he made occasional half-hearted searches, again with no luck.

It was therefore with some surprise that, three years after starting his quest, he received a call from a man called Alan, whose mother had picked up on the small personal column insert in the *Fife Courier*. Wondering whether it might be of interest to her son, she'd cut it out, put it in a kitchen drawer and never given it another thought until coming across the scrap of paper during a rummage for birthday cake candles.

When the phone rang, Rab was re-reading a newly published

book entitled *Diana: Her True Story*[2]. Supposedly sourced from the Princess's close friends and confidantes, the journalist knew that it hadn't been. This was despite denials from the palace that she'd had nothing to do with it. Rab had been following the speculation about the Wales's marriage and suspected this was just the start of a publicity war between the couple. He wasn't sure where his sympathies lay. Jeannie sided firmly with Charles and even more firmly with the idea of a republic.

Alan lived in Stirling, which thankfully wasn't too far away, and expressed himself willing to meet up, suggesting that his local golf club, the aptly named Blair Allan, would be a suitable venue. Rab would have preferred a pub, but beggars couldn't be choosers.

The man wasn't what the investigator expected, but why shouldn't someone who'd spent a summer during his youth hanging out at music festivals turn into a prosperous accountant? He'd had one and a half decades to effect the transformation.

Prior to the rendezvous, Rab had paid a visit to Malc, a mate who worked in a photography studio and who'd proved helpful now and then. He'd asked his friend to alter the photo of the presumed runaway by aging the face slightly and lengthening the short back and sides.

Rab held his breath as Alan studied the image. It was a long shot. But, almost immediately, Alan said, 'Yes, that's Pete.'

'Did you know him well?'

'I wouldn't have said we were best friends. But we hung out in the same group for a while. Pitlochry wasn't a huge event. It wasn't well organised, and bands seemed to turn up as and when. Not at all like Glastonbury these days.'

'Do you remember anything particular about him?'

'I have to admit that, some of the time, my recollections get a bit hazy. Literally so. There was a lot of the wacky baccy around. Pete was one of the ones who also popped pills. Uppers.

Downers. You name it. I was too chicken to try those, and stuck to the pot. Hey, you're not going to quote me on this, are you? I've got my reputation to think about.'

'You have my word that I won't, Alan. All I'm trying to do is find him. Any idea what became of him?'

'Sorry, not sure I can help. I returned home, went back to school like a good little boy and eventually transformed into the respectable citizen you see before you today. I've never come across anyone from that time since, not that I'd recognise them if I did.'

'Can I get you a refill?' Rab asked, noting that Alan's glass was almost empty.

'Please, but stick it on my tab again, will you? I'm on the Talisker. And have another yourself – maybe something a bit stronger this time?'

Given that someone else was paying, the journalist happily procured two single malts. This was much better than a local pub! As he was returning to the table, he noted that his generous host appeared to be meditating. The man, leaning on his elbows and with a balled-up fist covering each eye, was gently rocking to and fro. Rab stopped in his tracks. For a good three minutes, he stood still, unwilling to break the spell. Eventually, Alan emerged from wherever he'd been and shook himself, like a dog which had got wet in a pond.

'There were a few girls,' he began, once Rab had rejoined him. 'I had a bit of a thing for one of them. A wee lassie called Shonagh, from the Isle of Skye, who may well account for my taste in whisky. On a subconscious level of course. We couldn't afford the good stuff in those days.'

Rab, knowing an untimely prompt might send any resurfacing memories scurrying away, waited in silence. He waited in vain. At least the trip had cost him no more than half a tank of petrol.

26TH AUGUST 1992

COBOURG ROAD, BERMONDSEY

On 19th August 1992, 'the pictures they didn't want you to see' were splashed all over the front page of the *Daily Mirror*. These had been taken by an Italian photographer and showed a topless Sarah, Duchess of York, lying on a poolside sunlounger, having her toes sucked by Texan millionaire John Bryan. The pair, who were holidaying in St Tropez, were accompanied by two bodyguards (apparently literally caught napping), and by the young Princesses Beatrice and Eugenie. More sensational photos featured on nine inside pages.

Rab would have given anything to be a fly on the wall in the breakfast room at Balmoral. One of his favourite fantasies was that he could become invisible.

A mere four days later, *The Sun* newspaper published a front-page revelation of the existence of a tape recording. This was of a conversation between Diana, Princess of Wales, and a close male friend. A special phone line enabled the public to listen to the contents, assuming they were prepared to pay more than ten pounds for the privilege. Rab dialled the number, but failed to pick up on any gem worthy of pursuing.

Both Peggy and Lil also considered the cost of listening in to be a worthwhile investment. It gave them a lot to talk about when they met a few days later at Peggy's, although they didn't get onto the topic until Lil had looked through the latest photos of her 'great-nephew' Nathan.

Disappointingly, Freddie and Laura's son didn't share the same birthday as the royal twins, but he'd put in an appearance soon after midnight the following day, so the timing had been close-run. Lil had last seen the child on his first birthday, which had been celebrated at Ron's. Ron, of course, had always been party to the family secret and kept referring to Nathan as 'me great-great-grandson'. If Freddie and Laura noticed what, from their point of view, seemed to be an extraneous 'great', they didn't comment.

'Goodness, he's grown. They change so quickly at that age,' observed Lil, as she handed back the pictures. 'I expect he's into everything, now he's walking.'

''e certainly is. They've 'ad to put soft corners on all the low tables, which he keeps takin' off. There are locks on the kitchen cupboards and a gate to stop 'im climbin' the stairs,' Peggy confirmed. 'And they 'ave to remember to switch off the washing machine at the socket, because 'e 'as a fing about pressin' buttons and kept settin' it off. Freddie let's 'im turn it on when there's a load of washin' to do, as a special treat.'

'Freddie does the washing?'

'Yes. And 'e's a whizz wiv the 'oover an' all, apparently. It's all equality these days. Ralph never changed a nappy. 'e'd prob'ly 'ave put it on the wrong end.'

'Terry tried once, when I'd popped out and left him in charge. He forgot the plastic pants, so Janet needed to be wrung out by the time I got back. No marriage plans yet?'

'Never bin mentioned. I don't fink they'll be in any 'urry. It's only a ceremony, after all.'

'Can you imagine saying that even twenty years ago, Peg?'

'No, but you 'ave to move wiv the times. 'appiness is what matters. 'ow's Dad? Did you tell 'im I'll be round on Friday, as usual?'

Lil had called in on their father, before this visit to her sister's.

'Yes, and he's fine. Same as always. I know he misses Mum, but he seems to have got a lot of lady friends who are more than happy to cook for him.'

'I don't bovva takin' 'im food anymore, unless Ralph's made an extra portion of goat curry, which is 'is favourite.'

'Sounds adventurous for Dad. He's always liked his traditional grub.'

"e doesn't know it's goat. We tell 'im it's lamb.'

Lil sighed. 'Poor Mum. She'd have enjoyed saying "I told you so", now she's been proved right about Charles and Di.'

'Maybe she can 'ear us now from the spirit world. Didn't Di say somefin' about people she'd loved lookin' down on 'er?'

'And the rest. I can't make up my mind whether she's being treated badly, or whether she's paranoid. Or it could be a bit of both. I wonder why the man kept calling her Squidge, with a figure like hers. Not exactly a lot for a man to grab hold of.'

'You couldn't say the same about us, could you?' laughed Peggy.

'The royals seem to be having more than their fair share of scandals, don't they?'

'I'm not sure. I fink it's only because they *are* royals. If someone snapped me an' the milkman in a compromisin' position, it wouldn't make 'eadline news. An' I don't s'pose anyone's listenin' in to my phone calls eivva.'

'Let's hope Mum got it wrong about the King and Queen. I did wonder whether they were having problems before the kiddies arrived, but maybe that was just down to nature.'

The royal family had even more to contend with as the year wore on, when a curtain was ignited by a spotlight in the Private Chapel at Windsor Castle. The resultant fire quickly spread and, very soon, large parts of the State Apartments were ablaze. The conflagration took fifteen hours to bring under control, and there followed a public debate about who should meet the costs of repairing the extensive damage.

Princess Elizabeth, for whom the castle held many happy memories, dubbed 1992 her *annus horribilis*. The year had seen the divorce of her only daughter, and the separations from their wives of her two older sons. The one happier event had been Anne's second marriage in December, but this did not prove to be the hoped-for turning point in the Windsors' private lives.

18TH JANUARY 1993

KENSINGTON PALACE

1993 certainly started no better. A transcript of the so-called Camillagate tape was published in January. With its intimate content and references to tampons, the bedtime dialogue left no one in doubt about the passionate relationship between two lovers – who were both, at the time, still married to other people.

'You idiot!' said James. 'Didn't you learn from Squidgygate?'

'Actually, our conversation was recorded in 1989 a couple of weeks before Diana and Gilbey's,' Charles replied.

'Were they putting some libido-enhancing drug in the coffee at Kensington Palace at the time, or was it all down to seasonal lust?'

'Have you rung just to tear me off a strip? If so, join the queue. They've all been consulting the thesaurus for every possible synonym for "disgusting".'

'No, old boy. I was about to give you some avuncular advice. Disguise your voices next time and use false names. And try to steer clear of the graphic. Was it the same hacker?'

'Not sure, but does it matter?'

'I don't suppose so.'

'Where are you? It's a remarkably good line.'

'Guyana. Tropical climate, so the weather's nice and they

speak English. Democratic regime. Decent food, though the green beans could do with a haircut. Virtually impenetrable rainforests, which they're doing their best to protect. I can heartily recommend it, if you need somewhere ecological to escape to.'

'I don't think I have any option but to ride it out.' Charles did not sound happy. 'I've looked in on the girls, by the way.'

'Thanks. And how are they?'

'Fine. Their "Nanny Annie" is totally brilliant with them, isn't she? Tricky beings, nannies. Seems they have to be fond of their charges, but not too fond. It must be a tricky balance to strike.'

'More problems with the hired help? What's happened now?'

'Diana doesn't like Tiggy. Thinks she's too possessive with Wills and Harry, for starters. Same thing happened with Nanny "Baba". The boys adored her, and she was sacked without even being allowed to say goodbye. She was even banned from sending them so much as a postcard. It was a case of a mother figure vanishing into thin air, and it left them totally bewildered. Wouldn't you have thought that the whole point of having someone to look after your children is that they all get on well together? Remember Nanny Lightbody?'

'Who could forget? She really was daunting, and I don't scare easily. You said "for starters"? What did you mean by that?'

'Diana thinks I'm having an affair with Tiggy, and that Camilla is just a decoy.'

'Well if that's the case, she's a pretty damned convincing one.'

In July 1994, during the course of a television interview with Jonathan Dimbleby, Prince Charles admitted to adultery, but emphasised that this was only after his marriage to Diana had irretrievably broken down, despite their both having tried to make a go of it. The 'War of the Waleses' continued to be played out publicly. In 1995, Princess Diana featured on the BBC programme *Panorama* and told Martin Bashir that her husband's affair with Camilla made her feel worthless. She described her marriage as 'crowded', because there were three of them in it, and spoke of her bulimia and attempts at self-harm.

Shortly afterwards, Princess Elizabeth intervened and told the couple to get divorced.

1996

30

PORCHESTER GARDENS, BAYSWATER, LONDON

James was worried. Eustace's son Howard was in Saudi Arabia and, although summoned to return to Britain on the first available flight, might not arrive in time. Cathy, he knew, was already at the house in Bayswater, and the King had ordered a car to take him there immediately after Edith Heggarty, Countess of Willaston, had telephoned the palace.

Eustace was in the main living room, half sitting and half lying on a reclining chair. He looked comfortable and didn't appear to be suffering, though what could be seen of his face beyond the oxygen mask was a ghastly white, despite the warm glow of a living flame gas fire. The crinkled corners of his eyes were the only clue that he was smiling. James waved a dismissive hand as his mentor made to get up.

'I've brought your annual stipend,' he said, handing over a bag to Edith.

The Earl mumbled something unintelligible, so Cathy eased off the mask. 'Somehow, I don't think I'll be exercising my shooting rights at Balmoral this year, Your Majesty,' he repeated.

'Then I'll just have to shoot the little beggars on your behalf,

293

if you don't make it,' replied James, with a querying glance at the countess, who shook her head.

'I didn't fail you, did I, dear boy?'

'You most certainly didn't. You've always been there for me. No one could have wished for a wiser guide, or a better friend.'

'Forty-seven years ago to the day. Your father and I had such fun deciding what official role I could...' The words tailed off. Cathy reapplied the mask, and Eustace took several deep breaths before speaking again. 'You see, I always thought there was something you felt you couldn't tell me and, because of that, I wondered if I'd let you down?'

'No. Never. I'll tell you now what it was,' said James, and proceeded to do just that. The words fell on deaf ears. The Earl of Willaston had passed peacefully away, his wife and daughter both clinging to one hand – and his kneeling sovereign holding the other.

When James finally returned to Buckingham Palace, he braced himself and visited the late earl's apartment. There, on the table beside the gin bottle, was a lemon. At the sight of it, His Majesty broke down and wept.

2ND AUGUST 1996

BLAIR ALLAN GOLF CLUB, STIRLINGSHIRE

More than seven years on, his futile search for a missing boy was but a distant memory. The same applied to any number of other potential stories, all of which had simply faded into the mists of time. Rab's career as a freelancer was going nowhere. He should never have let his wife persuade him to give up his job with the *Evening Times*. It had, at least, provided a reliable source of income. He'd now completed three novels. In all of these, his fictional private detective had enjoyed far more success than his yet-to-be-published creator. But still Jeannie kept the faith and kept the new oven on low of an evening.

Then came an unexpected call.

'I had a dream!' declared the voice. Rab didn't recognise it.

'Who's speaking, please? Martin Luther King Junior?'

'It's Alan Smethurst. We met a few years ago. You were looking for Peter. Did you find him?'

'No.'

'Well, I had this dream last night. It was all very muddled. One minute I was in my own garden, digging up bags of fusilli pasta, then I was using them to fuel a camp fire, which we were all sitting round singing "We Shall Not Be Moved". Peter was there and some of the others. I've only remembered bits and pieces though, and probably nothing useful.'

Rab, who believed he was fairly skilled at getting people to retrieve information from their memory banks, knew that a telephone line was not the best conduit. With nothing better to do, he arranged to meet Alan later on and told him to jot down any further recollections in the meantime.

At his would-be informant's insistence, the venue for the meet would again be the golf club, and the drinks were once again on him. Despite the generous hospitality he was offering, Alan seemed apologetic. 'I hope I haven't dragged you here on a wild goose chase.'

'No worries,' said Rab, looking round. The place was busier than last time, probably due to the fact that it was a Friday afternoon, and the POETS brigade was there in full force. 'Piss Off Early, Tomorrow's Saturday' was a working-hours philosophy to which he necessarily couldn't subscribe. 'It's nice to have a change of scenery, not to mention a decent wee dram. And it's good of you to bother calling me, Alan. Not many people would have taken the trouble to do that.'

'Well, what I remembered probably doesn't amount to much. It's only really that Peter was close – closer than I ever managed to get with my lassie Shonagh – to one of the other girls. That's about the sum total of it. Her name's been on the tip of my tongue since I rang you, but I still can't for the life of me – '

'Steady on. Just take a deep breath, and try going through the alphabet,' Rab suggested.

Alan had a sip of malt, leant forward and stared at the section of wall just beyond Rab's left ear, concentration written on his face. The journalist, watching him nod for each letter, counted to twenty-six. There was a pause before the head movements resumed. This time, Alan hesitated after the sixth nod, then continued steadily onwards.

'Third time lucky?'

Again the rhythmic sequence briefly faltered after 'F'.

'Faye? Felicity? Frances?' Rab suggested.

'No. None of those. I keep nearly getting it.'

'Fiona?'

Alan stared morosely into his glass, swirling its contents.

'It wasn't a proper name. It was a sort of nickname… Got it! It was Fizz! Or was it Fliss? Something like that anyway.'

'What did this – let's call her Fizz – look like?' Rab felt a strange tingle run down his spine and was suddenly struggling to contain his excitement. If he was on the right track, the name was almost certainly not Fizz but something very close to it.

'Blonde. Not natural, I don't think. She was little. Not tiny but I'd say shorter than average, and she was a bit on the chubby side. Not my type.'

'Do you know where she was from?'

'Absolutely no idea.'

'Did she have a regional accent of any sort?'

Alan frowned in an effort to remember.

'Come to think of it, I don't think she did. Nothing obvious.

Not like Peter. He was as Glaswegian as they come.'

'Do you know where they were planning to go after Pitlochry? Another festival maybe?'

'Afraid not. A few were heading down to Devon, for some sort of folk gig, but I really couldn't say whether Peter was one of the ones planning on doing that. Sorry I can't be more helpful.'

'You've been very helpful indeed. Thanks, Alan. If I need to, can I get in touch again?'

With the glimmer of an idea, Rab was driven forward by pure instinct. Once back in his shabby rented office, he searched through numerous images on the internet, but none of them fitted the bill. There was no option but to travel to Aberdeen, which he did the following Wednesday.

The reference room in the main library there was hot and stuffy and, after several hours spent trawling through miles of microfilm, Rab was having difficulty focusing. Eventually, he found something that might do. It was a slightly fuzzy photo of a young dark-haired gymkhana winner. She was standing proudly beside her pony, which was apparently named Trixiebell. That fitted with what he already knew. The librarian, not pleased about having to put herself out, showed no enthusiasm for the task of providing a paper copy and barely glanced at what she was being asked to reproduce. As she handed over the result of her grudging endeavours, she was banging on about something to do with copyright charges.

Rab wasn't worried about that. He paid the basic fee, exited as quickly as he could and headed straight for the nearest pub. There, because he was driving, he restricted himself to a pint of shandy. Once settled, he drew out his purchase from its envelope. The low-resolution picture seemed even blurrier than before, but he knew he wasn't going to find anything better.

29TH AUGUST 1996

DRAWING ROOM, BALMORAL

'Enter a free man!' James greeted his nephew with more cheerfulness than he felt.

'What are you doing here?' asked Charles. 'I thought you were busy sorting out second-hand clothes in a Bolton charity shop?'

'It was Blackburn, actually, but a man needs to spend a bit of time with his family now and then. And the Countess of Willaston is up here for a few days. I thought a bit of Scottish air might do her good.'

'How is she?'

'Coping better than I am. I must apologise for my lack of sympathy when Uncle Dickie died. I know now how you felt. How long does it take to get over such a bereavement?'

'I'll let you know when I get there.'

'That doesn't sound good. So tell me, what's it like being divorced?'

'I haven't really taken it in yet. Andrew said it doesn't feel very different, but then he and Fergie always got along. They might still be together if she hadn't blotted her copybook in such a spectacular way. There's no chance she'll be welcomed back into the family fold.'

'Do you think there's a chance that Camilla might be accepted, in time?' James asked.

'No way. She'll be cast as the wicked witch forever. Can't see public opinion ever wavering from their adoration of St Diana. But at least I can carry on seeing her with a clearer conscience. Not openly, of course, but where's the story? If it's picked up that we're still close, that's all anyone will be able to report. The press can keep rephrasing it any way they like, till everyone starts saying "so tell us something we don't know". How's Dorothea?'

'Happily stitching away robotically. She's trying to teach Matilda and Eleanor, but neither of them seems interested.'

'Not thought any more about producing a son and heir?'

'I wondered about cloning. Like they did with that sheep.'[1]

31

30TH SEPTEMBER 1996

GLASGOW

Rab's friend in the photo shop had looked at the image with some surprise. 'Surely that's – ?'

Malc's observation was encouraging.

'Possibly. Can you do what I want, please? And not a word to anyone.'

'What are you up to, Rab? Planning a cartoon submission to *Private Eye*? And what's in it for me?'

Rab hesitated. 'Ten per cent of what I earn, if this comes off? Or a slap-up dinner later this month?'

'I'll take the dinner,' said Malc. 'A bird in the hand and all that.'

This would not turn out to be the wisest decision Malc had ever made.

Alan had needed only to glance at the doctored image before saying, 'Yes. That's her. Or it could well be.' On the basis of this affirmation, Rab spared no expense. Speed was now of essence. He paid a top-class researcher, who was sworn to secrecy, to get copies of what he needed. Meanwhile, he gave a lot of thought to the question of how best to play it.

Engineering an opportunity for outright confrontation

could be difficult. He didn't fancy marching up to imposing, and probably locked, gates and pressing an intercom, even though stating his business could well gain him access – or, then again, not necessarily.

A more devious approach seemed the better option, if he could think of a way of pulling it off. And it might prove more productive. As for bait, there were a couple of possibilities.

First, the Duke had just written a book about Scottish relics, and an extra plug for that might not be unwelcome. Secondly, His Grace was reportedly making a number of improvements to the jolly old ancestral home, with a view to opening it up to the public after Easter next year. There were also plans to take in paying guests. For an exorbitant price, people could join weekend house parties, which promised two days of 1920s-style decadence in the company of like-minded (i.e. filthy rich) companions. The word was that, despite the Duke's lofty connections, there hadn't exactly been a rush to sign up.

As Rab figured it, any positive publicity would attract more visitors. This would surely be a tempting prospect. He'd have to claim that he'd been commissioned by a major national publication to produce the article. To say he was writing anything as a freelancer, without the guarantee of getting into print, was unlikely to secure him an interview. It wouldn't be difficult to cobble together an official-looking letter from *The Times*. If he ran it through a photocopier or attached it to an email, any defects would be unnoticeable.

The scheme worked. Before the visit, Rab did his homework. He bought, and dutifully read, *The Stone of Destiny*, which was actually quite interesting.

In case he needed to confirm his credentials, he also put together a folder containing some of his higher-profile articles. His most impressive scoop, if you could call it that, had been a product of sheer good luck. He'd been in an Edinburgh pub and was waiting for Jeannie to finish shopping. There, he'd got into conversation with a crew member from the Royal Yacht *Britannia*[1]. The chap had been with the ship for almost twenty years, during which time he had heard many tales from those who'd served before him. These, together with his own first-hand experiences, meant that he was a treasure trove of untapped information.

Rab was the sort who inspired confidences, especially from those whose tongues had been loosened by alcohol. He also knew when to prompt and when to remain silent. As a result, he discovered that, when Princess Margaret and her new husband were aboard the ship, Her Royal Highness had always insisted that they both donned full evening dress for dinner. Tony Armstrong-Jones preferred a more casual approach to dining and had clearly disliked the formality. This was a private holiday, they weren't entertaining, so why on earth did they have to be waited on and act all stuffy? A few of the ensuing rows had been legendary.

The exact opposite, newlyweds 'Andy and Sarah' had enjoyed playing practical jokes on each other and had generally been 'good fun' passengers on their trip round the Azores. The informant also told Rab of his encounter on deck with a just-married and weepy Princess Diana, when she and Charles were sailing the Mediterranean. He hadn't been the only one in whom the young royal readily confided. For the duration of that voyage, the yacht had been nicknamed 'the ghost ship', so adept was the captain at dodging the press.

Mr and Mrs Mark Phillips had been blighted by the most dreadful storms on their first trip as a married couple, and spent the first week being seasick. A similar fate had befallen His Majesty and Queen Dorothea. Luckily, as they'd gone to the Western Isles, rather than to the West Indies, they'd been able to return to a British port after only three days at sea.

'Five royal honeymoons aboard *Britannia*' had proved a profitable piece. Rab had even managed to weave into it the old joke about Anne's asking Mark, 'Do you want the bridal suite?' to which he replied, 'No, I'll just hang onto your mane.'

All Rab's articles were written under his byline of Tim Rashbairn, an anagram of his real name. Another anagram, Martin Bashir, had already been taken. The folder that he assembled for his forthcoming encounter also contained copies of several crucial documents.

Finally, two weeks after those almost unbelievable papers had come into his possession, he found himself being warmly greeted by the owner of Kirknadrochit Castle.[2]

1ST OCTOBER 1996

COBOURG ROAD, BERMONDSEY

'One way or anuvva, we ended up with a load of kids in the fam'ly,' said Peggy. ''oo cares 'ow we're all related?'

It was the first time Lil had ever heard her sister almost acknowledge Freddie's origins, but she wasn't brave enough to openly lay claim to 'her' three great-grandchildren. Laura, who seemed happy enough to remain a partner rather than a wife, had gone into reproductive overdrive. Nathan, now five, had been swiftly followed by another brother, named Callum. The latest arrival, Oliver, was just six months old.

'I wonder if they'll keep goin' until they get a girl?' Peggy whispered.

'They might end up wiv a football team,' suggested Ron, whose ninetieth birthday they'd convened to celebrate. The only absentee was Janet, who'd visited the previous weekend but needed to get back to work.

'Nothing wrong with your hearing, is there, Dad?' said Lil.

'Would you like me to fetch you another piece of cake?'

A loud shout of 'no!' emanated from the kitchen. The normally patient Laura appeared to be losing control.

'Sounds like them boys are after finishin' it,' commented the family patriarch. ''cept they leave the cake and eat the icing.'

'Ow! Callum just hit me, Mummy!'

Peggy, who'd been cuddling Oliver on her lap, stood up. 'This one's ready for a nap. I'll go and put 'im in 'is buggy.'

'Where've Freddie, Terry and Ralph all disappeared to?' asked Lil.

'Upstairs. Terry's fixin' a socket in the spare bedroom.'

'And it takes three of them to do that?'

'Freddie's prob'ly 'idin' in 'is old room. It's the only place 'e can get a bit of peace an' quiet.'

Callum raced into the room, with Nathan in hot pursuit. A frazzled-looking Laura appeared in the doorway. 'I'll take them to the playground. They need to burn off some of that energy.'

'I'll join you,' offered Ron.

'They can all go,' decided Peggy, as she carried Oliver into the hall. 'Oi you lot! Get yerselves down 'ere. You're goin' for a walk in the park.'

32

KIRKNADROCHIT CASTLE

Before long, Rab was being taken on a guided tour of the ancient pile, which involved room after roped-off room. The Duke didn't speak as eloquently as he wrote, and the blow-by-blow garbled accounts of each section's history quickly became tedious. Maybe His Grace's slim volume on relics had been ghostwritten?

Buoyed up by the promise of coffee (surely this couldn't drag on much longer?), Rab feigned interest and jotted down a few squiggles in a notebook. The only time his curiosity was genuinely piqued was when he saw the original portrait of the Duke's mother and her twin sister.

To start with, his host had appeared gracious and hospitable. Knowing what was coming, Rab even felt slightly sorry for the man. Coffee was finally served in a room with splendid views of the River Don. There was further talk about the house party plans and some discussion about the book, which hadn't yet been touched upon. There was even amicable laughter about the theft, by some students, of the Stone of Scone back in 1950.[1]

However, the Duke's air of affability was about to wear thin, and did so rapidly once Rab felt it timely to change the subject.

'I understand that you and the Duchess didn't marry until after your daughter was born, Sir?'

'That's true. So what? It would have mattered to the inheritance of my title had she been a son but, as she wasn't, it is totally immaterial.'

'She was registered in just your wife's maiden name, I believe. Any reason for that?'

'Sorry to disappoint, but the reason's nothing remotely scandalous, if that's what you're hoping for. It was just a case of having to provide fewer details by doing it that way. I was out of the country, so my wife dealt with everything. Neither she nor I are enthusiastic about bureaucracy, so the simpler the better.'

'All of which resulted in a birth certificate that doesn't connect your daughter to you.'

'So? Not naming the father when registering a baby isn't against the law. Some women are unable to provide the name of a baby's father. But, in our case, there was never any doubt about paternity. I never denied it. And everything was legitimised with our wedding soon after. If you're digging for dirt, you're digging in the wrong place.'

'All I'm trying to do is clarify matters. I need to understand how a certain event which I believe took place, *could* take place, without raising questions and without anyone popping up later, having put two and two together.'

'I have no idea what you're talking about, man. It sounds like you've come here today on a muckraking mission, and I don't take kindly to that.'

'Just want to set the record straight, Sir.'

'Then let me set things straight, Rainsmith. My daughter's acknowledged pedigree is impeccable. Let's just remind ourselves who we're talking about here.'

'I have no reason to doubt her lineage, Sir.'

'Well then, get to the point man.' The Duke's face had turned an alarming shade of red.

'The point is Peter Lowry.'

Rab had seen plenty of people lose their cool after a shock revelation. He'd seen fingers being run through hair or around the inside of collars, instinctively defensive arms folding across chests, the onset of sundry nervous twitches and all manner of other body language that confirmed he'd hit the mark. But he had never before seen a ruddy complexion so instantly drained of blood.

'Who? I have no idea who you're talking about. Never heard the name. I'd like you to leave now.'

Rab didn't move.

'What happened to Peter, Sir? The last confirmed sighting of him was in June 1976 but a few weeks later, on Monday 16th August, he married your daughter at Coldstream registry office[2]. Her maiden name was given as Kennedy. If you haven't seen the original certificate, I have it here, Sir. You may be interested to know that she used one of your subsidiary titles – Banffshyre – as your surname, and your occupation was stated as farmer. I presume you do the occasional spot of soil tilling?'

'It's all arable,' barked the Duke, 'and this is a load of rubbish.'

Rab was unfazed. 'There is no record of any subsequent divorce. May I remind you that Peter's case is still officially open? The Greater Glasgow police will therefore be very interested in following up on what I've found out. So far, none of this has been passed on to them, but withholding information is a serious offence. I can't put it off indefinitely.'

'Are you trying to blackmail me, Rainsmith?'

The journalist calmly helped himself to more coffee.

'No, Sir. I simply want the truth.'

'I have nothing further to say to you,' said the Duke of Albemarle, adding stubbornly, 'Watch my lips. I do not know a Peter Lowry.'

Rab made a point of finishing his drink before rising to his feet. As a further gesture, he bent to grab a couple of shortbread biscuits from a plate on the low table, and made a show of casually putting them in his jacket pocket. Then he took a couple of steps towards the door.

'It will almost certainly be a murder enquiry, Sir. If your memory starts to improve, you have my card, which has my mobile number on it. I'll see myself out.'

Rab had taken his time after leaving the Duke. It had given him quite a thrill to be able to mention, in such a nonchalant manner, his newly acquired Nokia 1610. Only ten per cent of the population owned mobiles. He was thinking of doing a piece on how the world would be transformed once everyone carried such devices. He only hoped that the reception was good hereabouts. It wasn't reliable everywhere.

He'd found a loo – coffee always went straight through him – before heading to his car and driving off. There was a convenient lay-by about a mile away from Kirknadrochit Castle, where he pulled in, confirmed that there was a phone signal and switched off the engine. The call had come five minutes later, when he was halfway through the second biscuit. He finished it before turning the ignition key.

His Grace was still sitting in the same chair, in the same room with the view. It looked like he hadn't moved since Rab's departure, but he must have done.

'How much?' he began.

'I hope you're not trying to buy me off, Sir. That would be most unethical.'

'Look, Rainsmith, we're both men of the world. I'm sure this little matter can be resolved between the two of us. Shall we say half a million, shake on it and put an end to things once and for all?'

'What happened to Peter Lowry, Sir? Is he dead?'

Defeated, the older man slumped. 'No, he isn't dead, but he might as well be. He's in a nursing home near Inveraray – under an assumed name, naturally.'

'Naturally.'

'He's being very well cared for, at some considerable expense.'

'Funded no doubt via some offshore and completely untraceable account. Tell me what happened.'

'He took something. Had what I think they called a bad trip. It caused irreparable brain damage. He doesn't know who he is, or even what planet he's on.'

'And this was when?'

'A week after my daughter so foolishly eloped. She rang in a panic. I went and fetched them both. They were in a small, squalid encampment near Arbroath. Until then, I knew nothing about any of it. She was going through a bit of a wild-child phase. My wife and I weren't happy about that, but there didn't seem much point in creating a big fuss by trying to track her down. We thought it was just something she needed to get out of her system, like a lot of teenagers. All we could do was wait until she saw sense. We were sure it wouldn't be long before she missed her creature comforts and came running back home.'

'I can fill you in a bit about her time at the Pitlochry festival, if you're interested. My informant referred to her as Fizz but it would, of course, have been Fitz. If it's any consolation, she seemed very much in love with Peter.'

'So she said. She was distraught.'

'Now I have that final piece of the jigsaw, let me guess the rest,' offered Rab. 'Confronted by a messy situation, you considered arranging a divorce but, as that would have been a matter of public record, you thought it better to simply brush the whole affair under the carpet, on the basis that no one could possibly find out?'

'That just about sums it up.'

'Did she, or indeed does she, visit Peter?'

'She went once, early on. But it was too upsetting for her. I still don't know what put you on to it?'

'Perhaps that old Greek goddess Nemesis remains in the business of enacting retribution? Or maybe some other divine intervention showed me the way?'

'What a surprising man you are, Rainsmith. I've always wondered about the role of the Moirai. The Fates did seem to be with us to a certain extent. My daughter, fortunately, wasn't pregnant. Nor was she hooked on drugs. In that respect at least, she was being sensible – though how long her resistance would have lasted, I don't know. Luckily, she was jolted back to reality in time.'

'Luckily for some.'

The Duke glared at his interrogator. 'We were able to continue much as planned. She went back to school, followed by a stint spent being finished in Switzerland, and then got herself a little job at a London art gallery, as they all seem to do. That enterprise she went into was doing well. She certainly made damned sure she kept a fairly low profile and didn't get into any more scrapes. Do you have children, Rainsmith?'

'Sadly, no.'

'Then you'll have to take my word for it. As a parent, you'd do anything – whatever it takes – to secure your child's well-being. She was very young at the time. We didn't see why one silly mistake should ruin her whole life. Peter's life was already in tatters. We did arrange, via trusted intermediaries of course, to get the best medical opinions, but nothing could be done for him.'

'Didn't it occur to you that he was also somebody's child, and that they would be worrying?'

'Yes, it did. But we asked ourselves which would be preferable: to believe, or at least hope, that your son was still alive and well somewhere? Or to know that he was a vegetable, completely beyond help and, to all intents and purposes, dead? We were inclined towards the former.'

'How very comforting. So your daughter emerged as an eligible bachelorette, with her reputation undamaged. And then along came a suitor to claim her hand. He married her and they all lived happily ever after. Better still, her suitor happened to be King James III of the United Kingdom, making her Queen Dorothea of the United Kingdom, plus sundry Commonwealth realms. The couple went on to produce two beautiful children, one of whom is destined for the throne, unless a little brother turns up. Except – and here's the teeny-tiny flaw – that splendid Westminster Abbey ceremony, as watched by millions around the globe, was all a sham. You put on your new morning suit and proudly walked your daughter up the aisle, knowing that she was about to commit bigamy. I have a feeling that this story might warrant a few column inches in the tabloids, wouldn't you say?'

His Grace nodded miserably.

'I will give you credit for one thing though,' Rab said cheerily.

'And that is?'

'You arranged to have Peter cared for, rather than taken care of.'

'I'm not sure I understand.'

'You didn't arrange to have the poor boy quietly bumped off,' Rab explained.

'You may have a pretty low opinion of me, Rainsmith, but I wouldn't stoop to murder, whatever the circumstances. It never even crossed my mind.'

'I believe you, Sir. You've just made that abundantly clear. It can't have been cheap, either, keeping a man with the constitution of an ox in a private clinic all this time. I imagine some in your position might have acted very differently. If Peter had died of convincingly natural causes at any point before the royal wedding, Dorothea would have been a secret widow, instead of a secret wife.'

'Thank you for accepting I have some scruples. It's almost a pity I do. Then no one would have been any the wiser.'

'Oh, I would still have found out about the marriage. Once I was on the right track, it would inevitably have come to light, unless you'd found some means of getting his real name onto the death certificate and notifying the police – in which case, he'd no longer have been a missing person and I would never have picked up on him as such. But the scandal that's about to erupt would have been just that: one more royal scandal. And not a particularly seedy one either. People can be very forgiving, and most wouldn't condemn a youthful indiscretion. Barring a bit of fuss about her "spinster of this parish" status on the marriage certificate, in time it would have all blown over, and your dear little granddaughters would not be illegitimate. In fact, once the tea towels and mugs had been printed, you might even have been able to risk coming clean.'

Knowing it was hopeless, the Duke nevertheless tried one final throw of the dice. 'How does a million pounds sound?'

8TH NOVEMBER 1996

SITTING ROOM, CLARENCE HOUSE, LONDON

'You're looking cheery for the first time in ages, Cabbage,' observed the Duke of Edinburgh. 'Good to see.'

'That's probably because it's Friday night. The only thing in the diary for the next two days is tea with Mummy tomorrow afternoon,' commented his wife. She swung her legs from the floor and stretched out along the length of the sofa. On her feet were the furry corgi slippers that had been Anne's gift the previous Christmas. Everyone had received novelty slippers last year, but Phillip's had long since been chewed to shreds by one of the dogs. Sighing with contentment, Elizabeth sank back onto a pile of cushions.

'It's funny,' she said. 'Most parents would be delighted to see their children married, as indeed we were at the weddings. But, in the end, we were happier still to have them safely divorced. It's a relief, now I'm finally resigned to being a failure as their Mama.'

'You're no such thing. It's not our fault they made such bad choices, Andrew in particular.'

'Please don't go on about Sarah again. Hopefully, Anne and Timothy will prove a better match. And Sophie seems like a sensible girl. I wonder whether she and Edward will make a go of it, if he finally decides to propose and settle down?'

'Statistically they should. Three divorced children out of four already puts us way above the national average rate. Then there's your sister. At least James seems content.'

'Hmm. I'm not so sure about that.'

'Oh, I don't know. What's not to like about Dorothea? Maybe she's slightly lacking in the sense of humour department, but she's quiet, docile and dutiful. In short, she's an exemplary queen.'

'Which is exactly my point. She reminds me of Jane Seymour, and I'm not talking about the actress.'

'And Queen Jane also married a clever, spirited man, who was as keen as James is on dangerous sports. For speed boats, read jousting. She sat and did her needlework, and Henry didn't mind in the slightest. In fact, from what I recall from my history lessons, he happily sat and stitched alongside her.'

'Can you honestly see James' taking up embroidery?' laughed Elizabeth.

'Maybe not. But, like Jane, Dorothea produced an heir. And a spare as well. These days, gender doesn't matter like it did in Tudor times.'

'I certainly can't say I was sorry when our little nieces arrived, Phillip. Fifty-five and a half years as heir presumptive was quite long enough.'

'Well, you can afford to relax now that the spectre of the throne's no longer haunting us. This tea party tomorrow – I hope I'm not expected to attend?'

'No. It will just be Mummy, Margaret and me.'

8TH NOVEMBER 1996

GLASGOW

Once he'd put a bit of distance behind him, Rab telephoned Jeannie and told her not to bother cooking. They'd go to their nearest Beefeater restaurant. It wasn't exactly pushing the boat out, but he didn't want the formality of anywhere more upmarket, nor the hassle of needing to book a table. 'We'll take a taxi,' he declared. 'I could do with a drink.'

He broke the news after they'd eaten their main course. His wife had, of course, known he was onto something. Usually, the two of them discussed what he was currently working on. This time he hadn't said a word, which she put down to his being fearful that it would all fizzle out and turn into one more disappointment.

She listened with rapt attention, her mouth slightly agape. 'Bloody hell,' she said, when he'd recounted the dénouement, 'and you turned down a million quid? This story won't earn anything like that, even if your press agents are the best in the world.'

'It might. And, if it does, I'll be able to account for it on my tax return. A sudden influx of hush money wouldn't be so easy to explain. Besides, what else could I have done? I'd have been colluding in a crime.'

'So what's the penalty for bigamy?'

'Up to seven years in jail and/or a fine.'

'I'm sure the royal family can afford the fine, but are you saying that the Queen of England – sorry, the person everyone thinks is the Queen of England – could end up in prison?'

'It's possible, yes, but unlikely. There is some discretion about whether or not a custodial sentence is dished out. It depends whether it's deemed to be in the public interest.'

'I shouldn't have thought throwing poor Dorothea in jail would serve any useful purpose, though a perverse judge might want to make an example of her and demonstrate that nobody's above the law. But the Windsors will doubtless hire a whole team of top-notch barristers to make sure that doesn't happen.'

'But what sort of a defence could be put forward?' asked Jeannie.

'I've looked into the legal position. There was a 1977 Act in Scotland whereby the accused might prove they had no reason to believe their spouse was still alive after they'd been missing for seven years of more. As you might imagine, this has given rise to a few cases where someone's been presumed dead, but then turned out not to be.'

'Which isn't so very different from our case in point.'

'Except that Dorothea knows her husband is still in the land of the living. At least… Oh triple – '

'Fudge!' came the swift interruption. 'What is it, Rab?'

'If that were the case, the Duke would have said.'

His phone rang at that very second. He knew who'd be calling and why. Jeannie heard only one side of the conversation.

'Good evening, Your Grace… I can't say I'm surprised. What does surprise me is why you didn't mention it earlier…? I see. You forgot… I hope you had a secure connection when you and she were cooking this up. You know how easy it can be for hackers to eavesdrop… No, I won't… You'd lose, and you know it. Every word printed will be the truth and nothing but – '

315

Rab moved his mobile from his ear and stared at the device for a few seconds, as though mortally offended by it.

'What was all that about?'

'He cut me off!'

'What did he say?'

'Predictably enough, it turns out – ha ha – that he informed his daughter many years ago that Peter had died. He supposedly told her this because she was feeling guilty about not visiting, and he wanted to spare her further distress. In other words, he's planning to fall on his sword.'

'Do you believe him?'

'No. But others might. They'll undoubtedly want to. It would mean that Dorothea wed King James in all good faith, except for the minor discrepancy about her marital status, which I'm not sure would invalidate the marriage.'

'But, if she genuinely believed she was a widow, surely she would have come clean and not pretended to be a single woman. At the very least, she was party to a deception.'

'And that's where the Duke's fiction starts to unravel. To prove she was free to marry again, she'd probably need to have produced a death certificate. And, of course, there isn't one. True to form, her father will, of course, shoulder all the blame and say he advised her to keep schtum.'

'Do you think it will end up in court?'

'I haven't the foggiest idea. My role is to light the blue touch paper and stand well clear.'

'But, if those involved have to swear under oath that they're telling the truth, surely persisting in a lie would amount to perjury,' Jeannie suggested. 'Can you imagine Her "supposed" Majesty doing that?'

'She might, if she's as protective of her children as her father seems to be of his precious daughter. But I'm guessing it will all be handled as discretely as possible, in an effort to minimise everyone's embarrassment.'

'I hate to dampen your enthusiasm, Rab, but what would you do now, if you were the Duke? If Peter's languishing in a nursing home under an assumed name, and if no one can prove who he really is, who's to say he isn't dead? The Duke and his daughter could simply claim that he wandered off during the honeymoon and that neither of them ever saw him again. In that scenario, they'd be entitled to believe him dead by now, even if they omitted to go through the formality of having him declared as such.'

'If he'd said exactly that, and nothing more, during the interview, I probably wouldn't have got much further. Luckily for me, he couldn't think fast enough on his feet. Perhaps he was panicked by the thought of a police enquiry.'

'Even so, it could end up being the Duke's word against yours. He might deny everything he told you.'

Rab smiled and patted his jacket pocket.

'You canny beggar,' said his wife. 'You've got it all on that mini-tape recorder, haven't you? Didn't he suspect?'

'No, I'd been pretending to jot things down in a notebook, which I conspicuously put on the coffee table, in the hope he'd assume there'd be no record of our conversation.'

'At the very least, you've got cast-iron proof of the marriage. That must be a big enough story in itself. Better still, you also know about the clinic in Inveraray. It's not a big place, so that shouldn't be too hard to find. Nor should it be too difficult to confirm the existence of a male drug-addled patient, aged thirty whatever, who's been stuck there since a fairly specific time during the 1970s. Any high-powered official investigation would eventually get to the truth, no matter what name Peter was admitted under, or how convoluted the whole cover-up has been. You don't think the Duke will transfer him to somewhere else, do you?'

Rab pondered for a moment. 'No. In the circumstances, it would be a rather stupid thing to do. It wouldn't serve any purpose, other than to further demonstrate the level of His Grace's deviousness and desperation.'

'Why don't we try to locate the clinic and see what we can find out for ourselves?'

'I'd wondered about that, Jeannie. My exposé will give rise to a rush for the rich pickings. There'll be hordes of journalists crawling all over Argyllshire, and one of them could well strike gold ahead of any palace-instigated or police enquiry. But I think I'd be better off working on what I've got, just to make damn certain that anything due to go public is completely fire-proof.'

'Are you sure? Right now, we've got a head start. You know Peter's date of birth. You know, more or less, when he was admitted and why. Armed with all that, we could claim to be looking for a long-lost relative. Who knows? If we could blag our way in and actually see him, we might even be able to sneak a photo. What price a front-page picture of the Queen's real husband? And how sick would you feel if someone else nabbed such a nice little exclusive?'

'Put like that, it's tempting.'

'And don't forget that the people working at the nursing home, or whatever sort of institution it is, won't yet be on the alert. As far as they're concerned, their soon-to-be-famous inmate is simply some bloke they've been looking after for donkey's years. An ordinary-looking couple – that's us – wouldn't raise too much suspicion.'

'Good point, Jeannie. But we're still going to leave it. What I can do, though, is tip off the Duke. I'll tell him to make doubly sure that the staff are being ultra-vigilant and must blank anyone making enquiries. He might have done that already, though he isn't the sharpest tool in the box.'

'So what was that last bit of your conversation just now about?'

'He demanded to see the article before it went any further. And have the right to amend it as he saw fit. When I didn't agree, he threatened to sue me for defamation, as if I'd be that stupid.' Rab sighed. 'I guess he can't be blamed for one final show of bluster. Shall we ask for the sweet trolley?'

'Do they do cocktails here?'

'I don't think so. Why?'

'I just thought I'd get in a bit of practice, ahead of sampling a few on some exotic beach.'

'Don't you fancy a caravan in Norfolk again?'

'Not if we can afford the Caribbean instead.'

1997

33

MONDAY 6TH JANUARY 1997

'KING JAMES III IS DEAD

The whole nation is plunged into mourning at the news of King James's death yesterday afternoon, which was formally announced at 10 a.m. this morning, in a brief statement issued by Buckingham Palace.

There are no further official details, but it is understood that His Majesty was killed in a tragic accident on Coniston Water, just before 3.30 p.m.

The King, after spending Christmas and New Year at Sandringham House, Norfolk, travelled to Cumbria early last Friday. He and a small entourage checked in at Hillside Lodge near Ambleside.

It is well known that His Majesty was planning a challenge for the water speed record later this year, aboard a specially designed boat Velocitas, *which is Latin for 'speed'.* Velocitas *had been undergoing technical modifications at an undisclosed location and was being transported to Coniston today. The King and his development team were then due to resume trials following the Christmas break. A palace source explained that His Majesty wanted a couple of days to himself, ahead of everyone else's arrival, but added that he was very much looking forward to the next phase of testing.*

He owned a second commercially built speedboat named Limax *(Latin for 'snail')*, *in which he regularly took recreational trips on the lake. He was a familiar sight to locals, one of whom has since said, "I think he found being on the water relaxing, but he was probably also doing some reconnaissance of the geography. It's a popular area for walkers and, if he saw anyone, he often waved as he went past."*

The timeline leading up to the disastrous event has been pieced together. His Majesty left the hotel immediately after lunch, as he had done on the previous two days. At around 2.30 p.m., he was seen by a number of people driving his Jaguar through the village of Coniston. His boatyard is located close to the southern end of the lake, and his car was later found parked beside it.

Several eyewitnesses to yesterday's incident have confirmed that, to begin with, there was nothing unusual about the fatal run. But reports also suggest that the vessel seemed to pick up speed and was going "faster than usual" when it bounced and subsequently exploded.

Mrs Sheila Walters, who was walking her red setter in Torver Common Wood at the time, described herself as "still shaken and horror-struck". "It was obvious that no one could possibly have survived," she said. "I was too far away to hear a bang, but did see a flash and bits flying into the air. It all happened so quickly, I didn't take it in for a few seconds."

It would appear that "significant bodily remains" have already been recovered, along with several fragments of the craft. It is expected that, for an indefinite period, a search of the area will continue. Investigators are keen to retrieve as much as possible, in their efforts to identify the cause of the crash.

His Majesty's sister, Princess Elizabeth, Duchess of Edinburgh, has been declared Queen Elizabeth II.'

There had seemingly been nothing else on television for weeks, with no dearth of material for the media to analyse.

Prior to James's tragic death, people throughout the land had been bombarded with the fallout from Rab's sensational story, all of which had been verified by documentation and further confirmed as true by the Duke of Albemarle. His Grace was now facing criminal charges, though what these would amount to remained unclear.

The additional irony was that Peter Lowry, now located and correctly identified, was fading fast and could only be weeks, if not days, from dying.

What would happen to the King's wife, who was never his wife and therefore never the rightful queen? She was judged to be a largely innocent party in the whole messy affair. Would his four-year-old daughters remain with their mother? That seemed the natural conclusion, but where would they live, and what about their future relationship with the royal family, who could surely not be seen to be abandoning the two young girls? And what should their status be? Would they be stripped of their titles, or would they remain princesses, with or without the style of HRH? Numerous experts on constitutional issues had featured daily, giving their opinions on what they saw as the options. In such an unprecedented situation, there was a great deal of uncertainty. An announcement from Buckingham Palace had been eagerly awaited. So far, only a brief holding statement had been issued, indicating that a matter of such sensitivity was being given very careful consideration and would take 'some time' to resolve.

This was generally interpreted as meaning that thought was being given to what possibilities might follow Lowry's imminent demise. 'Queen' Dorothea would then become free to marry again. If she and the King were to go through another wedding ceremony – a proper one this time – their daughters would at least be legitimised[1], even if the girls remained ineligible to inherit the throne, due to the fact that they'd been born when their parents were not legally married. But any further children produced in wedlock would be rightful heirs. One had only to refer, the experts claimed, to the Lascelles' precedent.[2]

Much of this speculation was eclipsed, if not rendered irrelevant, by the shock and grief surrounding His Majesty's untimely death and by speculation about the manner of it. Was it an accident? Was it a disguised suicide? Had the recent turbulent revelations proved too much for one man to take, especially after the death of his acknowledged mentor, the Earl of Willaston, less than a year earlier? Eminent psychiatrists emerged by the dozen, offering their views on the differing means by which people cope with such a loss. Alongside these debates, conspiracy theorists were claiming that the late king's craft had been sabotaged and that he'd therefore been murdered.

None of the boffins, who were again rolled out from the cloisters of academia, disputed the succession of Her Royal Highness Princess Elizabeth as queen. Her reinstatement as first in line had been confirmed only a few short weeks earlier, just after the truth about her brother's sham marriage emerged. Equally undoubtedly, HRH Prince Charles was her heir apparent. As such, he was now rightly eligible to be Prince of Wales, and would additionally get an automatic entitlement to the Duchy of Cornwall.

15TH FEBRUARY 1997

LABURNUM CLOSE, EWELL

The establishment of a James III Memorial Fund was announced almost immediately after His late Majesty's state funeral. Called 'One Jump Ahead', it was to be launched, in a television broadcast to the nation, by HRH The Prince of Wales on the evening of Saturday 15th February – one day after what would have been James's forty-eighth birthday.

On a rare visit, Janet was home for the weekend.

'Aren't you going to watch?' asked Terry.

'It'll be starting soon,' said her mother.

'I'm not bothered. I'll take these trays through and do the washing up.' The Dagleys rarely sat at the table to eat these days. 'Do you want anything else?'

'No thanks, love,' her parents responded, almost in unison.

'Leave the trays for now and talk to us,' suggested Lil, 'We don't see nearly enough of you. Surely you're interested in what Prince Charles has to say. I hear the fund is all to do with your line of work. Didn't you nearly meet the King once?'

'I nearly met him twice, as a matter of fact. The time you're probably thinking of was a few months ago when he visited Liverpool, and I was off sick that day. I should have been showing him round one of the labs and telling him about the work we do, but my stomach upset was so bad, I couldn't have struggled in for a million pounds. It was all I could do to crawl out of bed to the loo and, in the end, I just stayed put there! The first time was just after I got the results of my finals. Remember?'

'I do now,' admitted Lil. 'I don't know what's happened to my memory these days. Your Aunt Peg and I always dreamed of shaking hands with royalty, but we never did. The only one in the family who actually managed it was your – er, cousin – Freddie. And that was accidental.'

'Oh please, not that Royal Knockout programme again. Every time I've heard the tale, it's become more and more embellished. To start with, there was a good chance that it wasn't even the King he met, but some weirdo pretending to be the King,' protested Janet.

'Oh, we're pretty sure now it was the real thing.'

'Or you'd like to believe it was. You and Aunt Peggy are obsessed with royalty. My money's on wishful thinking.'

'No. Your Aunt Peg and I got Freddie to go over it again, not so long ago. He's a typical male. When it comes to the finer points, you know men! '

Janet was acquainted with plenty of men. She'd dated several, but always felt she'd only ever truly known one.

'So let's start from the very beginning,' she said.

'A very good place to start,' trilled her mother, to the tune of 'Do-Re-Mi', a song from *The Sound of Music*.

'What was Freddie doing at the time? Serving burgers?'

'No, he was standing on his own eating one.'

'Where exactly?'

'How should I know?'

'I thought you said you'd got a blow-by-blow account Mum?'

'Yes, but we didn't ask Freddie to draw us a diagram. Backstage somewhere.'

'Okay. So Freddie's standing in some unidentified location, minding his own business, and what? Some bloke wanders up to him and says, "Hello, I'm King James. Who are you?"'

Lil hesitated. 'I'm not sure.'

'So was this stranger alone?'

'I think so.'

'That doesn't stack up, does it? Surely the King would have some sort of bodyguard with him.'

'I expect he did, but any escort wouldn't necessarily be visible. That's how these things work. If you look at any film of the royals on their walkabouts, they aren't surrounded by men in black. Those stay in the background and aren't noticeable.'

'Fair point. So a passing male person sees Freddie, wanders over and strikes up a conversation?'

'That's about it. Not such an unusual thing to happen.'

'And Freddie didn't recognise this man?'

'Not to start with, but he did as soon as the bloke took off his hat and glasses.'

'And why would anyone do that?'

'I don't know, but he did. And the way he spoke was right.'

'Any half-competent impersonator could do that,' argued Janet.

'But why would they?'

'To test out, with a random member of the public, how convincing their act was, perhaps? To see if the victim started bowing and stuttering when they found themselves in the presence of greatness? That seems plausible to me.'

'Freddie did say he looked very like the King.'

'So do a lot of men. Which brings us back to why His Majesty would wander up to my – OK, let's stop playing games here – my son, start conversing and, part way through, whip off his hat and reveal his true identity.'

'I don't know,' Lil confessed, 'but I'm sure that's what happened. And there was one detail which confirms it.'

'Which was?'

'After about five minutes, some burly official-looking chap emerged out of nowhere, pointed to his watch and said, "Sorry to interrupt, Sir." Imposters don't arrange for that sort of thing to happen, do they, whatever their game might be? It's what swung it for you, wasn't it, Terry?'

'Yes. It did. Like you Janet, I'd always taken the story with a pinch of salt. In fact, so much salt, it could have seasoned the whole of the North Sea. But it wasn't as though this encounter happened in any old place. There were royals in the vicinity, which could well account for the King's presence.'

'I always understood that he didn't want to have anything to do with the silly programme?'

'Officially, he didn't,' stated Lil, 'but there was an interview on the other day with that actress. You know, the one who played Lois Lane in the *Superman* films? She was on Prince Andrew's team. She said it was an open secret that the King was there beforehand. I can't remember her name, but it'll come to me.'

'And Freddie isn't stupid,' added Terry. 'Nor is he the sort to fantasise. In fact, I'm only sorry now I didn't believe him straightaway.'

'There, I told you!' said Lil.

Terry ignored his wife's triumphant outburst and continued. 'But whichever way you look at it, the whole thing was very odd. Why pick on our boy, when there must have been dozens of other people floating round? It's not as if Freddie was in any presentation line-up or anything. He just happened to be there helping out.'

Janet was thoughtful. 'Okay Dad. Let's say that if you're convinced, then so am I.'

'Thanks very much,' said her mother. 'You two always were thick as thieves.'

Once again, Lil's comment was overridden.

'So, if I suspend disbelief, could it be that Freddie wasn't picked out at all? Maybe loads of others believed they too had been specially selected? The King was a friendly sort, wasn't he?' Janet argued. 'They say he had a habit of chatting informally to people, and for too long, even when he was doing the official stuff and working to a deadline.'

Lil wasn't happy to believe her supposed nephew was merely one of many and put her case. 'Why are you being so obstinate, Janet? From the very first time Peggy told me about it, there's no doubt that he made a definite beeline for Freddie and that they talked for ages. It wasn't just a quick "hello" and "have you always been interested in catering?" either. His Majesty wanted to know his name, how old he was, where he came from, what his interests were and a whole host of other stuff.'

'Maybe that's how the conversation always went when he met people?' Janet suggested.

'And he shook Freddie's hand.'

'Lovely,' said Janet. 'I expect the King really enjoyed getting his palm covered in hamburger grease.'

'Did you watch "It's a Royal Knockout"? We did, didn't we, Terry?'

'We certainly did. It was a bloody embarrassment. All that sort of slapstick stuff is silly.'

'Ah well,' said her mother. 'It was all a good few years ago now.'

Terry patted the settee cushion next to him. 'Come and sit next to your old Dad, Janet, and relax for a few minutes. The programme's starting. You're always up and down like a yo-yo.'

Music, which sounded like the ominous film score from *Jaws*, began to play. A blob with spikes floated across the TV screen.

'Isn't that pretty?' commented Lil. 'I wonder what it is?'

'It looks like ZEBOV-Gab.'

'Can we have that in English, please?' laughed Terry.

'It's one of the Zaire strains of Ebola virus,' said Janet. 'Very deadly. We're targeting protein 24 to try to combat it.'

'I've got it!' exclaimed Lil. 'That actress was Margot Kidder.'

Charles had started to speak.

'In 1936, following the death of my great-grandfather King George V, a memorial fund was established to enable the creation of national playing fields. In 1952, another fund was started in honour of my grandfather, King George VI. This was to benefit the young and the old.

During his lifetime, my late uncle, King James III, supported many worthy causes. Notably, these included the Order of St John's Ambulance which, as its Sovereign Head, James espoused so enthusiastically. This was his particular tribute to our cousin, Prince William of Gloucester, who, some twenty-five years ago, also died in a tragic circumstances.

And yet, for all the splendid work done by the charities and organisations that were so dear to James's heart, I have no doubt whatsoever where he would have wished any monies raised to be directed.

It almost goes without saying that some will go to The King's Trust and to The Elizabethan Trust. So many thousands of people are treading the straight and narrow, thanks to a multitude of schemes targeted at the very young and their families. I shall say no more about this, because I need time to explain the second major theme of the fund.

From the tender age of just seven, James suffered from what he called "Cassandra Syndrome". No, this isn't some sort of obscure medical condition, even though it was increasingly a cause of real anguish to him. For those who can't quite place her, Cassandra was a Trojan priestess in Greek mythology, who was cursed to utter true prophesies, but never to be believed. I have no wish to criticise the dead, nor to embarrass the living, but certain recipients of well-considered kingly wisdoms chose to ignore the advice they were given. In some instances, this resulted in their fall from power. Worse still, in other cases, refusals to take heed were to the detriment of our fine nation's reputation and the well-being of its people.

So let us take heed now. The good cause I am about to describe may, to many of you, not sound like a glamorous one. It may certainly have no immediate impact on our lives and, in one particular respect, I hope that it never will. It was His late Majesty's firm belief that we should invest heavily in virology research. Viruses cause untold misery. Every year, millions suffer from colds and influenza. To recognise that the latter can and does kill, one need only look back to the aftermath of the First World War and the outbreak of Spanish flu, which afflicted up to a hundred million people worldwide.

But it doesn't stop there. They are responsible for a wide range of illnesses, some of which can be life-threatening or even fatal. Conditions can range from certain cancers to heart disease. Unlike bacteria, for which there are antibiotics, very little can be prescribed to combat them. Indeed, an individual may well be unaware that they have been infected.

These microscopic organisms, like all other animals, adapt and change. But, unlike other animals, they do not take centuries of evolution to do so. James, who at one time suffered an infection, became very knowledgeable on the subject. He believed that humanity needed to stay one jump ahead. His single overriding fear was that a brand-new strain of virus would one day appear out of nowhere and spread very rapidly, causing global devastation. I pray to God that this never happens. I pray we shall never have cause to be grateful for our late king's foresight, but I do share the firm belief that we should be prepared, in case the worst should happen.'

Janet stood up and collected a tray. 'You'll miss the rest, if you go now,' said Lil.

'No I won't,' her daughter replied, as she left the room. 'If it makes you any happier, I'll switch on the TV in the kitchen.'

'It is therefore,' Charles was continuing, 'my privilege to announce the creation of this fund, half the proceeds of which will go directly to the James III Institute, a facility to be developed at his *alma mater*, the University of Oxford. Not one single penny will be diverted from his cause, for he would have wanted no statues or other effigies as a memorial.

My uncle was also my dearest friend. He was your friend, too. Many of you, both at home and abroad, were presented to him on official occasions and will therefore have fond memories both of your sovereign and of the humanity he personified. What may also surprise you to know is that many of you met him without ever knowing it. He mingled amongst you unrecognised, and did so because he wanted to find out how people lived their lives and what really mattered to them. You may have encountered him in a pub or social club, or even on a picket line. You may have worked alongside him as a food bank volunteer, or chatted to him as he cleaned up litter on a run-down housing estate. I can tell you now that, if you ever met Fergus Carrick, you did indeed have the privilege of rubbing shoulders with a great king who was never afraid to be ordinary.'

Mr and Mrs Dagley were startled by the loud sound of shattering crockery, and they both rushed through to find Janet lying in a dead faint on the kitchen floor. Beside her were the broken remains of her mother's last two, and much-cherished, 'Homemaker' plates.[3]

34

BUCKINGHAM PALACE

The window of his Buckingham Palace office was wide open, and he could hear the sounds of London starting to wake up. The sky was blue and cloudless, with the promise of a beautiful day to come.

Sir Keith Bradshaw GCVO[1] had completed most of his friend James's early memoirs, but was still agonising about Saturday 24th June 1967. The diary entry, as written at the time, filled a full page, plus an extra insert. Tucked in were many other sundry jottings on additional sheets of paper, each bearing later dates. They were fastened together with a monogrammed clip, which must have been specially commissioned. There was also a dried-up daisy, pressed flat, and now so fragile that Keith was reluctant to even touch it, for fear it would disintegrate. He wondered whether an image of the flower would make a suitable front cover, but that depended on whether he included the section at all.

Was it a bit too intimate? A bit too personal? The book included plenty of other accounts of a young monarch's forays into the real world and of the people he'd met there, so there was no shortage of material.

A couple of the SO14 protection officers who'd conspired with and indulged their king were now dead. Keith had spoken to the others, all of whom had since retired and therefore had nothing to lose by the disclosure of the unorthodox parts they'd once played. Their revelations might prompt a Metropolitan Police Service investigation into the running of the Protection Command, but this could only be a historic review.

The record of that warm June evening and night told the story of how the King had lost his virginity. He'd been at a small informal folk festival, held in a corner of Bushy Park, where tents had been pitched and a makeshift stage erected. He couldn't remember which bands had been performing, and knew only that the psychedelic music was a mesmeric, and almost incidental, soundtrack. The dark-haired, blue-eyed girl had been staying in nearby Kingston, with a friend whose parents were away for the weekend. Kept on a tight leash by her own Mum and Dad, she made the most of any opportunity to stretch her wings and fly. Incredibly, she and James had only been yards from each other in 1964 when the Rolling Stones played at the Wimbledon Palais. How they could have been so close on that occasion, yet not been magnetically drawn together, seemed to be one of life's greatest mysteries.

James had returned to the diary entry many times since. One of the subsequent notes referred to the episode as *'the most wonderful few hours of my entire life'*.

He'd been whisked away just before an early dawn, leaving her sleeping. *'She looked so beautiful and so peaceful, it seemed a shame to disturb her. But oh how I wish I'd done so, and asked for her telephone number or address. It was a miserable journey home, because I knew it would be impossible to find her. Where could I even have started? There was no glass slipper to tout round on a cushion. My only memento was a tiny flower from the garland I made and crowned her with. I left her my lucky* shamrock charm. It was a silly prop I used to carry when I was being Irish Fergus. I hope she found it and kept it.'

In a rambling section penned eighteen months later, the King had again been berating himself. '*I knew the name of the town where she lived, so why didn't I engage a private detective to check out all the local grammar schools and ask to see the rolls of the pupils in their upper sixth forms? I could have provided a description, to match against every possibility. I'm no artist, but could easily have produced an identikit likeness from the image etched in my memory. But would the schools have been allowed to give details, or would confidentiality have been an obstacle? I don't know how it works. Is it too late to try?*' Dated two days later was a short despondent addition: '*They wouldn't have let me marry her anyway, but they might have been forced to agree, in time.*'

The last comments had been written on the day before his wedding. '*My wife-to-be looks a little like her but there the resemblance ends. If only Dorothea could inspire the tiniest fraction of the emotions I once felt.*'

The late king's loyal friend once more skimmed through the on-screen pages of the draft manuscript, smiling at the childlike innocence of some entries. '*They wouldn't buy me a Rottweiler for my birthday because it might attack the corgis. Corgis aren't proper dogs.*'

Keith was no longer worried that anyone might recognise themselves as characters from the many encounters he'd described. Some, including a bunch of ex-miners from his home village, certainly would. So what if they did? None of that really mattered now. The one thing that did matter was the chapter heading of a June 1967 date, followed only by a row of question marks. He wished Eustace had still been around to advise. What would the old Earl of Willaston's thoughts have been?

He stood up, walked to the window and leant on the sill. 'What does it amount to?' he imagined Eustace saying. 'You've written a fine series of adventures, dear boy. Some of them helped to shape a king. But where's the one which had the most impact? Which one forms the heart of your book?'

Returning to the old diary, Keith read once more the original entry that ended, *'All I knew was that her name was Jan and that she lived in Morden.'*

With a glance at the clip bearing intertwined 'J's, he started to type, having finally decided to publish and be damned.

EXPLANATORY NOTES

The essence of this work of fiction is to reconcile those events that really happened with those which might have happened had Her Majesty The Queen had a younger brother and, therefore, not acceded to the British throne in 1952, upon the death of her father.

From the start of King George VI's reign in 1936, the then Princess Elizabeth was heir presumptive. Had she been male, she would have been heir apparent. If her younger sister Margaret had instead been a younger brother, 'he' would have been heir apparent, and our present queen, although older, would have become second in line.

Princess Margaret was second in line until the birth of her nephew, Prince Charles, in 1948. She dropped another place upon the birth of her niece, Princess Anne, in 1950.

These notes clarify, where considered necessary, what is real and what is not real. They also provide additional information which the reader may find helpful or, simply, interesting. It has not been possible to include all details in the text, either because they relate to 'future' events, or because they would have unduly disrupted the narrative.

1948

CHAPTER 1

1 In private, Prince Phillip called the Queen by her family nickname of 'Lilibet' which, unable to cope with all four of the syllables in Elizabeth, was how she referred to herself as a child. He also called her 'Sausage' or 'Cabbage'. In French, 'mon petit chou' ('my little cabbage') is a form of endearment equivalent to 'sweetheart'.

2 Traditionally, the Home Secretary had to be present at royal births. This was to prevent the possibility of the baby's being substituted for another, as was rumoured to have been the case when, in 1688, James II's wife produced a son. (The baby was said to have been smuggled into the birthing chamber in a warming pan.) This son later became known as 'The Old Pretender' and claimed the throne of England and Ireland, as James III, on the death in 1701 of his deposed father.

Her Majesty's own birth in 1926 was witnessed. The last time a Home Secretary attended a royal birth was on Christmas Day 1936, when Princess Alexandra, daughter of the Duke of Kent, was born.

James Chuter Ede served as Home Secretary under Prime Minister Clement Atlee. Although the longest-serving Home Secretary of the 20th century, he is little remembered, despite his having pushed through a number of significant reforms.

3 The current royal dynasty remains the House of Windsor. Prince Phillip, who was from the German House of Battenberg, had taken the revised (Anglicised) name of 'Mountbatten' and was keen that his own descendants also use this name. Continuing pressure resulted in the adoption of the surname 'Mountbatten-Windsor' by some descendants of Queen Elizabeth II and the Duke of Edinburgh. It was first officially used by Princess Anne in 1973, on the occasion of her marriage to Mark Phillips.

4 Sir Norman Hartnell was a British fashion designer and dressmaker to both the Queen and the Queen Mother.

5 Prince Phillip's mother, Princess Alice of Battenberg, was a great-granddaughter of Queen Victoria and lived an eventful life. She suffered from congenital deafness, but learned to lip-read in four languages. During the Second World War, she risked her life saving Jews from extermination by the Nazis. For the last two or so years before her death in 1969, she resided at Buckingham Palace with her only son and daughter-in-law.

6 Prince Phillip was not present at the birth of Prince Charles, nor was he when Anne (b.1950) and Andrew (b.1960) arrived. He did, however, attend the birth of Edward (b.1964), at the Queen's request.

7 In 1995, UCL created its Constitution Unit, initially to conduct detailed research and planning on constitutional reform in the UK. This remit has since been extended to institutions worldwide.

8 Sir Hartley Shawcross served as Attorney General for England and Wales from 1945 to 1951. He was lead British prosecutor at the Nuremberg war crimes tribunal and was also Britain's principal delegate to the United Nations from 1945 to 1949.

9 Sir Alan Frederick 'Tommy' Lascelles was appointed Private Secretary to George VI in 1943, and held the same position under Elizabeth II until his retirement on 31st December 1953. This courtier, depicted in early episodes of the Netflix production *The Crown*, was a cousin of the Harewood family.

10 After two short-lived daughters, William IV's wife last gave birth in 1822, to stillborn male twins. Had they survived, the elder would have become the rightful king. Beyond any living issue of William and Adelaide (male or female), nobody stood in Victoria's way. Her own father was, by then, dead, and that left only younger uncles. Even if these uncles had produced sons, Victoria would still have been heir, in the same way that Queen Elizabeth II was heir presumptive, and not the sons of her uncles who were younger than George VI (i.e. the Dukes of Gloucester and Kent).

   With Victoria's accession to the throne, a special provision ('the saving') was made in the wording of the accession declaration to provide for the possibility that William's 44-year-old widow was pregnant. It is not known whether, on George VI's death in 1952, any consideration was given to the remote possibility that his widow might be pregnant with a son. HM Queen Elizabeth The Queen Mother was 51 years old at the time.

11 George VI described his wife as 'the most marvellous person in the world in my eyes'. However, as the 24-year-old Duke of York, he became infatuated with the 'Queen of Musical Comedy', Evelyn Laye, and this devotion endured for the rest of his life. 'The Beautiful Boo' remained discrete about their relationship. When the text of a proposed article about her mentioned the King's 'fervent admiration' of her, she struck out the passage and wrote in the margin, 'Not in the Queen Mother's lifetime'. Laye died in 1996.

12 During the war, the government decreed that all goods made in factories must have a practical purpose. This instantly eliminated ornamental objects and items such as vases. To get round this, Woolworths reclassified flower vases as utensils by adding the back stamp 'CELERY'. Even so, there were severe shortages but, by 1948, supplies (many via the company's Republic of Ireland store in Dublin) had begun to increase.

13 Woolworths is usually spelt without an apostrophe, but sometimes 'Woolworth's' is used. The chain was often fondly referred to as 'Woolies'. Until more recently, the shop signs read 'F.W.WOOLWORTH CO'. Deptford High Street, where a branch of Woolworths was located, was the 'Oxford Street' of South London in the 1890s, so prosperous that many of its working-class shopkeepers kept domestic servants. Over the years, it became progressively shabbier.

14 Standford Street is a fictional street just off the real-life Evelyn Street, a main thoroughfare through Deptford named after the Evelyn family. Seventeenth-century writer and diarist John Evelyn acquired, by marriage, Sayes Court, a house with surrounding grounds situated in Deptford. He meticulously laid out splendid gardens at the property.

Many of the streets in the area were torn down 'for redevelopment' in the early 1960s. Some residents who refused to leave ended up living in isolated houses, surrounded by rubble. Others waited, in a state of uncertainty, to be rehoused.

15 The 'canary girls' were British female munitions workers during the First World War. They handled TNT, a toxic explosive, exposure to which could turn the skin an orangey-yellow colour.

CHAPTER 2

1 The creation of a Prince of Wales has no statutory basis. There has been considerable legal argument about whether custom or tradition can acquire the status of law *sui generis* (as one of a kind) simply by virtue of having been practised without disturbance for a long time.

2 'The law is an ass' is a statement generally attributed to Charles Dickens. It was uttered by the character Mr Bumble in *Oliver Twist*. However, it features much earlier in the play *Revenge for Honour*, published in 1654.

3 'Ich dien' is the motto of the Prince of Wales. It is German for 'I serve'. Together with the symbol of three feathers, it dates back to 1343 and the time of Edward the Black Prince. According to legend, both motto and emblem were chosen as spoils of war, following an English victory over King John of Bohemia. However, neither was used by the Bohemian king, so this explanation is unlikely. Another theory is that the motto derives from the Welsh 'Eich Dyn', meaning 'your man'.

4 For centuries, a system of male-preference primogeniture governed the line of succession to the throne. Under the Act of Settlement (1701), this principle was not expressly stated, but it is deemed to have been implied under English common law. This meant that younger sons always took precedence over older daughters. Although almost unimaginable in 1948, this was changed in 2011 under the Perth Agreement, which also provided that those who married Catholics would no longer be excluded from the line of succession. As the Queen is head of state of sixteen Commonwealth realms (including Canada, Australia, New Zealand and Jamaica), all had to sign up to the agreement. In 2020, Barbados announced its decision to become a republic.

5 *Nova constitutio futuris formam imponere debet non praeteritis* is the legal maxim that governs almost every Act of Parliament. It essentially means that a new law ought to impose form on what is to be done (or is not to be

done) in the future, not the past. There have, however, been rare examples of retrospective legislation – usually made to correct practices which have been found to be illegal, or to validate (or arguably clarify) activities which have no statutory basis.

6 The Privy Council is a large advisory body to the monarch. Its current membership (on which there is no limit) is 715 (more than double that of 1952), but it can function with a quorum of only three.

Members include senior UK politicians (all cabinet ministers and the leaders of the major opposition parties), the Church of England's three senior bishops, senior justices, some Commonwealth politicians and certain officials. As membership is for life, there are an awful lot of counsellors who never attend. (On rare occasions, privy counsellors have, however, been removed, or have requested to be removed.) Privy counsellors are addressed as 'The Right Honourable'.

'Privy' means private, and members take an oath, or make an affirmation, requiring them to keep secret all matters committed to them. It meets about once a month, with usually only a handful of attendees, in the presence of the monarch. A full meeting of all counsellors is held on only two occasions: the accession of a new sovereign (which last happened in 1952), and when an unmarried sovereign announces his or her intention to marry (which last happened in 1839, when Queen Victoria wanted to marry Prince Albert). Even then, not everyone attends.

The Privy Council forms an important link between the executive powers of ministers and the constitutional authority of the sovereign. In theory, the extent of royal prerogative and a monarch's statutory powers is enormous. In practice, this authority is almost never exercised, and there would be shockwaves if it ever were. The system is essentially a mechanism whereby government ministers recommend pieces of proposed legislation (which have already been agreed) and, on their advice, the monarch says 'approved.'

The Privy Council's other roles include extending legislation to British Overseas Territories, ratifying legislation from Crown Dependencies (e.g. the Channel Islands) and, via the Judicial Committee, acting as the highest court of appeal for certain Commonwealth countries.

7 The saying 'It's easier to ask forgiveness than it is to get permission' (and its many variations) is commonly attributed to Grace Hopper, a US navy officer and early computer programmer. She first quoted it in 1986. However, the adage dates much further back than this. The words 'It being less difficult to obtain forgiveness for it after it was done, than permission for doing it' featured in an 1846 work of fiction by Agnes Strickland. Versions also turned up in a Pittsburgh newspaper story (1894) and in a 1903 novel by Mrs Edward Kennard.

8 Letters patent (always plural) are open documents and legal instruments by which the sovereign's will is enacted – for example, to confer an office or create a new peerage. Letters patent were issued in 1958 when Prince Charles was created Prince of Wales.

9 The Welsh newspaper reacted as stated. Prince Charles' investiture took place on 1st July 1969.

10 Phylip with one 'y' is the Welsh spelling of the name.

CHAPTER 3

1 Large families were almost a tradition in the royal family. Queen Victoria had nine children (four boys and five girls). With three boys and three girls, Edward VII was the father of six, as was George V (five boys and one girl).

There are several theories as to why George VI and his wife had only two children. One suggestion is that George contracted mumps in 1911, while he was at the Royal Naval College in Dartmouth, resulting in reduced fertility. Another is that because the Queen Mother, after difficult pregnancies, twice gave birth by caesarean section, she was advised against having further children. The simplest explanation is that the couple simply felt their family was complete. They never expected to become king and queen and, even when George was thrust upon the throne, they had 'an heir and a spare'.

It is rumoured that Edward VIII, also exposed to mumps at Dartmouth, became infertile as a result.

2 The Dukedom of Cornwall can only be held by the oldest living son of the monarch, who is also heir apparent. It cannot be held by other males (e.g. grandsons or nephews), even if they are heirs apparent. Prince Charles became Duke of Cornwall in February 1952 when his mother became Queen and was officially proclaimed as such in 1973. His feudal dues included gilt spurs and greyhounds, a pound of pepper and cumin, a bow, a salmon spear, wood for his fires and silver shillings.

Dukes of Cornwall also hold the titles which used to be given to the heirs to the Kingdom of Scotland.

3 After the Second World War, National Service was a form of peacetime conscription whereby all able-bodied men aged between 18 and 30 years were called up for a period of 18 months (increased to two years during the Korean War, 1950–53). The last National Serviceman was demobbed in 1963.

CHAPTER 4

1 Jiminy Cricket is a character invented in 1883 by Carlo Collodi for his book *The Adventures of Pinocchio*. This was turned into an animated Disney film in 1940, which featured a cartoon version of Jiminy, who was appointed Pinocchio's official conscience.

2 Lionel Logue was an Australian self-taught speech therapist, who helped George VI to overcome a severe stammer. Their relationship was the subject of the film *The King's Speech*. Logue died in April 1953, aged 73.

3 The term 'role model' was coined by American sociologist Robert King Merton (1910–2003). He is also credited with developing the concept of the 'self-fulfilling prophecy'.

4 Sir Clarence Henry Kennett Marten KCVO (Knight Commander of the Royal Victorian Order) was subsequently appointed Provost (chairman of the Governing Body of Eton College) in 1945. He was co-author of *The Groundwork of British History* (published 1912), which became the standard school textbook on the subject. He died in December 1948.

5 The heir to an earldom is a viscount. A viscount's title can be either a
surname, or a place name, or a combination of both. When Princess
Margaret's husband, Anthony Armstrong-Jones, was created Earl of
Snowdon in 1961, he chose Linley for the viscountcy (after his maternal
great-grandfather) and Nymans in the County of Sussex for the territorial
designation (after a garden close to where his mother had grown up).

The creation of new earldoms is rare, especially in the circumstances
described here, but not unheard of. The most recent (excluding Prince
Edward, Earl of Wessex) is the Earldom of Stockton, which was created
for former Prime Minister Harold Macmillan, whose heir was Viscount
Macmillan of Ovenden, of Chelwood Gate in the County of East Sussex
and of Stockton-on-Tees in the County of Cleveland.

From 1974 onwards, the counties of Wales have undergone a number of
boundary adjustments, mergers, separations and name changes. Hanmer,
near Wrexham (Wrecsam in Welsh), is in a county now called Clwyd.

CHAPTER 5

1 From the mid-1960s, Down (or Down's) syndrome was increasingly used
to describe the genetic condition formerly known as Mongolism or
Mongoloid idiocy. The obsolete medical terms are now considered to be
misleading, offensive and wholly unacceptable. The chance of having a
baby with the syndrome increases with maternal age. At 45 years old,
there is a one in thirty risk; this is roughly 50 times greater than it is for a
woman in her early twenties.

2 King George VI enjoyed visiting his horses in training and at stud, but
wasn't the racing enthusiast that his wife and daughter turned out to be.
Upon his death, the Queen inherited his horses, as well as his racing
colours of a purple jacket, scarlet sleeves and gold braid. The Queen
Mother's own colours were first carried on Manicou, her second
steeplechaser and the first one she owned outright.

3 Monaveen – bought from a West Ham greyhound trainer and owned in
partnership with her daughter – and all the Queen Mother's subsequent
horses (until 1973) were trained by Peter Cazalet at his Fairlawne country

house at Shipbourne in Kent. Lord Mildmay was his stable jockey. She spent many happy weekends there with celebrity guests (such as Elizabeth Taylor), with entertainment provided by Noël Coward. Sometimes a day's racing at the nearby 'leafy' Lingfield Park was included.

Fairlawne was sold in 1979 to Prince Khalid Abdullah (d.2021), who founded Juddmonte Farms – one of the leading organisations in thoroughbred horseracing.

4 A lighter is a flat-bottomed barge. The term 'lighterman' usually refers to workers who operated unpowered lighters in London's docks. The job was highly skilled. The lightermen, steering by means of oars, used the River Thames' currents to travel westwards on the incoming tide, and eastwards on the ebbing tide. Their function was to transfer goods between ships, quaysides and factories along the river. With the advent of containerisation and the closure of London's major central docks, their trade largely disappeared.

5 High street betting shops were not introduced until 1961.

6 GPO stood for General Post Office. A monopoly, it was the state-run postal system and telecommunications carrier in the UK. In 1969, its assets were transferred to the Post Office. In 1981, the functions were split.

7 After D-Day (4th June 1944), Hitler ordered the long-range bombardment of England, as a last ditch attempt to win the war and as an act of vengeance.

V-1s, the so-called doodlebugs, were pilotless planes that made a droning sound. When the sound stopped, it meant that the engine had cut out and that the missile was about to drop. Around 25 per cent crashed before reaching their targets and over half the remainder were brought down by fighter aircraft, anti-aircraft guns or massed barrage balloons. There were over 9,000 V-1 attacks on London alone.

More advanced than the V-1s were the silent and deadly V-2 supersonic rockets. They were the world's first long-range guided ballistic missile, and there was no defence against them. However, due to false intelligence fed to the Germans, a number failed to reach their targets. The V-2 rocket was first deployed against Paris on 7th September 1944. The last V-2 strike was in March 1945, when 134 people in Whitechapel, London, were killed.

The Woolworth's New Cross store was not rebuilt until 1960.

8 Oxford shoes are lace-up brogues. Women's styles usually had 2- or 3-in. stacked heels. In the 1940s, they were sturdy, practical, comfortable and long-lasting. Almost everyone had at least one pair in either black or brown leather.

CHAPTER 6

1 Her Majesty owns all the swans in England, and there is an official role of Queen's Swan Marker, who is responsible for the birds' welfare. He also organises the annual Swan Upping ceremony on the River Thames, when all mute swans are rounded up and ringed. This is done so the population can be monitored.

A statute passed by Edward II in 1324 also means that the monarch owns all sturgeon, dolphins, porpoises and whales within three miles of the coast. If any are washed up, they must be offered to the reigning king or queen as a gesture of loyalty.

2 Beeston Castle is located in Cheshire. It was built in the 1220s and kept in good repair until the 16th century. It is now in ruins but enough of it survives to provide a good indication of how it once looked. Now owned by English Heritage, from it can be seen the Welsh mountains and the Pennines.

3 'Plates' means feet ('plates of meat'). Cockney rhyming slang was developed in the East End of London during the mid-19th century. It is not known exactly why, but it was useful for traders in market places, enabling them to collude without customers' knowing what they were talking about. It could also be used by criminals hoping to confuse the police. The language relies on pairs of words, the second one of which rhymes with the intended meaning. Thus, 'me old china' means 'my old mate' (derived from 'china plate'), 'loaf' means head (from 'loaf of bread'), 'apples' means stairs ('apples and pears'), 'whistle' means suit ('whistle and flute'), 'butchers' means look ('butcher's hook') and so on. Usage is not as common these days as it once used to be.

CHAPTER 7

1 Lewisham Municipal Maternity Home was opened in 1918 by Queen Mary. It is presumed to have closed as a result of the outbreak of war in 1939, and its use in this book is a fictional device.

2 In the 1950s and most of the 1960s there was a spike in March weddings due to a tax rule whereby a married man could claim a full year's allowance, even if he married only a day before the end of the financial year (around 5th April). The married man's allowance was over 50 per cent more than the single man's allowance. This was changed in the 1968 budget.

3 Temple Bar is the ceremonial entrance to the City of London from the City of Westminster. It marks the dividing line between the Strand to the west and Fleet Street (the centre of British printing and publishing from the 16th century) to the east. When George VI was travelling to St Paul's for the opening of the Festival of Britain, he was presented with a sword. This was handed back in a symbolic demonstration that he was entering the City of London in peace.

CHAPTER 8

1 In the UK, a regent is someone who acts on behalf of a king or queen because that monarch is a minor, absent or incapacitated. The best known regent in British history was the future George IV, who held the role when his father (George III) was incapacitated by mental illness.

There have been a number of Regency Acts over the centuries, usually passed when necessary. In December 1936, Edward VIII abdicated after reigning for only 10 months. (For this reason, 1936 is referred to as 'The Year of the Three Kings'.) George V's second son became king. The new monarch's heir presumptive (Princess Elizabeth) was only ten years old. General provisions for all eventualities, including a minor acceding to the throne, were therefore needed.

The 1937 Regency Act was thus passed. It provided that the regent shall be the 'next eligible' person in line to the throne. To be eligible, that person had to reside in the UK and be aged 21 years or over. In 1937, the next in line after Princess Elizabeth was Princess Margaret, her younger sister, then aged six. Third and fourth in line were the George VI's younger brothers – the Duke of Gloucester and the Duke of Kent. (George, Duke of Kent, who was the fourth son of George V and Queen Mary, died in a plane crash in 1942. An officer in the Royal Air Force, he was the first member of the royal family to die on active service for more than 450 years.)

Thus, had George VI died while Princess Elizabeth was still a minor, the Duke of Gloucester would have become regent.

2 Counsellors of State can act on behalf of the monarch and, in this book's scenario, on behalf of a regent. The Counsellors of State are the monarch's consort (if there is one) and four others, who are the next four eligible royals in the line of succession. The age of eligibility is now 18 years old.

For the purposes of this work of fiction, the order of succession upon the death of George VI would have been as follows (Counsellors of State underlined):

1. HRH Princess Elizabeth (b.21st April 1926)
2. HRH Prince Charles (b.14th November 1948)
3. HRH Princess Anne (b.15th August 1950)
4. HRH Princess Margaret (b.21st August 1930)
5. HRH Henry, Duke of Gloucester (b.31st March 1900)
6. HRH Prince William of Gloucester (b.18th December 1941)
7. HRH Prince Richard of Gloucester (b.26th August 1944)
8. HRH Prince Edward, Duke of Kent (b.9th October 1935)
9. HRH Prince Michael of Kent (b.4th July 1942)
10. HRH Princess Alexandra of Kent (b.25th December 1936)
11. HRH Princess Mary, Princess Royal (b.25th April 1897)
12. George Lascelles, 7th Earl of Harewood (b.23rd February 1923)
13. David Lascelles, Viscount Lascelles (b.21st October 1950)
14. Tinkerbell Lascelles (b.21st August 1924)

Charles, Anne, the Duke of Gloucester's two sons, and the three Kent cousins were all too young in 1952 to be eligible. The Counsellors of State therefore included Princess Mary, the only daughter of George V and

Queen Mary. In reality, her son, George Lascelles, who was the seventh Earl of Harewood from 1956 until his death in 2011, was also a Counsellor in 1952.

3 Before becoming Queen, Elizabeth was occasionally referred to as 'the Princess Elizabeth, Duchess of Edinburgh'. The Duke of Edinburgh was given his title upon the couple's marriage.

4 As she was no longer Queen Consort, the Queen Dowager automatically lost her role as Counsellor of State upon the death of George VI. As the new Queen Elizabeth II's consort, Prince Phillip automatically became a Counsellor in 1952. This resulted in a situation whereby her husband could act on the Queen's behalf, but her mother could not.

Had the Queen died or become incapacitated while Charles was still a minor, Princess Margaret would, under the 1937 Act, have become regent (as the next eligible person in line of succession). This was changed under the 1953 Regency Act, which provided that the Duke of Edinburgh would assume the role until Prince Charles reached the 'royal' age of majority, which, in his case (but not yet for the population at large) had been reduced from 21 to 18 years.

Pressure had obviously been brought to bear to regularise the Queen Mother's position because, on a personal basis for her lifetime, an exception was made under the 1953 Act and she was reinstated as a Counsellor of State.

The current Counsellors of State are Princes Charles, William, Harry (although living in the United States, he is still technically 'domiciled' in UK) and Andrew.

5 The Royal Collection is the largest private collection of artwork, furniture and jewels in the world. Most of the collection is held by the Queen 'in right of the Crown' (i.e. for the duration of her reign). The value of it is traditionally viewed as 'priceless', but recent estimates indicate that it is worth up to £12.7 billion. Six hundred drawings by Leonardo da Vinci alone are valued at £3.22 billion.

Queen Mary (consort of King George V) was an avid collector, and sometimes paid well over the market value to acquire an item she wanted. One of her best known pieces is the palatial dolls' house designed by leading British architect Sir Edwin Lutyens. It features electricity, hot and cold running water and working lifts. Every fully-furnished room is accurate down to the last perfectly scaled detail. George V was himself a keen philatelist who, in 1904, paid £1,450 (well over £1 million in today's money) for a single stamp (a Mauritius two pence blue).

CHAPTER 9

1 'Utterly oyster' was a favourite phrase of the Queen Mother. It described being clammed-shut (i.e. saying nothing). In 1949, she used it when she was attempting to dissuade Marion Crawford, the former governess of Princesses Elizabeth and Margaret, from accepting a lucrative 'tell all' story deal from an American publisher. 'Crawfie', as she was known, went ahead and was, as a result, completely ostracised by the royal family.

2 The Queen Mother bought the Castle of Mey in 1952 and spent a huge amount of her own capital restoring it. In 1954, she had a Frigidaire refrigerator installed there. This is still going strong after almost 70 years and is thought to be the oldest working fridge in the country.

Despite this evidence of her supposed frugality, there is no doubt that she was the most extravagant member of the royal family. Constantly bailed out by her daughter and, later, her grandson Prince Charles, upon her death, she had a multi-million pound overdraft with the royal bankers Coutts.

3 In heraldry, the term 'couchant' means lying down, and 'rampant' means standing up. The coronet of a British earl bears eight strawberry leaves (four visible) and eight silver pearls around the rim (five visible). Coronets are rarely worn, except at coronations.

CHAPTER 10

1 Photographs featuring George V's children show that all four of his sons (the future kings Edward VIII and George VI, the Dukes of Gloucester and Kent, and Prince John) had hair which parted naturally on the left. Photos of a very young Prince Charles suggest a parting on the right, but

this was quickly switched. Prince Andrew's parting was on the left from the outset. The only one of the Queen's sons to sport a right-sided parting in adulthood is Prince Edward.

Both Prince William and Prince Harry followed the family tradition, and both also seemed to go through phases of having no discernible partings at all. However, Princes George and Louis of Cambridge seem to have bucked the trend by taking after their mother, whose parting falls naturally to the right. It will be interesting to see whether this changes as they grow older.

2 The striking of Edward VIII's coinage was not due to begin until January 1937, by which time he had abdicated. A very few pattern pieces (effectively samples to evaluate the design) were struck. The same image of Queen Elizabeth II has been in use on postage stamps for more than fifty years. In 2011, with the possibility of the Royal Mail's being sold to foreigners, Parliament passed a law stating that the monarch's head must always feature on British stamps.

3 George VI was known to have occasional angry outbursts.

4 A special coronation issue of two National Savings Stamps, depicting the royal children, were issued on 1st January 1953. There were further issues with updated images in 1954 and 1960. The value of the Prince Charles stamps was 2/6d (12 and a half pence in today's currency), while the value of the Princess Anne stamps was 6d (2 and a half pence). The stamps, which were stuck in a special book, were popular with children. Completed books could be exchanged at post offices for a National Savings Certificate. The scheme lasted until 1978.

5 Capital punishment for murder was abolished in Britain in 1969 (1973 in Northern Ireland). The death penalty for certain offences (such as treason) remained on the statute books until 1998.

1954

CHAPTER 11

1 Harbingers of the 1950s teenage revolution, Teddy boys were youths who wore long draped jackets that resembled those favoured by dandies of the Edwardian period (thus giving rise to the 'Teddy' nickname). Favoured footwear included suede shoes with thick crepe soles (nicknamed 'brothel creepers' or 'beetle crushers'). Their upswept pompadour haircuts became iconic. They were associated with early rock and roll, jazz and skiffle music. Widely viewed as bad or dangerous, they were forerunners of the 1960s rockers. There were also Teddy girls.

2 Group Captain Peter Townsend was a British RAF officer who served gallantly as a squadron leader during the Battle of Britain. He is credited with shooting down at least eleven enemy aircraft. In 1944, he was appointed equerry to King George VI, and he served in the royal household until 1953. He and his wife of eleven years divorced in 1952. Soon after, he became romantically involved with Princess Margaret, and the couple got engaged in 1953. The proposed union caused a constitutional crisis, because the Church of England refused to accept the remarriage of the divorced.

The Queen is Supreme Governor of the Church of England and, under the Royal Marriages Act of 1772, her consent was required while ever her sister was aged under 25 years old. Winston Churchill's Cabinet also refused approval. When news of the relationship appeared in the press, Townsend was posted to the British Embassy in Brussels. The British public were largely in favour of the match, and the Queen wanted Margaret to be happy. In October 1955, a compromise emerged enabling a civil marriage, subject to the princess' relinquishing her rights to the succession, but she later announced her decision not to marry, citing her duty to the Commonwealth as one of the reasons.

Although Townsend later claimed that their feelings for one another remained unchanged, there has been speculation that, on her side at least, this was not the case.

CHAPTER 12

1 The Walthamstow Hoe Street bombing happened in broad daylight at 10 a.m. on Saturday 16th August 1944. A huge area was devastated by a V-1 flying bomb, and there were many casualties and fatalities.

2 The Co-op on Grand Drive, Lower Morden, is still there.

3 Anthony Eden, regarded as one of the least successful British prime ministers, was created Earl of Avon in 1961, and died in 1977.

1958

CHAPTER 13

1 Heatherdown, near Ascot, was a preparatory school regarded as a 'feeder' for Eton. Both Prince Andrew and Prince Edward went there, as did Princess Alexandra's son James and the Duke of Kent's son George. The school closed in 1982. Cheam School still exists.

2 The wedding of Princess Margaret and 'Tony' Armstrong-Jones took place on 6th May 1960. The bride, whose dress was designed by Norman Hartnell, was given away by her brother-in-law, Prince Phillip. The groom's best man was Dr Roger Gilliatt, son of royal gynaecologist Sir William Gilliatt.

Kingsley Amis thought Princess Margaret's marriage a dreadful symbol of modern Britain, 'when a royal princess, famed for her devotion to all that is most vapid and mindless, is united with a dog-faced, tight-jeaned fotog of fruitarian tastes such as can be found in dozens of any pseudo-arty drinking cellars in London. They're made for each other.'

3 The Queen's third child, Prince Andrew, was born in February 1960.

4 The Rolling Stones' song 'Mother's Little Helper' was recorded in March 1966 and referred to the increasing usage of tranquilisers, such as Valium, amongst housewives.

CHAPTER 14

1 The 'Great Nine' public schools of England are Eton, Harrow, Winchester, Charterhouse, Merchant Taylors', Westminster, Shrewsbury, Rugby and St Paul's.

2 *Time* magazine reported of the Sixties, 'The guards now change at Buckingham Palace to a Lennon and McCartney tune, and Prince Charles is firmly in the long-hair set.' (Maybe his fringe had grown a bit...?)

1965

CHAPTER 15

1 On 26th February 1965, the Duke of Windsor was admitted to the London Clinic, where he underwent an eye operation to correct a detached retina. A further two procedures followed. He was discharged on 28th March, and returned to Paris.

In 1972, Prince Charles and the Queen both visited the Windsors at their Paris home, a few days before the Duke died. The Duchess of Windsor insisted on being styled HRH in her own household.

2 The Duke and Duchess of Windsor were friends (and, in rural France, neighbours) of Sir Oswald and Lady Diana Mosley. Sir Oswald Mosley, leader of the British Union of Fascists, had been imprisoned during the Second World War. Diana was one of the famous Mitford sisters. In 1989, she appeared on *Desert Island Discs*, a radio programme which began in 1942. It was arguably the most controversial episode ever. In the broadcast, she claimed that the number of Jews exterminated by the Nazis was exaggerated. When she died (in 2003), amongst her personal effects was a diamond swastika brooch.

3 Coronation is possible at any age. However, as the ceremonial involves the taking of an oath, the ability to speak is handy. In the past, being crowned gave a monarch added security of tenure.

Minors who became king include:

Edward III, aged 14. Crowned immediately.

Edward V, aged 12. One of the murdered 'Princes in the Tower'. Never crowned.

Richard II, aged 10. Crowned immediately.

Edward VI, aged 9. Crowned immediately.

Henry III, aged 9. Crowned immediately.

Henry VI, aged 8 months. Crowned aged 7.

4 The Family Law Reform Act 1969 reduced the age of majority in England from 21 to 18 years. On 1st January 1970, everyone aged 18, 19 and 20 years old 'came of age'.

5 The Queen's 1953 coronation took fourteen months of preparation.

6 King George II was the last British monarch to lead his troops into battle. This was during the War of the Spanish Succession, at the Battle of Dettingen (1743).

CHAPTER 16

1 England's third goal in the 1966 World Cup final was controversial and prompted German claims that the Soviet linesman was biased (West Germany had knocked out the USSR in the semi-finals). For a goal to be valid, the whole of the ball must pass over the goal line. Modern technology indicates that only 97% of it actually did. However, if the referee decrees a goal to be a goal, then it *is* a goal.

2 Her Majesty The Queen presented the cup and the medals. On her right was her cousin, the Earl of Harewood, who was president of the Football Association.

3 In 1980, a children's book written by HRH Prince Charles was published. Titled *The Old Man of Lochnagar*, it was based on a story devised to

entertain Princes Andrew and Edward. Proceeds from the sale of the book go to the Prince's Trust.

4 Timbertop, an outpost of Geelong Grammar School, Victoria, was attended by Prince Charles for six months (February to July) in 1966. The Queen Mother visited Australia while he was there. Charles later said that the time he spent at the school was the most enjoyable part of his whole education. British Prime Minister Boris Johnson took a gap year as a teaching assistant at Timbertop in 1983.

5 Prince Charles is known for his love of plants and does much to encourage the planting of trees. When he has planted one, he often gives one of its branches a friendly handshake to wish it well. He is patron of a number of environmental and horticultural organisations, including the Delphinium Society (for those interested in delphiniums) and the British Pteridological Society (for fern enthusiasts).

CHAPTER 17

1 At Oxford University, housekeeping staff are known as 'scouts'. Elsewhere, they are known as 'bedders' (short for 'bedmakers').

2 During the 1960s, unmarried mothers were generally viewed with intolerance and stigmatisation. 1968 was Britain's peak year for adoptions, with well over 16,000 in England and Wales. Some sources put the figure as high as over 24,800. Almost 40% of babies were adopted by a girl's own parents, meaning that slightly more than 60% were adopted by other relatives or non-related people.

Culturally, a pregnancy out of wedlock was something to be hidden, and many girls were sent to mother and baby homes until their confinement. There were 172 such homes in England in 1968.

The situation began to change with the wider availability of birth control, which led to fewer illegitimate pregnancies, although social disapproval remained. By 1980, the number of registered adoptions had more than halved, to 10,600 and had reduced again to 4,300 by 1998. The adoption figures include children, as well as babies.

The 1967 Abortion Act (effective from 1968) may also have had an impact on the number of unwanted pregnancies. It certainly went a long way towards eradicating backstreet abortions and their inherent risks.

3 In 1967, all colleges at Oxford and Cambridge were either exclusively male or exclusively female. The first female students were admitted to a handful of formerly male-only Oxford colleges in 1974, James's *alma mater* Hertford amongst them.

The Hertford College Penguin Club was not formed until 2009. Its notorious initiation ceremonies reputedly included swimming in the River Cherwell, dancing naked around Oxford smeared with goose fat, and eating raw squid. The club, closed by college authorities, was short-lived. Drinking clubs, often characterised as retreats for the over-privileged and hedonistic public school fraternity, have always been a feature of Oxford University life.

4 Monaveen's victory in the race at Fontwell Park in 1949 initiated the Queen Mother's total of 457 victories over the years as a racehorse owner. Her interest in jump racing expanded after the death of her husband. She still had twelve horses in training – shared between Nicky Henderson and Ian Balding – upon her death in 2002.

She was said to prefer the exuberance and informality of National Hunt racing, as it offered 'a bit of danger, a bit of excitement.' She was at Aintree with both her daughters for the 1956 Grand National, when Devon Loch inexplicably 'slipped up' close to the finish.

The Queen Mother Champion Chase trophy – the Grade 1 highlight of the second day of the annual Cheltenham Festival, held in March – was named in her honour from 1980, though victory there eluded her.

1970

CHAPTER 18

1 In 1970, goal difference was not applied when determining the relative position of teams on an equal number of points. Had it been, England would have been declared winners of the 1970 Home Nations contest.

2 To mark the Queen's coronation in 1953, a football tournament was held at Hampden Park. This featured English and Scottish teams competing for the Coronation Cup. The winning team, Celtic, became unofficial champions of Britain.

3 The Lilleshall estate is located in the county of Shropshire. After the Second World War, it was left in ruin and was proving expensive to run. In 1949, it was sold to the Central Council of Physical Recreation, which was seeking a second National Recreation Centre to serve the north of England. Its purchase was made possible by a financial gift from the people of South Africa. The new Sports Centre was opened by Princess Elizabeth in 1951. The England 1966 World Cup squad trained there.

4 The Queen's Anello and Davide shoes are worn in by a junior member of the palace staff, whose feet are exactly the same size as Her Majesty's. This servant, nicknamed 'Cinders', wears socks to perform the service and walks only in carpeted areas.

5 After the Queen's accession, her mother took well over a year to vacate her apartment at Buckingham Palace. Eventually, she reluctantly relocated to Clarence House, which she described as 'this horrid little house'. She spent £1 million on refurbishing it, stripping out all Prince Phillip's installations. She also maintained four other residences, all kept fully staffed. These were the Castle of Mey, Birkhall (on the Balmoral Estate), Royal Lodge (in Windsor Great Park) and Walmer Castle (acquired when she became Lord Warden of the Cinque Ports).

Once the London residence of the Dukes of Marlborough, Marlborough House was home to both Queen Alexandra (widow of Edward VII) and

Queen Mary (widow of George V). Since 1965, it has been leased by the Queen to the Commonwealth Secretariat.

CHAPTER 19

1 The coronation of Her Majesty Queen Elizabeth II took place on Tuesday 2nd June 1953. The event was televised live, and many people bought or rented television sets in order to watch it. Three lots of film were jetted direct to Canada so that Canadians could see the event on the same day. Music was specially commissioned, and there were celebrations in all the Queen's realms, the rest of the Commonwealth and elsewhere across the world.

2 All located on the Old Kent Road, the Frog and Nightgown, the Dun Cow and the Gin Palace pubs have, respectively, now been demolished, converted into a doctors' surgery or become flats. The Razala Ritz never existed.

3 The Queen, Prince Charles, the Duchess of Cornwall and the Duke and Duchess of Cambridge are the only royals who get round-the-clock protection. The Princess Royal, and the Earl and Countess of Wessex are guarded only whilst carrying out official duties and engagements.

4 From the start of 1962, the Celsius scale was given after the Fahrenheit scale in weather forecasts. From 15th October of that year, the Celsius measurement (referred to by most people as degrees centigrade) was given first. The change to metric was accomplished very rapidly.

5 On 21st April 1983 (Her Majesty's 57th birthday), the first £1 coins were issued in the UK. These ultimately replaced £1 banknotes. The reverse design was the Royal Coat of Arms. In 1984, the theme was Scotland, and the thistle was featured. In 1985, it was the turn of the Welsh leek. Third in the series was the Northern Ireland flax (1986). In 1987 came the English oak tree. In the 1990s, the Scottish lion, the Welsh dragon, the Northern Ireland Celtic cross and Broighter collar, and England's three lions appeared. Bridges and cities have since featured. The Broighter collar (or torc) is a large tubular neck collar which was part of a hoard of

Iron Age gold artefacts. This was discovered in 1896 in the north of Ireland. Such collars are associated with Celtic kings and gods.

The twelve-sided 2021 pound coin was designed by 15-year-old David Pearce, who won a competition run by the Royal Mint. On it are the Tudor rose, a leek, a thistle and a shamrock.

1974

CHAPTER 20

1 Miners' pay, which had been relatively high at the start of the 1960s, started to fall below that of other workers over the course of the decade. In 1971, the National Union of Mineworkers (NUM) demanded a 43 per cent pay rise, and miners voted to take industrial action if they didn't get this. A strike followed in early 1972, but the acceptance of an offer, together with the establishment of the Wilberforce Enquiry into miners' pay, resulted in a return to work. The episode demonstrated Britain's dependence on coal, given that most electricity was generated by coal-fired power stations.

The NUM became increasingly militant in 1973, and further pay increase demands were rejected in November 1973, leading to an overtime ban aimed at halving coal production. In December, Prime Minister Edward Heath announced that commercial electricity consumption would be limited to three consecutive days a week (with certain exemptions). These restrictions came into force on 1st January 1974 and lasted until 7th March.

On 24th January, 81 per cent of NUM members voted for a strike, which began on 5th February. Heath called a snap general election, basing his campaign on the slogan 'Who governs Britain?' Labour under Harold Wilson won by a narrow margin, and miners' wages were immediately increased by 35 per cent.

2 The Beatles did play in Sheffield in 1964, and they stayed at Park Hall. All the places mentioned in Killamarsh still exist.

3 The actual date of Ian Ball's kidnap attempt on Princess Anne was 20th March 1974. In a hired Ford Escort, he drove in front of the princess's car, forcing it to stop. Anne's protection officer, her chauffeur, a tabloid journalist and a police officer were all shot during the incident. Ball told the Princess to get out of the car, to which she replied, 'Not bloody likely.' A passing pedestrian, former boxer Ronald Russell, punched Ball in the back of the head and led Anne away. Ball fled the scene but was caught, arrested and subsequently pleaded guilty to attempted murder and kidnap. Evidence suggested that he planned to demand a ransom payment of millions of pounds which, he claimed, he intended to give to the NHS.

   Those involved in thwarting him received awards. When the George Medal was presented to Ronald Russell, the Queen said, 'The medal is from the Queen of England, the thank you is from Anne's mother.' Her Majesty also paid off Russell's mortgage.

4 Whilst most of the media were opposed to the NUM strike, the *Daily Mirror* proved an exception and ran an emotive campaign supporting the miners.

5 Someone *does* iron Prince Charles' shoelaces!

6 Sir Nikolaus Pevsner (1902–83) wrote and compiled *The Buildings of England*, a series of forty-six volumes covering the individual counties of England, published between 1951 and 1974.

7 In 1984, Charles made an 'open attack on modernism' at the Royal Institute of British Architects' 150th anniversary celebration at Hampton Court Palace. He unexpectedly criticised ABK's proposed extension to the National Gallery in Trafalgar Square, calling the design 'a monstrous carbuncle on the face of a much-loved and elegant friend'.

   Charles went on to be heavily involved in the Poundbury development just outside Dorchester, on Duchy of Cornwall land. Initiated by the architect Léon Krier, it was built in accordance with Charles' extremely traditional principles.

CHAPTER 21

1 In 1953, the Queen decided to replace the Tudor Crown on telephone boxes with the St Edward's Crown used for coronations. The EIIR cipher does not appear on pillar boxes in Scotland because some Scottish people do not accept the current queen as the second monarch of her name. Earlier boxes, which did feature the cipher, were vandalised or even blown up. Instead, the Scottish Crown is depicted. The 'R' stands for *Rex* or *Regina* (Latin for 'king' or 'queen').

2 Lucia Santa Cruz, daughter of the then Chilean ambassador to London, was reportedly Prince Charles' first serious girlfriend. The two met at university in 1967, and it was she who supposedly introduced him to Camilla Shand, as someone he might get on well with. Lady Jane Wellesley followed Camilla (1973–4), then Davina Sheffield, whose boyfriend was powerboat racer James Beard. The next romance was with Lady Diana's older sister, Lady Sarah Spencer (1977). Lady Sabrina Guinness (1979), heiress to the Guinness brewery, was next and may have been ruled out due to reports of a racy past. Charles proposed to Lady Amanda Knatchbull (Lord Mountbatten's granddaughter), who turned him down because she did not want to live with all the media attention. He also proposed twice to Anna Wallace (known as 'Whiplash Wallace'), the daughter of a wealthy Scottish landowner, who also rejected him. That relationship ended when he took her to a ball and spent most of the time dancing with Camilla. Anna told him, 'No one treats me like that – not even you.' Charles thus failed to meet a self-imposed deadline of marrying by the age of 30.

3 By a considerable margin, the 1970s has been voted the most tasteless decade in terms of home décor. In particular, coloured bathroom suites, often with patterned matching tiles, characterised many trendy properties. Avocado green was especially popular, but turquoise, pink, maroon, chocolate brown, pampas and apricot (Sun King) were also very popular. On new housing estates, when a choice of fittings was given, purchasers were rarely offered the option of plain white sanitary ware.

4 Founded in 1956, the Duke of Edinburgh's Award Scheme benefits 14- to 18-year-olds. The programme involves three progressive levels of achievement – bronze, silver and gold. It encompasses a wide range of activities under the headings of volunteering, physical, expeditions, and the acquisition of skills. Since its inception, the scheme has expanded to 144 nations.

5 In the 1970s, there were very few charities devoted to family relationships. The Tavistock Centre for Couple Relationships (1948) existed, but Relate wasn't founded until 1983. OnePlusOne, with its emphasis on early intervention, also dates from the 1980s, and Family Lives goes back no further. The Family Welfare Association (founded as the Charity Organisation Society in 1869 and renamed in 1946) did much to support families. In 1975, it organised the UK's first family therapy conference – relatively unheard of at the time. It is now called Family Action.

6 In 1954, the Queen Mother undertook a lengthy solo trip to the USA. To Americans, she was a symbol of British resistance during the Second World War. She appeared, from the newsreels, to be having fun but, in a letter to the Queen, described her travels as hard work and 'hell'. It was the first of more than forty visits abroad. She was patron or president of about 350 organisations.

7 The BBC Sports Personality of the Year awards began in 1954. In 1971, the winner was HRH Princess Anne, who'd been individual gold medallist at the European Eventing Championships earlier that year. Anne went on to participate in the 1976 Montreal Olympic games.

8 Australian Ken Warby still holds the water speed record (317mph), a feat he achieved in October 1978 when piloting his *Spirit of Australia* craft. Prior to that, it was held by American Lee Taylor (288mph), who broke Briton Donald Campbell's 285mph record. Both Taylor and Campbell died in pursuit of the record, Taylor during a test run in 1980. Only one other attempt at the record has been made since Warby beat the 300mph barrier (in 1989) and, again, this resulted in a fatality. Despite the risks, there are several ongoing projects, and the record remains coveted by enthusiasts.

1979

CHAPTER 22

1 Lord Louis Mountbatten was Charles' paternal great-uncle. Appointed Chief of Combined Operations in 1942, he organised the highly successful raid on Saint-Nazaire, a French port on which the Germans placed heavy reliance. He also planned the disastrous raid on Dieppe. As Supreme Allied Commander South East Asia Command, he oversaw the recapture from the Japanese of Burma and Singapore. He was appointed Viceroy of India in 1947 and was charged with achieving a transition to independence which maintained that country's integrity. As there were two opposing political factions, the outcome was a swift and bloody partitioning – and the creation of the separate state of Pakistan.

In 1974, Charles first broached the subject of marrying Mountbatten's granddaughter, Amanda Knatchbull. She was his second cousin and had just turned 17. Her mother thought she was too young at the time. 'Uncle Dickie' advised him as follows. 'In a case like yours, the man should sow his wild oats and have as many affairs as he can before settling down, but for a wife he should choose a suitable, attractive and sweet-charactered girl before she has met anyone else she might fall for.' Mountbatten, keen to stay close to the crown, did everything possible to promote the match, and the couple were reputedly very fond of each other.

In August 2019, FBI files became public. These showed that Mountbatten was an alleged homosexual and paedophile. There have been a number of suggestions that he frequented gay brothels and had a perversion for young boys.

2 On 28th August 1972, Prince William, the Duke of Gloucester's older son, was killed when the Piper Cherokee aircraft he was piloting in a competition crashed.

3 The Toxteth riots in Liverpool occurred against a background of accelerating economic decline and increasing anger about the way the police handled minority communities, with criticisms ranging from clumsy

to downright racist. In early July 1981, there was full-scale rioting involving the use of firebombs and missiles such as paving slabs. When the police failed to drive back the attackers, tear gas was deployed. A second wave of rioting took place in late July. The Scarman report, primarily directed at the Brixton riots which had taken place earlier in the year, recognised that the rioting was a product of social problems. The government's response was to send Michael Heseltine, nicknamed 'Tarzan', to Liverpool and charge him with setting up a task force. Heseltine was the right man for the job and spent a long time walking round housing estates and talking to people.

4 Prince Charles did take Camilla's gift on honeymoon. His new bride found it and also discovered the photos of Camilla, which he kept in his wallet.

5 On 22nd June 1948, the HMT *Empire Windrush* passenger ship – a German-built ship which was claimed as a prize of war – docked at Tilbury. Amongst those who disembarked were 802 people from the Caribbean (mainly Jamaica). The new arrivals were housed temporarily near Brixton, South London. This marked the start of mass immigration from Commonwealth countries to Britain, which was facing a shortage of labour. Workers, most of whom settled permanently, were needed to help rebuild the country after six years of war. Other sectors (such as the NHS and transport) were also suffering from a dearth of workers. The newcomers were often referred to as 'coloureds' (which many mistakenly considered kinder than calling them 'black'), or by the extremely offensive terms 'darkies' and 'coons'.

The first migrants anticipated the passing through Parliament of the British Nationality Act 1948, which gave them the status of citizenship of the United Kingdom and Colonies. In 2017, it emerged that hundreds of Commonwealth citizens were being discriminated against due to the 2012 introduction of stricter immigration controls, which made life in Britain almost unliveable for some of those who could not prove their citizenship rights. Affected were many 'Windrush generation' migrants who'd arrived on their parents' passports and were therefore 'undocumented'. The situation has not yet been fully resolved, despite attempts to simplify the application process and to compensate those who suffered losses because they could not demonstrate their right to live in the UK.

CHAPTER 23

1 The Falklands War (never officially declared as such) is deemed to have started on 2nd April 1982, when Argentina invaded and occupied two British dependent territories located in the South Atlantic. Britain dispatched two task forces – surface ships and submarines – and provided air cover from Ascension Island. It was a difficult undertaking: 255 British servicemen lost their lives, but the British succeeded in recapturing the islands, and the conflict ended on 14th June. Despite the government's apprehension, the Queen insisted that her son be allowed to remain with his ship, HMS *Invincible*, and HRH Prince Andrew saw action as a Sea King helicopter co-pilot. The outcome contributed to an overwhelming Conservative majority in the general election that took place the following year. Argentina still disputes sovereignty.

2 'Quango' (first coined in the 1970s) is not an official term. The acronym stands for 'Quasi Autonomous Non-Governmental Organisation'. Often seen as wasteful bureaucratic bodies, quangos are deemed to be undemocratic because, although substantially funded by government, they enjoy relative freedom from political considerations. This, however, can be advantageous, and some bodies undoubtedly have useful roles in providing specialist expertise.

1985

CHAPTER 24

1 The Dukedom of Albemarle became extinct in 1776. There is an Earldom of Albemarle, associated with the Keppel family. George Keppel, third son of the seventh earl, married Alice, who was a mistress and confidante of King Edward VII until his death in 1910. Camilla, Duchess of Cornwall, is the couple's great-granddaughter. It has been reported that, when Camilla first

met Prince Charles, she reminded him of her great-grandmother's relationship with his forebear and asked, 'So what about it?'

2 Despite his sponsorship of the equal pay for equal work bill, Willie Hamilton, Member of Parliament for Fife Central, is best known for his anti-royalist views. He has called the Queen 'a clockwork doll', labelled Princess Margaret 'a floozy', and declared Prince Charles 'a twerp'. However, he admired the Queen Mother. 'May she live to be the pride of the family.'

In 1957, the Queen's public manner had been cruelly attacked as that of 'a schoolgirl, captain of the hockey team, a prefect and a recent candidate for confirmation.' This prompted a spate of further verbal onslaughts. Her Majesty responded by making a few modest reforms to court life, which included dispensing with the practice of debutante presentations. Princess Margaret had already criticised these events as attracting 'every tart in London'. Inside the palace, the powdered wigs worn by footmen were also done away with.

CHAPTER 25

1 Kensington Palace, sometimes referred to as 'KP', was for a long time regarded as the dumping ground for minor royals. Edward VII referred to it as the 'Aunt heap', and it has also been called the 'dowager dumping ground'. Latterly, it has had more glamorous residents. The Duke and Duchess of Cambridge and their family currently reside there (along with the Queen's Kent and Gloucester cousins).

1987

CHAPTER 26

1 Sarah Ferguson surprised everyone by using the word 'obey' when she spoke her wedding vows. Diana, Princess of Wales had omitted it and, in later years, so did the wives of her sons, Princes William and Harry.

Sophie Rhys Jones did, however, use the word when she married Prince Edward in 1999.

2 The brainchild of Prince Edward, who was keen to develop a career in theatre after leaving the Royal Marines, the *Grand Knockout Tournament* (often referred to as 'It's a Royal Knockout') was recorded on 15th June 1987. The venue was the lakeside lawn of the Alton Towers stately home and theme park. The show was broadcast by the BBC on Saturday 19th June. Each under the captaincy of a royal family member – Prince Edward, Princess Anne, Prince Andrew and Sarah Ferguson, the now Duke and Duchess of York – there were four teams of celebrities, actors and sportspersons famous at the time. The one-off event, based on the popular and long-running television series, raised over £1 million for four charities.

3 On 15th April 1969, 18-year-old Princess Anne and some friends paid a surprise visit to the American musical *Hair*. At the end of performances, the cast (some naked) routinely invited members of the audience to dance with them on stage. The Princess obliged, but did not remove the navy blue trouser suit and white blouse that she was wearing. The musical spawned the songs 'Hair', 'Aquarius' and 'I Got Life'.

CHAPTER 27

1 The King's Cross fire began at approximately 7.30 p.m. on 18th November 1987 at King's Cross St Pancras tube station. Starting under a wooden escalator serving the Piccadilly line of the London Underground, it erupted in a flashover into the ticket hall. Thirty-one people died and 100 more were injured.

2 There are two Royal Standards (flags) in the UK. At first glance, they look similar, but the one used in Scotland features the Scottish lion rampant (upright) twice and the English three lions couchant (lying down) once (five lions in total). The opposite is the case for the English standard (two sets of three English lions and one Scottish lion; seven lions in total). The fourth quadrant (bottom left) contains an Irish harp. The Scottish

standard is flown above royal residences north of the border, except when Her Majesty is in residence.

3 There have been reports that, in 1985, Diana had an affair with Barry Mannakee, a Royal Protection Squad Officer. He may or may not have been the unnamed man with whom Diana was said to have been 'deeply in love' around this time. Mannakee died in a motorcycle accident in 1987 and Diana is rumoured to have said that she thought he'd been 'bumped off'. The James Hewitt affair followed. He was deployed to serve in the Gulf and she felt very let down when he later told all. James Gilbey, an old friend and heir to the Gilbey Gin company, was named as the man to whom she was speaking in a conversation recorded on New Year's Eve 1989. This was the so-called Squidgygate affair (initially dubbed 'Dianagate').

In 1992, just after her father's death, Oliver Hoare was allegedly found semi-naked behind a potted plant in a palace corridor during a fire alarm. An affair with him was never confirmed, beyond the existence of 'a spark', and he apparently refused to leave his wife for the Princess. In 1995, Diana met Will Carling, who denied two trysts. The rumours caused the break-up of his first marriage to Julia. From 1995 to 1997, Diana was romantically involved with heart surgeon Hasnat Khan. She called him 'Mr Wonderful' and begged her 'soul mate' to marry her, but he feared he could not have a normal life if they wed.

Her final liaison was with Dodi Al Fayed, who invited her and her sons to spend the summer of 1997 on his yacht. She later returned alone to join Al Fayed in August.

4 Princess Margaret was very fond of Charles and has referred to him in letters as 'my heavenly nephew'. He called her Aunt Margot, and his sons (Princes William and Harry) both called her 'Great-Aunt Margot'. Her Majesty The Queen is called 'Mama' by her children.

5 The Prince of Wales is believed to have coined the family nickname 'Fog' for Princess Anne's husband Mark Phillips, on the grounds that he was 'thick and wet'. (Charles is also said to have nicknamed his daughter-in-law Meghan 'Tungsten' because, like the strong metal, she is 'tough and unbending'.)

6 In 1985, Mark Phillips fathered a daughter (Felicity) as a result of an affair with a New Zealand teacher named Heather Tonkin. DNA testing confirmed his paternity in 1991. Anne had started an affair with the Queen's equerry, Timothy Lawrence, whom she married in 1992.

7 The Duke and Duchess of York's first child, Princess Beatrice, was born in August 1988. After the birth of the couple's second daughter, Eugenie, in 1990, it was said that Andrew was spending only forty days a year with his wife.

8 This line is a gag from the 1980 spoof disaster film *Airplane!*.

9 Phil Collins did indeed organise and play at Prince Charles' 40th birthday party. He also provided the entertainment for Princess Diana's 30th birthday luncheon at The Savoy in July 1991. He played his saddest, 'most break-up-y' songs, and recalls Elton John and Fergie 'sharing tiara tips at the side of the small stage.' His description of the event is included in his autobiography *Not Dead Yet*, published in 2016.

He has been personally involved with the Prince's Trust for over forty years, and the prog rock band Genesis have donated over £1 million to the cause.

1992

CHAPTER 29

1 When Prince George (first son of the Duke and Duchess of Cambridge) was born on 13th July 2013, a 41-gun salute was fired in Green Park – the customary twenty-one round royal salute, plus an extra twenty rounds because it took place in a royal park. His birth was also marked by sixty-two rounds fired from the Tower of London – the usual twenty-one rounds, an extra twenty because the location was a royal palace, and a further twenty-one because the salute took place in the City of London.

An amazing 124 rounds were fired at the Tower whenever Prince Phillip's birthday (10th June) coincided with the Queen's designated official birthday (which falls on one of the first three Saturdays in June and is marked by Trooping the Colour). Each event merited sixty-two rounds.

Gun salutes occur on the anniversary of the Queen's accession to the throne, on her real birthday (21st April), on Coronation Day (2nd June) and on Prince Charles' birthday (14th November). They also happen upon the State Opening of Parliament, when Parliament is prorogued, when a head of state is meeting the sovereign (in London, Windsor or Edinburgh) and on the occasion of royal births. In each instance, blanks are fired.

2 On 16th June 1992, *Diana: Her True Story*, written by Andrew Morton, was published. Although denied at the time, the Princess of Wales had contributed much of the material for it.

1996

CHAPTER 30

1 Dolly the sheep, born on 5th July 1996, was the first mammal ever cloned. The cell used to clone her was taken from the mammary gland of an adult sheep, and she was named after Dolly Parton, because her creators couldn't think of a more impressive pair of glands than the singer's.

CHAPTER 31

1 The Royal Yacht *Britannia* was commissioned in January 1954 and decommissioned in 1997. During its years of royal service, the ship sailed the equivalent of a round-the-world trip every year and called at more than 600 ports in 135 countries. The floating royal residence hosted four honeymoons, as described. It is now a major tourist attraction in Edinburgh.

2 There is a village in Inverness named Drumnadrochit. In Gaelic, 'drum' (druim) means 'ridge', and 'na drocaid' means 'of the bridge'. 'Kirknadrochit' (church of the bridge) doesn't exist.

CHAPTER 32

1 The Stone of Scone, used for the coronations of the kings of Scotland, was installed at Edinburgh Castle on 30th November 1996, 700 years after it was taken to England by Edward I. Its location since 1296 had been King Edward's Chair in Westminster Abbey.

2 Before 1929, a girl of 12 and a boy of 14 could marry without parental consent under Scottish law, although this rarely happened. The legal age was raised to 16 in 1929 and, in Scotland, this remains the case. It explains why couples eloped from England and Wales (where parental permission was required if either party pre-1970 was under 21, and under 18 after 1970) to Gretna Green, the most southerly village just over the Scottish border.

1997

CHAPTER 33

1 There have been two separate claims that Prince Charles fathered children. One was made by a former Canadian navy lieutenant Janet Jenkins, who claimed to have been Charles' lover for 16 years. Her son, Jason Jenkins, was born nine months after a supposed liaison with the Prince at his Highgrove home, while he was still married to Diana. The second claim came from an Australian, Simon Dorante-Day, who believes he is the son of Charles and Camilla. The couple were allegedly spotted together as long ago as 1965 (!), after which Camilla is reported to have disappeared for around nine months. Neither claim has ever been commented on by the palace.

2 Lascelles is the family name associated with the Earldom of Harewood. In 1922, Princess Mary married Henry, 6th Earl of Harewood. She was the only daughter of King George V and Queen Mary, and was given the title 'the Princess Royal' (the title now held by HRH Princess Anne).

David Lascelles, 8th Earl of Harewood, is a first cousin (once removed) of the Queen. He has a daughter and two sons. The older son, Benjamin, was born in September 1978, five months before his parents married in February 1979. Although legitimised by the marriage, he is not eligible to inherit the earldom. His younger brother Alexander, who was born in 1980, is therefore heir apparent. As such, he holds the title Viscount Lascelles. He is currently 64th in the line of succession to the British throne.

3 Woolworth's buyers sometimes visited art colleges in a quest to find new designs for their tableware. 'Homemaker' was created by a young student called Enid Seeney. The black-and-white pattern featured cartoon-like drawings of 1950s furniture and was originally overlooked by the buyer, who was persuaded to trial it in a few stores. It was an instant success, and a complete range of crockery was soon in all the stores. Miss Seeney earned very little from her inspired design.

CHAPTER 34

1 GCVO (Knight or Dame of the Grand Cross) is the highest grade of the Royal Victorian Order – an order of knighthood – and its holders have the prefix Sir or Dame. Membership is conferred by the reigning sovereign upon those who have performed personal service.

ACKNOWLEDGEMENTS

My thanks go to the following:

As always, the whole team at Unicorn Publishing and to proof-reader extraordinaire Michael Eckhardt, without whom Rab Rainsmith would have taken eight days to travel by car across Scotland. Credit also goes to amazing typesetter Matt Wilson, especially for coping so patiently with the vagaries of the Cockney vernacular. The sequel may well see Ron killed off and Peggy attending elocution classes.

Steve and 'voice of Wales' Eurgain Baker for their sustained enthusiasm and encouragement, from the first premise onwards.

'Frantic Scribblers' Anne Mawdsley, Bev van Hoof, Julie Crookes, Moira Brimacombe and Peter Borchers – all masters of the descriptive. It is probably not evident that their requests for 'more context' were actually heeded. In terms of supportive fellow writers, the helpful Facebook community created by Max Gorlov also deserves a mention.

Trusted readers Mark Thompson, Lorna Grant, Vicky Penn and Stephanie Fauset – and Paul Fauset, too, for his positive reaction to the initial idea.

Rob and Tricia Rowbotham, whose memories stretch far

enough back to enable them to pinpoint instances of 'they wouldn't have used that phrase in those days'.

Viv (a one-time resident of 'Glenholme' Road) and David Howard, especially for prompting one very timely way forward.

Dr Bob Morris of UCL, for his thoughts on 'the saving'.

Finally, praise is due to my husband Stephen, for patiently discussing plot development – 'Haven't we got anything else to talk about?' – and for countless hours spent going through the evolving manuscript, identifying duplicated words, spotting inaccuracies and formatting text. But for his unstinting help, this book couldn't have happened.

Maggie Ballinger
Sheffield
January 2022